9/20

PRAISE FOR
ETIQUETTE FOR RUNAWAYS

"Deeply compelling characters intertwined in a story steeped in history, international travel, jazz, secrets, passion, addiction, heartbreaks, temptations, and more...An exceptional debut novel from a very capable storyteller who has perfected her craft."

—DIAN GRIESEL, a.k.a. @SilverDisobedience,
author of *The Silver Disobedience Playbook*

"Exquisitely written, Liza Nash Taylor's *Etiquette for Runaways* is a powerful tale of seeking absolution and pursuing dreams. It's a magnificent, special novel that I didn't want to end."

—ALAN HLAD, international bestselling
author of *The Long Flight Home*

"Taylor's sweeping coming-of-age story is utterly engrossing, exquisitely rendered, and deeply felt, with a rich cast of characters that linger in the heart and mind long after the final page is read. May Marshall is a heroine for any age—Jazz or otherwise—and her battles feel as intimate and immediately recognizable as our own."

—STEPHANIE BARRON,
author of *That Churchill Woman*

"Liza Nash Taylor has written a dazzling book that explores the hidden dreams and shifting sorrows of an amazing character, May Marshall. Taylor weaves May's travails, travels, and triumphs into a multiplicity of wonders: generational mystery, moonshine intrigue, mother-daughter heartache, Jazz Age glitter, and a love story that lingers long after the last page is turned. *Etiquette for Runaways* is a must-read, remarkable, and sumptuous debut."

—CONNIE MAY FOWLER,
author of *Before Women Had Wings*

ETIQUETTE FOR RUNAWAYS

Liza Nash Taylor

ETIQUETTE FOR RUNAWAYS

BLACK STONE
PUBLISHING

Copyright © 2020 by Liza Nash Taylor
Published in 2020 by Blackstone Publishing
Cover and book design by Alenka Vdovič Linaschke

"What'll I Do?" by Irving Berlin © 1924 by Irving Berlin
All rights reserved. Used with permission.

Any historical figures and events referenced in this book
are depicted in a fictitious manner. All other characters
and events are products of the author's imagination, and
any similarity to real persons, living or dead, is coincidental.

Printed in the United States of America

First edition: 2020
ISBN 978-1-982603-94-6
Fiction / Historical / General

1 3 5 7 9 10 8 6 4 2

CIP data for this book is available
from the Library of Congress

Blackstone Publishing
31 Mistletoe Rd.
Ashland, OR 97520

www.BlackstonePublishing.com

For Rocky, with gratitude
for his loving and benevolent disinterest.

PART I
DOG DAYS

"When the ancients first observed Sirius emerging as it were from the sun . . . they usually sacrificed a brown Dog to appease its rage, considering that this star was the *cause* of the hot sultry weather . . . and they . . . believed its power of heat, conjoined with that of the sun, to have been so excessive, that on the morning of its first rising *the Sea boiled, the Wine turned sour, Dogs grew mad,* and all other creatures *became languid . . .*"

John Brady,
Brady's Clavis Calendaria;
Or, a Compendious Analysis of the Calendar,
Volume II, London, 1813

ONE

It was a small drama, glimpsed by chance. The hawk winged upward, rising over the hayfield. As it receded toward the fence line, May could see that it held some prey—a small rabbit or a squirrel. Fresh-cut hay meant exposure. Easy pickings. She craned forward over the kitchen sink toward the open window, hoping to catch sight of it again. Raising her heavy braid, she let the breeze cool her tanned, sweat-dampened neck. The calico curtain fluttered inward like a limpid wave, then billowed away from the window with a sudden gust. The air moving over the mountains carried the sweet green scent of the field along with the charge of a summer storm. Inside, it picked up the odors of cold breakfast bacon and a single rotting onion hiding in the pantry. Winding through the farmhouse kitchen, it nudged open the screened door a few torpid inches—warped wood scraping over the patch where the linoleum had worn through.

The hawk was gone. The field was as before, rolling green up to the tree line. Beyond, the Southwest Mountains appeared to pulsate with humidity and heat.

The telephone jangled in the hall, interrupting the metronomic droning of cicadas that was the anthem of the dog days. Sometimes, if May allowed herself to listen, a half hour might pass. Truth be told, she didn't mind losing time here and there. These little respites helped the days go by. Morning, she was nearly through. Afternoon and night would come and go, and then it would all begin again. Delphina would ask once more, *what's wrong, Chérie? Why won't you eat this, why won't you talk to Byrd when he calls, why won't you leave the house* . . .

Mostly, she kept it where it belonged—the dark time. Still, there were moments when memory caught her unawares and despair perched on her shoulder, weighing her down in oppressive blackness. Plucking at her collar, she fanned herself, willing the pressure behind her eyes to cease. Her dress was loose, gaping to expose a pale crescent of flesh around the neckline. A year ago, the dress had fit perfectly. She had spent the previous summer sewing—every moment she wasn't working at her father's market—and when she was there, standing behind the counter, she sketched the stylish dresses from *Vogue* on paper bags and butcher paper. She had saved her wages for dress fabric, and at the beginning of August, she bought a stylish straw cloche with a ribbon that matched the green of her eyes, and white gloves with a pearl button from Miller & Rhodes, because that was where the smart Richmond girls shopped. The college girls.

But that was last summer. The dress that hung on her now had not become larger. It was May herself who had . . . *What's the word?* She shook off the cicada song. *Diminished*, she thought, smoothing her collar. *Yes, diminished. What a perfect word.*

The telephone stopped and she wondered, idly, who had called. There was no one she wanted to speak to. From the front hall, she heard Delphina's voice saying, "Marshall residence," but May couldn't make out the rest.

The kitchen door swung inward. With a declarative, "*Mon Dieu!*" Delphina pushed it open with her hip, her hands occupied in knotting a scarf at the back of her neck. Beneath the scarf, her hair was graying, but her light-brown skin was taut on her tall, narrow frame.

May turned on the water, letting it run cool over her wrist. Delphina gave a final tug to her scarf then deftly fastened an apron, turning her back as she tied the strings behind her. "Blue says you'd best get over to the Market. Says there's two carfuls of revenue agents out front, banging on the door."

May's hand froze on the tap. The bowl overflowed in the sink. *Revenue agents? It's Sunday morning, for Chrissake.* "He's sure?"

Delphina quirked her mouth. "They're shouting, 'Open the door; Bureau of Internal Revenue!' That might've given him a hint. Lord have mercy. I told you . . . How many times have I told you not to get mixed up in this mess? Just another one of your Daddy's crazy ideas. All these years I've worked for him he has never had a single lick . . . not one single, solitary lick . . . He wants to take risks, it's his business, but it's another thing convincing Blue . . . and now you too! I told you it was foolishness, but no, oh, no, you had to go and . . ." She flicked her hand toward the door. "Get on over there."

May clutched her braid as if she were climbing a rope, as if a trapdoor might magically open above her. Her eyes flitted from the line of mason jars on the kitchen table to the wall clock, and back again. "I need to get Daddy up. Is there coffee left?"

Delphina began assembling canisters and utensils, her movements swift and stiffly efficient, her mouth a tight line. Without looking up, she pointed a wooden spoon toward the ceiling. "Dead asleep." She raised one eyebrow. "I heard the truck come in around sunrise. He won't be stirring anytime soon." Waving the spoon toward the jars, she said, "Get those smelly things out of my kitchen. I already told you yesterday. And shut that water off."

May closed the tap and glanced at the clock again, steeling herself. *Why didn't we come up with a plan?* Breathing hard, she banged through the swinging door into the hall, tugging the knot of her apron. It fell behind her as she bolted up the stairs, wresting her dress over her head until a button popped, pinging against the steps. Crossing the upper hall, she took aim, heaving the wadded dress against her father's closed door. With an unsatisfying whisper, it slid to the floor like a deflated balloon.

In her room she rifled through her closet, tossing her good shoes over her shoulder. There was no time for stockings. Sweat beaded on her forehead as she raked a brush through her hair. She sniffed an armpit, then doused herself with eau de cologne. The buttons of her second-best dress were suddenly cumbersome, the buttonholes a little too small. Shoes and gloves in hand, she hurried breathlessly back downstairs, snatching her cloche from the coat rack.

In the kitchen, Delphina tapped flour through the sifter, humming with an affected disinterest that was, May knew, intended to *convey a message*. She understood the message as well as if Delphina had shouted it, but now was just not the time. There was a *situation* to be dealt with, and she had no plan. May sat to fasten her shoes, and the buckles seemed to fight the straps. She said, "If I'm not back in an hour, wake Daddy and tell him to call the lawyer—that's Mr. Honeycutt—damned shoes—but if he's still drunk, I mean Daddy, not Mr.—*christ* a'mighty—if he's still drunk, do *not* let him call the Market. And put caps on those jars for me, in case they come to the house. Oh Delphie, *please?*"

Delphina parried her spoon in May's direction, narrowing her eyes. "If federal agents come to this house, *I* will not be here. Today's my day off, anyhow. I am not even here right now. You understand me?" Her mouth puckered and she resumed her humming, a little louder than before.

May pulled on her gloves and as the screened door slammed behind her, Delphina called from inside, "Bring me back a pound of butter, if they don't arrest you."

On the long porch, a brindle-and-white bulldog lay panting, leaning against the clapboard. Tail thumping, she raised herself and lumbered down the steps. Above, the storm clouds that had looked so promising earlier were moving away across the mountains, as if fleeing the scene. The dog trotted behind May and jumped into the cab of the farm truck, settling herself heavily against the passenger door. The seat was hot against May's legs, the steering wheel hotter, even through her gloves.

"Sweet, tiny baby Jesus," May said to the dog, "Blossom, we should've had a plan." Her father had told her, in June, *those revenue agents won't bother with us; oh, no, we're small potatoes. They go after the big operations. This is only temporary, a little boost. Quick cash. Help me out this summer. Quick cash. Anybody shows up asking questions, just stay cool and talk real slow. I'll handle it. The less you know, the better.*

Holding her breath, May pushed the starter switch. *Please, god-of-all-truck-engines*, she implored, *not today*. On the third attempt, it roared to life. It was a short drive to her father's market, and she accelerated, lurching over the long, rutted driveway toward Route 22. At the

end of the drive, a peeling white sign hung on a post: Keswick Farm &
Orchard. Below was a rusty mailbox, and on a wooden stake closer to the
road stood May's home-painted sign, now covered in a layer of road dust:
Sewing and Alterations, Inquire Within.

She pulled onto the road, heading eastward. Fitfully, she circled one
wrist with the other. Would they use handcuffs? They might. They might
have already searched the Market. They might have been tipped off. There
could be reporters and photographers. She checked the rearview mirror;
the road behind was clear.

Dread wedged in her throat like a cherry pit, along with an
all-too-familiar sick humiliation that settled low and cold and heavy in her
stomach, as it had on another Sunday morning, a few months before—
that lovely, late-April morning that had seemed so glorious. Then, all May
had been able to do was stand there, frozen by the shock and disappointment in her French teacher's eyes, when there was no possible explanation
as to how May happened to be exiting an off-campus hotel at 7 a.m. on the
arm of a young man—the hotel that was right next to the church that celebrated Mass at six. She had remained frozen while the teacher insisted she
come immediately to the Dean's office, while Amory backed away, hands
raised, then turned and left her there on the sidewalk. *Amory? Amory, where
are you going? You have to come with me, you have to explain to the Dean that
we're . . . Amory, please, come back!*

The teacher's look turned to pity. May had stood mute, as the
Dean—a smear of shaving cream still quivering on his neck—telephoned
her father, tersely explaining that her scholarship was revoked. *Come and
once, Mr. Marshall. Take your daughter home. She has no place here.*

May banged the steering wheel. *Another stupid, stupid decision, May.*

She had started out following the rules, *No riding in automobiles
with gentlemen without a chaperone; no unescorted trips off campus;
hats, gloves, chapel on Sundays.* And then, along came Amory Whitman, with trouble written all over him.

And then, the dark time had come.

TWO

Keswick Market stood at the crossroads of Stony Point Pass and Route 22, closer to Charlottesville, Virginia than Gordonsville. It wasn't a big place—one story with a white clapboard front and a rusting tin roof. A single gas pump stood outside, and barrels alternated with rocking chairs across the wide, neatly swept porch. A Closed sign was visible through the glass of the front door. May slowed to pull in. Two men in suits stood on the porch, peering inside. Two more sat in rocking chairs with arms crossed identically, rifles resting across their laps. The truck hissed and bucked to a halt in the gravel. As the dust settled, she glanced again into the rearview mirror. There was no need to pinch her cheeks, they were flaming. She fumbled with the door latch and climbed out to stand on the running board. Blossom bounded from the cab and waited, raising her snout to sniff the air.

"Good morning!" May waved, stepping down with exaggerated daintiness, aware of the shrillness of her voice. Squaring her shoulders, she smiled. *Stay cool and talk real slow.*

"Can I help you, gentlemen?" She sauntered toward them, pulling her gloves from her hands, finger by finger. "Y'all need directions somewhere?"

The man who seemed to be in charge wore a sheriff's badge. He hitched his lapels and came down the steps then stopped, standing with arms akimbo and legs apart. His brown suit was wrinkled, his trousers tucked into knee-high leather gaiters with mismatched laces. Pushing his fedora back on his freckled forehead, he squinted, first at May, then at the door of the truck, with its fading lettering: KESWICK FARM ORCHARDS, KESWICK, VIRGINIA. "Well, no, miss." His voice had a syrupy, studiously unhurried deference. "We ain't lost a-tall. I'm Hiram Beasley, County Sheriff for Albemarle. I don't believe we've met. And these gents are from the Prohibition Unit of the Bureau of Internal Revenue." He spit from the side of his mouth and a brown puddle appeared in the gravel. Working the wad of tobacco in his jaw, he jerked his head toward the Market. "We're looking for Henry Marshall. We have a warrant to inspect the premises."

May matched his cordiality. "Good gracious! Daddy's not here." *True.* "He's over in Crozet, at a tent revival." *Untrue.* "He'll be back in time for supper if y'all would care to wait, but I'm May Marshall. Do come inside, out of this dreadful heat, please." She walked slowly up the stairs to the front door, fanning her face. "I believe we have some lemonade in the icebox, or at least I can offer y'all a cold Co-Cola." She rattled her key in the door, buying time. *Real slow.* "My grandfather built this market in 1900. Only, as you can see, we're closed, being it's the Lord's Day. I was just stopping on my way home from church to pick up some butter." She touched her fingers to her chest. "Such a shame, y'all having to work on a Sunday, 'specially with it being so hot and all." Shading her eyes with her hand, she affected an expression of puzzled sympathy, looking each of the men in the eye in turn. The seated agents stood up, and one doffed his hat and bobbed his head. As the door swung inward, the little bell above jangled and in the sudden dimness, May waited for her eyes to adjust. Blossom leaned hard against her knee. The men followed her inside.

"Blue?" she called, "You back there? We have some gentlemen here, from the government." The agents began walking the aisles, peering behind shelves and beneath baskets. They opened pickle barrels and hefted sacks of grain. May called again, "Blue?" The overhead lights switched on, and the canvas curtain that closed off the back rooms parted.

Blue held his suspenders and nodded, unsmiling, toward May. "Morning."

The agents stopped and waited as Beasley approached, his eyes narrowing as he looked the larger Negro man up and down. "Why didn't you answer the door, boy? You deaf? Couldn't you hear us knocking?"

May began, "Listen, mister . . ." before Blue shot her a stern look. Beasley shoved his hands into his pockets and leaned back, jingling something metallic. Blossom stiffened, growling, her hackles rising. Across the room, one of the agents raised his rifle to his shoulder, fixing the barrel on the dog. No one moved.

"Now, now," May said, evenly. With her eyes on the gun barrel, she moved her hand slowly until it was in front of Blossom's face. She took a single step forward. The dog stayed. "Sheriff Beasley, sir, we have a policy. Blue doesn't answer the door when we're closed. What with hobos, and . . . and, well, you never know, do you, who might come knocking? Forgive me, I didn't introduce you properly. This is Mr. Blue Harris. He's run the Market for years. He makes all the pickles and preserves himself." She indicated stocked shelves behind the counter, lined up with neat rows of canned goods and mason jars of Keswick Farm products. She looked toward Blue, forcing a smile. "How come you're cooking on a Sunday? Supposed to be a day of rest."

Blue's voice was impassive. "All those peppers come ripe this week."

Beasley put his face close to Blue's. "Well, *Mr.* Harris, we'll need to see the back room and the cellar. We've had a call that y'all might be running moonshine out of this place."

Blue's jaw twitched, but his face was otherwise expressionless. "Ain't any cellar," he said. Stepping back, he held open the curtain.

In the kitchen, pickle brine steamed in an enamel pot on the stove and the air was redolent with vinegar and cloves. A basket of bright bell peppers sat on a long worktable, along with a short, curved knife and a pile of stems and seeds. Beasley put his hands to his hips as he surveyed the kitchen, then fixed his gaze back on Blue. "You ought to open the door to Federal agents, boy. Show some proper respect. And I reckon you don't know a *damned thing* about any moonshine, do you?" Laughing, he looked toward the agents. "That's all right. You don't have to talk to me. Least not right now, anyhow. Hear no evil, speak no evil." Beasley pointed in turn at Blue and May, and his face was serious again. "But if these agents here should *see* any illegal liquor, or *hear* any more rumors about this place? Things won't go too well. Now, I, myself, can see just fine. And I never forget a face."

May opened a bottle of Coca-Cola and offered it to Beasley, keeping her arms tight to hide the crescents of sweat staining her dress. The others watched to see if he would accept it, and he did, leaning back against the table, draining half the bottle in a gulp then suppressing a belch with a fist to his chest. The agents continued to search the kitchen and the storeroom where Blue lived, flipping the mattress and peering into each of the crockery vats that stood in a line against the wall. Blue began to chop peppers with slow precision. Steam rumbled the lid of the pot on the stove, and May moved away from the heat, avoiding eye contact with Blue. Focusing on the wall clock, she concentrated on keeping her face neutral. *Whoever turned us in doesn't know about the jars. These agents would know exactly where to look. Only they don't.*

Fifteen long minutes clicked by. One by one, each agent looked at their leader and shook his head. When Beasley, red-faced, jerked his chin toward the front of the Market, the agents filed outside. May stood at the front counter, watching, waiting, willing the sheriff to follow. The rhythmic *thunk, thunk* of Blue's knife counted off the seconds. Beasley stood beside May in front of the counter, uncomfortably close. He took a mason jar from a pyramid-stacked counter display and hefted it. "Huh," he said, "My grandmother used to make corn relish."

May held out one hand in appeasement. "Please, take that, with our compliments." She passed him the jar and took two more from the display.

He pointed to another jar with an expression of distaste. "But I never could stand apple butter. Always tasted gritty."

"I know what you mean," she said, attempting a smile. "I can't abide the smell of it myself. But some folks like it. It's one of our most popular products."

"Listen, missy," he leaned forward, resting his crossed arms on the countertop. "you tell your father I'll be back tomorrow, and I expect he'll be here to meet me and nine o'clock sharp. We're watching. The Sheriff's department and the Internal Revenue Service of the United States will *not* be made fools of. You understand me?"

May nodded like a wide-eyed marionette, and Beasley held her gaze. One of his eyelids twitched. She willed herself to be still. The sheriff's eyes never left hers as he leaned over and shoved the stacked display jars back, over the far edge of the counter. *Pop, pop, pop!* Like gunfire, twelve jars hit the floor in an explosion of glass. May gasped, her hand at her throat, choking on the sudden, intense odors of vinegar and cinnamon and sweet apples. Blue came to the curtain and looked down at the mess, standing tall and silent. May took his cue and didn't move.

As Beasley strode outside the little bell tinkled above the door, and she listened for the sound of an engine. Trembling had begun in her legs and moved its cold fingers up her back to her shoulders.

Blue leaned against the door frame, shaking his head. "Where the *hell* is Henry?"

May tugged at her braid, watching the road through the window. The agent's cars crested a hill and dipped out of sight. She breathed shallowly, her senses still on high alert. Blossom pushed open the screened door and trotted off into the pinewood bordering the back of the Market, in search of the next interesting scent. May laid her palms on the smooth, worn oak of the countertop, attempting to draw from its solidity. *That horrible man is gone. Blue is here. I'm fine, I'm fine, I'm fine.* She said, "Last night was Hog and Hominy Club. You know how that goes. He's sleeping it off. You think somebody called them?"

"That, I do not know. I do know that Henry'd been paying that bastard, up till June. All the small operators do 'cause he can keep the feds away. Protection money. Only since y'all came up with the new package, Sheriff Beasley can't find a thing here. Not one drop. 'Bout to drive him crazy. Him showing up with agents is nothing but intimidation."

"Daddy's been paying that man? He didn't tell me."

"He says the less you know, the better."

"Does Beasley know where the still is?"

"Must not, else he'd have gone there first, I reckon. Heh, heh. But I tell you what, they weren't expecting to come up against a pretty girl." He smiled, his face creasing into deep dimples. "You did fine, May. Fine. We'll be all right." He held her gaze for a long moment.

May was unable to summon any expression of triumph. "Things could have gone bad, Blue. I can't believe Daddy didn't tell me about this."

Blue rubbed his neck and lifted one side of his mouth like a shrug. "I bet you we ain't seen the last of Sheriff Beasley. He's crooked as they come. But long as he doesn't find anything, he can't do squat."

Back inside, May pulled off her gloves and set about putting things to rights. She worked automatically, unable as yet to process the events that had just occurred. Behind the counter, she scraped up glass and muck then built another pyramid of jars, exactly as it had been, while Blue pushed the heavier bins back into place and filled a mop bucket.

Steadier now, May stepped up the short ladder and aligned jars on the shelves behind the counter. Exploded mess flecked some of the canned goods. Can by can, and jar by jar, she wiped clean the spatters, attempting to order the chaos in her mind.

On the third shelf, pint and quart-sized jars labeled Keswick Farm Apple Butter were lined up in a row. The labels bore a pen-and-ink rendering of the white clapboard farmhouse with twin chimneys and neat, green-black shutters. In small type, below the house, was printed: Made with Pride, since 1849. Similar jars held preserves, chutneys, and pickles. What Sheriff Beasley had not known was that beneath the counter, identical-looking quart jars with the same label held something far more potent than apple butter. Inside of each was a smaller, cylindrical baby bottle with a flat cap, filled with liquor. It had been May's idea to coat the inside of a mason jar with an opaque mixture of apple butter and glue. The production of the dummy jars had become just another chore—two dozen jars a day, five days a week. It was messy and it smelled terrible, but it meant she could work alone, at home.

May collected Delphina's butter, and outside, she whistled one long note. Blossom bounded from the woods and jumped into the truck, sniffing the paper-wrapped block.

Blue leaned one arm on the truck window frame. "You best get that to Delphina before it melts. I need to get back to my pepper jelly. Today was just a bump. Sorry you had to see it." He leaned back, crossing his arms. "You ought not be mixed up in this business."

"Neither should you."

"Henry and I've been working together one way or another since we were boys. We've got things covered. I'm gonna buy myself a little place where I can retire."

May smiled at him. "You're not old enough to retire."

"Ten years or thereabouts, I will be. What about you?"

"What do you mean?"

"I mean, what're you doing with yourself? You going back to school somewhere? You're too smart not to. You're wasting yourself here. Delphina says you never leave the house."

May looked down, concentrating on peeling a sliver of paint from the steering wheel. "I started my alterations business."

"How many customers have you had?"

"Two."

Blue rubbed his chin. "Let's see . . . so, one customer a month? You must be real busy with that, then."

"I'm exploring other opportunities."

Blue snorted. "Is that right? Well. Glad to hear it." His voice turned quiet, gentle. "It's not natural for a gal your age—pretty young gal—to be closed up like you been. You ought to be out kicking up your heels. You know I'm right. Henry's worried about you; Delphina too. I've known you all your life. You want to talk, come find me. I'm good at listening."

May couldn't meet his gaze. Tears were too close. She blew out her breath. "Thanks. I'll have a talk with Daddy."

"You do that." He smacked the side of the truck and smiled, waving, then went back inside. The truck engine whined and died, and May rested her damp forehead against the steering wheel, feeling defeated. After two more tries, the engine finally turned over.

Turning onto Route 22, the perfume of honeysuckle and wild roses growing tangled along the road was intensified by the heat, and slow-flying bees attended the last tired blooms of August. Leaning toward the window, she let the warm wind flow over her face. Farm signs flashed by—Cloverfields, Harkaway, Tall Oaks, Chestnut Grove. Like Keswick Farm, they had been owned by the same families for generations. Out of long habit, May checked the telegraph lines that paralleled the train tracks, looking for the red-tailed hawk that often perched on a particular pole. She passed the train depot and the Keswick Post Office and the Gothic Revival Episcopal Church. The church bell was ringing as the minister stood by the open doors, shaking hands and patting children on the head as the congregation filed out.

May hadn't been inside the church since she was seven years old—not since her baby brother's funeral. She would never forget the impossibly tiny white coffin, smelling of fresh paint, and how tightly her father held her hand as they processed behind it. Her mother had locked herself in her room and would not come with them. When Doctor Sawyer came to the house, he had to speak to her through the door. Her father began to sleep in the spare room.

Ahead on the road, the farm turnoff came into view. Something flat lay in the road ahead and as she watched, a car coming from the opposite direction drove over it; split pieces skittering away. Her alterations sign. Her impulse was to drive right past—past the sign in the road, past the farm—to keep going as far as a tank of gas would take her and see where she ended up. It didn't matter where, as long as she could escape.

Escape. *Well*, she thought, *I tried that, didn't I?* She had been waiting for something to happen, some divine tap on the shoulder. She needed a plan.

THREE

The truck clattered back over the long driveway to the house. May hit the first deep rut and bounced on the hard seat. The jolting impact suited her mood. Blossom put her ears back, bracing herself. Shifting gears, May slowed the truck and glanced at the familiar scene in front of her. Beyond the chestnut trees in the yard were hayfields, bordered by rail fence. In the late summer pasture, where hay had been baled, black-and-white-spotted cows stood vivid against yellowing grass. In the background, above her father's orchards, the mountains loomed a lush, steamy, darker green. Deep within those woods, in a gully that ran along a streambed, Henry Marshall's still was hidden.

From a distance, the farmhouse appeared much as it did on the canning labels: neat and white, surrounded by boxwood and camellia bushes. May had been six when her mother had drawn the label illustration and she had a distinct memory, as clear as a photograph—her mother, like a flower, in pink linen, sitting in the front field with her sketch pad. As a child, May believed that her mother's pen had magically repaired the rusted tin roof and sagging porch of the old house, its deft strokes filling in the missing slats of the shutters and reviving the aged, fractured oaks in the yard. A six-year-old could believe in magic, having no idea that such a belief was a luxury of innocence; once extinguished, it could never be rekindled convincingly.

May parked at the back of the house and slammed the truck door. Relief was supplanted by rising indignation. The screened door opened into the kitchen with a rusty complaint and Delphina looked up from the lattice of her piecrust to ask, "*Veux-tu déjeuner?*"

May laid the butter beside the sink and responded, "Don't fret about luncheon for me, thanks." Her eyes met Delphina's briefly; she read the concern there. "They didn't find anything." The furrows between Delphina's eyes relaxed.

May walked heavily through the swinging door, then stomped up the stairs. Outside her father's bedroom, she bent to retrieve the dress she had thrown earlier. It felt heavy in her hand.

She shoved the door open. The handle banged the wall. Odors of liquor and stale sweat blended sourly with hair tonic. Light filtered through the window shade, illuminating faded wallpaper and clothes strewn across the floor. She crossed the room and yanked the shade cord, sending it clattering to the top of the window. Below, in the yard, her mother's roses were overgrown, tenaciously covering the front wall of the wash house.

"Jesus, little gal, shut the damned shade," her father said hoarsely, squinting into the flood of sunlight. May turned from the window. His graying hair hung in clumped strands over his forehead. Pushing it back, he propped himself on his elbows. Henry Marshall had been a handsome man in his youth, and May had inherited his strong brows and high cheekbones. But years of sun and bouts of bitter drinking had taken their toll. At forty-eight, he looked ten years older. Blossom nuzzled his hand and he scratched beneath her collar, saying, "Mornin', girl."

May moved to the foot of the bed. She hated the tremble in her voice—the constriction of her throat that was the choking of frustration. "It's *afternoon*, and guess where I've been?" Henry's head swayed slightly. She stamped her foot, and her voice rose. "Revenue agents came to the Market, with the sheriff. I had no idea you'd been paying him! You said you'd take care of things, didn't you?" She held the brass rail of the footboard and shook it.

Henry winced, holding up a palm. "Calm down, for Chrissake. They find anything?"

"No, but you weren't there! You didn't see how awful that Sheriff Beasley was to Blue."

"Listen. Blue knows the risks." May bit her lip. He continued, "I never planned on you being part of this. We were doing fine. You were off at college. I wasn't expecting you back home so soon." She stepped back, flushing; stung, as if he'd slapped her. Instantly, she was back in the darkness of disgrace when he *ought* to be telling her that everything would be all right, that she had saved the day and been brave and clever. Her mouth opened, then closed.

In the shadowed corner behind the wardrobe, Shame leaned against the wall and crossed its arms, nodding, as if to say, *Well played, Henry. Well played.*

Henry said, "We'll just have to be a little more careful."

May's hands dropped from the bedrail. She raised her chin, working to steady her voice. She spoke quietly. "You're supposed to be in charge. We didn't even have a plan. They had guns, Daddy." Turning stiffly, she walked out, leaving the door open. Blossom followed her across the hall, her nails tapping the floorboards.

For the past twelve years, the door to May's mother's bedroom had been kept closed. She turned the door handle and when she went inside, the dog sat at the threshold and would not follow.

The mahogany bed had been brought from New Orleans when Ellen Valentine became Ellen Marshall. Now, the lace net canopy drooped, fogged with dust, and the carved feather fronds and pineapple finials that crowned each post had lost their beeswax sheen. On the dressing table, a silver brush and matching repoussé mirror had blackened with tarnish. The perfume flacon held only a brown stain on the bottom, and when May removed the stopper the residue smelled cloying and rancid. In an oval silver frame, her mother looked young and hopeful in her wedding dress and long pearls, with orange blossoms in her hair. *Why aren't you here, Mama? Parents are supposed to watch out for their children.*

Beneath the window, a wheeled, wicker bassinette still stood. May picked up a tarnished rattle from the yellowed blanket. It had been her own, first, and was dented from her teething. Then it had passed on, to baby Henry. She had been so happy to have a little brother. She had promised to behave like a big girl.

But then, her mother had run away. Every time May had tried to ask when she was coming back, her father shook his head and left the room. Eventually, she stopped asking and, at an early age, she learned that the remnants of the Marshall family did not discuss painful subjects. Grief was to be borne with quiet dignity. Anger was not to be expressed in shouting. Love was a stiff hug at birthdays or Christmas, a word to end a letter. It was never declared aloud. In those early days, after her brother died and her mother left, Delphina took over. May spent more and more time with her friend Byrd Craig, who lived next door. Byrd's parents were warm and kind, not distant and silent as her father was, not always closed away in their room, as her mother had been. Mrs. Craig was generous with her plump-armed hugs that smelled of flowery talcum powder. When Byrd's older brother, Jimmy, had been killed in France, in the War, May had witnessed the grief his family expressed. Byrd cried openly, and his mother wailed at the memorial service, clutching the triangle of American flag to her breast. The gold star of remembrance still hung in their window.

Since May had come back home in April, she wouldn't come to the phone when Byrd called her. When he dropped by unannounced, she was distant, refusing to go swimming with him, or riding, or any of the things they had done every summer since they were small. It was as if that girl had ceased to exist.

May laid the rattle back in its place, listening to her father's careful, heavy tread descending the stairs, then the quiet click of the front screened door as he eased it closed. He would not run the one-woman gauntlet of Delphina's disapproval by passing through the kitchen. He would slink back in at suppertime, acting like nothing had happened.

FOUR

At breakfast the following morning, Henry sat at one end of the long pine table. As May came in from the hall, he took a slow sip of coffee, appraising her over his cup. She appraised him too, without meeting his gaze directly. *Freshly shaven, clean shirt, steady hands, bloodshot eyes.* May set her cup and saucer on the table and pulled out her own chair, opposite his. Delphina placed a plate in front of her while tension hovered around the perimeter of the room like nervous, unwelcomed guests.

With a placating smile that was not returned, Henry asked Delphina, "What's the grand occasion, having breakfast in here?"

Delphina filled his coffee cup. "Kitchen table's covered in those jars again. Until they are removed for good and all, meals will be in the dining room." She turned and left.

Henry cleared his throat and popped open the newspaper. *Go ahead and hide*, May thought. She picked up her knife and began cutting precise, translucent slivers of butter, relishing the grating metallic rattle of the knife edge against the butter plate. *Slice, clack! Slice, clack! Slice, clack!* She tucked the butter between the steaming hotcakes, pouring molasses over the top.

Henry pointed to something in the paper. "Looks like after those agents left the Market, they busted Bose Shifflett at Bacon Hollow. Somebody must've peached him, or else he owed Beasley."

May's voice remained level. "How'd you get mixed up with him in the first place?"

"He came in sometime in April, found the hooch stashed in the storeroom. I wasn't doing a very good job of hiding it. I'd heard of him, of course. He told me he could protect us from the feds, in exchange for regular cash. Well, I stopped paying him after you came up with those jars; told him I'd quit the business. Figured I'd get a break. Somebody must've let him know we're still producing, only he can't find anything now." Henry laughed, then he sighed and leaned forward, letting the paper collapse into his lap. "Look, I'm sorry you were there. Truth is, moonshine's bringing in more than anything else right now. If that Farm Relief Bill had passed, we'd be sitting in clover. Coolidge might've sent Albemarle Pippins all over the world." His arm arced a broad angle. "They're going to propose it again, though."

"That plan was for wheat and corn, Daddy, not apples. Stop trying to change the subject."

"See! It's a good thing we're not raising corn. And that goddamned Piggly Wiggly in town . . . Look at this advertisement here. Goddamned balloons! Today, they're giving free balloons to every child who goes in there. I swear. It can't last, though. People don't want to pick out their own groceries, they want *service*. You know I'm right. Just a flash in the damned pan. But we've got a fine apple crop coming in this year. A doozy. If we get a good harvest, we'll cut back on the hooch. Maybe we can stop after Christmas. Maybe New Year's." He scratched his chin. "Be a real shame, though, to lose that holiday business." May hacked her soggy stack of hotcakes into a neat grid of small squares. Henry sighed again, then continued, "Now listen, little gal, you don't have to help if you don't want. But you can't complain about the money, not that I've seen you spend any of it."

From the front porch, a piercing, "Yoo-hoo!" rang out and reverberated through the house.

"Aw, hell," Henry muttered, rising. "That's Aggie."

"The jars!" May hissed, rising and starting for the kitchen. Through the butler's pantry door, Delphina gave a quick nod, then tossed dish towels over the mason jars. May turned back and her father's chair was empty, the newspaper abandoned on the seat.

"How *dooo*? Henry?" The voice grew closer, cutting off any chance of escape upstairs. "May? You out here, honey?"

May groaned, quietly. *No, I don't want to help with the Baptist clothes drive, or the quilting bee, or your coffee hour.*

Delphina whisked away the plates, disappearing into the pantry as May's aunt came into the room. May said, "Look who's here!" *Go away! Leave me alone! I don't want to sew rag dolls for poor children!* "What a nice surprise." She could see her father out the dining room window, already halfway across the yard, trotting toward the barn, arms pumping at his sides.

Agnes Waddell clutched a bundle of mail against the shelf of her bosom. She looked like a slightly older, heavier version of her brother Henry. She said, "Thought I'd stop in on my way to the church, to say how-do, see how you're gettin' on this week. Bless your heart." She cocked her head to one side, smiling beatifically while the bunch of celluloid cherries on her straw hat bobbled like insect antennae. "Hope I didn't disturb your breakfast. But I do have something to discuss with Henry." *Bobble, bobble.* She handed May letters and a small parcel. "Brought your mail from the box. Looks like you got something from that *cute* Elsie Carter. She's just the dearest girl. Such a fine family, those Carters. Nice she keeps in touch. Reckon she's heading back to school soon . . . that time of year and all." May half-smiled, setting the mail on the table. Agnes continued, "Henry here?"

"You just missed him." *Now GO.* "But you might catch him at the Market."

"S'pose I've got a few minutes to visit. Catch my breath. Any Co-Colas in the icebox? Oh, my heavens to Betsy, I am *parched*. Can't hardly speak."

"Let me get you one. I'll meet you on the porch."

The kitchen was deserted. On the cooling stove, a frying pan held hotcakes, cooked on one side.

On the back porch, four dark-green rocking chairs sat in a row. The first, her father's, had sturdy oak slats and a rush seat that had molded to fit his backside. The guest's chair was almost pristine, with an awning-striped seat cushion. The third had been her mother's—painted wicker with dainty scrollwork and a faded, ruffled chintz cushion—a coquette of a rocking chair. May settled into the last chair, a smaller version of her father's.

The guest's chair creaked as Agnes settled herself. "Git, you!" She flapped her hands as Blossom nosed the hem of her dress. "Nasty cur. Bless your heart," she said, taking the bottle from May.

"I heard you've been on a trip," May said, steering the conversation from herself, ". . . a revival, wasn't it?"

"Yes, yes. Sorry I didn't stop by last week. I know you don't get to see many folks these days. But you know, the Lord directs us, and we must obey. I went to Little Rock with the church circle. That's in Arkansas, of course." Her eyes flicked upward. "Thank you, sweet Lord Jesus for safe travels, amen. Did you ever wonder why Kansas is just *Kansas*, but Arkansas is *Ar-can-saw*, not Ar-*kansas*?" Agnes held the icy bottle to her forehead, pushing her hat back over her tight, steel-gray curls and sending the cherry bunch into a frenzy of activity. "Laws, it's hot."

"It is," May said. "Delphina's making a terrine for lunch."

Agnes spoke in a dramatic whisper, with one side of her mouth pulled down. "I didn't want to say anything, but I thought I smelled something strange in your kitchen. I wouldn't eat that with a ten-foot pole. *Terrine.* Must be one of those French things your girl makes. Those French folks eat snails and frogs, for pity's sake." She opened her handbag and pulled out a cardboard fan, imprinted with an image of Jesus, hovering above the Stony Point Baptist Church, where she worked in the office. "Never could tell what your mother was going to serve for dinner." She fanned herself energetically.

May inhaled, letting the comment pass. *Don't stir the pot.* "A cold lunch is nice when it's so hot, don't you think?"

"Well, can't you come up with an American name for it? No need to keep up all that French mumbo gumbo anymore. You're affluent in English too." May looked down, covering her smile with her hand. Agnes stopped her fan, pointing it at May. "I keep telling you, you ought to make Delphina talk English. It's the American way."

May looked out toward the mountains and exhaled, her patience waning. "You know she speaks perfect English. I *like* speaking French with her. It keeps me in practice. I'd like to go there, to France, someday. All that beautiful art and architecture. They make the most gorgeous dresses in the world there, in Paris—the ones in the magazines."

"Lordy, don't I remember, your Mama and her fancy French dresses and her New Orleans airs. Henry fell for it hook, line, and sinker."

Stop saying bad things about my mother. Do you think I don't remember her? "Wouldn't you like to go there—to France, or to England, or South America—and learn about someplace new?"

"No," Agnes said, flicking her fan. "Though Little Rock was right far. Anyhow, I need to get on over to the church. The Lord's good work is never done! The altar guild's meeting at ten thirty. Why don't you come over and sign up? You spend so much time in that garden anyway; put some flowers where other folks can seem 'em." Raising herself from the chair, she shot a warning glance toward the dog.

"I told Daddy I'd help out with the canning this week, but you're sweet to think of me."

"Aw. Bless your heart." Agnes patted May's arm. "You know, the church will always welcome you. Thanks ever so for the Co-Cola."

May walked her to the front door then onto the front porch. Agnes held a hand up to shield her eyes, saying, "Tell Henry I came by. I wanted to ask him what he knows about those agents."

May gripped the porch railing. "What agents?"

"It was all in the paper this morning. Federal Agents, all over Bose Shifflett's place. They hauled him off to jail! Poor Myrtle. Honestly, what that woman endures. She certainly doesn't deserve *that*." Agnes shook her head, setting the cherries aquiver again. "*I* say, a godless man like that goes and breaks the law, he ought to get what's coming to him. Henry might be next."

"I don't know what you're . . ."

Agnes held up a halting hand. "I came by to be helpful. Folks *talk*, May. It's shameful what Henry's got up to. Shameful and common. And Lord knows, the last thing *you* need is . . . well." She raised her eyes, then hitched her handbag over her elbow and marched to her car and drove off, leaving a trail of dust.

In the kitchen, Delphina had returned. She stood at the sink scraping the frying pan. May said, "I didn't know she knew. Did you hear all that?"

Delphina said, "Enough. That woman needs to stay away from here. All the time poking her nose into folk's business, being so *helpful*."

May cut the twine on her parcel and tore through the stiff brown paper. With a pleasant frisson of anticipation, she unfolded the letter inside. Delphina said, "It's nice of your friend to keep on writing to you. When are you going to write back?" Without waiting for an answer, she patted May's shoulder and left the kitchen.

August 14, 1924

Dearest May,

Guess who bobbed her hair last week? All the smart girls down here are doing it. Mother's hairdresser refused, so I had to go to the barber. Of course, Mother and Daddy were appalled. It was so amusing. I'll send you a photograph for your scrapbook.

Mother is starting to pack my trunks, and don't I wish you were coming back. Do you suppose I'll be able to pass Domestic Science this year? Of course, I'll be perfectly hopeless in French without you there to tutor me. I had a letter from my new roommate. Her name is Eunice Goode, and she's from Burnt Chimney, Virginia. Sounds like a horrid place to come from, don't you think? She plays the oboe and has asthma, so I bet she'll turn me in for smoking.

I'm throwing a house party at the river over Labor Day. I want you and Byrd to come, and I won't take no for an answer! I'll drop him a line to invite him properly. We'll have a swell time, and there's a dance contest at The Jefferson Hotel that Friday night, the 29th. Why don't you ask Byrd to drive you? I heard something about him seeing Charlotte Penrose. (Remember her, from Mary Baldwin? She had all those extra clothes racks in the hallway.) You could stay here for the week and take the train back. Think about it, won't you? It would be perfectly splendid, I promise!

I think about you every day, old girl, and I'm going to keep on writing and calling until you answer back. You must give me a chance to atone for introducing you to that cad, Amory. You were such a wily thing; I had no idea you were so over the moon for him. I blame myself for not warning you off. At least now he's engaged and won't be breaking more hearts. His dreadful fiancée, Bitsy Ragsdale, was in the

*newspaper last week. A big photograph of her christening a ship at the
Newport News Shipyard.*

    *Now then, so you don't forget everything you learned at college,
here is a book of crossword puzzles. They are all the rage down here.
I got a tiny little crossword dictionary that goes on my arm like a
wristwatch! And here's the latest* Vogue. *Please come visit.*

                    Your pal, Elsie

May let the letter fall to her lap. She should have confided in Elsie.
Amory. When she thought of him now, it was with disdain. He was a
coward. And now he was engaged to someone called *Bitsy*, who was, no
doubt, rich and pretty. May hoped that *she* was old news now in the gossip
circles of Richmond. Elsie sounded like her same, buoyant self, full of
news. She missed her friend. She missed the late-night talks and parties.
She missed the way Elsie could sit down at a piano and have everyone
dancing to ragtime in minutes.

    It was time to write back. *Oh, Elsie, I miss you, and I miss being at Mary
Baldwin. I'd give anything to be able to go back; to do it over, differently.
Anything.* But there was no sense in putting down on paper something
that could never be. That would require the sort of magic that only a
six-year-old could have faith in.

    May rifled the pages of *Vogue*. The model on the cover wore a haughty
expression, with long ropes of pearls and organdy, in a shade that was
called "ashes of roses." Studying the design of the dress, May ran her finger
along the line of a seam. *So much for sewing and alterations.* She had, in
fact, told Blue a fib. She hadn't had a single customer in the two months
the sign had been out by the road. Who was going to drive by *here* with
a fancy dress to be hemmed? *I should work for a dressmaker. One of those
places in Washington or New York, where Elsie orders her clothes from.* It was
the kernel of an idea, maybe even the start of a plan. She searched her
memory for the name of the shop—Madame somebody? *Something* de
France, or de Paris? Elsie said all the Senator's wives had their clothes made
there, after the Paris collections.

    The events and interactions of the morning and previous day had left

May drained. Her ability to converse and respond had grown rusty in these reclusive months. She tied on a faded calico apron and took her straw hat from its hook beside the back door. From the shed behind the house, she collected a basket and continued, still musing about the Washington dressmaker, to the garden at the farthest reaches of the backyard. Her refuge. Blossom ambled ahead, settling herself in the shade of a large boxwood bush, in a hollow of dirt she had dug out early in the summer. The cicadas were singing, and in their song, May could hear her mother say, *"Would you look at this tea rose, May? Did you ever see such a shade of yellow? Just like butter and sunshine. Don't cut it yet. We'll wait till it's opened a little more. We'll have a whole house full of roses."*

The picket fence surrounding the garden had long ago weathered to gray. May's mother had spent hours there, often starting work at dawn to avoid the heat. After she left, it had fallen into neglect and over the years, grass had grown tall and unruly around the pickets. Thorny weeds and sunflower stalks obliterated the paths, and the gate was secured only by a tenacious snarl of morning glories. When May returned home from Mary Baldwin at the end of April, she pulled away the dead vines and decided to resurrect the garden. Her father had seemed preoccupied, and neither forbade her nor offered help.

It hadn't taken long for her to figure out what he was up to—the crates of mason jars, the odor of fermentation on his clothes. When she asked, he denied nothing. He boasted about how much he was getting for his premium applejack and shadblowberry cordial. He scoffed at the common corn liquor made by his peers. May didn't argue with him. She only wanted to be left alone. In the rawness of fresh heartbreak, she sought solace in wresting stubborn saplings and weeds from the dirt. The effort calmed her. As the days passed and Amory did not call, she retreated more and more to the garden. In her impotent rage, she hacked at overgrown rose canes until her arms were scratched and bleeding. The mild spring days passed. She ate when Delphina called her to meals, but she felt no hunger. She grew thinner. Some afternoons, she worked together with Otis, an orchard worker who was some sort of cousin once removed of Blue's. The fact that he was mute had been a source of respite. They labored together in companionable silence, leveling the brick paths and dividing peonies. By the end of June, the unruly plot had been tamed, and May had found a way to make the days pass.

When her father had proposed her helping with the moonshine business she had agreed, readily. It would bring money she could save, and she wouldn't have to pass pleasantries or fend off prying questions from market customers about why she was home.

And now, it was mid-August. Inside the fence, the heartier flowers flourished—golden sunflowers towered, fortresslike, beside iridescent black-red hollyhocks. A rabbit skittered from beneath the arbor as May entered, and a mockingbird remonstrated from its perch on the opposite side of the fence. Far overhead, a trio of buzzards traced wide circles in the cloudless sky. She gathered hollyhock seeds and cut faded blooms. The heat was intensifying; Blossom had returned to the porch. May cut the last of the rosebuds and a handful of the fragrant lemon balm Delphina used to make her Van Van oil. Latching the gate behind her, she carried her basket up a small rise in the pasture.

A stately chestnut stood alone, enclosed within a rusted ornate iron fence. In the patch of shade were three graves. Ochre-colored lichen bloomed over the two older stones, and the edges of the carvings had softened over the years. These were the graves of her father's parents. Beside them, a small marble figure of a lamb reclined on a plinth. HENRY MARSHALL III—1912 was carved on the flat surface. Drawing her knees up, May leaned against the tree, holding the flowers like a bridal bouquet. She dreamed sometimes about her mother and baby brother. In her dreams, her mother was stroking May's cheek while telling her, in French, what a clever girl she was. Always in French. After the dreams, May was left with a longing, grasping at something beautiful that constantly moved out of reach. They were in the front field. Mama was beckoning. May ran, but her mother got farther and farther away. As the years passed the dreams came less frequently, and her mother's voice became less distinct, until, finally, she seemed only to be mouthing words.

Memories of her brother were hazy. At four months, he cried most of the time, and the doctor called it colic. Her mother began to lock herself in her room, only allowing the bassinette to be rolled in at night. At times, May woke with a cold stone of dread lodged in her chest, remembering the morning her father had said, *Little Henry has gone to be with the Lord,* and May had asked, *When will he come back?*

When she had those dreams, she did not tell her father, but Delphina seemed to know, and would hug her and rub her back. How could she know what May had dreamed?

In the distance, a train whistle sounded as it passed, heading west, going somewhere that was not *here.* A place where a person could start fresh and work up to something, be *worth* something. May wished she were on that train. She divided the flowers among the headstones and turned to walk back to the house.

FIVE

Late the same afternoon, May reclined on a wicker swing that hung from the ceiling of the shady upstairs porch. The house was quiet, and she wished, as she often did, that they owned a radio. Using her foot, she maintained a lethargic rhythm, pushing off against a post. A sprig of mint wilted in an empty glass on the floor, where Blossom lay. May chewed the end of her pencil and dropped her crossword puzzle book. She was being self-indulgent, but her chores were done. No one required her presence or knew where she was, and there was something vaguely satisfying in that. Her thoughts kept returning to the morning's letter, to Elsie's offer of a visit.

May remembered, vividly, her own preparations for college. With anticipation, she had studied Mrs. Post's etiquette manual, then scoured the Richmond newspaper society columns for mention of girls who would be attending Mary Baldwin. She had packed her things, folding her home-made dresses in tissue paper with her secret, timid aspirations tucked in between, like sachets. Then, finally, departure day arrived. Her father had loaded her things into the truck. Staunton was forty miles away, but it might as well have been another continent. The fact that her belongings were packed in fruit crates and a single battered suitcase went unremarked by her new roommate. Elsie Carter's monogrammed trunks and matching hatboxes were stacked outside their room by a chauffeur.

In May's then-naive estimation, the dresses she copied so painstakingly might have passed for Paris-made; with the neat French seams and smartly fitted pleats that Delphina had taught her to sew. She had not known that her dresses wouldn't pass muster. She hadn't known that being a scholarship girl was not a badge of pride, but rather a label of poverty. Much of what she had learned in eight months of college had little to do with academics.

Still, it felt like a new beginning. Nobody there needed to know that her mother had run away, or that her father drank. After Christmas, May had attended Elsie's debutante ball in Richmond, where she met a charming Hampden-Sydney College graduate who was escorting his sister. When Amory Whitman had written the next week, inviting May to a party, she thought she'd died and gone to heaven. After that, he had driven over to Staunton, and she sneaked out of her dormitory to meet him in Gypsy Hill Park. They wandered through the trees and held hands and then kissed behind the bandstand. Her first kisses. His letters brought equal parts thrill and dread—thrill that he was paying her attention, and dread that she would reveal herself to be unworthy. She wrote little lists of conversation topics and tucked them into her purse. In a matter of weeks, she was besotted to the point of recklessness.

Over spring recess in March, she had gone to stay with Elsie in Richmond, where she could spend whole days alone with Amory. She didn't confide to Elsie that things seemed to be progressing quickly from necking to petting. She didn't ask her friend what was proper, because she would not risk losing Amory. When he told her she was special and beautiful, she bloomed at his touch. She didn't listen to the rumors. After Easter, he told her he wanted to have a talk with her father. Then, that last weekend in April, he asked her to meet him at the Riverside Hotel in Staunton. And because she possessed neither the confidence nor the ingrained morality to say no, May said yes.

May recognized the sound of Byrd's Studebaker chugging up the driveway and wondered if she could hide, right where she was, and just not answer the door. It was too hot to move, even in the shade, with the ceiling fan whirring. The only stimulus that could cause Blossom to exert herself was an ice chip, proffered from May's glass. From her place on the swing, she listened. The car stopped at the end of the front walk. A single door slammed. Byrd's voice called, "Afternoon, Delphina."

Delphina called back, "Afternoon, Byrd. She's up on the porch, there."

Charles Byrd Craig had played football for the University of Virginia, and now had a year to go in the School of Law. May had sat with his parents, cheering him on at his home games, the way a sister would. He had taken her to fraternity parties and taught her the latest dances. He had encouraged her to apply for a scholarship and driven her to Staunton for her interview at Mary Baldwin College. With unspoken understanding, he had not brought up the subject of her expulsion and, though she did not tell him, she was grateful.

His footsteps tapped up the outdoor staircase that connected the lower and upper porches. Blossom raised her head, thumping her tail as he came through the screened door, but she did not rise. Neither did May. She did not react to his handsomeness the way other women did. His looks were as familiar to her as the view. Delphina said it was the sleepy, morning-glory-blue eyes. Aunt Aggie said it was the dimples and the perfect teeth. Elsie said it was the waves in his sandy blond hair.

"What's doing, gal?" Byrd removed his hat, swatting May's leg with it.

"I've been gardening. Tore my hands up clipping roses. See?" She held out her sunburned arms. "Pour yourself some tea."

He loosened his tie and unbuttoned his collar. "Let's go to Fry's Springs Club. You haven't been swimming all summer."

"Not today, but thanks."

He settled into a wicker armchair with a languorous grace, propping his feet on the railing. "Heard y'all had some visitors at the Market."

"Who told you?"

"Word gets around." Byrd put his feet down and sat forward. "Thought I might try to talk some sense into your dad. This is dangerous business. Y'all heard they raided Bacon Hollow? Bose Shifflett's in jail."

May nodded. "I know. I already talked to Daddy. He says we'll stop when the apple harvest is in, only I'm not sure I believe that."

"May, he needs to understand. Once those agents start watching . . ." He shook his head.

"I know, I know." She pushed the swing, willing herself to be more pleasant. She said, brightly, "I got a letter from Elsie today. She invited both of us to a house party over Labor Day."

Byrd picked up the crossword book and frowned at it. "There's a big dance contest in Richmond that weekend, at The Jefferson."

May made a sour expression. "You-know-who will probably be there."

"Amory? Come on now, that's all blown over. He's an ass." The ceiling fan clicked, *tock, tock, tock*, as it rotated with a barely discernible wobble. Byrd leaned his head back against the clapboard. "It might not seem like it now, but getting expelled isn't the end of the world. Something else will come along."

"Aren't you the wise one?"

Byrd was watching the fan; his voice sounded sad. "There are worse things."

"Oh, Byrd." May sat up, swinging her legs forward, stopping the swing. She reached toward him, resting her hand on his arm. "I'm sorry! Jimmy. To*day*. Oh, Lord, I forgot. Forgive me."

"Mother's been in bed all day."

"I know you miss him. I do too. He was so funny."

Byrd nodded. "Six years. It's nice to be able to talk about him. I told Mother I want to go to France and see his grave." In the distance, a train whistle sounded. "That was the worst day of my life."

May nodded. She and Byrd had been thirteen and fifteen that summer of 1918. They had been riding all morning and were walking back to his house from the barn when the black sedan came up the drive and stopped at the front door. His parents weren't home, and Byrd took the telegram. They sat together on the front steps, she with an arm around his shoulders as he tore open the envelope. ". . . *deeply regret to inform you that Private James Craig, Infantry . . .*"

She had been awestruck by the weight of it—by the responsibility of possessing that awful knowledge before Byrd's parents did. Now, six years later, to the day, the silence between them was heavy with emotion. Added to the memory was the prick of guilt, that her friend had sought her out on this sad anniversary, and she had been so self-absorbed as to forget it.

After a minute, Byrd snorted. "We're a couple of live wires, aren't we?"

May said, "I'm sorry. I've been a poor friend lately."

He sighed and sat up, smacking his hands on his knees. "Well, it's time you got out of this house. Let's go to the pictures Friday night. That new Louise Brooks is playing, and another one with Douglas Fairbanks is coming to the Lafayette. Don't tell me no again."

"*The Thief of Bagdad*?"

"You know about it?"

The swing creaked. She continued to push with her foot. "I saw it in the newspaper. I do like that Douglas Fairbanks."

"That's the spirit. We can go to the Fat Man's Club after."

"Don't push it, buster. Is that the place you took me last summer, the one that smelled so bad?"

"Yeah, only they had a raid and had to move. I hear they have a new pianist. And maybe, just maybe, I can convince you to enter that dance contest with me. I know we're out of practice, but there's a cash prize."

"How much is it?"

"Twenty-five dollars, each."

"Really?" May said, "And it's not a marathon?"

"Nope, a contest. And I tell you what: if we win, you can have my share."

SIX

When the picture let out at ten o'clock, May and Byrd strolled up Main Street with the dispersing crowd. She had been grateful for the darkness of the theater, for the dramatic organ music and the fantastical story, transporting her to somewhere new and exotic. Byrd imitated Douglas Fairbanks wielding a cutlass, refusing to stop until he made her laugh. The night was sultry, and purple-gray clouds skittered in front of the new moon. The pavement was dark between the streetlights, and somewhere between Tenth and Eleventh Streets Byrd took her arm, leading her down a narrow alley. As they descended a dimly lit stairwell, a distant strike of lightning illuminated the sky.

"Watch this." He knocked a tattoo on a black door. A brass peephole clicked. An eye appeared. The peephole snapped shut, then the door swung open.

The Fat Man's Club held the dubious distinction of being Charlottesville's first speakeasy. Despite the inferred glamor of its exclusivity, there was something entirely unwholesome about the place. The Fat Man himself, Byrd whispered, was never seen and it was rumored that he was, in truth, a thin person; the name only a decoy for the authorities.

The long, dim hallway smelled of full ashtrays and beer. The ceiling was low, the floor stained, and the brick walls had small, high windows covered in black cloth. The greatest appeal of the place was its proximity to the University—within stumbling distance of the dormitories and fraternity houses. When classes resumed, Byrd explained, it would be standing room only, every night. The doorman showed them to a table and a waiter approached, mopping his brow. "What can I get you folks?"

"A couple of Bitter Blows, if you don't mind," Byrd said. The waiter nodded and turned away.

May folded her arms on the table. The surface was sticky. "What, dare I ask, is a Bitter Blow?"

"Shadblowberry cordial, moonshine, soda water, and a dash of bitters. I'm going to have to catch you up on a few things before we get to Richmond." The musicians began to play, and as they watched, three couples shuffled aimlessly around the small dance floor. Byrd leaned closer, to be heard. "I'm glad I got you to come out tonight."

Their cocktails arrived and May took a tentative sip, then said, "This isn't bad."

"Thought you'd like it. Dance with me?" She took a gulp of her drink. It had been months since she had danced, but they fell into step with ease. Noticing them, the piano player grinned and began to play something livelier, his fingers springing off the keys. By the time the set had finished, the other patrons were applauding as they stepped off the dance floor. As they sat, Byrd said, "Come on. Say you'll go to the contest."

Fanning her face, May flushed with a tiny, hopeful, quivering droplet of pride. It had been a long time since she had felt proud of herself. They *did* dance well together. People probably assumed they were a couple. *Maybe I could.*

She said, "Wouldn't you rather have a real date?"

"No, as a matter of fact, I would not. You're the best dancer I know."

She crossed her arms over her chest, and the drop of pride fell into a vat of cynicism. Richmond was Amory's town. "Did Charlotte Penrose turn you down? I heard you've been seeing her. I think her father owns a slew of coal mines."

"Don't be snide. She's a nice girl."

"One of the 'Penrose Pearls.' Five sisters, and two of them were at Mary

Baldwin. They were roommates, and I remember they kept getting in trouble because they had such loud fights and threw each other's things out of the dormitory window. One of their shoes hit the house mother on the head!"

"May, stop." Byrd's eyes crinkled. "You're terrible."

"I'm not fooling. She needed stitches." *Maybe I could, if I had Byrd and Elsie there.*

"Charlotte is good fun."

"So you *have* been seeing her." *Elsie will know about that dressmaker.*

"On and off."

Don't ask. Just don't. "How many girls did you go out with last week?"

"Three."

May wagged a finger at him, narrowing her eyes as she smiled. "Ha! You are *such* a parlor snake. You're like one of those revolving doors! If you were a girl, they'd call you fast."

Byrd leaned back, holding up a palm. "Sheath your claws." He smoothed his hair and grinned. "If I didn't know better, I'd think you're jealous."

"Well, you do know better. Who else but me will give you a hard time?"

"Listen, we'd have a good chance at that contest. Think about it. That's a lot of money."

May leaned forward, swishing the ice in her glass. "And you'd really give me your share?" *I could leave. I could get a little room.* She held out her glass. "Hell, give me another one of these."

It was shortly after midnight when Byrd dropped May back at the farm and they ran together, laughing, through the rain to the front door. "All right," Byrd said, "You keep those dancing shoes polished up. I'm not going to let you off the hook now. We'll need to practice if we're going to win."

May gasped, breathless from running. She held her wet dress away from her body. "You bet we're going to win. Thanks for tonight. It was nice. It felt good."

As he drove away, she switched off the front light and watched the sky through the screen, flashing silver on indigo. Sparks of hopefulness lit in her consciousness. She had ventured out, and it had gone well. Now she had agreed to go to Richmond. If they could win, and she had another fifty dollars, and she could arrange a job interview in Washington . . . *One step at a time.*

Her father's voice carried through the hallway from the back of the house. May followed it, calling, "Hi Daddy, I'm home." Her father sat alone on the porch, his rocking chair stilled, one arm draped over Blossom's back. The big dog sat close, leaning against his chair, panting, her ears pulled back. Her tail thumped as May leaned down to scratch an ear. "You scared, old girl?" May said, "It's only a thunderstorm."

May took her usual seat. Watching a summer storm pass seemed a perfect way to end the night. The air felt static; the breeze picked up as the sky lit with another distant flash. Rain sheeted off the roof's edge. Henry leaned forward in his chair, his arms resting on his knees. He said, "Tell me about the picture you saw tonight. I like those pirate stories."

As May began to explain the plot, the telephone jangled from the hallway. "I'll get it," she said, pushing herself up.

"Hello?" she asked, tentatively, knowing that a ringing phone at midnight would not bring good news. "Marshall residence, this is May speaking."

There were a series of clicks, then crackling, as thunder boomed in the distance. The voice of the operator came over the wire: "Please hold to be connected."

A deep male voice came on the line. "Tell Henry Marshall to expect a visitor at the Market tomorrow morning."

"Who is this?"

"A friend." The line clicked and began to buzz.

SEVEN

Ten minutes later, Henry pulled the truck behind the Market and cut the engine. Through sheeting rain on the windshield, May could see the light above the back door, haloed in yellow. Below, the kitchen door swung inward as a light switched on, throwing Blue into silhouette inside. May and Henry exchanged hopeful looks in the dimness of the truck cab. Over the rumble of thunder, Henry said, "I wish you'd stayed home."

May said, "It'll go faster with three of us. Come on." She pushed open the truck door and dashed for the market, gasping as a white slash of lightning fractured the sky. Inside the kitchen, she and Henry stood dripping on the floor. Blue, roused by Henry's call minutes before, was pulling his suspenders over his shoulders.

Henry said, "How many cases here, Blue?"

"Twenty, maybe? We going to the still?"

Henry nodded. "Gonna be messy getting down there, in this."

May said, "Do you think they'll go there too?"

Henry said, "If agents knew where it is, they'd have raided us by now. Far as I know, the only ones who know are the three of us and Otis. May, fill up the cartons from the shelves. Blue and I will take it out to the truck. This shouldn't take long. Then I'm taking you home. The two of us can unload."

In the front room, May went up and down the stepladder, ferrying

Apple Butter jars from the shelves nearest the ceiling while her father and Blue came and went from outside.

Fifteen minutes later, May carried the final, partially filled carton outside. Warm rain dripped off her nose and ran into her eyes. The smell of oily gravel mixed with pine and cedar from the surrounding woods. She set the carton on the open truck gate and stopped to wipe her face as two yellow beams cut through the darkness, curving around the side of the Market toward them. Headlights.

"Run, May!" Henry called from the kitchen door, "Get yourself home!"

May ran across the gravel, avoiding the oncoming lights. Ahead of her, the twin beams played off tree trunks. Reaching the edge of the parking area, she entered the woods. She paused behind a thick oak, looking back. The car stopped, its lights fully illuminating the back of the truck, where eighteen cases of moonshine were stacked. Her calf muscles twitched with the impulse to flee. A train whistle pealed in the distance, becoming louder as the train neared a crossing, its brilliant light blinking through the darkness ahead of her. May ran along the gravel edge of the track, staying low at first, the clamor of the train masking her heaving breath. The huffing engine passed in a blur of yellow light and vibrating cacophony. The beam receded, and in the sudden darkness she tripped on a root, her arm dragging against rough pine bark as she fell. She pulled herself up and leaned against the tree, gulping the hot, acrid, metallic air.

The tingle of abraded skin began to register as needle pricks of pain. Her chest burned; she could not fill her lungs. She pushed her dripping hair from her face. A rustling in the underbrush caused her to jump, and she held her breath. A deer emerged from the rise across the tracks and looked down on her, its tail twitching. May blew out a long, shaking breath, and the doe froze, then bolted. Wiping her eyes again, she tried to orient herself in the darkness. If she followed the tracks, they would intersect Black Cat Road in a quarter mile. From there, it would be another quarter mile home across the Craig's front field. May's dress clung to her chilled skin and her teeth began to chatter.

By the time she reached the farm drive, the sky was clearing and the moon was out. Everything looked peaceful—the dripping trees, the house with the porch light glowing. Mud sucked at her shoes, and she could hear Blossom's deep, alarmed barking.

"That you, Chérie?" Delphina called into the darkness from the porch, her voice alarmed. "*Mon Dieu*, child, what happened?"

May sank to sit on the steps, drained and cold. Water dripped from her hair onto her face. "Is Daddy back?" The call-and-answer of tree frogs and rain dripping from the gutters punctuated the quiet.

Delphina put her hand on May's forearm, saying, "I came over to hush the dog. She's been carrying on and wouldn't quiet. I thought maybe somebody had got in the house or something. Then I saw the truck was gone. The phone started to ring, and it was Blue. He said I should be looking out for you, and Henry'd be back real late. He said to tell you everything's fine. Said you'd know what he meant. Let me see that scrape on your arm."

"It's nothing." *Nothing. Nothing. Everything's fine. I'm fine.*

Delphina turned May's arm over, examining it. "I hope you didn't get into poison ivy or chiggers. And Lord have mercy, look at your good shoes! Leave 'em on the porch and come right this minute and let me see to this arm."

Like a dutiful child, May trudged behind Delphina, crossing the yard to her cottage.

In the small garden plot outside, Delphina picked a handful of leaves by moonlight. May followed her inside. She rarely came into Delphina's private space. A big cooking fireplace of old Virginia brick took up one wall, and from rough-hewn rafters, herbs and plants hung in bunches to dry, along with a snakeskin. "Hold this," Delphina commanded, passing the fresh leaves to May.

May sniffed the bundle. "Smells nice."

"Just plain old comfrey and chamomile. Good for bruising." Delphina began pounding the leaves in a mortar, mixing them with green powder. She wrapped the crushed leaves in muslin. "I am not asking why you came through the woods like that. I do not want to know. But I ought to put you over my knee for worrying me so."

"I'd like to see you try." May tried to laugh and instead found herself choking back tears.

She sank onto a cane-backed chair, feeling weak and very, very tired. She studied the glass and earthenware jars that lined the mantel—Delphina's herbs and cures. From behind a jar, the edge of an old photograph showed. She said, "What's that?"

"Come over here and let me wrap that arm."

May stood and reached for the brittle, faded picture. Holding it with her fingertips, she said, "Delphie, this is you! I've never seen a photograph of you. You look so young. And who is . . ." May turned the photo over. Written in sepia-toned ink was

Ellen and me, 1902

"This is Mama?" The young woman in the photograph had dark hair waving down to her waist, she was emaciated and hollow eyed, leaning hard against Delphina—a younger, darker-haired Delphina, less severe looking than she was now, but with the same regal bearing. May looked up, waiting. "Why haven't you ever shown this to me?"

"Give that here. You know your Daddy doesn't allow . . ."

May moved toward the table lamp, looking more closely. "What was wrong with her?"

"Come over here."

May carried the photo and laid it on the table beside the muslin. Delphina tied her arm as she continued to study the photograph. "Delphina . . ."

"She'd been sick for a while." Delphina pulled the muslin knot.

"Tell me."

"She'd been sick. Nothing to tell."

"I'll ask Daddy." May watched Delphina's face as she loosened the fabric and knotted it tighter.

"Don't you go and stir that pot." Their eyes met. May could not tell if she saw pleading or warning or both before Delphina took the photograph and tucked it decisively into her apron pocket. "Lord," she said, returning to her usual brusqueness, "you're a nosy one. Now, you get to bed before you catch your death. It's one thirty in the morning."

May paused at Delphina's door, her hand on the handle. "Thank you." She glanced back at the photo. "When I was little, I used to think you could read my dreams. Was that magic?"

"Nah," Delphina's expression softened. "That was just me reading your sad little face."

EIGHT

May's clock read 7:30 a.m. Morning sunlight streamed through the windows of her bedroom. The night before, she had lain awake, too exhausted to close the blinds, waiting for the sound of the truck and her father's return. But restless sleep had won out.

Now the events of the previous night lingered in her muscles and blood like venom. She pushed herself up from the mattress with a groan. Barefoot and foggy, she trudged down the stairs and to the kitchen. Delphina worked at the sink, scouring a pot with savage energy. Silently, May took a smaller pot from the drainboard and began to dry it, setting normality into motion.

"Let God dry 'em this morning," Delphina said, turning off the taps. May sat heavily in a kitchen chair and rubbed her palms over her face before examining the tender scratches on her legs and arms. The truck's noisy brakes ground to a halt outside. "There's Henry now," Delphina said, "He didn't come back last night. Now don't you go asking him about that picture, you hear me? You know how worked up he gets if you ask about Ellen. He's got enough on his plate this morning. I got to gather the eggs." Delphina strode from the kitchen, basket over her arm.

May held the porch door open as Henry carried two cardboard cartons inside, then set them on the table. She recognized the rattle of empty mason jars. Her father touched her arm, frowning with concern. "You all right, little gal? Bet we scared the devil out of you last night."

"Who was that, in the car?"

He patted her shoulder, then crossed to the sink to wash his hands. "Just a customer wanting some hooch, name of Chessie Mackenzie. He's a regular—said he was passing and saw the lights on. I told him he scared us silly. I called to you, but you couldn't hear me for the rain. I knew you'd get yourself back. All the hooch is out of the Market. I'll keep it down at the still." He glanced up at the clock. "I need to get back and open up."

"And you *promise* you don't owe that Beasley?"

"Yes, ma'am, I promise."

May said, "We need to stop—not just selling out of the Market—we need to stop making it. Last night was a warning."

"We'll talk later, alrighty? You take it easy today." Henry grabbed a cold biscuit and bit off half of it.

"No, I want to be there if Sheriff Beasley shows up."

"Absolutely not. You're out of this now. He doesn't need to see you again."

"Telephone if you need me." May followed him out to the porch and sat in her rocker, drawing her knees up beneath her nightgown. A red-winged blackbird settled on the fence rail, its plaintive cry sounding like a fretful baby. The landscape looked as if it had been washed clean in the rain, with tufts of vapor, like cotton candy, rising through the trees on the distant mountains. When Blossom nudged her, May rubbed the bony furrow between her eyes.

Her father's promises, she knew, were given with conviction, every time. His inability to maintain those avowals was another matter. Clarity, unlike self-deception, was harsh. No wonder he had become so adept at blurring the lines. He wouldn't change. This *place* was not going to change. Scratches and bruises now marked her as fearful and powerless. To sit and wait and hope this didn't happen again was like sticking her head in the sand. Luck wasn't going to walk up on the porch and shake her hand and give her a hundred dollars. Decisions needed to be made.

"Blossom," May said, "It's time I got out of this puddle of self-pity. I've been rolling around in it for too long. I've got it all over me, like a shoat in the mud." She looked over at her shoes from the night before. Delphina must have tried to clean them, but the pale tan calfskin was splotched and ruined. Blossom regarded her with a doleful look. May rocked forward forcefully, propelling herself to her feet. "First of all, I am going to Richmond." The dog put her ears back. "And you know what? I hope I see Amory Whitman at that contest. I will hold my head up and look him in the eye, and he can go straight to hell."

She marched upstairs, opened her desk, and pulled out a box of writing paper, then scrawled a hasty letter.

August 23, 1924

Dear Elsie,

I was so pleased to get your letter. Forgive me for not writing before. I can't wait to see your haircut. I'm sure it looks very smart, and it must be nice and cool in this beastly heat. I love the crossword puzzles! I got Byrd to try one, but he said he didn't see the point.

We are coming to your house party, and we'll be at the dance contest on the 29th, with bells on. I'm going to make Byrd practice with me every day, and I'll get him to bring his gramophone records, and I'll bring my scrapbook.

I have a favor to ask of you. Well, actually, of your mother. I'd like to keep it between us for now. I was thinking of applying to work for that dressmaker you like in Washington, I think the name was Véronique de Paris? Wasn't her salon on Connecticut Avenue, near Elizabeth Arden?

I was wondering if your mother might write a reference for me. I'd like to set up an interview during my visit with you.

Tell your dear mother I'll bring her some preserves and some shad-blowberry cordial. I'll see you next week!

Love, May

NINE

A week had passed, and May stood on a low stool in the upstairs sewing room, in front of a long mirror. "Was that the telephone?" she froze, listening.

"Stop fidgeting," Delphina murmured, through a mouthful of pins. She pinched the excess fabric of May's dress. "You've been jumpy all day."

"Guess I'm nervous about the contest." *Partially true.* She was equally anxious to hear from Elsie. May had considered telling Delphina her idea, but she kept it to herself.

A wasp-waisted dress form stood at attention in a corner, and on the walls, framed watercolor sketches of her mother's elaborate designs for Mardi Gras costumes hung—a jester, a flower fairy, an exotic bird, and May's favorite, a tiered aperture that made the wearer look like a fountain, dripping crystal beads. At the top of each sketch was printed: C.M. VALENTINE & CO. FANCY DRESS COSTUMES AND FINE SEWING, and at the bottom: 521 N. HENNESSEY STREET, NEW ORLEANS. "Do you remember these costumes?" May asked.

"Course I do," Delphina said, "Folks would wait two years for a costume from Valentine's." Tilting her head toward the fountain sketch, she said, "That one there? We stayed up *all* night stringing those crystals. But it won a prize. Your Mama was right proud." She tugged the dress, and May did a quarter-turn. Delphina continued, "When Ellen was a bitty thing she'd beg to go to work with your granddaddy, to play with all the beads and make paper dolls. When she got older, she'd draw pictures of the most outlandish costumes to show to him when he came home. He'd just laugh, and say, 'That's impossible,' but then she'd explain to him how it would work. And I tell you what—it always did. The patterns looked like puzzles to me."

"Why did she stop?"

Delphina clucked her tongue. "Turn again. Hold still. She met your Daddy, he brought her here. Then you came along."

"Not so tight there," May said, "It has to swirl when I spin." The lilt in Delphina's voice meant she was keeping something to herself. Avoiding something.

"Turn." Delphina continued to pin. May was facing the mirror again. She regarded her face, thinner now than it had been the last time she had worn this dress. Her cheekbones were more pronounced. She tilted her face. Delphina told her that she had her mother's fine complexion. Holding her dark hair above her head, she fanned the ends over her forehead.

"Think I ought to bob my hair?"

"It's fine like it is." Delphina did not look up.

May peeked from beneath her false bangs. "Elsie did it. Sure would be easier to wash, wouldn't it? Might be nice to look different." She thought of Louise Brooks, so modern with her glamorous silky bob and flirty bangs. A star in the pictures. Had she ever looked ordinary? And what would Amory think of her with bobbed hair? *He might not even be there*, she told herself, yet again. She had composed a litany of reassurances over the past week: *It's just a silly little contest. Byrd will be there, and Elsie. Byrd and I dance well together. No one needs to know if I have a job interview in Washington. If it doesn't work, I'll come home on the train. Nothing ventured, nothing gained.*

"All right, then." Delphina rose, slowly, holding a hand to her lower back. "Careful of those pins." May pulled the dress over her head then sat at the sewing machine and adjusted the delicate fabric. As she re-stitched the seams, Delphina looked over her shoulder, saying, "You sew beautifully, Chérie. Like your Mama. Now, then, how many dresses are you taking?"

"Two evening and three day." May snipped a loose thread. "I'm going to give you the telephone number for Elsie's parents' house. I don't know if they have a telephone at the river." She looked up at Delphina, scissors poised, "Promise you'll ring me if there's any trouble."

"Things will be fine here."

"I hope so. Damn, look at that. It's almost half past three! Is the iron still hot? I've got to wash my hair. If I cut it off, I could be ready in no time, probably. Oh! Was that the phone? I'll get it."

May ran downstairs in her slip, snatching up the receiver on the third ring. "Hello?"

A gravelly female voice responded, "Hello, yourself, old dear!"

"Elsie!" May said, glancing toward the stairs.

"Just wanted to let you know that everything's set. Mother posted a letter to Véronique and then I telephoned. You have an interview on Tuesday at two. Véronique may spell her name the French way, but I suspect she's Veronica from New Jersey. She likes that you speak French. I'll drive you up there and we could do luncheon before, if you like? Anyhow, you're terribly clever to come up with this."

"Oh, thank you! I'm so excited. And please tell your mother how much I appreciate her help. I'll write her a note."

"Marvelous. Listen, I must run, but we'll see you tonight. Kisses!"

May replaced the receiver and hugged herself as she ran back up the stairs. Her plan was in motion.

After her bath, she dressed, then laid her suitcase open on the bed. A sudden waft of mildew reminded her that she hadn't used it since returning from Mary Baldwin. She folded a nightgown, then pulled a small black velvet pouch from her top drawer. Her mother's pearl necklace. She'd been told they were fine pearls and now, they would be her insurance. If she and Byrd didn't win, she could pawn them in Washington. Opening the drawstring, she poured the strand into her hand. Rolling pearls between her fingers, she was caught in a memory.

She was seven, and restless. "Where do pearls come from, Mama?" They had been napping on Mama's bed, shutters closed against the heat. Now, she wanted to go downstairs to see baby Henry or at least play at Mama's dressing table.

Mama's sleepy voice. "The ocean, Chérie. Deep in the ocean. From a place far, far away."

"But how do they get them from the ocean?"

"Pearls are mermaid's tears. They save them on a string, see?" Her mother, eyes closed, dangled the strand for her to grasp.

"What makes the mermaids sad?"

"So many questions . . ." An edge of irritation. *"Get Mother's tonic, won't you? Go on downstairs. That's a good girl."*

May had never learned the answer to her question about the mermaid's tears—and there were so many more that could never be asked. She weighed the necklace in her palm, then clasped it behind her neck. *All you left me was pearls, Mama. Did you think they'd be enough? I sure hope so.* Her mind went back to Delphina's photograph. Holding up the long skirt of her dress, she quickly crossed the hall. In her mother's room, she picked up the wedding portrait from the dressing table. The photo was from 1903. Delphina's was dated 1902. Something—some span of time—was missing.

From the lower hall, the grandfather clock chimed five. May carried her suitcase downstairs and left it in the hallway. When she called out to her father, Delphina responded from the kitchen, "He's not here."

The kitchen smelled of honey and baking. Delphina tucked a cloth over the top of a basket. May said, "There's something I don't understand."

"What's that?"

"Why aren't there any photographs of Mama in Paris?"

Delphina fussed with the cloth. "She didn't bring them here."

"That photograph you have, with Mama. The date on it was the year before she married Daddy, the year she was supposed to be in Paris. Only *you* weren't there with her. But you're in that picture from 1902."

Delphina swallowed visibly. The *ah-oo-gah, ah-oo-gah,* of a car horn sounded, coming down the driveway. Delphina said, "There's Byrd now."

A car door slammed. Delphina's eyes flitted to the hallway. She licked her lips and said, "She was sick. She was in a hospital."

Those vacant eyes. "What was wrong with her?" May said, "What was the name of her illness, Delphina? Should I ask Daddy?"

Delphina blinked slowly. "Your father doesn't know about it."

"You mean, he believes she went to Paris for a year before they met, but she didn't. And what else haven't you told me? Do you know where she is?"

"No. I don't know."

"Where was she when she sent me that doll?"

Byrd called from outside. "Hello?"

Delphina picked up the basket. "I don't know where she is now. That's the truth. We can talk about it when you get back, only don't ask Henry." She marched out, leaving the kitchen door swinging behind her.

Worrying her pearls through her fingers, May followed through the hallway to the front door. She could demand answers from her father. She was an adult now. Delphina was hiding something. But it would have to wait.

On the porch, Blossom's tail began to thump, increasing its tempo as Byrd strolled up the walk. He wolf-whistled, then bounded up the steps to take her suitcase. He kissed her cheek and said into her ear, "You look like a dream. And you smell good too. Ready?"

Was she ready? All week, the anticipation of competing on the dance floor had caused her chest to seize a little with anxiety. Imagining the scene produced an instantaneous, defensive detachment, wherein she was able to project the events in abstract flashes, not entire sequences. To visualize outcomes meant to envision the possibility of mortification—slipping and falling, or tripping on the hem of her dress, or forgetting the order of steps in any particular dance. She breathed deeply and smiled.

The evening dress she was wearing had been her favorite. A deep blue crepe, printed with calla lilies, with a low, draped back and a fluid skirt that was perfect for dancing. Adding to her detachment was the discomfiture of wearing formal clothes during daylight hours, as if she and Byrd were playing dress-up, posed within a big, shiny soap bubble. It was necessary, she knew from past experience, to maintain the semblance of calm, to complete each separate, tiny motion that would propel her on to the next scene, in hopes that the imagined script would prove true. May started down the steps, calling over her shoulder, "You look pretty dapper yourself, mister." Byrd's black dinner jacket fit him perfectly; the satin lapel accentuated the dark flecks in his eyes. "The girls will be all over you to sign their dance cards."

Delphina passed the basket to Byrd. "For the drive."

He peeked beneath the cover. "What a treat! Nothing in the world better than your ham biscuits. Thank you."

Delphina said, "You take care of my girl, you hear?"

"Delphie," May said, "do you know where Daddy is?"

Delphina's eyes had a pleading expression. "Saw him walk up to the graves a while ago."

"I just want to say goodbye." Kicking off her shoes, May gathered the skirt of her evening dress in one hand. Blossom followed her.

Beside the grave of his son, Henry sat with his back against the trunk of the chestnut tree. He held a bottle. May's steps quickened and she stood in front of him, hands clenched at her hips.

"Hey, li'l gal," he said. "Ain' you a sight for sore eyes."

"How could you do this today?" She stomped her foot in the grass, knowing she sounded petulant and childish.

"Now, you listen." Henry shook an unsteady finger. "Don' you be fussin' at me." He rubbed a palm over his face.

Her voice rose unsteadily. "I'm right *here*! Why can't you talk to me instead of sitting up here alone and . . . so . . . ." He looked up at her and she could not say the word, *pathetic*. She said, instead, quietly, "I know you miss Baby Henry. I miss him too."

"You were too small . . . You were too small to remember."

"I *do* remember him." May was pleading now. "And I remember Mama. I remember the good things. And I've never been able to understand why you won't tell me about her."

Henry ran his hand over the top of his head and rubbed the back of his neck. He looked old and worn out. "Did my best with her."

"Do you know where she is?"

He shook his head, holding up a palm in pledge. "She's dead to me."

"That's not an answer. I deserve to know."

From the house, Byrd called, "May? You need any help?"

May's fingernails bit into her palms as she turned her back on her father and walked away.

Byrd was leaning against the side of the Studebaker, chatting with

Delphina and finishing a biscuit. "Ready?" he asked, dusting crumbs from his hands.

May nodded, not looking him in the eye. "Let's just go. Please."

"I'll watch him," Delphina whispered. "Y'all go on and have a good time." May climbed into the car and Byrd closed her door.

"You all right?" He asked as they pulled away. The scenery flashed by and May's vision blurred. Byrd spoke quietly. "What happened?"

"He's getting worse. He sits up at the graves and drinks and talks to himself." May inspected the reddened crescent marks on her palms. "And something strange happened. Delphina has this photograph of herself with Mama. Only it's from the year when my mother was supposed to be in France, before she married Daddy. There's something Delphina's not telling me. It's been twelve years since she sent me that doll, and not a letter since, or a birthday card, or anything."

"Maybe when you get back you can try to talk to him. Or maybe both of them together. I could ask him, if you want." Byrd hesitated, then said, "Do you still want to go? I know Elsie's looking forward to having you. And I'm counting on us winning that contest, much as you made me practice." He looked over at her and his smile faded. "Now what's wrong? What'd I say?"

May fiddled with the window crank. "Nothing. I mean, yes, I do want to go, and I want us to win." She wiped her cheeks with her palms, concentrating hard on counting telegraph poles. "Do you think he'll be there with his fiancée? The paper said she was 'Deb of the Year.'"

"Amory? *Pfft*. Are you kidding? Bitsy Ragsdale's perfect for him—socially ambitious and shallow as a puddle. Deb of the Year will probably be the greatest accomplishment of her life. You don't really want to be like those Richmond girls, do you?"

"I thought I did." May sighed. "I *liked* being with those girls. I wished I could be a debutante and be celebrated for nothing more than who my family happened to be. I hadn't seen that life before college—I mean, I knew about it, but I hadn't seen the way they *live*. Now I have, and it's like looking through the window at a party I'm not invited to." She laughed derisively, volatility turning to sarcasm. "And what's wrong with having a wardrobe from Paris and a new roadster every year and a Grand Tour, and never having to worry about paying the goddamned mortgage? Those are the sort of girls you take out all the time. You were in Richmond last week. Who were you with?"

Byrd tugged at his collar. "Patsy Wrunkle."

"*No.* Not Rodney Wrunkle's sister?"

"Yes."

May snorted. "Lord. I had forgotten about him. Elsie used to call him Rotten Wrunkle behind his back, because he always had the *worst* bad breath. Does Patsy have it too? Maybe it runs in their family. Wouldn't that be awful? To have inherited bad breath? And you know how he laughs like a donkey?" May leaned back her head and brayed. "Does she laugh like a donkey?"

"You're terrible." Byrd leaned over the steering wheel, laughing. "She's actually a nice gal. Goes to Hollins."

"Ah," May said, nodding. "And did you know that their father is called the Peanut Baron of Suffolk? Another suitable candidate to be the future Mrs. Byrd Craig."

Byrd sat back, seeming to relax. He reached across the seat to pat May's hand. "Nah. You know I'm waiting for you."

She slapped his arm with her gloves. "Phooey. You want a proper girl who's rich and doesn't break the rules."

"I like you the way you are."

You have no idea.

May turned toward him. "Well, look out then, 'cause I've got nothing left to lose in Richmond. Let's see what happens if I keep breaking the rules."

TEN

The Studebaker pulled up to the entrance of The Jefferson Hotel at half past seven. Sleek automobiles disgorged groups of fashionably dressed young people while shrill laughter and shrieked greetings rang out into the sultry evening, adding to the atmosphere of anticipated gaiety. A smiling attendant opened May's door, and she waited at the foot of the wide steps, scanning the courtyard as she pulled on her evening gloves. She would not be caught unawares.

As they stepped inside the lobby, she took Byrd's arm. Her eyes were drawn up the sweeping twin marble staircases to the sparkle of crystal chandeliers forty feet above. At the top of the steps was the Palm Court, where The Jefferson's signature pair of alligators swam in lazy circles around a center fountain. May searched passing faces while affecting an air of ease that she did not feel. Almost immediately, a young woman grasped Byrd's other elbow, pulling him toward her, saying, "Why, Byrd Craig, what a *perfectly* lovely surprise!" May knew at once who she was and tightened her own grip. Bitsy Ragsdale was petite and pretty, in a tensely brittle way. From her blunt-cut bob to her jutting elbows, she was made up of angles. The line of her gunmetal satin dress was punctuated by the jut of her hip bones and a silvery fabric band was tied around her forehead. She patted Byrd's lapel. "What have you been up to?"

"Well, Bitsy. Hello. And Maude," Byrd took a half step away from Bitsy and his brilliant smile turned like a spotlight toward an awkwardly tall young woman who stood close by. She started and squinted, as if the unexpected beam of his attention was too bright to bear. He said, "How are you this evening? You look very nice. What do you call that color?"

Her cheeks blotched. "Puce. And fine, thanks, Byrd. I mean, I'm fine tonight, and . . . thank you for asking." She took a large swallow from her glass.

"Ladies, this is May Marshall, from Keswick. May—Bitsy Ragsdale and Maude Whitman."

May nodded. "Lovely to meet you both."

Bitsy frowned as if she were puzzling something out. Her eyebrows shot up and she raised her glass to her lips. She smiled—a slow smile that progressed no farther than her mouth. She held her glass in place long enough for May to notice the large emerald she wore over her evening gloves, on her left hand. *The Whitman emerald*, just as Amory had described it. "I've heard of you before," Bitsy said, coolly.

Maude, Amory's younger sister, had prominent gums and a weak chin. Her stooping posture and expectant expression seemed to convey, in equal parts, hopefulness and a resigned aura of inadequacy. She squinted at May, saying, "Are you dancing in the competition?"

May leaned her head briefly against Byrd's shoulder. "Byrd and I are partners tonight. How about you?"

Maude's dance card, with its little silk tassel, dangled dejectedly from her wrist. "My brother will be representing the family."

May smiled weakly. *Oh, my family will love you,* Amory had said, *You'll meet them as soon as they come back from Europe. We'll keep this our secret, for now.*

"How nice," May said. "It's been *lovely* chatting, really, but Byrd, darling, let's get a drink."

"Good luck, then," Bitsy said, in a singsong voice, waggling her fingers so that her ring flashed. May fluttered in response and continued to squeeze Byrd's arm as they worked their way through the crowd into the ballroom.

"Byrd, *darling?*" he said.

"I was polite, wasn't I? God, I need a drink."

A pretty girl called from across the lobby, waving an arm above her head, "Hey there, Byrd! Save a dance?" Several female heads swiveled toward them, casting admiring glances toward Byrd. May was proud to be on his arm. She had felt the same sort of pride with Amory. To be attached to him was to be inside of his nimbus—anointed—one of *his crowd*, always ready to laugh before the joke was told. She craned her neck in search of Elsie. But who was she kidding? It was Amory she was looking for.

Byrd patted her arm. "How about a Bitter Blow?"

"May!" A feminine voice boomed, "*So* glad you made it!" Elsie enveloped her in a bear hug, whispering, "I haven't breathed a word to anyone." She winked, then, removing her long, gold cigarette holder, she gave Byrd an exuberant smacking kiss on the cheek, leaving a vivid-crimson lip print. Her gestures were expansive, and her distinctive, raspy voice made everything she said sound naughty and enticing. "We *just* walked in! We'd have been here sooner, only I got pinched for speeding on the way, didn't I, Archie? I've got a table for us over here. You remember my date, Archie Nelson?" She waved her cigarette, yelling hello to friends who passed by. Elsie Carter wasn't strictly a beauty; instead, she was one of those refreshingly rare young women who thought nothing of making a fool of themselves or being the butt of their own joke.

"Now, then. May, you sit here, next to me, so we can catch up." Elsie stood behind a chair, directing her guests and dropping ashes on the floor. "Byrd, you *divine* thing, you sit over there across the table so I can look at you. Listen, everyone, we're throwing a party at Mother and Dad's afterward, and Cook will make us a big breakfast when we get there. You'll come, won't you Byrd? We'll leave for the river in the morning."

"Only if you promise to play the piano."

Elsie smiled her wide, slightly buck-toothed smile. "Splendid. Anything you want to hear, as long as it's ragtime or Jazz. I want to see you two come home with that trophy over there." She gestured toward a table near the orchestra, which displayed a large silver loving cup and several smaller trophies. "Too bad Archie's a gimp, or we'd give you a run for your money, wouldn't we, Arch? Be a darling—get me another packet of smokes, would you?" Archie gamely rose and limped across the floor. Elsie leaned toward May, saying, "Polio. Still, he started on the football team at VMI. He's a jolly fellow, even if he is a tad quiet. By the way, old girl, you're looking *awfully* svelte. And those cheekbones!" Elsie held May's chin. "What I wouldn't *give* for those cheekbones. And here I eat nothing but grapefruit and do slimming exercises every day, and I'm still stout."

"You look gorgeous. Your dress is divine. Is it Véronique? And Elsie, I can't thank you enough, or your mother. I hope it works."

"Why all the secrecy?"

May toyed with her napkin. "If I don't get the job, I don't want anyone to feel sorry for me, you know? I'll go back home like it never happened, and no one's the wiser."

The orchestra began playing, and the clumps of young people divided as couples took to the floor. Elsie and Archie remained at the table, with Elsie regaling her guests with anecdotes while Archie watched with apparent amusement. May danced a foxtrot with Byrd, then a polka with someone else from their table. Siphons of soda water and bottles of ginger ale were in constant demand from the harried waiters, as young men and women brought out flasks of liquor and jars of moonshine. By the third Bitter Blow, May's nerves seemed to be less of a problem. Byrd mixed a round for their table while Elsie showed off the silver flask she kept tucked into her garter, and the hollow walking stick she had given Archie, twisting the brass knob from the top, then pouring out a shot of gin. The bandleader tapped his baton and announced a break, saying that the contest would begin when they resumed. May continued to scan the ballroom. She had rehearsed carefree expressions in the mirror at home, in preparation. She wanted to be sure she was laughing or smiling when Amory noticed her. She wanted him to think she had never cared.

The bandleader read off the rules and the order of events then thanked the patrons of the contest: Miller and Rhodes Department Store and the E. A. Whitman Tobacco Company. Four couples would dance in each round, the winners competing in successive rounds. When he tapped his baton on the podium, the ballroom became quiet.

Byrd led May onto the floor for the first round as the music began.

She knew he would lead her without hesitation or error. His effort-less grace and good looks made him a pleasure to watch. They won the round, then waited at the sidelines, catching their breath and watching the other groups compete. As the fourth group took to the floor, May finally saw Amory.

Watching him dance, she remembered how flustered she had felt trying to keep up with him. It wasn't only the dancing. She had been so overwhelmed as to find it nearly impossible to make conversation. Even with her little lists of topics she often ended up nodding, staring like a fool, and the more foolish she felt, the harder it was to speak, and she knew, as if she were watching a ship sink, that she was not *doing her part*. She was, on a social level, *a disappointment*.

The more May thought about it, the more determined she became. It wasn't only the prize money she wanted, she wanted to beat Amory Whitman. As she watched, he spun Bitsy, and when he looked over her shoulder, May caught his eye. He froze for an instant and paled. Bitsy jerked back toward him, a half beat out of step. His face recovered its bland expression. Her mouth twitched, remembering how he used to look at *her*, and how she had gazed back, feeling desirable, feeling adored.

The contest continued with a waltz, then a Charleston. Four couples remained when the bandleader announced that the final dance would be a Tango. A murmur rose from the crowd as the music began, the tempo slowly building and becoming more complex. Byrd's arm was at May's waist. She knew exactly where Amory and Bitsy were standing. She locked eyes with Byrd, and they began. *Sweep, turn, halt.* The desired facial expression for the Tango was one of intense concentration and fixation on one's partner. They were playing parts, alternately dominant and submissive; defiant and acqui-escing. *Sweep, turn, halt.* Her skirt swirled around her legs, one beat behind. *Sweep, rotate, sweep.* Their heads turned stiffly in unison as their bodies moved sinuously. Faces in the crowd slid by in a centrifugal blur. *Click, click, freeze.* Like marionettes. Then the slow, sensuous folding backward into a dramatic dip. *Trust. Melt. Hold. Breathe.* The crowd erupted in cheers and applause. Byrd pulled her upright, squeezing her hand. They were both flushed and beaming. May did not look toward Amory and Bitsy. She didn't need to.

After the noise died down, the bandleader thanked the sponsors again, and the crowd hushed as the winners were announced. The third-place couple received a gracious round of applause and a small trophy. A flash went off as a reporter from the *Richmond Times* scribbled names on his pad. May and Byrd were announced in second place. Several seconds passed before the applause began sporadically. The crowd began to hum. May stood there, clutching Byrd's arm as she maintained her now-frozen smile and that living part of her that had danced and hoped and laughed, retreated. It was as if she watched from the chandelier above, looking down as Bitsy and Amory were announced as grand prize winners. She registered no reaction as the applause turned tepid, mixing with an increasing conversational buzz. Bitsy flashed a triumphant smile.

When Byrd went to shake hands with Amory, May refused to follow. Disappointment quickly replaced the detachment that had shielded her from the initial blow. This was one outcome she had not imagined. Of course, she had allowed that there might very well be better dancers than she and Byrd, but the idea of being bested by Amory and Bitsy was a humiliation she was utterly unprepared for. At the table, she put the trophy down and slid into her seat, reaching for her glass.

Elsie leaned toward her and hissed, "That was fixed!"

May tossed back the remains of her drink and watched as Bitsy and Amory held the loving cup aloft, beaming into the camera's flash. Bitterness, and yes, she had to admit, a degree of jealousy rose from the soles of her feet, creeping upward. Her breath was shallow, her jaw clenched with it. It wasn't that she still wanted Amory; she didn't. She wanted the prize; she wanted to get the better of him. What she wasn't ready to admit to herself was that somehow, she had convinced herself that if he saw her win, if he saw her succeed on her own terms, she would be validated—with past mistakes struck off the record. *Social mistakes*, she corrected herself.

"His *father* was the sponsor," Elsie continued, "Y'all danced circles around them! That Tango! Gawd," Elsie fanned her face. "I told Archie I was holding my breath, it was so *steamy*. Wasn't it, Arch?" She leaned in closer to May, and said, "You know, I heard tonight that their wedding invitations went out yesterday." Elsie's eyebrows rose. "Apparently they had to move up the date, if you catch my drift."

May fanned her cheeks. "I need another one of these." She shook the ice in her glass, then caught Byrd's eye across the table and shrugged. Best to feign indifference. He was patting his forehead with his handkerchief. The man next to him leaned over to say something into his ear.

Elsie leaned toward May, whispering, "What a rotten thing, huh?" She poured gin into May's glass and continued, "Really, old girl, that darling man is mad for you." She waggled her brows and puffed her cigarette.

"Byrd? Oh, go on," May said. "We're like brother and sister. And he's got a new girl every other week."

"The way he *looked* at you while you were dancing . . ." Elsie tapped ash onto the tablecloth.

"That's just acting. Besides," May raised both hands, "I have sworn off men. God, I'm ready to get out of here."

Someone tapped her on the shoulder. Conversation ceased as she half turned in her seat, looking up at Amory's sister, who stood, weaving unsteadily, holding the back of May's chair with one hand and a champagne glass in the other. Maude made an exaggerated sad face, saying, "S' too bad for you, toots." May blinked slowly, regarding her without expression.

Byrd stood. "Let me help you to your table, Maude. Waiter, bring some coffee for Miss Whitman, please."

"I dunneed any coffee," Maude said, "I'm *jesh* fine." She put her glass down on their table.

Elsie said, "She's just squiffy, forget it."

Maude flapped a hand at Byrd, then shook her index finger in May's face. "You're not gon' win *hanything* in this town, sister."

May rose to face the taller girl, drawing herself up, trying to process this affront. Telling this person, *I don't believe I deserve that*, or *That hurts my feelings*, or, *You're drunk and mean*, were not options that May could access at that moment. Defensiveness turned quickly to righteous anger. They stood almost touching, eyes locked, breathing at each other, and May realized she was slightly unsteady herself. She said, "I'd *never* want to be your sister. Don't you *dare* call me that."

May leaned in another fraction of an inch, still not touching Maude. With an expression of surprise, the taller girl swayed backward, releasing her grip on the chair. She fell, and as if in slow motion, her arm knocked a waiter's tray, sending glasses and soda siphons crashing to the floor at the same moment the drummer beat a final stroke on his cymbals. The ballroom fell silent as the tinny chime faded out, then a collective gasp was audible from the onlookers. Maude sat like a rag doll, legs splayed before her, blinking up at May. She looked down, then screamed, holding up her hand, which was bleeding onto her dress.

As the scream died out, May could hear Bitsy Ragsdale's strident voice as she pushed through the throng, demanding, "Get *out* of the way! Idiots!" Amory seemed to follow reluctantly.

Byrd came around the table and grabbed May's arm. "What are you doing?"

May's chin jerked back. "Nothing! I didn't do anything. She came at me!"

Elsie leaned in, nodding. "She did."

Bitsy grabbed a napkin and wrapped Maude's hand, attempting to help her rise, but Maude outweighed her considerably, and Bitsy only succeeded in raising her a few inches before she plopped down again. Bitsy turned to Amory. "Amory, you fool, *do* something!" Maude clutched her hand and began to keen and rock. Bitsy glared at May. "Look what you've done!" she shouted, "You don't belong here, and you never will." Maude had fainted and was being hoisted up by a waiter, assisted by a beet-red Amory. The rest of the ballroom was in a state of suspended animation and the orchestra had not begun a new number.

Elsie rose slowly, her hands flat on the table, her cigarette holder clenched in her teeth. Her voice sounded like a growl. "Listen here, Miss Bitsy Ragsdale, this gal's worth ten of you, any day, and don't you forget it." In a louder voice, she said, "Everybody here knows who really won that contest."

Byrd said, "Elsie, Elsie, calm down. Everybody, calm down."

Bitsy stomped to where Elsie stood beside May and glared up at her. Elsie and May exchanged looks, then Elsie lowered her chin and blew a slow stream of smoke into Bitsy's face.

"Girls!" Byrd said, "Amory, take your sister home, for God's sake."

Craning forward, hands on her hips, Bitsy defied her diminutive nickname. She shoved Elsie. Archie rose from his chair. Elsie laughed, and May yanked Bitsy's headband down over her eyes. Bitsy reached out as May shoved her back with both hands. With arms wheeling like a toy soldier, Bitsy slipped in the spilled mess and went down. Onlookers called out, raising glasses.

"Let 'er have it!"

"Catfight!"

"Five bucks on the little one!"

"Amory!" Bitsy cried, blindly feeling the air around her, "Amory Whitman, help me right this minute!"

May stood with her hands on her hips, Archie and Byrd flanking her. Around them, there were hoots from the crowd. They were all watching her. She hiccupped, and her stomach lurched. Things were getting whirly.

"Come *on*, y'all," Elsie said, grabbing her evening bag. "We need to get out of here right now. This party is over." She marched out of the ballroom while Archie hurried to gather her belongings as two officious-looking desk clerks pushed through the crowd in search of the source of the commotion.

Byrd took May's arm, steering her through the buzz. "Damn it, May, what were you thinking?" She jostled along beside him, out of step. In the Palm Court, the alligators continued their laps, oblivious to the drama. At the reception desk, Byrd spoke to the clerk while May drooped against the counter, looking up at the chandeliers and stained-glass skylights high above the floor. The brilliant colors expanded and contracted, doubled, then recombined like a kaleidoscope. Byrd spoke tersely to the clerk. "Would you have my motor brought around, please, and cancel my room for this evening? The name is Craig."

"Wait a min', Byrd," May covered her mouth with her hand. "*Hic.* Oopsie! Hey, aren't you coming to Elsie's party?"

His voice was quiet and stern. "You've had enough party for one night."

"Spoilsport." May held up one unsteady index finger. "I'm goin' to the party."

"You'll do nothing of the sort. I'm your escort and I'm responsible for you. I'm taking you home. You made a scene."

"Ah." She swayed. "I'm not a sore loser. That Bissy's jus' a lil' bitch is all."

Byrd guided her toward the stairs. The vine pattern of the red-and-gold carpeting seemed to grow as she watched, twining down the stairs forever. Two flights down, jovial-looking clumps of people milled around. On the first landing, May tried to pull away from Byrd. "I'm not goin' home." She stamped her foot.

His voice was a hiss. "Yes, you are. I'm not about to leave you here."

May's voice rose. "You don' know what's best for me." She reared back. "You think you know me, but you don', mister. I . . ." She stopped. People were watching. And there, again, was Shame, sitting down there in the lobby, grinning up at her, pounding out some raucous song about bluebirds all day long on the big, glossy grand piano. Byrd took her arm again.

Outside, Elsie stood with Archie on the steps, waiting for her car. She took May's arm and said, "Come on home with me, old girl. We'll have some Bromo seltzer and eggs Benedict, then sleep it off. Byrd, you come too."

"Thanks, Elsie," Byrd said. "I had a room booked here, but I think it's best if we head home tonight." He motioned to the parking attendant.

May watched the headlights of an oncoming car and stumbled slightly. Catching Elsie's eye she mouthed, *Help!*

Elsie said, "C'mon, Byrd, it's midnight already! You can't drive back now. May's supposed to stay all week." Byrd's face was stony. May wanted to curl up on the little strip of carpeting they were standing on. Couples were exiting the hotel, and Elsie's roadster arrived, followed by Byrd's Studebaker.

Elsie hugged May and kissed her cheek. "Ha! It's a damn good thing I made my debut last year. They'd blackball me now, sure as shooting!" She put a hand on Byrd's arm, saying, "Sure you won't change your mind?"

May put her head against Elsie's shoulder, leaning heavily on her friend. "It's true, what they said. I don' b'long here."

"Archie," Elsie said, "Give me your handkerchief." She mopped May's face, then held her by the shoulders. "Your mascara is a proper mess. But listen to me. *You* can get along anywhere, sugar pie, don't you doubt it for a minute. I'll ring you tomorrow, about our *plans*. It'll all work out; trust me." She flicked the ash from her cigarette toward the entrance and laughed. "We gave Bitsy the what for, didn't we?"

Elsie and Archie waved as they drove off, and Byrd helped May into the car, tucking the hanging hem of her dress inside. The door slammed and she leaned her head against the seat back and closed her eyes. She had never seen Byrd so angry. Silent, harsh self-recriminations swirled and re-combined in her mind. Many were familiar old chestnuts; she had told them to herself with slight variation dozens of times. Reciting them was comforting, in a sick sort of way: *You're fooling yourself; no one really likes you; if you hadn't come with Byrd, you'd never have been asked by anyone else. He only asked because he felt sorry for you, because you're so pathetic.* And now, something new to add to her collection: plans for her interview post-poned, maybe ruined.

Byrd started the car, and May opened her eyes and looked over at him. Even whirly as she was, she knew to give him time to cool off. They drove through Richmond. After a few minutes, he said, "I'll need to get some gasoline."

For the next twenty miles they did not speak, until May sat up, sud-denly, and said, "Oh . . . oh, I need to . . ." She leaned toward the door and vomited, half in and half out of the window.

"Dear God, May," Byrd said, veering the car to the side of the road. "You could have warned me."

"I'm sorry," she said, sobbing and wiping the sick from her mouth, "I'm so sorry . . ."

Byrd stopped the car and came around. He told her to lean against the car while he rifled through Delphina's basket. May bent forward, heaving again into the grass until she felt like she could not catch her breath.

"Here, here," Byrd said, kinder now, "Stand up." He wet a napkin with iced tea from a flask. "Rinse your mouth." He wiped her face and dabbed at her dress. She leaned back against the car, swiping the hams of her hands over her face. In the harsh light of the streetlamp, she regarded her reflection in the side window glass—stained dress, swollen eyes, tracks of mascara and smeared lipstick. Back in the car, the odor of vomit was still pervasively sour. She leaned against the window frame, inhaling the balmy night air. They were in the country now. Byrd cranked the engine, and she reached for his arm.

"Wait," she said, quietly, "please?"

"You going to be sick again?"

"No . . . no. I'm sorry about your car, and—there's something else. I want to explain." She inhaled, then let out a shuddering breath.

Byrd let out a long sigh as he pulled back onto the road. "What is there to explain?" He raised one hand from the steering wheel and let it drop back. "You drank too much, we didn't win, and you weren't very ladylike about it. In fact, I'd have to say you were a poor sport. I'm disappointed in you, frankly."

"Welcome to the club. I seem to disappoint everyone." May squeezed her eyes shut, sober enough, now, to regret her behavior. "I'm sorry I spoiled your evening. Honestly, I am."

"What got into you?"

"When I saw Amory . . ." May took a deep breath and tugged at the pearls around her neck. "I never heard from him after . . ."

Byrd glanced at the dashboard. "Hang on, we're almost out of gas. There's a filling station up there."

Stop. Right this minute. He would never understand. No one would.

Light glowed from inside the station, and three men were assembled outside, around the door. One sat on a metal kitchen chair that was canted backward on two legs, against the building. He called over, "No attendant after eleven, mister. Pump your own." Big moths and insects swarmed around the solitary light above the twin gasoline pumps.

Byrd waved an assent then reached for his billfold. "Want a ginger ale or something?"

"Yes, please," May said, "My dress is a mess . . ."

"What were you saying, about Amory?"

"Nothing. It was nothing."

"Be right back." Byrd started the pump, then went inside. Two of the men followed him. May looked out into the night, wondering, cynically, if things could have gone any worse. She giggled over the memory of Bitsy Ragsdale on the floor. Tomorrow, she knew, she would have a sore head and tender stomach. There was one thing she could salvage, though. She would go home tonight, and in the morning, she would call Byrd to apologize—or better yet—do it in person. She would eat crow. Then she would take the train back to Richmond, and have Elsie take her to her interview on Tuesday. If she was offered the position, she imagined herself finding a clean, yet charming, little room—maybe with patchwork quilts—in some nice widow's cozy house. And for nest egg money, she had her pearls. How, she wondered, did the pawn system even work? Could you get your things back? *Hock* was such an unpleasant name for a business.

From outside, the odor of gas and oil and tire rubber wafted on the humid night air, giving it weight. May held her pearls to her nose and sniffed. *God, I smell disgusting.* At one side of the station was a coiled water hose. She took the dish towel from Delphina's basket, then watched the man in the kitchen chair. When he turned his head toward the station door, calling out something she could not hear, she slipped from the car and hurried across the lot, undetected. Crouching behind a pile of tires, she turned on the hose. The water was icy, bracing; the wet front of her dress clung to her as she scrubbed it. *Great. Now to get back to the car without giving a peepshow. Where is Byrd?*

As she wrung out the towel, headlights shone across the gravel and a black Ford pulled into the station from the opposite direction. It stopped under the light at the pumps. May stepped back into the shadows, watching. Byrd now stood in the doorway, talking with the man in the chair. *Come on! Don't be so damned friendly!*

A man in a hat got out of the Ford. With his back to May, he tossed something flat into the back, then removed his rumpled suit coat, folding it and laying it on the back seat. He turned to start the pump and she saw that he wore brown gaiters over his trousers, from ankle to knee, with mismatched laces. *Sheriff Beasley.* May's hand wandered up to her mouth. She peered around the corner, hoping to signal Byrd, but he was deep in conversation, his back to her.

Beasley put both hands on his lower back and leaned into them, stretching. Sweat stained the back of his shirt. He shuffled across the lot to a clump of bushes opposite where May hid and turned his back with his hands in front of him. Staying in the shadows, she hurried back to Byrd's car, gesturing, simultaneously trying to catch his eye while not calling attention to herself. *Stop talking! Come on!* She danced from foot to foot, pinching the thin wet fabric from her skin.

Byrd held up a finger, *One minute!* Beasley was still seeing a man about a dog. May glanced into the sheriff's car. The light above illuminated the interior, and there, on the back seat, peeking from beneath his coat, was a black ledger with red corners. A single bill stuck out of the top. May leaned closer. *A fifty.* At the station door, the seated man leaned forward, his chair now upright. He rose, taking Byrd's money. Byrd followed him inside.

Watching Beasley over the top of the car, May reached into the open window of the Ford and snatched at the fifty-dollar bill. Byrd came out and strode toward her, a ginger ale in one hand. She tugged, and the ledger slid across the seat, closer. The bill, she now saw, was secured with a paperclip. Beasley's back was still turned. He hitched his shoulders. As Byrd approached the Studebaker, May grabbed the ledger, opened her car door, and slid inside. She shoved the ledger under the seat as Byrd opened his door. Leaning forward, she kept her head down, wiping the floor of the passenger side with the towel. Byrd passed the ginger ale to her.

May faked a yawn. "Where are we?"

"Nearly to Gordonsville. Something's happened."

ELEVEN

Byrd pulled onto the road, accelerating rapidly, tires squealing. May grabbed the window frame, saying, "What on earth?" Her heart thumped in her chest.

He said, "Listen, those men back there were talking. Your dad's still was busted tonight."

"Oh, God." May put a hand over her mouth.

"They were talking about it when I walked up. When I heard your father's name, I didn't say anything. He's in the Charlottesville jail."

"That man—that man who pulled in after us, in the Ford? It was Sheriff Beasley!"

"I don't know if he was in on it or not. There were federal agents."

"What will happen? Was Blue there?"

"They only mentioned your father. I didn't want to ask too many questions." May couldn't think. Byrd continued, "Late as it is tonight, we can't do anything." She closed her eyes, willing her other senses to focus, to process this, come up with the right answer, to come up with a plan.

Byrd said, "They might be looking for you too."

"Me?"

"No telling what they know, if they found the still. It's best if you lie low while we find out the details."

"But where . . ."

"It's almost two now. Everybody thinks you're in Richmond, right? So if they're looking for you, they'll start there." Byrd ran a hand through his hair, then tapped the steering wheel. After a moment he said, "I have an idea. I don't think anyone will look for you west of Charlottesville. My dad has that hunting lodge, in Bath County? We'll go there. It's about four hours from here."

May held her fist over her mouth. They drove on in silence, and in that quiet, her mind was shrieking. An hour later, as the car shuddered up the road over Afton Mountain, a heavy fog slowed them down. May rolled up her window and pressed her forehead to the glass. She did not trust herself to speak. She would fall apart.

At the Craig hunting lodge, the sun was rising, and birds stirred in the woods. At 6 a.m. the temperature was cool, about ten degrees cooler than Keswick. May wrapped Byrd's dinner jacket around her as she picked her way over the slate path, the heels of her satin dancing shoes sticking between the stones. The wide porch wrapped two sides of the building, with railings and posts made from rough cedar trunks. Spaced among them, wide spider webs sparkled with dew. Byrd retrieved the key from its hiding place and unlocked the stout plank door. "Dad's had this place since before I was born," he said. "But we haven't been up here much since Jimmy died. Mother would never stay here. She'd only come if Dad got her a room over at the hotel." Sunlight streamed through, illuminating dust motes in the air. Byrd ushered May in, then went from room to room, propping open windows, dispelling the odors of mildew and cedar. In the large, pine-paneled main room, a gun rack took up most of one wall. Iron hooks held fishing creels and heavy plaid jackets. Comfortable looking, faded easy chairs and worn hooked rugs surrounded a large fieldstone fireplace, stacked with logs. From over the mantel, the head of a large buck gazed down with a stern expression, seemingly irritated at having been shot and stuffed.

From a hallway, Byrd called, "Told you it was rough. There's a pump out back, and an outhouse." Returning to the main room, he handed her a towel and bar of soap. "Pick any bedroom you like. I keep some clothes here. I'm going to change, then go over to the hotel to call Blue." Byrd paused, his hand on the door frame. His tuxedo shirt had lost its starched pleats and his hair was disheveled. His voice was quiet when he said, "I'm sorry about this."

May looked at the floor. "I'm the one who's sorry. You must be exhausted. It's been such a night." She rubbed her crossed arms. "I want to go with you. Let me get out of this evening dress."

"No, you stay here. I'll get some food on the way back. There's a little market up the road that opens early. You've had a shock. Go have a lie-down."

"Where are the sheets? I'll make the beds." She stared at the buck's head, as if it might answer her.

May made beds and found a broom to brush away cobwebs. She found a bucket on the back stoop and filled it from the pump, pouring out the first rusty bucketful. When she heard the car, she hurried back inside. Byrd was coming in with a paper sack. He sank into a kitchen chair and May pulled out the one across from him.

She asked, "Did you reach anybody?"

"I got Blue, at the farm. He said that last night he was out making deliveries after closing. When he got back, they had padlocked the Market. Now, there's a handbill pasted to the front window that says, Closed Until Further Notice. He said they caught your father at the still and—get this—they found guns there. And at the Market they found two of your fake jars, under the porch. Blue said they knew right where to look."

"Guns? There are no guns at the still . . . and there were no jars left at the Market. I'm certain of that."

"I'm sure they were planted."

"Did Blue know who turned Daddy in?"

"Not yet."

"Was Beasley there?"

"Yes. But nothing will happen until Monday or Tuesday, with the weekend, and Monday being Labor Day. Blue says he'll stay at Delphina's and keep an eye on things. I told him I'd call again tomorrow; he said he'd be there at noon."

May looked down. "Uh, there's something . . . Oh, hell. There's something I'd better tell you. Hold on a minute."

She pushed back from the table, then went outside and returned with the ledger and held it out to him. With hands clasped behind her back, she looked at the floor, like a naughty school child. She explained how she came to have it.

Byrd shook his head in apparent disbelief, "May, for God's sake."

"Nobody saw, I swear. And even if Beasley saw your face, he doesn't know who you are. I'll throw it away."

"Why'd you *do* this?"

I was mad at you, I was drunk, I wanted to run away. She held out the fifty-dollar bill. "This was sticking out of the top."

Looking up at the ceiling, Byrd raked both hands through his hair, then dropped his hands onto his knees. "Let me see that," he said, taking the ledger. He flipped pages quickly. "Do you know what this is? You know he's crooked, right?" She nodded, biting her lip, waiting to be chastised. Byrd said, "This looks like records of payments. Oh boy, look here." He pointed to a line, then to another, several rows down, they both read, *Agnes Waddell, $25.00.*

They looked at each other. May said, "Aunt Aggie's been paying Beasley? What on earth?"

"No, see—it's in *expenses.* He's been paying *her.*"

"Wait," May said, flipping pages, "maybe there's more money in here."

"You can't keep it, May."

"Why not? You said it yourself, he's crooked and he deserves . . . Can't I just keep a little? Maybe ten, or twenty? Five?"

"This is evidence of corruption. You have to turn it over."

It was well past noon when May awoke with a start, not remembering at first where she was. She had been dreaming she was at The Jefferson. The police had handcuffed her and were trying to push her into the alligator fountain. Bitsy and Maude were laughing and pointing, with diamond rings on every finger.

She smelled bacon cooking. Byrd had left a new bottle of aspirin on the bureau and filled the ironstone ewer. She splashed her face in the washbowl, then took stock of the contents of her suitcase. Besides her interview dress and the clothes she had packed to take to Elsie's, she had underwear and toiletries, her mother's pearls, and her crossword puzzle book. Tucked into a corner, she found a small muslin bag, tied with a scrap of ribbon. Holding it to her nose, she smiled. It was one of Delphina's "keep-safes"—a sachet of fragrant herbs and dried flowers, meant, Delphina always said, as a good luck charm. Each one was blended for its intended recipient, and the charm lasted as long as the scent remained. May inhaled freshly cut grass and roses and lemon balm, and had a sudden, clear vision of her mother, smiling, the sun making a halo of her wide straw hat.

Inspecting the bedroom, it was clear that this was a man's place; the scratchy plaid blankets and absence of ornamentation, save mounted taxidermy and some prints of dogs playing poker. Hooks on the paneled walls served as a closet, and a brass spittoon sat in the corner. The door hinges creaked as May eased it open. In the kitchen, Byrd stood flipping bacon with a fork. He wore a plaid shirt and moleskin trousers with red suspenders. "How are you feeling?" he asked. "Hungry?"

"Famished." She rummaged in drawers, then set two places at the table, where a jar held daisies and Queen-Anne's lace. Byrd spooned eggs onto plates, and they sat. He said, "Now listen, I don't want you moping around all day, fretting. We'll talk to Blue again tomorrow. You need some distraction. How about if we go for a swim at the Homestead pool, or you could help me fish for supper? I got some bloodworms at the market, and I can fry trout to beat the band."

May made a face. "You catch our dinner. Would you mind if I took a walk in the woods? I saw a path out back."

In a silence punctuated only by a tinkling stream and the cries of birds, May made her way along rough trails. A canopy of leaves dappled the ground in shadows, and she wrapped Byrd's flannel shirt around herself and sniffed the collar, comforted by its familiar scent. Much of her consciousness was attuned to keeping her bearings and negotiating the paths.

She felt dwarfed by the trees and distant blue-gray mountains. As she replayed the previous night in her mind, she squatted beside the stream, ferrying leaves out into the water. They twirled and bobbed, and either continued downstream or caught against the mossy stones, flattened as the water moved past.

It was nearly five when she returned to the cabin. She heated a pot of water and had what Delphina called a bird bath. Somewhat refreshed, she tidied the lodge and swept the porch, then sat on the steps with her chin in her hand. After a while, she heard the rattling of Byrd's car making its way up the dirt road. He got out, holding up a wicker creel. "I got some gorgeous trout, and fresh corn from a stand by the road. We'll eat like kings!" He dropped the creel on the porch and joined her on the steps, taking his hip flask from his pocket. "Hair of the dog?" With a grimace, May shook her head no. "You're awfully quiet," he said. "Did you have a nice walk?"

"It was lovely. I met some chipmunks."

"When'd you get back?"

"A little while ago."

"You started to tell me something last night, right before we stopped for gas. What was it?"

"Oh . . ." May looked down, brushing imaginary dirt from her ankle. "Oh, it was nothing. I don't even remember now." Without looking at him, she said, "What's going to happen, at home?"

"Too soon to say." He removed his cap and pushed his hair off his forehead. "Usually, the fine is two hundred bucks for a still and sixty days in jail. But listen, about that money—if you need it that badly, let me loan you some."

May held out her hand and he passed her the flask. She swallowed and coughed. She said, "That's generous of you. You're always generous. But no. I'm grateful for all that you've done. And I'm grateful you brought me here. While I was walking, I had a chance to think—about a lot of things. You can't afford to get involved any further. You've got to start a legal career soon." She poked her finger into her chest. "You're harboring a fugitive, or something like that. This is *my* problem."

"Let me help you." He leaned closer and began to rub her back and she folded into his embrace like a cat, eager for comfort and touch. "May, listen to me," he pushed back, his hands cupping her shoulders. "I know you've been through a rough patch, but we can get through this together. I'd marry you tomorrow if you'd have me. You know I would."

She crossed her arms over her chest, as if she were shielding her heart. *Oh, no, you wouldn't.* She leaned away from his grasp, looking out toward the woods. "Right." Her voice was bitter. "For Chrissake, who wouldn't want the notorious moonshiner's daughter?"

Byrd's posture stiffened as his hands dropped in a gesture of frustration. He stood up and returned his flask to his pocket. "I need to clean those fish." He went inside.

May stayed on the steps, watching night fall. *He only asked because he felt sorry for you.*

Pots banged in the kitchen.

TWELVE

The next morning, May was roused by the muffled metallic thuds of rain on the tin roof. A strip of pale light outlined the closed shades. The moments of half-waking were a respite, and she pulled the blanket over her head and drew her knees to her chest, entertaining the idea of hiding beneath the covers until everything made itself right again. The events of the past two days played over in her mind. She had wanted to win the dance contest, but now that was utterly trivial. And what would happen with her interview now? Maybe she *should* let Byrd solve her problems. That seemed the simplest solution, didn't it, to let a man make the decisions? Well, hadn't she tried that with Amory? *I will not allow anyone to control me like that again.*

Byrd had been so honest it was painful. And in that moment where he laid himself bare, she had balked. She could have told him what happened in June, but she didn't start, and the moment passed. How much disappointment in her could he take before he, too, would turn his back? Better to keep going as if nothing had been said, no declaration made. Deal with in in the Marshall manner—minimal eye contact, never bringing up the painful subject again, no apologies, no explanations, no emotion. As the rain became a steady thrum, the aroma of coffee brought her fully awake and she threw off the blanket.

In the kitchen, Byrd cracked eggs into a bowl. May was rubbing her face with a small towel as she came in. "Coffee smells good," she said, hoping to set a light tone. "Give me a job to do."

"Scramble the eggs?"

"You're on." He poured the thick coffee. Behind him, the pan began to smoke. May wafted the burning odor away. "I want to go with you when you telephone Blue. Do you think I could heat up enough water for a bath? Or I could just stand outside in this rain."

Byrd turned to face her. "I can do better than that," he said, matching her bravado, "You've got your swimming suit?"

Despite its cozy name, The Homestead was a sprawling, graciously formal brick building with a long, wide porch furnished with rows of rocking chairs and clusters of wicker furniture. Triple-sash windows offered glimpses inside into the luxurious, spacious lobby. Outside, a group of bellmen in smart uniforms huddled by the wide double doors, trying to avoid the downpour. The parking area was filled with expensive automobiles that had delivered their owners to the resort for the Labor Day weekend. A chauffeur in khaki livery stood outside of one, holding an umbrella over an arriving couple. A bellman hurried to open May's door, asking Byrd, "Any luggage, sir?"

Byrd said, "We're only here for the day."

In the lobby, fires burned in twin fireplaces, warding off the chill of the rainy morning. Guests sat sipping coffee or milled among the potted palms. An exasperated-looking nanny shushed and shepherded a gaggle of towel-dragging children past the sign pointing to the indoor pool. While Byrd spoke with a clerk, May read a placard announcing the activities for the week: Tea dances, golf matches, and shooting were all on offer for the active set. For the more sedate there were bridge lessons, mah-jongg, or china painting, with kite making for the children. Observing the hotel guests, May was uncomfortably aware of her wilted appearance. Byrd's seersucker suit was out of press. Still, he held himself with his usual self-confident grace as he escorted her through the main building, past tea salons, game rooms, a beauty shop, and barber. At a door marked Ladies Baths, he said, "I'm going to have a shower and a shave. I'll be waiting here at noon, and we'll call Blue, all right? When I stopped at the desk, I arranged for a little something to relax you. They have your name."

Byrd walked away down the long hallway. May let out her breath and her shoulders dropped. Under the light breakfast banter, there had been tension. These hours alone together had brought out things she hadn't expected. Byrd was one of her few remaining allies. She couldn't lose him.

The spa was silent and sterile looking, with white-tiled floors and walls. Two middle-aged women sat in wicker chairs in the reception area, wearing white bathrobes, their hair turbaned in towels. They glanced up briefly at May, then resumed their conversation. She took a seat and thumbed a fashion magazine, not wanting to have to make small talk. On a small table, there was a white telephone. She should telephone Véronique de Paris and postpone her interview. Or maybe just cancel it. Then she remembered that it was Sunday, and tomorrow a holiday. The shop would be closed.

A ruddy-faced attendant, barefoot, in a spotless white uniform, consulted a clipboard and gave May a robe, instructing her to leave her clothes in a locker. "You'll be having the Swiss Treatment today, yes, madam?" she asked, in German-accented English.

"I don't know," May said. "Whatever I'm signed up for is fine."

"Very well. Please, this way. Have you had before this treatment?" the attendant asked, leading May into a small, tiled cubicle.

Hugging her robe around herself, May counted twelve showerheads, pointing ominously inward from every direction. "Um, no," she said, "Do I have to?"

"It is most therapeutic madam, for the lymphatic system," the attendant said, "Please remove your robe." Indicating some industrial-looking cranks and dials set into the tile, she continued, "I will be standing here. Hold the bars."

Blushing and naked, May faced the wall and held tight. What was a lymphatic system? She was afraid to ask. Behind her, the woman was muttering in German and making adjustments. A mechanical hissing began, followed by a loud *whoosh*, and May was hit by a jet of water so powerful it nearly buckled her knees. She heard, over the roar, "Turn around now." Through strands of dripping hair, she could now see her assailant, forearms bulging, wielding what looked like a fire hose. Did people actually *pay* for this? After a few minutes it stopped, and May exhaled, her body tingling and glowing pink. *Thank God*, she thought, *it's over*.

The attendant raised her eyebrows. "Is madam feeling vigorous? Now, this way for your salt massage."

May had lost her dignity. She submitted. The woman's hands were strong and efficient. "You are very tense?" she asked, kneading May's shoulders. The rasp of salt on skin was just short of painful. She allowed her thoughts to drift, determined to enjoy the experience. Being touched, even by a stranger, felt good. She felt human. The attendant gave her shoulder a final gentle squeeze, saying, "Now come with me, please."

She led May down a tiled corridor, into a dimly lit enclosure. The air was warm and fragrant. Steaming water filled the largest bathtub May had ever seen. The tap ran on, the water lapping gently, overflowing onto the slanted floor where a tiled trough carried it away. The attendant emptied a vial into the water and the sweet pungency of lavender filled the small space. She said, "I will leave now. Take as long as you wish. Have a lovely day, madam." Making a slight bow, she departed, closing the curtain behind her.

May entered the tub gingerly, then lay back, floating her arms in front of her, cocooned by the heat. The lavender scent filled her head, at once clarifying and relaxing. She held her nose and dunked her head, swirling her hair around her. When she opened her eyes underwater, the lights above glowed like beacons through fog.

Memory.

June. Another bathtub, two and a half months earlier.

May came up, gasping, holding tight to the edges of the tub. The overflowing water sloshed over her hands in waves. Memory had been jarred, teased, and provoked, and now, it broke through and would not be denied. Unleashed and without mercy, it played in her head.

Home. Sundown, a Sunday evening in the middle of June. Hot and quiet in the countryside, except for crickets and the occasional coal train in the distance. In the kitchen, she scraped the cold supper that had been left for her into Blossom's bowl, then closed her in the pantry.

Upstairs, as the bathtub filled, she had unpacked a paper bag, lining up the contents on the glass shelf above the sink with deliberate precision: a pint mason jar of clear liquid, a brown glass bottle, a flat, rectangular tin with a bright label. Catching a glimpse of reflection in the mirror, she glanced away, a hot flush staining her cheeks. If she had allowed herself a frank assessment, she would have to notice the oily darkness of her unwashed hair, the puffiness around the eyes, the dullness of the changeable green irises. She hadn't been able to look at herself for weeks—not her face, and certainly not her body. She had tried to ignore the soreness in her breasts and vague queasiness at the smell of coffee.

Finger by finger she ticked off the weeks. How many times had she counted, hoping for a different result? She had thought it was from not eating, from all that crying, but now there was no denying that she was eight weeks late.

Holding the brown bottle up to the light, she tried to read the doctor's script on the faded label. Her father's prescription from a double tooth extraction. Just one pill had made him sleep all day. She hoped they were still as potent. She had considered rat poison, and lye. Efficacious, yes. But she had seen rats die. She would fall sleep in the bathtub, and no one would have to know.

Two, four, six, eight. *She swallowed the tablets, grimacing at their bitterness. Then swallowed four more and studied the circular white stains left on her palm, briefly mesmerized by the idea that everything she was doing in these hours, she was doing for the last time. Her hand didn't feel like her own; it was as if she was watching someone else.*

And some of these. *The lid of the tin opened with a* pop *that made her start. With shaky fingers, she picked out the small brown pills—patent medicine that Delphina gave her for headaches.*

Now, something to wash them down with. *She filled the bathroom* tumbler with gin and downed it fast, shuddering, willing away the urge to vomit, pressing the back of her hand hard against her mouth.

Her father would find her. It was not too late to leave a note, but everything she could think to say was a cliché: *I can't go on. Life is not worth living.*

No. Absolutely not. Amory Whitman would not define her. He didn't know, and he never would. She would make sure of that. He had taken too much already, and she knew, in her shame, that she had offered too much, wanted too much. She had allowed herself to imagine a beautiful life, a family like Byrd's family—a big, lovely house and beautiful clothes like Elsie had.

Steam enveloped the bathroom in an ethereal, otherworldly softness. The damp heat had weight. She removed her wristwatch, propping it beside the tin. Quarter after nine. An hour? Two? Three?

Dying is the only way, she had told herself, over and over, because otherwise, *the rest of my life will be defined by one mistake. One spectacular lapse in judgment.* She had understood, too late, that if there was a scandal, the girl almost always paid the price. The man might be called a rake, or maybe even a cad. But the girl became damaged goods.

She truly believed that she was *damaged goods.* Irreparably so. Her heart was shattered, her pride flattened, hopes for her future; razed. She might have made Amory marry her, but that would have been a bitter, lonely victory. Her father, if he knew, would put on his suit and drive to Richmond and march righteously into the Whitman's big house on River Road and demand . . . demand what? That Amory behave like a gentleman? That he make an "honest woman" out of his daughter? Everyone would say she'd tricked him, trapped him. But that had never been her intention. She thought she loved him. In fact, she had been nothing but a conquest.

Now, she would be a tragedy. The idea that her death would haunt him forever gave the whole thing a sort of romantic dignity. She had heard those whispers on the dormitory hall, about that girl some years ago—the one who hadn't waited—the girl who hadn't said no enough times. How had she imagined herself smarter or luckier than that girl? Well, that girl had taken poison, and now she was a legend.

Steam continued to fill the bathroom as she undressed. Droplets of condensation gathered and rolled like tears, down the tile walls. Clutching the sides *of the tub she lowered herself, ever-so-slowly, into the water, panting as steam filled her lungs. Her hair swayed like seaweed as her skin flushed deep red. Sweat pricked her scalp as the gin began to do its work, creating a distance between the present moment and what she imagined would be left behind.*

White, white, blue. *She counted tiles on the wall.* White, white, blue, *until steam obscured the grout lines between. When her skin faded to pink, she pulled the plug and ran more hot water. She had taken all the pills in the bottle. Another swallow of gin. Easier to get down this time.*

She had imagined that she would just become sleepy and slip beneath the surface of the water, quietly submerging into blackness without a whimper. Already, things seemed out of focus. Squinting at her watch, she was surprised to see that it was after ten. The water turned tepid; she was relaxing. Reaching to turn on the tap, she gasped. Deep inside her body, a new heat rumbled—a fierce, twisting vice that took her breath as her mouth filled with saliva and her stomach contracted in searing pain. Another cramp cut through the haze. With panicked clarity came the realization: there was no going back. If she screamed, no one would hear. Her father was at his poker game and would be until late, and it was Delphina's day off. She would be in town at the pictures.

She raised herself, skin steaming, lightheaded, holding the edge of the bathtub, feeling her way to the toilet. Doubled over, retching, she sobbed entreaties to a God she rarely consulted. Please, let me die. Please. She had not anticipated pain. She hadn't expected to bleed.

Some hours later, she opened her eyes. Cold. The tile was cold as she rolled, naked, dry-mouthed, empty, onto her side and tried to focus on the clawed foot of the bathtub; the flecks of chrome, pockmarks of rust. The smell of vomit caused her stomach to contract, but there was nothing left.

This was not the afterlife. This was the bathroom floor.

A series of sounds intruded—tiny hammers in her skull echoing—plink, plink, plink. When she pulled herself to her knees, a veil of black stars clouded her vision and her head throbbed. Pain was something she could grasp. She tightened the tap; the noise stopped. She rose slowly, shivering. Everything hurt. In the now-cold bathwater, she washed herself, silently assuring herself as the pink-tinged water drained away, that she would try again, tomorrow or next week, whenever she could find more medicine. Or maybe now she would die of an infection, because she certainly was not going to a doctor. She wasn't going to tell anyone—not her father, or Delphina, or anyone, that she had tried and failed to die, that she had started bleeding instead. There couldn't be anyplace lower than rock bottom, save for hell, if a person believed. That was a small consolation, and at that moment, she knew it was the only consolation she had.

THIRTEEN

May stepped from the bathtub, shaking, repeating to herself, *I'm here. I'm here, in the ladies' baths, at The Homestead. Byrd is waiting. I'm here. I'm here.* The room was too small, too close; a cave. Swaddled in the thick robe, she found her way to the dressing room and sat at a dressing table, unaware of time, staring into the mirror without seeing herself. When an attendant came in and began to gather towels, May began yanking a comb through her tangled hair. The red eyes she could blame on the bathtub. She pinned up her hair and dressed, then stood, somewhat shakily. Smoothing the front of her dress, she reassured herself that she was *here.*

In the hall outside the baths, she found Byrd lounging in an armchair, reading a newspaper. She squinted in the sunshine pouring through the long row of windows, her eyes smarting. He folded the paper and looked up, a smirk playing about his mouth. "Did you enjoy that?"

May looked at him. Her lower lip trembled. *Stop! Stop it right this minute.* She dug her nails into her palms.

Byrd pushed himself up from the chair saying, "Are you all right? They didn't hurt you, did they? Mother takes that treatment every time she comes here. Good for the glands, or something. Dagmar is supposed to be the best."

May swallowed. The sun was a harsh floodlight; it allowed no shadows. She raised her chin and smiled. "It was heavenly, really. Thank you.

And next time *I'll* choose a treatment for you, mister. There's a telephone; what time is it?"

"Twelve forty-five. I didn't know you'd be so long in there, so I called."

A family passed with two small girls and a barking Labrador. Byrd said, "I'll tell you about it over lunch, or we could have a swim first, if you want."

"I've had enough water for one day, I'm already a prune."

They strolled through gardens with flowers that seemed, to May, garishly bright and impossibly perfect, like a stage set. The brick paths had not a weed nor fallen leaf. Byrd held her chair at a table on a broad terrace with a panoramic, picture-postcard view of the Blue Ridge mountains. He said, "Blue says your father is fine. Tim Honeycutt has agreed to represent him, and I offered to clerk. Sounds like this might take more than a day or two to straighten out. They're holding your Dad without bail, on account of the firearms charge." May put her fingers over her mouth.

Byrd held up a hand. "But listen to this. A man came to the farm last night. Blue knew him—says he's a pretty regular customer. His name is Chester—Chessie—Mackenzie. Does that ring a bell?"

"No, but we have lots of customers."

"He wanted to talk to you. Blue said he had a badge—he's an undercover federal agent, working for the Bureau of Investigation. Blue said he didn't know where you are, and this fellow Chessie gave him a card and said for you to call him as soon as possible, about the case. He told Blue he knew the guns and jars were planted. He said you might remember him as 'a friend.'"

May dropped her napkin. "We need to call him."

"I did. He sounds believable—says you need to stay away from home. He's meeting us here, in the lobby, tomorrow morning at eleven."

When the waiter appeared, Byrd ordered without consulting the menu. Platters of oysters on the half shell appeared, and May smoothed her napkin over her lap, pondering what she had just learned. Forking an oyster into her mouth, the burn of horseradish heightened her senses. Around them, couples and families enjoyed the holiday, oblivious to the drama that was playing out at her table. It was like a costume party; some were dressed for shooting and others for golf; a pair of ladies dressed for tennis and another for riding. *Like they haven't a care in the world.*

FOURTEEN

May and Byrd arrived at The Homestead at ten forty-five the next morning. She realized, as she scanned the lobby, that they didn't know who they
were looking for. Any of these men could have been customers. Byrd led
her to a chintz-covered sofa that faced the entrance and she perched on the
edge of her seat, trying to keep her hands from fidgeting. She wore white
gloves and a linen dress. Byrd wore his seersucker suit and carried Beasley's
ledger. They looked like any other young couple on holiday. Byrd picked
up a discarded newspaper and pretended to read it. Minutes ticked by.

May whispered, "Do you think he knows what I look like? I might
have met him. I don't know, I mean, I can't remember. What if this is some
sort of setup, and he's really going to arrest me? I bet they do things like
that, you know, the Bureau of Investigation. Maybe you should hide that
ledger under the sofa cushion, just in case. You didn't tell him about it, did
you?" She tugged her skirt over her knees, rocking slightly.

"Calm down, calm down. He'll find us. I didn't tell him. We'll see
what he has to say."

A waiter came over, momentarily blocking May's view of the doors. As
Byrd ordered coffee and sandwiches, she craned her neck. Signs on easels
stood by each door, advertising a trunk show of French fashions in the dress
shop: From Saks Fifth Avenue, in New York City! Another showed a famous

orchestra, slated to perform in the ballroom: All the Way from New York City and the Roseland Ballroom, Eddie Lavalle and His Vallettes!

The waiter bowed and turned to go. A wiry man, as small as a jockey, came through the doors. He swiped off his hat, revealing glossy black hair cut very short on the sides, graying at the temples. He scanned the lobby and caught May's eye, then started toward them. As he neared, she could see that he was older than he looked from a distance—maybe forty-five. May leaned toward Byrd, poking him in the side.

"I see, I see," Byrd whispered, "Calm yourself." As the man got closer, Byrd jumped up and held out his hand. May rose, smoothing her dress, offering a tentative smile.

The man gave Byrd's hand a single, hard shake, saying, "Mr. Craig? Chessie Mackenzie." He turned to May, taking her hand lightly for a moment. "And you're May Marshall. Sorry I'm late. These country roads are always slower than you think." He sat in an armchair across from the sofa, hitching the pants of his rumpled blue suit. The waiter returned, and as everyone exchanged awkward half smiles, coffee was set up and poured, seeming to take an hour instead of minutes. Mackenzie balanced his cup and sat forward; arms propped on his knees. May held her hands together in her lap.

Finally, the waiter departed, saying he would return with their sandwiches. May wanted to scream at him, *Go away! Can't you see this is important?*

"Well," the agent said, "I'm glad I was able to track you down, Miss Marshall. You did a pretty good disappearing act." May didn't know whether that was a compliment or not. He continued, "I'm sure you're wondering why I'm here. Let me get right to the point. I approached your father recently, after Sheriff Beasley found out about those jars you've been making. Pretty clever, I must say." Again, she didn't know how to respond. He continued, "Anyhow, your father has been helping me—me, and the Bureau. We've been working on a case now for almost a year—and, by the way, this is all hush-hush—concerning a ring of local officials. So far, they've defrauded the US Government out of over a million dollars in whiskey excise taxes." He paused to stir his coffee.

Byrd whistled low, and said, "Is this nationwide?"

"No," Mackenzie said, "There might be similar things going on else-where, but our case is concentrated here in Virginia—mainly Franklin County. They don't call it 'the moonshine capital of the world' for noth-ing. There are some bad characters over there, let me tell you."

The waiter returned with a wheeled trolley, then held out a tiered tray and a pair of silver tongs. Byrd said, "Just leave them, please." Macken-zie reached for a tiny sandwich, stuffing it into his mouth, saying, "Sorry, didn't get anything before I left."

"Please," May said, "Go on."

"Anyhow, as I said, we've been working the case. The Governor sent out an order months ago that sheriffs were supposed to be collecting fees from moonshiners instead of arresting them, on account of how backed up the court dockets are with cases, and the jails being so full. Only some of these local guys decided they'd shake down the small operators, like your father, offering them 'protection' from the feds in return for bribes, when, in fact, the 'shiners didn't need it. Your father is one of twelve infor-mants we've been working with to gather evidence."

May's eyebrows shot up and Byrd leaned closer to Mackenzie. He continued, "He couldn't tell you about it, for your own safety. We knew Beasley found his still. We know the guns there were planted, as were the jars at Keswick Market."

Byrd turned to May; there was a silent question in his look. May said, "Agent Mackenzie, I should probably tell you that um, well, I have some-thing that might . . ."

Byrd pushed the ledger across the table between them, saying, "Have a look at this. It's Beasley's."

Mackenzie shifted his gaze from Byrd to May and back again, then put down his plate and opened the ledger. He flipped pages, scanning, then stopped. "Where did you get this, Miss Marshall?"

May bit her lip, looking to Byrd for guidance. He spoke, sounding like a lawyer. "Let's just say she came across it by chance, in the early hours of Saturday. Beasley has no idea that it is in Miss Marshall's possession."

Mackenzie nodded, rubbing his chin. "All right. I guess I don't need to know that right now. This is in*credibly* valuable. We've been looking for a break like this for months. I'll have to take this with me."

May exhaled, flooded with relief. "There are payments listed in there to my aunt, Agnes Waddell. I think she turned Daddy in."

Mackenzie tapped the ledger, then he nodded slowly. "Waddell, Waddell . . . Ah! I knew I'd heard that name before." He clucked his tongue. "Mrs. Waddell is friendly with the Sheriff's wife. In June they were serving lemonade at the county courthouse, when that Klan lecturer from St. Louis spoke on 'Americanism.'" He sneered.

Byrd said, "I saw that, in the *Daily Progress*—that's the Charlottesville newspaper."

"That's right. We're watching two local KKK units, around Charlottesville. There were a couple of flaming crosses in June, but no violence—least not yet. The WKKK—the women's branch—has almost a half-million members nationwide. They have a magazine called *The Kluxer*, with recipes and sewing patterns, if you can believe that. It's dangerous propaganda, disguised as housekeeping hints. It's frightening to see this kind of intolerance being promoted as normal and patriotic—even more frightening to see how many 'average' folks swallow it." Mackenzie held up one hand. "But don't get me started . . . Your aunt and Mrs. Beasley have become recruiters."

May's mouth opened, then closed, as replayed conversations and seemingly casual comments clicked into place, suddenly forming a clear and ugly picture. She said, "I don't want to believe that about my aunt, but I do. It's terrible to think that's happening, at home or anywhere."

"You're right there. Now, about this ledger . . ."

May opened her handbag and passed the fifty-dollar bill to the agent. "This was inside. I suppose it's evidence too."

He smiled and tucked the bill into the ledger, snapping it closed. "Miss Marshall. Someday I want to hear this story."

May felt herself blush. "Agent Mackenzie, when will my father get out of jail? They've closed down our market, you know."

"He needs to stay put for a bit, I'm afraid. If we let him out, Beasley will be on to us. He thinks he has a tight case." He tapped the ledger.

"With this new evidence, we can lay a trap. In fact, Miss Marshall," he glanced at his wristwatch and seemed to ponder something, ". . . you could be of great service to us—help your father's case. Are you willing to help?" May nodded. She would agree to anything if it meant she wasn't in trouble. Mackenzie went on, "Here's what I'm thinking . . ." He stopped, wolfing down another perfect triangle of sandwich while looking around him. "We need to ask if we can have access to an empty office or something—surely they have one in this joint. I want you to try to telephone Sheriff Beasley. I have his home and office numbers on me." May's eyes widened. Mackenzie wiped his fingers on his napkin. "I'll be right there beside you. I'll write out a script. Remember, this will help your father."

Half an hour later, May sat at a wide mahogany table with Byrd beside her. Mackenzie sat across from her, hastily writing notes. She took a deep breath and blew it out as she listened to the operator, then the sounds of ringing.

"Hello?" A woman's voice came on the line.

May said, "May I speak to Sherriff Beasley, please?"

"Mercy," the woman said, sounding exasperated, "is this official business? Hiram's 'bout to go down for a nap. It's a national holiday, for pity's sake." May glanced up at Mackenzie, and he nodded.

"Yes, um, Mrs. Beasley? It's important."

"Hold the line, then." May waited, hearing the clatter of the other receiver, then a distant call, "*Hi-ram? Hi-ram! Somebody on the telephone for you.*"

Two minutes passed like years, then, the sleepy-sounding voice, "This is Beasley, who's this?"

May breathed again and dove in headfirst, reading from a ledger page, altering her voice to sound expressionless, "Bose Shifflett, Bacon Hollow, May fifteenth, forty-five dollars. Sam Rives, Earlysville, May fifteenth, twenty-five dollars, owes two weeks. Monroe Curtis, Stony Point Pass—"

Beasley almost shouted. "Who the *hell* is this?"

May put her hand to her chest, startled, but kept on, "Walter Wheeler, Chopping Bottom—"

"What do you want?" Beasley's voice sounded murderous.

May swallowed, then continued, "You missing anything, Sheriff?

You need to drop the charges against Henry Marshall, the sooner the better." May laid the receiver in the cradle, listening to the click. Her hands were shaking.

Mackenzie and Byrd were smiling at her. The agent said, "Well done, well done. Now we just have to wait and see what his next move is. To drop the charges, he'll have to make the evidence disappear. We'll be watching."

Byrd said, "Is May safe, Agent Mackenzie? What if Beasley figures out she called? It wouldn't take a genius."

Mackenzie said, "Beasley's no genius. Miss Marshall, it's best if you don't go back home right now. Mr. Craig is right. For one thing, there's a warrant out for you. It might not be safe. I didn't tell you that those jars we found under the market porch on Friday were full of wood alcohol. If anybody died from drinking it . . ." May blanched. Mackenzie continued, "Moonshining can be a deadly business. I've seen it. You ought to get away for a while—least a few weeks, while this sorts itself out and we wait for the sheriff to make a move. We'll keep an eye on your farm and market in the meantime."

May tried to take it all in. Byrd patted her arm. She said, "Well, I did have this idea, it was sort of a plan, actually, to go to Washington tomorrow with my friend Elsie . . ."

Byrd frowned, as if to say, *What, you didn't tell me?*

May licked her lips. "I was going to apply for a job at a dressmaker. It's set already."

Mackenzie shook his head. "Not far enough. This ring is statewide, up in northern Virginia too. Beasley has eyes and ears too close to Washington." He held out his hands. "Any family you could go to?"

"I have some family in New Orleans, only we haven't been in contact for years . . ."

After months of avoiding decisions and interaction, May felt bombarded, and no single idea seemed able to take hold, as if she were grabbing for one particular raindrop in a downpour.

Mackenzie looked at his watch again. "Listen, you ought to leave tonight, and Mr. Craig, you ought to get back to Keswick, carry on as if you don't know anything. Miss Marshall, you send me word by your boyfriend here, letting me know where you'll be. I've got to get back to Richmond. Holiday traffic will be hell. Thank you for your help. Good day to you both. You'll be hearing from us."

The trio walked back through the lobby, saying goodbye again at the doors. Mackenzie headed out, holding the ledger aloft briefly, in salute. Byrd ran a hand through his hair, saying, "Whew. That was something, huh? I'm going to get a train schedule from the desk. Be right back."

He walked away and May stared fixedly at the exit, trying to quash the impulse to bolt, to run away and hide. A bellman came through the door, tipping his hat. May smiled absently, and her gaze shifted toward the posters and schedules beside the doors, looking for guidance, for a sign.

CHESTER LAVALLE, FROM NEW YORK CITY, SAKS FIFTH AVENUE, PARISIAN FASHIONS!

The bellman now carried suitcases on his way back outside. He paused beside the poster, and said, "Mr. LaValle just checked in. If you have the chance, miss, you ought to hear him tonight. That New York jazz is something else."

Byrd returned, unfolding the schedule pamphlet. May said, "Let me see that." She traced a finger across a line—*Hot Springs, Alexandria, Washington, Baltimore, Philadelphia* . . . "Byrd," she said, "I'm going to New York. See, there's a train at six thirty tonight. Is your bathing suit still in the car? I'm dying for a swim."

FIFTEEN

Elaborate tile mosaics decorated the walls of the indoor pool. Huge ferns and lush tropical plants surrounded the large, greenhouse-like enclosure. In the shallow end, a patient father stood, coaxing his wary little boy to jump in. The son held his nose and crouched at the edge, then retreated, flapping his small hands.

"The water is lovely, isn't it?" May said, lowering herself from the ladder.

Byrd dunked his head and slicked back his hair. In the reflection of the water, his eyes turned aquamarine. He said, "This whole pool is filled by the hot springs. Smell the minerals?"

May sniffed. "A little bit." They treaded water. "You know, Elsie told me that when she went to Virginia Beach, the bathtub in her room had a spigot for salt water, right from the ocean." She sculled her hands beneath the surface. "It seems strange to be here, doesn't it? At this fancy resort. Like we were on vacation, or . . . something."

"It is odd." Byrd's gaze moved across the pool, to where an amorous couple cavorted, dunking each other and embracing. The woman's shrieks of laughter echoed in the enclosure. Byrd began to swim laps, and May watched his muscular arms slice the water. She floated, looking up at the glass panels of the ceiling. Even while her ears were submerged, she could hear the couple laughing together. There was no doubt in her mind that they would go to their room and make love. She swam to the side and rested her arms on the ledge, kicking lazily. The little boy approached the side again, holding his nose. He jumped, and his father held him aloft, looking triumphant. The amorous couple climbed out, and the man put a towel around the woman's shoulders. He kissed her neck, then whispered into her ear and they left. The boy jumped again and went under the water. He bobbed up, sputtering, and began to cry. His father carried him away. After a few minutes, Byrd ceased his laps and stood in the chest-deep water, breathing hard. The pool enclosure was silent, save for the sound of water dribbling from fish-shaped spigots. They were alone. He said quietly, "You're sure about this? About going to New York?"

"Yes. I think I can get a job like I wanted in Washington, at least temporarily. I've always wanted to go there, anyhow. This seems as good an excuse as any." She smiled, and Byrd smiled back at her irony. Droplets of water glistened on his forehead and cheekbones. May wanted to trace them with her fingers.

Byrd swam to the side of the pool and laid his cheek on his arms, looking away from her. She moved behind him and put her arms around his chest. The wool jersey of his swimsuit was scratchy, but he was warm, and his scent made her feel safe. The water lapped against them as May laid her cheek against his shoulder blade. When he spoke, his voice was so quiet she wasn't sure she heard him. "I meant what I said, about getting married."

She shook her head, her chin tracing *no* on his back, then pressed her mouth against his shoulder and tightened her arms around him. She wanted to comfort him. She wanted him to know she was sorry for the things she could not say.

His chest contracted beneath his jersey. "May," he said, "Don't." She released him and pushed away, stung. He turned, catching her by the wrists. "Listen." She struggled, but he held her. "Stop this." His voice was resigned. "I'm not a fool. You made it clear you aren't interested. I don't want sympathy from you." When he released her, she crossed her arms over her chest, unable to look at him. The door from the locker room burst open, banging against the tiles. Three children ran out and jumped into the pool at once, whooping and splashing with their mother behind them, stridently admonishing them to slow down.

After they dressed again, Byrd met her in the lobby. They drove to the lodge without speaking. The car slowed, and as Byrd pulled the brake, May began to open the door. "Wait," he said, taking her hand.

Raising her eyes to meet his, she saw regret and sadness and something that must be love, while Shame, her cold companion, got comfortable on the seat between them. May smiled, wanly, saying, "I owe you so much. Forgive me?"

"We're friends. We always have been. I hope we always will be." He squeezed her hand. "Let's go in. It's getting chilly and your hair is wet."

Inside, she closed the door to her room. Byrd's door closed down the hall, and there was silence. She crawled beneath the blanket and stared at the ceiling for a long time. Nothing she did seemed to be right. She would go to New York, and maybe, just maybe, something good might happen there. At least she and Byrd would have a chance to get back to where they had been before.

May pulled her scrapbook onto her lap. Its original neat, flat shape was distended with ribbons and corners of yellowed envelopes peeking out. The tang of mildew wafted from the first page. A photograph of herself at six, smiling broadly, holding a strand of popcorn. Beside her, wearing a sailor suit, was Byrd, one front tooth missing, holding the other end of the garland. She traced the line from herself, to Byrd, to her pregnant mother. Their last Christmas together. *I needed to ask you about things, Mama. Maybe things would have been different.* Another photograph showed May at eight, with Byrd and Jimmy, all on ponies. Beaming, Byrd held up a ribbon from the Keswick Horse Show. He had given her the ribbon afterward, solemnly asking her to marry him.

She paged through brittle paper dolls with elaborate costumes, drawn by her mother. More photographs; Mama, in her garden, baby Henry's christening. Only Mama wasn't in that photograph. She had locked herself in her room.

After the baby died at four months, and her mother left, there were no photographs taken until May went to college. Then the scrapbook pages began to fill again, with dance cards and invitations to the men's colleges nearby; pressed corsages, box tops from candy sent by beaux, all pasted in place. She smiled at a photograph of Elsie, starring in the class theatrical, wearing a Grecian costume May had sewn. Elsie again, at the Richmond Debutante Ball, arms full of flowers. She held a long-stemmed rose in her teeth, while the other debs stood, stiff with unsmiling dignity. *The night I met Amory.* From between the last pages, she withdrew an envelope, addressed in a crablike hand.

January 2, 1924

My Dear Miss Marshall,

It was my great pleasure to meet you last week. I so enjoyed our dance together. Would you do me the honor of coming to Richmond for a Cotillion on the 12th? I could book a room for you at Mrs. Kendall's boarding house. If you could make the morning train, we could have luncheon at The Jefferson.

Yours very truly,
Amory Whitman

Slowly and very deliberately, May tore the letter in half, then into quarters, and eights, and sixteenths. The pieces fluttered over a black page. The last quarter of the scrapbook was empty. The blank pages seemed to accuse her, taunting her to do something to fill them. With great care, she loosened the photograph of herself and her mother from the first page. This, she would keep with her. The rest, she could leave behind.

The room was becoming dim when Byrd tapped on her door.

"Be right out!" she called, knowing her cheerful tone rang false. The bedsprings creaked as she pushed herself up. The lodge had grown chilly, and branches slapped against the windows. Turning up the lantern on the bureau, she ran her fingers through her damp hair. Rain had begun again, pattering on the roof. She pulled Byrd's shirt over her wrinkled dress. He had lit a fire in the fireplace, and she stood beside it, warming her hands.

He was in the kitchen. She ought to go in and help, she knew, but it was as if an unsteady boulder had wedged between them, filling the space with tension. They had to navigate carefully around it to get to any other point. If they knocked against it, everything would turn to dust.

At the train station the following evening, May waited in the Studebaker while Byrd bought her ticket. When he returned, they sat in nervous silence on the front seat, until he opened his flask and held it out, saying, "Found some bourbon at the lodge." As she took it, she pulled her hat low over her eyes. "Don't act so guilty," he whispered.

"How long till the train arrives? I left my wristwatch at home."

"Five or ten minutes."

"I'm a little scared."

Byrd took a drink and wiped the back of his hand over his mouth. "Still time to change your mind."

"About New York?"

"About everything." He put his arm around her and smiled, but his jaw was tense. "You know how to get along. If you get into trouble, I'll hop on the first train, all right? There's a hotel for women called The Allerton. I don't know exactly where it is, but you can ask at Penn Station. Write to me at the University as soon as you arrive, but don't telephone. No telling who's listening on the party line."

May sipped from his flask. The whiskey left a pleasant taste in her mouth and warmed her chest. Streetlights winked on, glowing yellow against the darkening sky. "I wish the train would get here," she said. "Listen, Byrd, I don't know how to thank you . . ." He leaned toward her, placing his hand tentatively against her cheek, then tucked her hair behind her ear, smoothing it. She leaned toward him, and they kissed. His mouth was warm, and his natural fragrance was everything good about her childhood, distilled into one scent. Her thoughts lost their sequence, shifting like a weathervane, and kissing Byrd was suddenly the most important thing in the world.

They both jumped at a clanging noise, their faces illuminated by flashing red crossing lights as the track barriers dropped and the train rumbled into the station. After it huffed to a stop the conductor unfolded the steps, calling out, "Hot Springs! Hot Springs, folks!"

Byrd carried May's case to the platform, and she stood on the first step of the train car. He fumbled in his pocket, avoiding her eyes. "Remember," he said, "The Allerton. Wait, take this. Sell it if you need to." He pressed a folded banknote and his gold pocket watch into her palm.

The conductor shouted, "All aboard!" A bell dinged, followed by an eruption of steam and the sound of gears engaging.

"Byrd, I can't take this, it was your brother's!" May shouted, over the increasing clangor. As the train began to move, Byrd followed along, still pressing the watch into her hand.

"Bring it back to me, then," he said, finally meeting her eyes. "I'll wait."

PART II
BAD MANNERS

"Someday, perhaps, the ten years which followed the War may be aptly known as the Decade of Bad Manners."

Frederick Lewis Allen,
Only Yesterday, 1931

SIXTEEN

Steam belched from beneath idling train cars as May stepped from the *Capitol Limited*, holding her breath against the acrid odors of the tracks. The air of the cavernous train shed shimmered hot, humming with the determined intent of arriving and departing passengers. Clutching her suitcase, she was propelled by the masses up two flights of iron stairs then funneled through a gate, following the tide of Panama hats and straw boaters into Pennsylvania Station. As the crowd flowed on, dispersing, she paused, unsure of where to go. A man bumped her from behind, cursing as he moved around her. "Sorry . . ." she started, but he was gone. To remain still, she realized, was to be noticed—*spotted*—so she continued.

Holding her hat in place, she stared up at the vaulted ceiling of the concourse. From arched windows high above the floor, sunbeams streamed down like holy spotlights. Her eyes adjusted to the brightness. In every direction there were tracks, ticket windows, and exits. The public-address system reverberated with announcements, competing with the hubbub of the crowd. A porter approached, whistling, pushing an empty trolley. "Need some help, miss?"

"Please, yes," May said, gratefully, "I need directions to the Allerton Hotel."

"On 22nd?" he asked.

"I suppose so."

"You want a taxi? Traffic the way it is today, though, probably faster to walk." The porter wrote directions on the back of a claim check, and May wondered if he expected a tip. Before she could open her handbag, he disappeared into the crowd. Everything in New York seemed to happen too fast.

A revolving door opened onto Seventh Avenue and a line of broad-fluted, pink-granite columns. At 11:00 a.m., the air was already oppressive—heat overlaid with a stale, almost rancid odor. To the north, towering buildings—*skyscrapers*—blurred gray and brown. She had seen photographs in magazines, but in person they were difficult to fathom. Flags drooped on poles projecting over the street. Buses and automobiles clattered along the wide avenue in a constant stream. Car horns blared and brakes screeched—insistent and imperative. Diners and restaurants with colorful signs lined the avenue; aromas of meat and exotic spices weighed the air. People spoke in languages May could not identify, and even English, with a New York accent, sounded foreign and discordant. So much happened on the sidewalks—a sea of drab-colored suits flowed in both directions, punctuated by bright summer dresses. There were shoeshine boys; newsboys calling out lurid headlines, wearing that day's paper folded into a crown; men passing out flyers, encumbered by sandwich-board advertisements strapped to their shoulders. The weight of May's suitcase and pinching of her shoes went unnoticed, until, at the corner of Eighth Avenue and 22nd Street, she saw the sign for The Allerton Hotel. A frisson of triumph—mixed with the anticipation of a bath and a clean bed—propelled her up the brownstone steps.

The vestibule was well-worn and musty, and blessedly quiet after the overwhelming streets. An earnest-looking young clerk looked up from the desk, pushing spectacles up the bridge of his nose. "Can I help you, miss?"

"Good morning." May exhaled. "I'd like to take a room, please. A single?"

"Sorry, miss. This hotel is for gentlemen only. You must be looking for Allerton *House*. The ladies' hotel."

"Oh," May said—a deflating sigh rather than a declaration. "Is that close by?"

"Fifty-Seventh, East Side. You can take the El or the subway."

There was pressure behind her eyes; she blinked rapidly. "Could you help me, please, sir? I've just arrived. I don't know about the subway." Her stomach growled with an embarrassingly protracted noise like a drain emptying.

The clerk seemed mesmerized for a moment, then began tapping his pencil in a nervous tattoo against the desk. His voice became sympathetic. "Let me ring them for you."

When he hung up, he said, "Allerton House is booked. They can put you on the waiting list, but it'll be at least a week before something becomes available." He sat up in his chair. "But you might try the Martha Washington. Let me call them—save you a nickel." May waited, grateful for the kindness of strangers. He hung up and smiled. "You're in luck! They have a vacancy if you get right over there. It's on 30th, right off Fifth."

"Fifth Street?"

"No, sorry, Fifth Avenue. See . . ." The clerk sketched a grid, labeling the avenues. "You could take a taxi or the subway, but it's probably about as quick to walk."

With the crude map from the hotel clerk, May set out. The heat of the day had intensified. A vendor turned sizzling sausages on a brazier on a street corner, and she inhaled the rich aroma as she passed. *Soon*, she told herself, *soon I will eat, and bathe, and sleep for days.* Her shoulders ached, her palms, inside her gloves, were damp and hot.

At the Martha Washington Hotel, the female clerk was not helpful. May would have to provide proof of employment to get the room. An off-the-cuff fib about working as a dressmaker was rapidly and professionally rejected by the shrewd woman with a look of triumph, leading May to wonder if any hopeful young ladies had collapsed on the carpet in helpless tears upon hearing this news, because that was what she felt like doing just then. Outside again, her suitcase felt heavier, and she walked on aimlessly, her linen dress wilting in the heat. There was very little green in the city, she noticed. Stunted trees strained toward light and even the heartier ivy was grayed with dust. The high, glinting windows of a skyscraper drew her eyes upward and she stumbled, lurching forward over a drifting newspaper. Gasping, instantly mortified, she regained her balance, glancing left and right to see if anyone had noticed. No one stopped. No one, it seemed, *saw* her at all.

She needed to sit. She needed to think. She needed a plan. Following a stream of people, she pushed through the glass doors of Grand Central Terminal and stopped, awestruck, at the top of a wide marble stairway. Heavy, carved balustrades led down from the street, into the main concourse. The ethereal blue-green ceiling was mesmerizing with its celestial zodiac painted in gold. Sounds reverberated upward into the cool blue ether, turning to murmurs. The four identical faces of the clock above the information desk stood at ten minutes past four o'clock.

A porter passed. "Help you, miss?"

Help. Yes, please, help me! "Yes, please," May said, almost overcome with gratitude, "I'd like to store my things. Just for the day."

He pulled out a claim check. "Name?" May hesitated, and he looked politely impatient. "Miss . . . ?"

Name? Name. "Valentine," she said, "Miss May Valentine."

Someone had left a folded newspaper on one of the pew-like benches, and she picked it up, feeling lighter but somehow more vulnerable without her case. A pair of policemen crossed the broad floor with billy clubs swinging from their belts, and May shielded her face with the paper until they passed. Across the concourse, a sign read Biltmore Coffee Shop. As she entered, the mingled aromas of coffee and food cooked in grease made her mouth water. From the far end of the counter, a voice boomed, and she jumped. "Whatcha having, doll? We got some nice pie today." A waitress with brightly dyed yellow hair worked her way down the counter with a gray rag.

"A glass of iced tea, please?" May took a stool and pulled off her gloves. Her feet began to throb.

The waitress cocked a boomerang-penciled eyebrow. "Looks like you could use a little somethin', hon. Piece of pie? Lemon's good."

"Please." May blotted her face with her handkerchief. *A plan. No more of this flying by the seat of my pants.* The waitress sliced the pie as May watched, absently running a finger over her handkerchief, tracing the scalloped edges and hand-sewn embroidery on one corner. *May Marshall*, in script, an amateurish attempt wrought in pink chain stitch. When she was eight, Delphina had begun to teach her, patiently making time when May begged for lessons—satin stitch, feather stitch, backstitch, then on to the tricky French knot. Patience was required, and taught, along with tearing out and doing over, until she mastered each stitch. With a pang, May realized, *I don't think I ever thanked her.* She traced her name again. *A Plan. No more May Marshall. I'll be May Valentine.*

"Where you from?" The waitress poured tea from a sweating pitcher. "You sound like one a them Georgia peaches." She put the glass down, with a check, and said, in a kind tone, "Just got here, huh?" May nodded, chagrined at her transparency.

The waitress was called away and May opened the newspaper. *The New York Evening Post's* headline proclaimed: THE PRINCE OF WALES'S UPCOMING VISIT TO NEW YORK STIRS GREAT INTEREST! She wondered if there were photographs of her father and herself, in the paper at home. FUGITIVE FROM JUSTICE, MAY MARSHALL!

She took a bite of pie, tooth-achingly sweet and tart, then devoured the rest of the slice and drained her tea. Pushing away her plate, she folded the paper, scrutinizing advertisements for hotels and the employment listings. A position selling gloves at Gimbel Brothers Department Store caught her eye, and one as a bank teller. Circling these, she sat with her chin in her hand. Fatigue settled over her like a leaden blanket, and her shoulders drooped. *I need a place to stay.* She turned over the check. *Seventy cents? For pie and iced tea? That's twice what it is at home.* She counted a dollar and five cents, remembering Mrs. Emily Post's edict of etiquette, that no matter how insubstantial the bill, the minimum acceptable tip was a quarter. She lined the coins up on the counter. The waitress waved as May rose, steeling herself to take on New York City.

A man in coveralls was cleaning a glass door opposite the one she had entered. He tipped his cap, holding the door open. May took it as a sign. As she entered the lobby of the New York Biltmore Hotel, cooled air tingled her damp back. The assertive sweetness of lilies beckoned from a towering vase on a center table. With dramatic flourishes, a man with patent-leather hair played a grand piano. The marble floor gleamed, and an ornate gilded clock hung above the front desk. Sprinkled around the lobby were groupings of plush sofas and armchairs where fashionable-looking ladies and gentlemen sat, plucking delicacies from tiered silver tea trays. Two women stood to leave, and May perched on one of their empty chairs, hands clasped in her lap. *I'm waiting for . . . my terribly wealthy, doting old aunt who lives in a skyscraper. We'll have afternoon tea and then go shopping for horribly expensive ugly hats.* From beneath the brim of her cloche, she observed the scene, but no one seemed to notice her. No one asked what she was doing there.

"Miss? You can't sleep here." May jolted awake, disoriented and frightened, to find a man in a dark suit with a Biltmore nametag scowling down at her.

Sitting up straight, she put a hand to her throat, as if she could physically subdue her racing pulse. "I was just . . . waiting for someone." The gilded clock chimed six. The guests having tea had all been replaced by people wearing evening clothes and sipping cocktails.

May rose, smoothing her skirt, and the scowling man watched as she moved toward the entrance and down the marble steps. The stair rail was brass; so highly polished that she hesitated to touch it, lest she mar its perfection with a wayward glove print. Through the glass doors ahead, heavy raindrops bounced off the steaming sidewalk as the doors revolved, disgorging damp-smelling people who shook umbrellas and mopped wet faces. As May ducked into the ladies' lounge, two women followed, exclaiming over the downpour. While they passed their umbrellas to the matronly, brown-skinned washroom attendant, May went into a stall. She could hear the attendant say, "Yes in*deed*, madam. It certainly is coming down. Would madam care for another towel? Why thank you, ladies. Have a lovely evening." There was quiet, and the attendant began to sing softly, her voice low and serene and familiarly southern.

May came out and regarded herself in the mirror over the basin. *Really,* she thought with some detachment, *I'm a sight.* Disarrayed pins stuck out of her hair, and something gray smeared her cheek. The small, gelatinous blob on her dress was lemon pie, she decided. As she washed her hands, the attendant ceased singing. Proffering a damask hand towel, she suggested, "Is miss in need of a hairbrush?" She indicated a tray with powder, pins, and combs. May reached for the towel and black spots swam in her vision. She swayed and the attendant grasped her arm.

"Whoa, honeychild. You best sit a spell." With strong arms, she steered May to a stool in front of a dressing table. "Sit. You want me to call the house doctor?"

"No, no. I'm fine, thank you. Just a little dizzy." She began to rise, and the woman pushed her back down. Her nametag said, *Florence*, and she had kind, deep-brown eyes.

"Sit. Hear me? Catch your breath." Florence leaned closer. "You going to be sick?"

"No." May pinched the bridge of her nose. Her voice cracked. "No."

Florence leaned forward, patting May's back. "There, there. Don't cry now."

"I'm just—" May exhaled "—so tired."

"When'd you eat last?" Florence gently pushed May back and held up a finger. "Look here." She sat on a straight chair and lifted the skirt of the dressing table, revealing a tiered tray of finger sandwiches and delicate pastries. Lifting the top plate, she glanced over her shoulder toward the door, then offered it to May. "Only a little bit dried out. I finished all the egg salad."

A moment later, Florence pushed herself up to take a woman's dripping umbrella and offer a towel. May hunched over the plate of sandwiches, wolfing them down. When the woman retrieved her umbrella, Florence made a small bow, receiving her tip with gracious servility. She returned to her chair, landing with an *uumph*. "Better?" she asked.

May nodded, swallowing. "Thank you." She opened the clasp of her handbag, and Florence made a face and waved her hand dismissively.

"Keep your money. Looks like you need some help. I can always tell. You're a little old for a runaway. You got a place to stay?" May shook her head. "Humph. You best get something right quick. It's going on seven. Ain't safe for a pretty thing like yourself to be roaming the streets. You look like a nice brought-up girl." Swishing her fingers in the direction of the lobby, she continued, "You march yourself on out there and take a room. Everything will look brighter in the morning. If you want, come back tomorrow after four, and let me know how you're getting on. Come after six, I'll have my sandwiches. Now, I'm going to sit right here and say a prayer that Jesus keeps you safe."

May nodded, almost overwhelmed with relief and gratitude for instructions on how to exist in this strange new universe. She thanked Florence, then returned to the lobby. The scowling guard was nowhere in sight. The piano played a waltz, and a woman in a pink raincoat passed, carrying a tiny, fluffy dog with a rhinestone collar and a little raincoat of its own. A clerk glanced up with an appraising eye as May approached the desk. "I'm interested in taking a room," she said, trying to muster a semblance of dignity in her state of disarray. "Could you please tell me the rate for a single with a private bath?"

He blinked slowly, looking as if he smelled something unpleasant. "*All* of the accommodations at the Biltmore have private baths, miss. Our rates start at eight dollars. That's per day, not per *week*. Did you write ahead, to tell us of your arrival?"

May thought again of Mrs. Post's rules. *No, obviously I did not write ahead. Eight dollars? The Allerton was two! Three, for deluxe with breakfast and a shoeshine!* She raised her chin and held his gaze. The clerk, she knew, was waiting for her to skulk away, defeated, *unworthy* of the New York Biltmore Hotel. She placed her handbag on the counter and stood at her full five-foot-six inches, looking down on the man. "I'd like a room on a high floor, please."

"Certainly." When he held out the register, she wrote, *Miss May Valentine*. "Any luggage?"

"I left it at Grand Central."

"If you have your claim check, I can have it delivered to your room."

"Is there an extra charge for that?"

"Gratuities are at the discretion of the guest. And how long will you be with us," He lifted his spectacles to scrutinize the register. "Miss Valentine?"

Eight dollars. Damn. "I'm not exactly sure." The key he passed across the desk was heavy, made more so by an oval fob with a script *B* embossed on the silvery metal.

The corridor that led to the elevators was lined with small shops, all closed for the evening; a tailor, an antiques dealer, a jeweler. May stopped to look at the jewelry on velvet pedestals—succulent rubies; sapphires with layered depths of blue; emeralds that defined the color green; and diamonds that gave off a brittle gleam that said clearly, *I am rare, near per-fection, not for the likes of you.* A long strand of pearls draped over black velvet, and she laid her hand against the glass.

The elevator doors were bronze, sculpted with mythical figures and animals. May pressed the call button and leaned closer, studying the design. A bell dinged, and a handsome young Negro elevator operator in a khaki uniform was smiling at her. "Floor, miss?" She stepped in and stood behind him, clutching her handbag and key.

"Twenty-second, please." *Twenty-eight stories. How do they build something this tall?*

She regarded her reflection in the mirrored paneling with dismay, attempting to smooth her hair. The elevator rose as lights illuminated behind the floor numbers: *nineteen, twenty, twenty-one . . .*

"Here you are, miss, twenty-two." The operator made a small bow as May exited.

The hallway was eerily silent after the streets and the lobby. Her shoes sank into the plush carpeting. In her room, she looked down from the window, awed. She had never been so high. Below, automobiles looked like toys. Above, storm clouds skittered away, leaving an amethyst evening sky and raindrops dotting the window. A wave of vertigo passed over her, and she backed away to sit on the bed, running her hands over the cool, puffed beige satin of the coverlet. She pried her shoes off and fell back, arms outstretched.

She had done it.

She had gotten herself to New York City, and she had no idea what to do next.

There was a tap on the door. "Bellman!"

"One moment!" The bellman put her suitcase on a rack, and she tipped him. He left, and she counted the money in her purse. She had left Hot Springs with seventy-six dollars. She counted out enough for a ticket home and folded it into one of the hotel's envelopes and pushed it through the ripped seam in the quilted lining of her suitcase. She pinned the tear closed, hoping it was safe.

In the bathroom, the black marble tile felt deliciously cold against her feet. Like a bonbon, an oval soap bar sat on a paper doily on the edge of the tub. It smelled of cloves. The towels were thick, with an embroidered *B*, and a matching bathrobe hung from a hook. While May soaked, she tried to formulate a plan. *Eight dollars a day . . . and then there's food . . .* She soaped herself, listing things to fret about, adding to the list as she shrugged into her nightgown and climbed into bed. Beneath the satin coverlet, she felt swaddled and protected. She hoped that Florence's prayers really would keep her safe.

Waiting for breakfast to be delivered the next morning, May perched on her windowsill and watched the street below, no longer feeling the initial dizziness. At 9 a.m., the city had a rhythm, a faster pace than she was used to, but she liked the speed. When the waiter knocked, she wondered if it was proper to answer the door in one's bathrobe. Sitting cross-legged on the bed, she poured coffee from the shiny little silver pot. The tray held a silver toast rack with perfectly browned triangles and three different jams, none of which, she decided, could hold a candle to Blue's. While she ate, she studied the classified advertisements in the morning newspaper. One made her stop and put her coffee down:

SEAMSTRESS—NEW YORK BILTMORE HOTEL. FULL TIME. MUST HAVE EXPERIENCE IN DARNING AND ALTERATIONS AND BE ABLE TO OPERATE A SINGER MODEL SEWING MACHINE. INQUIRE IN PERSON AT THE PERSONNEL OFFICE, 6TH FLOOR, BETWEEN THE HOURS OF TEN AND FOUR O'CLOCK. ASK FOR MR. GRAY.

With a series of little claps, May squealed. *Right here, at the Biltmore! It's a sign! And I have a Singer at home. How swell to work at such a beautiful place—air conditioning and fancy silverware and all the nice soap.* Farther down the page, another listing caught her eye.

SEAMSTRESS—CARLISLE CUSTOM COSTUME MAKERS, 315 W. 27TH STREET, 2ND FLOOR. MUST BE EXPERIENCED IN BEADING, PATTERN MAKING, FITTING, AND ALL FANCY SEWING TECHNIQUES. TELEPHONE FOR INTERVIEW. HERALD 3880.

Beadwork? Yes! And fittings; yes! Pattern making. Hmm. Haven't a clue. Damn. What fancy techniques? She reached for the bedside telephone and asked to be connected to the costume shop. As the call went through, she sat back on her pillows, twisting the phone cord in her fingers, imagining herself a film star, waiting for her maid and limousine. *A girl could get used to this.*

"*Cah-lisle's*," a gruff, irritated-sounding voice answered.

"Good morning!" May sat up. "This is Miss May Valentine calling, and I wanted to inquire—"

"You calling about the ad in the paper?"

"I *am*, sir, and I'd like to arr—"

"Filled yesterday. You shoulda called sooner."

"Oh, I see—" *Click.*

May stared at the buzzing receiver, affronted.

After she dressed, she sat at the small desk by the window and opened each of the drawers, finding freshly sharpened pencils, notepads with an illustration of the hotel at the top, a telephone directory, and picture postcards of the Biltmore. There was letter paper with the hotel insignia and a neat stack of matching envelopes. She laid one of the sheets on the blotter, and wrote:

September 3, 1924

Dear Mr. Craig,

Your friend "Miss Valentine" arrived safely to you-know-where. The train trip was dull, and I wished I had a good book to read. I changed in Washington with no problem. I found that hotel you told me about, but did you know that there are two different Allertons? Anyway, I did get a room at this pretty swanky place. I'm enclosing a postcard so you can see it better. I'm on the 22nd floor. So far, I am doing fine. I'll send more later.

Your old pal,
Miss V.

At five till ten, May left her room. At the end of the hall, she dropped her letter to Byrd into the mail slot in the wall between the doors of the twin elevators. Through the glass cover, she watched it fall from sight, wondering where it would land. Would it be damaged after a twenty-two-floor fall? The bell dinged, and she stepped into the car, clutching the folded newspaper. The operator smiled as the doors closed. She recognized him from the day before.

Facing forward, he asked, "Lobby, miss?"

"Sixth, please."

"Personnel," he said. "Looking for a position?"

"As a matter of fact, I am. There's a listing for a seamstress in the newspaper. Do you know if it's still available?" She attempted to peer around his shoulder to catch his eye, but he kept one gloved hand on the control knob and the other behind his back.

"Couldn't say, miss."

"Oh, is this yours?" Stooping, she picked up a brass button from the floor. "Look, it's from your uniform."

The operator faced her. "Thank you kindly." He took the button and tossed it and caught it in his white glove. "You sound like a southern gal. I'm from Tennessee myself. Here you are, sixth floor." As May stepped out, he offered a small salute. "Good luck, now." The bell dinged as the doors *whooshed* shut. In the hallway outside the personnel office, May pinched her cheeks and smoothed her dress. Her breakfast was a brick in her stomach.

Ding! The elevator doors slid open. "You again!" May said.

The operator smiled. "How'd you do?"

"They hired me!" She said as she stepped into the car. "Just in the laundry, as a seamstress, but that nice Mr. Gray said I can start the day after tomorrow. Now I have to go to the basement and get a uniform." She put her gloved palms over her cheeks. "I've never had a real job before. I mean, not one that I found all by myself. But I showed Mr. Gray that I had made my dress. And I did. Make it myself, I mean."

"Congratulations," the operator said, "and welcome to the New York Biltmore. You'll be working for Mrs. McPhatter." He held up an index finger. "Don't be late, and don't give her any sass. You should get along fine."

"Gosh. Thanks. Now, if I can find a place to stay, I'll be *all* set." May clutched her handbag and rocked on her heels.

"You know, I heard about a place, right on 36th? Not as posh as this joint, though."

"You don't say?" May craned forward. "Honestly, I can't afford anything fancy . . ."

"Not to worry. Listen, my shift ends at four. I'll take you there if you like. Meantime, I can show you around the hotel. On the q.t., of course."

"And I can sew your button on for you. My name is May Valentine. This is my first visit to New York. I did go to New Orleans once, on the train? Only they didn't have buildings as tall as this." She scrutinized his name badge. "*Throckmorton.* Is that your first or last name?"

"Throckmorton C. Pendergrast, at your service." He whisked off his cap and bowed. "Of the Memphis Pendergrasts. You can call me Rocky, if you like. So you're new to the city."

May opened her mouth, then closed it. What was she *thinking*, blathering on to this stranger? This *would not do.* She needed to come up with a plausible story about herself.

May spent the afternoon exploring the hotel and riding the elevator with Rocky. When they were the only occupants of the car, he told her the ins and outs of the Biltmore, how to use the subway and elevated trains, and how to hail a taxi. They went up the North Tower, then Rocky traded elevators to take her up the South Tower. Between the towers was a formal garden, which, he explained, was transformed into an ice-skating rink in the wintertime. May listened, nodding, offering no more information about herself. From the roof, they had a panoramic view of the city, and Rocky pointed out Central Park, lush and green in the distance. At four o'clock, she rode down again to the basement and waited as Rocky changed out of his uniform. They exited from the employee's entrance, and he pointed out landmarks along the way, stopping at the doorway of 151 East 36th Street.

"This is the place," he said, "It opened last year, and I hear it's real clean. It's run by a church or something. I can't go in with you. Ask for Miss Wiggins. Good luck, Kiddo. I'll see you around the hotel."

SEVENTEEN

It was rumored, May would hear later, that Miss Adelaide Wiggins was a former nun. She might have been any age from thirty to fifty; it was impossible to say. As she bustled about her office, May sniffed discreetly. *Camphor? Lilac?* Pale and plump, Miss Wiggins had robust eyebrows, partially obscured by steel-rimmed spectacles with thick lenses, which caused her eyes to appear unnaturally large and startled. When she said, "Have a seat, dear," her voice was surprisingly warm. "Now, tell me about yourself." Miss Wiggins sat, folding her hands primly on her desk.

May perched, stiff-backed and ladylike, on the edge of the chair, clasping her gloved hands. Her mouth was dry. *Talk real slow.* She recited the lie she had contrived: "Well, ma'am, I arrived a few days ago, from North Carolina. I'm hoping to attend secretarial school, but for the time being, I have a job at the Biltmore Hotel."

"I see. Miss Valentine, The Roberts House is owned by the Ladies' Christian Union. We accept only unmarried young ladies between the ages of eighteen and twenty-five. How old are you?"

"Nineteen, ma'am."

In stern tones, Miss Wiggins recited, "Our mission is to provide moral and religious guidance for young women who are dependent upon their own exertions for support. Misbehavior is not tolerated. Gentlemen callers may be received in the visitor's parlor. Our girls are expected to keep their rooms tidy, and their appearance neat. The rent is ten dollars per week, payable in advance. That includes breakfast and dinner, except on Sundays. Here is a complete list of rules." She pushed two mimeographed sheets across the desk, and rose, jingling the large ring of keys that hung from her waist.

Sounds like Mary Baldwin. Or a convent. Or a prison. Or maybe a prison for criminal nuns. "Yes, please, ma'am. I promise I'll obey the rules."

"You seem to be a well-bred girl. We usually have a waiting list, you understand, but a young lady was evicted earlier this week because she missed curfew too often." Miss Wiggins paused, as if to make sure that May understood. "Come with me." May followed up a flight of stairs then down a long hallway. Unlocking a door at the end, Miss Wiggins stepped back, revealing a cell-like room that smelled sharply of disinfectant. The floor was linoleum and the furnishings simple—an iron-framed bed, a sink, a bureau, a chair, and night table—all in shades of gray. The window curtain was sheer and dingy white. May peered down into a small court-yard that was shaded by a chestnut tree.

"That's our little garden," Miss Wiggins said. "In the winter, we roast the chestnuts in the parlor fireplace."

"It's lovely. What color are your roses?"

Miss Wiggins lingered at the window. Her face softened. "Red, mostly, but a few pink. You may move in in the morning. Welcome to the Roberts House, my dear."

May tilted her head in her best imitation of an endearing Mary Pickford. "Miss Wiggins, do you think I might possibly be able to move in today?"

May hurried through the lobby of the Biltmore, not making eye contact with anyone. In her room, she wrapped the clove soap in its paper doily and tucked it into her bag along with the Biltmore letter paper, telling herself that it was the same as using it while she was a guest. She picked up the telephone receiver, but when the operator asked for a number, she hung up, struck with the frightening, heavy certainly that she was truly disconnected from home, and completely on her own. Why on earth had she thought this was a good idea?

On her way back through the lobby, she stopped in the ladies' lounge, but Florence was not there. Exiting the hotel, she looked for the landmarks Rocky had pointed out. She crossed 42nd Street, avoiding a policeman on a corner. When she saw the sign for the Pierpont Morgan Library, she turned east onto 36th Street, and was able to find the Roberts House again without asking directions. There was some small consolation in that accomplishment.

With ten dollars in her pocket, she returned to the Roberts House office. The door was open, and Miss Wiggins was writing at her desk. When May tapped the doorframe, she looked up, closing a black ledger with red, pebbled-leather corners. May stared, startled. The ledger on the desk was exactly like Sheriff Beasley's. Miss Wiggins said, "Hello again, dear. Fill in your name and home address here." She held out an index card. In her other hand, she dangled two keys, knotted on a black ribbon. May hesitated for only a moment, then quickly filled in *123 Marshall Street*. Had she mentioned a city? She continued: *Charlotte, North Carolina*.

In room sixteen, May shed her hat and gloves and opened the window. City smells wafted in, blending with the tang of disinfectant. She bounced on the bare mattress, then examined her keys, running a finger over the grooves. For the first time since leaving Hot Springs, she allowed herself to feel a tiny bit optimistic, and, for a few minutes, safe. The room was monastic—a sanctuary, and Miss Wiggins her guardian. Was this the way to a fresh start—this bare canvas of a place—where no one knew anything about her past except what she chose to tell?

Rocky had told her how to get to Macy's Department Store at Herald Square. The sidewalks were crowded, and the late afternoon sun cast a harsh, metallic light. May moved among strangers, telling herself that it was impossible that anyone was searching for her in New York. On 34th Street she saw shops selling everything from candy to women's foundations to hardware. Boys in scruffy knickers shined shoes on every corner while overhead, the elevated train rattled uptown. Crossing the street, the signs for Macy's flashed and beckoned. Such a huge store. Who on earth kept track of all the things they sold?

A white-gloved doorman in livery ushered her inside. Crystal flacons of perfume lined the counters and scented the air. Leather gloves as smooth as melted chocolate were stacked in neat rows of pastel colors, alongside matching feathered hats. Mannequins with haughty plaster faces peered down at her from pedestals, each dressed in the latest styles. May wandered through the stationery department, pausing to inspect a small diary with a tiny brass key on a green, tasseled cord. Like her unfinished scrapbook, the blank pages seemed like a taunt. Five lines per day. Should any particular day prove to be momentous, its memory must be condensed to fit into the allotted space. *But life just isn't that neat.* She replaced it on the shelf, then rode the escalator to the housewares floor. A motherly saleslady helped her choose pink towels and a chenille coverlet with pink roses, then wished her well at secretarial school.

Back on the ground floor, May juggled her purchases, now neatly wrapped in brown paper and twine. A slim young woman approached, holding a black-and-gold atomizer. She had short, marcelled blond hair and large green eyes. With her pencil-thin brows raised, she inquired, "Try a new perfume, miss?" She squeezed the bulb, spraying May's wrist, then stepped back, assuming a studied pose with one toe pointed, the atomizer perched on her flat palm. She blinked, holding her pose.

"Oh." May's eyes fluttered. "It's heavenly." The scent was delicious—orange blossoms and violets.

The girl smiled then, displaying dimples and a gap between her upper front teeth. She recited, "This particular scent is called *Amour Amour.* That's French for *love.* It's the very latest, from Paris. By Jean Patou. He's a famous couturier, and it costs sevenny—seven*ty*—dollars for a bottle." May thanked her, marveling at the price as she continued out of the store, her head full of the sensuous perfume.

At the door of the Roberts House, May juggled her purchases, attempting to fit her key into the lock. "Hey, hon, lemme get that." An arm reached around and grabbed the door handle, and May was facing the gap-toothed blond from Macy's. "Forgot my keys, anyways," the girl said, shrugging. Her voice was different, less refined than it had seemed at Macy's. She continued, "Hey, I remember you. You must be the new gal." She held out her hand. "I'm on the second floor myself. Room twelve. Name's Dora."

"I'm May. I got here yesterday."

Dora helped carry the parcels to room sixteen, then stretched out on the bare mattress, propping her feet on the foot rail. "Whew! My dogs are barking. Standing in heels all day's rough, you know? They make us wear heels. What brings you to New York?"

"I'm hoping to be accepted at The Katherine Gibbs School, to become a professional secretary." Lies, May was realizing, came more easily with each telling, and should not be presented over eagerly, and probably not with that questioning lilt. Secretarial school seemed a modest, ordinary goal. "Meantime," she said, now moderating her tone, "I'm working at the Biltmore, in the laundry." She watched Dora, attempting to gauge the plausibility of her story.

Dora raised herself onto her elbows. "If you're in the laundry, why'd you come to Macy's for sheets? Shoot, you could a lifted some from the Biltmore. Save yourself a little dough. And always check the lost and found." She rubbed her thumb against her fingers. "So . . . when you do get the chance, don't forget your friend Dora, okeydokey? I bet they have nice towels there."

"Where are you from?"

"Poughkeepsie. My Ma died, and I had to go live with my uncle." She made a face. "Didn't go so good, so I jumped a train."

May leaned forward. "You jumped a train? Really? How do you *do* that?"

Dora examined her fingernails. "Well, maybe I didn't specifically *jump onto* the train, but I did hide in the toilet. I got all the way here without buying a ticket! I can handle myself. I'm only at Macy's till I get my big break. I'm saving up to go to Hollywood." She fluffed her hair. "Unless the Prince a Wales or a Rockefeller proposes first. Ha! What's your story, hon? You talk like a smart gal. Hey, maybe you can coach me? The floor manager says my accent is low-class. And you know, I could teach *you* to have a little style, okeydokey? You're real pretty, but honestly, you ought to bob your hair. You got a smoke?"

"I don't smoke. Besides, you can't in here. It's against the rules."

Dora waved dismissively at the closed door. "*Rules.* Rules are just suggestions, in my book. Old Wiggie can jump in a lake. Blow the smoke out the window, and nobody's the wiser. An electric fan is even better. Only, not if your room faces into the courtyard, 'cause she can see, but the girls who face the street do it all the time."

"Are the girls here nice?"

"It's like this—some of 'em are prissy missies, and some are fun." Dora put her palm on her chest. "A bunch of us are going to see Rudolph Valentino on Saturday. You could come along."

May sat on the bed beside her. "The *real* Rudy? Didn't you love him in *The Sheik*?"

"Rudy in the flesh," Dora said. "It's called a premiere. That's when a picture gets shown for the first time. With a little luck, we'll meet some gents and they'll take us to a club. You need to get dolled up."

"That sounds swell," May said, "Only, I need to watch my pennies."

Dora hopped up. "Suit yourself. But let me know if you change your mind. A girl's gotta have a *little* fun. I'm gonna get a shower before the hot water runs out. Middle shower is best. See you around."

May held her wrist to her nose. The scent of *Amour Amour* was fading. She made the bed and hung up her pink towels, arranging the Biltmore soap beside the sink. *There. It looks more cheerful already.* She hung her clothes in the closet, then wound Byrd's watch and propped it on the bedside table, next to the photograph of her mother.

In the dining room the next morning, a few somber, studious-looking girls sat alone, reading as they ate. "The eggheads," Dora whispered, "and over there . . ." She nodded toward one table, then another. ". . . the snobs, and the foreigners." She led May through the cafeteria line, expertly pocketing illicit butter pats and rolls, to serve as lunch.

After breakfast, May sat in the garden and wrote to Byrd with the Roberts House address, then used a postcard from the Biltmore to write to Elsie with a brief apology for missing her interview. No doubt she would have heard of May's predicament by now. The chestnut tree reminded her of the farm, and looking up through the branches, she noticed Miss Wiggins gazing down from an upper floor window. May gave a small wave, and Miss Wiggins retreated, her magnified eyes blinking slowly behind her thick lenses.

EIGHTEEN

In the basement of the Biltmore, the steamy, hot air smelled of bleach and damp cement. Above, white-painted pipes crisscrossed the ceiling, intersected with steel beams. Below, a row of ironing boards lined one wall, with black electrical cords snaking from steam irons up into a flexible coiled arm that moved back and forth with the motion of the iron across a shirt or nightgown, each iron propelled by a woman in an identical short-sleeved white smock. There were mangles, and deep sinks, and rows of zinc-topped tables, each stacked with precisely folded white sheets, or towels, or damask napkins. Rolling laundry carts bore stenciled floor numbers. May saw no sign of air conditioning or fresh flowers, nor clove-scented soap.

The laundry was running at full tilt, and Mrs. McPhatter explained that May would wear a hotel uniform instead of the white smock, because she would be sent to guest's rooms from time to time. She led May on a brief tour, while the other workers laughed and talked, timing their sentences around the rhythmic click and hiss of the steam presses and the drumming of the dryers. May took up her post at the sewing table that faced the back wall. The other workers seemed to take no interest in her. It crossed her mind that perhaps, below stairs, a hotel uniform set her apart. Maybe there was some hierarchy that she was unaware of. She would be friendly, and they could respond, or not. Through the morning and into the afternoon, she bent over the sewing machine darning holes in bedsheets. It was uninteresting work, and with her back to the room, she had nothing to look at. She resolved, before her first morning was finished, that she would find something better. She was relieved when she was sent to a suite on the fourteenth floor to pin the hem on a guest's evening gown. Walking through the lobby in her uniform, May smiled to herself. The desk clerk who had checked her in watched her pass, his brow furrowing, and she could tell that he recognized her from somewhere but couldn't quite place her. It was as if she were in disguise. She could probably walk right past Sheriff Beasley unnoticed.

By the time her shift ended, May's shoulders ached, and her eyes were red from the constant irritation of borax and bleach. Leaving the employee's entrance, she squinted in the sunlight. At the Roberts House, she greeted the receptionist and checked the mail cubby for room sixteen, even though she knew she shouldn't expect a letter yet. Passing the telephone table, she imagined that she was already forgetting voices from home. In her room, she kicked off her shoes and sat on the bed, rubbing her eyes. Being in prison was probably similar to the basement of the Biltmore—windowless, colorless, and monotonous—and lonely, even though there were other people around.

When the lunch bell sounded on May's fifth day in the laundry room, she hurried outside to sit on the low wall outside the employee's entrance for her forty-five minutes of respite. The heat and humidity of early September seemed balmy after the basement. The door swung open, and Rocky came out, loosening his bow tie. "Look who's here!" he said. "Did you get the room?"

"Yes! I've been looking for you, to thank you." While he smoked, May ate a roll and told him about the girls at the house, grateful for conversation. She said, "How did you know about that place?"

Rocky took a long pull on his cigarette. "Sometimes, it's good to be invisible. People don't really see elevator operators. It doesn't occur to them that we're listening. But we do. Where are you from, anyhow? You have a southern accent, but it's not Alabama or Mississippi."

"Vir—North Carolina. And you're from Tennessee, right? What brought you to New York?"

"There was nothing keeping me in Memphis," he said, shaking his head. "Soon as I finished school, I jumped a freight train and headed north. That was five years ago. I don't have to look out for anybody but myself, and I like it that way." He threw down his cigarette, grinding the butt with his shoe.

"Sounds like you have a plan."

"You bet I do. I'm going to be the hairdresser to the stars, in Holly-wood. *Everyone* will want a hairstyle by Mr. Throckmorton." He wagged his finger. "I've been taking night classes at Madame C. J. Walker's Academy of Hair Culture, in Harlem. You been to Harlem?"

"I haven't been much of anywhere yet."

"Ah. There are some ripping Jazz clubs. You like to dance?"

"Yes! Do you know the Charleston?" May sat forward, tapping her feet on the cement. "My friend Dora wants to go to Hollywood, too, to be an actress in the pictures. She says I ought to bob my hair. What do you think?" May stroked her long braid.

Rocky nodded slowly. "You've got a classical bone structure. That was our lesson, last night, about facial structure. See, a simple Dutch bob would frame your face. If you want, I could do it for you. What do you say?"

May toyed with the end of her braid, then tossed it over her shoulder. "Why not, Mr. Throckmorton? But where?"

"Right here, in the basement. I'm off duty. Let me change out of my uniform."

"But I only have thirty minutes left."

"Not to worry. Come on." Inside, Rocky switched on the light in a storage room, where folded cots stood in a row. May sat on a stool in front of a cracked mirror and he fastened a sheet around her shoulders, then turned her so she could not see her reflection. With the first click of the shears, a dark-brown hank fell heavily to the floor like a dead bird. With each successive snip, her trepidation gave way to a novel buoyancy.

"Voilà!" Rocky stepped back, holding out his comb and shears. "*Très chic!*"

May's bare neck felt naked and exposed. "Do you speak French?"

"Don't I wish? It's so highbrow." As she began to turn toward the mirror, Rocky held out his hands. "Wait! We're not *quite* finished. Um, speaking of brows . . . is it all right if I . . . ?" He held up a pair of tweezers. "I mean, not that, you know, intense eyebrows aren't distinctive, but I was picturing less Charlie Chaplin and more Greta Garbo."

He looked so earnest that May burst out laughing. "I'm guessing your Academy hasn't had a lesson in bedside manner yet."

"Close your eyes."

When Rocky finally turned her to the mirror, a sophisticated looking stranger with large eyes and prominent cheekbones looked back with an expression of delighted surprise. She whispered, "I don't look like me anymore." Patting her new bangs, she leaned closer, indulging in a moment of undiluted vanity. "But I like it. Oh, I *do*. Thank you!"

Rocky looked pleased. "How about if we go out dancing and show off your new look?" His expression of pride turned to bashfulness. "I mean, you know, as friends. How's tomorrow night?"

"That'd be . . ." In the mirror, she caught his eye and her smile faded. "I mean, at home, it would be a problem for us to go out, even as friends. It would cause trouble."

"I get it." Rocky held up his hands. "Forget I mentioned it." He began to sweep up the hair from the floor, his back stiff.

"No. You're making it sound like I don't want to, but that's not true." May took the broom from him and knelt to use the dustpan. "It's just how things are at home."

"So we can be friends in the basement, but not out in public. Is that it? It's the same way where I came from. The whole reason I came to New York was to get away from the way things are *at home*. And where *is* home for you, anyhow? Which was it? North Carolina or Virginia? If you went to college, why would you be wanting to go to secretarial school? Your story doesn't add up. If we're going to be friends, you have to be honest with me."

May looked down. "I left home to get away from some trouble I got myself into. I'll tell you about it sometime, but you have to promise to not tell anyone."

After a long moment, he nodded. "Fair enough. Everybody's got their secrets."

May blanched. *My past is my own business. Nobody needs to know.* She asked, "Is it really different here? It's all right for Negroes and whites to dance together?"

"Not everywhere. But there are certain clubs, called 'Black-and-Tans.' My favorite is the Catagonia. On Fridays, they have a great crowd."

Walking home that night, May sought her reflection in every window along the way, eyeing herself at different angles while affecting a range of expressions, trying to appear nonchalant. At the Roberts House, she went straight to Dora's room. "Look at you, doll!" Dora said, "You look like a million bucks." Her hands were wet from washing something in her sink.

May rubbed the back of her neck. "My friend Rocky cut it, at the Bilt-more. And look at my eyebrows! He says the redness should go away soon."

Dora leaned closer. "You're like . . . exotic or something. You look like Louise Brooks."

"Do you think you could lend me a dress to wear Friday night? I think the evening dresses I brought with me are out of style now."

"You don't waste time, do you? Who you going out with?" Dora continued to wring her washing.

"Rocky asked me. He's from Memphis, and he's a real cutup. You could come along. I'm sure he wouldn't mind."

"So where you going?"

"The Catagonia Club. Have you been?"

"The *Catagonia* Club?" Dora dropped her washing into the sink and turned. "Honey, I hate to be the one to tell you, but that's a club for darkies."

"It's a Black-and-Tan. Rocky says they have a great floor show, with lots of chorus girls and a big orchestra."

"Hold on a minute." Dora held up her hands; soapy water dripped to the floor. "Are you telling me you're going out with a *Negro*?"

"He's really nice. You'd like him."

"I got enough friends, thanks," Dora muttered, turning back to the sink.

"Oh. Well, all right." May shifted from foot to foot, debating how to say what she really wanted to say. "What I meant was . . . I didn't mean to say that it's all right. Rocky is my friend, and you haven't even given him a chance. I wouldn't judge your friends that way. Come with us."

"I'm sure he's a peach. I've got plans already."

"I was hoping you might lend me a dress."

Dora wrung out her slip and draped it over the back of her chair, then dried her hands, saying, "Well, I guess you gotta start somewhere." She took two dresses from her closet, dangling a hanger from each hand. "Have your pick."

"These are gorgeous!" May fingered the price tag on a sleeveless, ice-blue dress with heavy crystal beads. "But you haven't even worn this."

Dora shrugged. "I'll wear 'em once, and sneak 'em back to the stockroom at Macy's. You gotta pin the price tag back on after, and you better not spill anything."

"But what if you got caught?" May laid the dress on the bed with care. She envied Dora's unapologetic nerve. "On second thought," she said, "this isn't a good idea. I mean, if anything happened, I wouldn't be able to pay for it. But thanks, all the same."

"Haven't got caught yet. I got a system." Dora poked her thumb toward her chest. "A girl's got to look for opportunities. These dresses are a way to create opportunities. You go out looking a certain way, you attract a certain type of gentleman. Think about it. Let me know if you change your mind. You'll learn for yourself soon enough; New York is mostly window dressing."

NINETEEN

Early Friday evening, May sat on her bed in her slip and stockings. The ice-blue dress hung on her closet door. She hugged her knees, watching the beads shimmer in the light while the price tag dangled from its string, attached by a little brass pin. The sparkly dress reminded her of something Elsie would leave on the floor after a night of dancing, taking for granted that she would always have a closet full of beautiful dresses. May had been allowed, briefly, to taste that life, and she had wanted more. She had wanted to gorge herself on that life. Sitting there on her bed, she debated whether she should go out at all. Just a few hours' distraction—was that so bad? If Dora was right, then going out could lead to opportunities. And she had told Rocky she would meet him; it was too late to back out. She didn't want to admit to herself that her qualms were insincere. She really did want to wear that dress.

A single rap on the door announced Dora, her hands full of small bottles and brushes. With a cigarette wedged into the space between her front teeth, she painted May's fingernails a color called Vermillion Millions. "Nail varnish covers the smell of smoke, trust me," Dora said, waving the nail brush. "Let 'em dry, and do not *move* until I say." She made up May's face, then helped her into the dress and buttoned up the back.

May turned a slow circle, as Dora sat back on the bed, appraising her handiwork and nodding in approval. "It's heavy!" May said, "All these beads. It took somebody forever to sew them all on. A lot of work goes into a dress like this."

"Yeah, well, you better take care of it. You're gonna turn some heads for sure. Create some opportunities."

May studied her face in the mirror, the heavily lined eyes, the Cupid's bow Dora had made of her mouth. She ran her painted fingernails over her cheeks and down her neck. The makeup dramatized the change in her appearance. She watched her lips move as she spoke, with the eerie sensation of commanding a puppet—as if she were someone other than May Marshall from Keswick, Virginia. Here stood a stylish, expensively clad girl, who might be Debutante of the Year—brimming with verve and promise. She held out the velvet pouch of pearls. "Clasp these for me, would you?"

Dora dangled the strand on a fingertip. "Ooh. How pretty. Are they real?"

"They were my mother's."

"Is your mother . . . not . . . alive?"

"I don't know. She left when I was seven."

"Jeez. That's so sad." Dora fingered the pouch. "Hey, what's this?" She held up a shard of porcelain. "Part of a doll's face?"

"It's nothing." May took the shard from Dora. No one was invited to touch this talisman. No one. May traced the edges of the fragment, so worn that the only paint left on it was the bright crimson of the lips, frozen in a tight little smile. Dora became engrossed in painting her own nails. May dropped the shard into her drawer and shoved it closed, her fingers clutching the knobs as if she could physically contain the memory that slipped out like a genie from a lamp. The one, single time she had seen her father's fury. She was seven.

Backed against the wall at the top of the steps, she was hugging a new doll. Delphina stood on the landing, hands clasped in supplication.

Her father on the top stair. His face red. Frighteningly red. "Give it to me," he commanded.

"Please let me keep it, Daddy! Mama sent it!" He reached for the doll,

catching its arm. Fabric pulled taut, then a terrible snap as the arm tore away. "Nooo, Daddy!" She clutched the doll tighter, eyes squeezing shut.

"Mr. M., please," Delphina said, taking his arm, "The box came while I was feeding the chickens." He shook her off and grabbed the doll, then threw it over the banister.

A sickening thud; the splintered notes of shattering porcelain. She plugged her ears with her fingers and kept her eyes squeezed shut. Holding her breath, she tried to block out the sour smell of liquor and the sound of his heaving breath.

The following day, May found the shard. Something glinted, partially hidden beneath the grandfather clock in the downstairs hall. She knelt to look. It was a piece of porcelain that had skittered across the floor. A fragment of the doll's painted face. She hid it, afraid to show it to anyone.

When May turned from her bureau, Dora was looking at her quizzically. "You all right, toots?"

Stepping back, May's hands moved to touch the cool smoothness of her pearls. There was nothing to be gained by revisiting dark corners. She kissed Dora's cheek, leaving a red lip print, and said, buoyantly, "I'm going to kick up my heels! Maybe next time you'll come along. Thanks for everything."

"You're welcome, but next time, I'm taking you to a proper club. You can do better. Let me fix you up."

May paused in the doorway. "Dora, listen. I like you, and I hope we'll be good friends. But I don't want any advice about who I go around with. Okeydokey?"

Following Rocky's instructions, May took the El to West 133rd Street. At the Catagonia Club, he waited outside the door, standing tall in a pearl-gray suit and derby hat. May told him that he looked as handsome as Duke Ellington, only without the mustache. Entering the foyer of the club, the outside world seemed to dissolve behind them. While Rocky spoke to the maître d', she studied her reflection in the entryway mirrors, hardly recognizing the girl who looked back. The girl in the mirror sparkled with anticipation. She was quite glamorous, actually. May stood straighter, lifting her chin. Now the girl looked confident. She gave herself a secret wink. No one would recognize the frightened girl who came on the train from Virginia.

The maître d' led the way through a smoky, perfume-and-liquor-smelling labyrinth, then paused, looking for a table. Even though Rocky had explained the premise of a Black-and-Tan club, seeing white people and Negroes sharing tables and dancing together seemed both pioneering and terribly sophisticated. In a corner, a young woman in a fringed silver dress sat on an older man's lap. When she threw back her head, laughing, the feather plume of her headband ruffled and settled. Her companion rolled up a banknote and passed it to her. Leaning forward, the girl's breasts almost spilled from her neckline as she sniffed up a line of powder from the glass tabletop, then whooped, wiping her nose. As she leaned forward again, her eyes caught May's and she lifted her chin in invitation, holding out the rolled bill. May shook her head and looked away, and the girl whooped again. Rocky leaned close and said, "Cocaine."

"She looks like she's having fun," May said.

The maître d' summoned them to a table near the stage and held May's chair. He bowed slightly, then disappeared into the crowd. She leaned forward, covertly watching the girl with the headband. She wanted to absorb every new thing. This sophisticated girl in the ice-blue dress needed some lessons in city life. "Have you tried it?"

"Yeah," Rocky said, "Makes you feel all jazzed up." He tapped a cigarette out of the pack. "Folks get dependent on it. And it's expensive. Listen—there are plenty of temptations in this world. A thing like that is just the thin end of the wedge. Cigarette?"

"No, thanks. What does that mean?"

"Well, you try something once, and maybe you like it. Then you try something else—a little bit riskier—and before you know it, you're living on the street. Sometimes, things that feel good are dangerous, you know?"

"But you tried it."

"I did. That I did. And I can tell you, it was something I had to walk away from."

The spotlights surrounding the stage flashed twice, then the room went black. A saxophone wailed a single, prolonged, mournful note. As it receded into the dark, the crowd was hushed—expectant, for one long beat; two; three.

With a startling blare of horns, the lights came up, and a line of chorus girls in sparkling costumes kicked and shimmied onto the stage. They kept time, operating as a single, mechanical force, at once graceful and strong. May tapped her foot to an exuberant thrill of rhythm as vocalists alternated with dance numbers. Each time the chorus appeared in new costumes, she was further enchanted—by the beautiful, sweating bodies of the dancers, the swing and glitter of their costumes, the musicians—so obviously enjoying themselves—asking and answering each other through their instruments. She glanced around at the audience, each person either ignoring or picking up the vibration, responding or not responding. There were eyes bright with cocaine, eyes lidded with boredom or drink, or both.

Rocky was watching her. "You seem to be enjoying yourself."

May sat forward eagerly, her palm on her chest. "I've got goosebumps! Oh, thank you for bringing me here. This place is . . . it's absolutely magical. The dancers—and those gorgeous costumes! You know, my mother designed costumes. You wouldn't believe the work that goes into them. That would be a swell job to have, wouldn't it?"

Rocky sat back and crossed his arms, smiling benignantly. "You should see your face right now. Why not give it a go? Apply to work at a costume shop. What have you got to lose?"

With a sudden, vertiginous dropping of her heart, May lowered her hand. *What do I have to lose? That, my friend, is a very good question.* The nightclub had transported her far away from the world she had left behind. She toyed with the stem of her glass, saying, "I just want a chance—you know, to make something of myself? I want to find where I fit in."

Rocky nodded, clinking his glass against hers. "Absolutely. Here's to chances, Kiddo. I put in three applications this week for hairdressing positions. *You* are going to apply at a costume house. Try for something better than the laundry."

May raised her glass. "To chances."

TWENTY

Saturday's early mail brought two letters, propped in the mail cubby for room sixteen. Girls were beginning to line up outside the dining room for breakfast, so May went to the bench in the quiet garden, where late-season roses bloomed in Miss Wiggins's carefully tended plot. The serene green space was a refuge from the clamor and relentless gray of the city. It had never occurred to her that trees and birds and flowers could be luxuries. She weighed the envelopes in her palm, afraid to open the one with the return address: *Honeycutt & Nash, Attorneys at Law.* As long as she did not read it, there were no emotions to be felt, save anticipation. For as long as it remained sealed, she was disconnected—she was May Valentine—with a clean slate. The division between her two identities was widening every day, and at the deepest reaches of that divide—between who she had been and who she hoped to become—lay the darkness of regret. It had traveled with her, over time and distance. She tore at the flap of the lawyer's envelope. It contained a handwritten sheet in her father's blocky hand.

September 9

Dear Little Gal,

It is a sorry state of affairs when your father is writing to you from a jail cell. I slipped this letter to Byrd, and I trust it will find you. I am not the least bit happy to hear that you decided to go to New York City. That place is full of all sorts of bad characters. I want you to come home as soon as you can.

Yesterday, I was formally charged with operating an illegal still, selling intoxicants, possession and manufacture of alcohol, avoiding taxes, and possession of illegal firearms. You've been charged with impeding an official investigation and aiding and abetting. No word yet on a trial date, or even if it'll come to that. Honeycutt says that on account of the courts and jails being so congested, it might take a while. My only real worry, aside from you being in that damnable city, is that if they keep the Market closed, things will get tight. Blue is doing the canning from the kitchen at home until we can reopen. Delphina is taking care of the house. I sure hope I get out of here before the apple harvest and get you home where you belong. I will wait for news from Byrd about you. Please be careful.

Love, Daddy

May folded the letter and pressed it against her chest. *Formal charges. Aiding and abetting.* Seeing it on paper made it real. *Here I've been, wearing sparkly dresses and dancing and making friends. And Daddy is sitting in a jail cell.*

Elsie's letter was in a thick, gray envelope with her monogram engraved in silver.

September 10, 1924

Dearest May VALENTINE,

Gracious, my darling, haven't you gotten yourself into a royal pickle! And your poor dad. And you're using an alias! How wonderfully adventuresome. When Byrd told me you had run off to New York, I could scarcely believe it! SO much more exciting than college. I've only been here three days, but I'm already missing you dreadfully.

As you might imagine, Domestic Science is an utter disaster, once again. I did cause a bit of a fire, though not as big as last year. Honestly, I keep telling them I don't need to know how to cook or sew. There are people who do those things for one.

Before term started there were ripping parties though, and I've been to all of them with Archie. Guess what? He PROPOSED to me last Sunday! I had such a wretched hangover I told him to go jump in a lake. He was a good sport, though, and I told him we could just forget about that nonsense. Now everything is going along swimmingly, though he pouted for a while.

Invitations to the debutante balls are already arriving, and I can name three girls who've asked Byrd to escort them. I can't imagine how he's going to handle them all, but he always does. I heard he's taking Charlotte Penrose to the steeplechase races next weekend.

Please write to me often and let me know your news. Really, old dear, I am frightfully worried about you.

Love, Elsie

May smiled as she folded the letter. It amused her to think that Elsie envied her, when she herself had always been the envious one. And she was hardly being adventuresome, working in a hotel laundry.

When May looked up, Dora stood in front of her, arms crossed over her chest. "Big news?"

"Oh, no . . ." May startled, arranging her face into nonchalance. "Nothing important. It's always good to hear from the folks at home, you know?" She folded the letter, holding it so that the address was concealed.

Dora shrugged. "Well, I'm glad it's nothing bad. How was your night out?"

"Oh, it was *such* fun. My ears are still ringing. And your dress is in perfect shape."

"So tonight, how 'bout I'll show you a *proper* club—the Hotsy-Totsy. We can get in free, on account of my boyfriend works there. He likes when I bring fun gals along."

"But I just went out last night! I was going to stay in, to write some letters. Maybe we could go out for an ice cream?"

Dora made an *are you crazy?* face and said, "Yeah, sure, and I'll show you my stamp collection." She cocked her head, holding out a flat palm in one of her Macy's poses. "It's Saturday night, for Pete's sake, and Fletcher Henderson and his orchestra are playing."

"Really? I've heard him on the radio." They walked together into the dining room.

Dora said, "Be ready to go at seven thirty, okeydokey?"

"Who's there?" Dora called, when May knocked.

"Only me." May opened the door and Dora turned from her dresser, wiping her nose with a handkerchief. May said, "Are you all right?"

Dora giggled, holding up a small brown vial. "Peachy. You want some?"

May pressed the door closed, whispering, "Is that cocaine?"

Dora shrugged. "Wacky dust. Gives you pep."

"Oh. I . . . I've never tried it. I think I'll pass, but thanks." She eyed Dora, then the vial, with the wide-eyed fascination of an eavesdropper.

"Suit yourself." Dora pulled a box of cigarettes from her nightstand, flipping her hand for May to lock the door. Sinking onto her bed, she exhaled a stream of smoke toward the open window. "God, I hate this joint. What do you say you and me look for an apartment?"

"Oh," May sighed, sitting on the edge of the bed, "wouldn't that be swell? Only I'm not sure how long I'll be here, and this place is about all I can afford."

"You got a fella back home?"

"A boyfriend? No." May glanced warily toward the door, then said, "Could I try a puff of your cigarette?"

Dora rubbed her chin and held out her hand. "Ha. I made you blush!"

Inhaling, May coughed, momentarily light-headed. Shaking her head, she passed the cigarette back. "Thanks."

"Want one?" Dora cocked an eyebrow.

"A boyfriend?"

Dora rocked forward, laughing. "You crack me up! A *cigarette*. Oh, look at the time!" She jumped up and ran water over the cigarette, then dropped the butt into a cold cream jar.

"Now, then," she grinned and opened a red garment bag, "wait till you see this dress."

The Hotsy-Totsy Club was on Broadway, between 54th and 55th Streets. Dora exchanged familiar greetings with the doorman, and they were immediately shown to a table. Inside, the walls were draped in swathes of satiny gray, and tufted, purple velvet banquettes surrounded the walls. The male clientele wore dinner jackets, but the women ran the gamut from flashy, eager girls in skimpy dresses to subdued, sleek-haired matrons in dark chiffon and important jewels. Waiters maneuvered, trays aloft, while a busty cigarette girl in a tight costume circulated, her tray on a strap around her neck, a tiny fez perched atop her head. Dora waved to a table of people and sat, saying, "Joey said he'd be here by nine." A pair of broad-shouldered twins approached and asked Dora and May to dance. After two turns around the floor, Dora excused herself and her twin moved on. From the dance floor, May watched her speak with a burly young man with slick, black hair. A doughy bulge of flesh projected over the back of his collar. They disappeared, and May returned to the table alone.

After fifteen uncomfortable minutes, she took a cigarette from Dora's pack and lit it, observing how the women at surrounding tables gestured and raised their chins to exhale. Some looked quite elegant, actually. After five more minutes, she wondered if she should leave, and if she had enough money to cover the drinks on the table. The cigarette girl passed, and May asked her for a pack of Chesterfields, thinking they sounded more sophisticated than Lucky Strikes or Camels. What was the appeal of a cigarette named after a beast of burden, anyway? Would anyone ever buy Mule cigarettes? Oxen? She was searching her handbag when Dora returned and patted her shoulder, saying, "Sorry, doll. Joey couldn't stay." She was flushed, and her eyes glittered like green glass. Drumming her fingers on the table, she spoke rapidly. "Put your money away." She took the Chesterfields from the cigarette girl and handed them to May, saying, "These are on the house. Our tab is taken care of."

She took her seat and leaned closer, "Joey gave me a little present." She giggled and pulled out a small vial. Holding it below the tabletop, she tapped out a line of powder on top of her hand. She inhaled, then slipped the vial to May, raising her chin toward the stage. "Come *on*. All the chorus girls do it."

May rolled the vial in her palm. Just ordinary brown glass. Just white powder that looked like talcum. If she didn't like it, she wouldn't do it again. It was that simple. One line.

The powder burned at first. She fought the urge to sneeze. Her teeth tingled, then numbed. A bitter taste moved down her throat. Her chest constricted and her pulse began to thump inside her skull. Thoughts came faster. Her hands went cold and her feet would not be still. The stage lights glowed now, with beautiful silver-blue halos. Colors vibrated; her velvet chair could not contain her, and suddenly, music was the marrow of her bones, pulsing with electricity. When she danced again, her energy was limitless. Her dance partner was terribly amusing, and she was chatty and clever, and another line made her even more so. She was May Valentine. Eager young men bought her drinks, and she allowed a hopeful gallant to kiss her, though she declined his requests to see her again, telling him she was in town for a few weeks before departing on a grand tour. It was *all* working.

At ten thirty, she and Dora reluctantly gathered their things. May felt cheated. She was just getting warmed up. In room sixteen, she lay awake until late, tapping her toes beneath her covers. While she had been dancing, she hadn't thought about the troubles at home. There was something entrancing about this city, she decided, and within this city, Dora had shown her a magical place. And she liked it.

TWENTY-ONE

Sundays at the Roberts House were somber, as a rule. A schedule of nearby church services was posted in the vestibule. At Miss Wiggins's decree, the beau parlor radio remained silent all day. The dining room was closed, so May spent ninety cents on a milkshake and an apple, then walked to Central Park. Along the way, the streets were eerily quiet and still, as if the city was actually resting. At 59th Street, the landscape expanded. The open, green space and expansive sky of the park seemed to change these city people. In the bright, mid-September afternoon, couples held hands as they walked the paths, families spread blankets on the grass as barefoot children ran and laughed. A pickup baseball game drew cheers from a small crowd of onlookers. May observed and felt isolated, surrounded by people, sitting alone on a bench. A mother sat cross-legged on a blanket, plaiting two perfect braids into her daughter's long, blond hair. May watched her hands, deft and lovingly gentle. When she finished, the little girl leaned her head back and the mother kissed her forehead. Her mother used to braid her hair like that, didn't she? Or was she wrong, and it was Delphina's hands she recalled?

Might her mother be here, in New York? She could be sitting under a tree right across the way. May wondered if she was lacking some sort of familial intuition. She imagined what her mother might say about her newly hatched idea to try to work for a costume house. It was too soon to call it a plan. She couldn't make real plans until things at home were resolved.

May bit into her apple, finding it bruised and mealy, nothing like the tart, juicy Winesaps she could pluck from a tree at home. She tossed it into a trash can and started back to 36th Street, encased, again, in the hard-edged, colorless city. Walking down Fifth Avenue, she passed well-dressed families, strolling and window shopping. On 50th Street, she lingered at each display window at Saks Fifth Avenue and picked one thing she would buy if she could: a wide ivory bangle, a peacock-blue hat with a long feather, a pair of emerald-green evening shoes with rhinestone clasps.

Walking to the Biltmore on Monday morning, May stopped to buy a copy of *Variety*, but it proved a disappointment; the only costume house listing was for a pattern maker. In the basement, Mrs. McPhatter wheeled a brimming laundry cart over to the sewing machine, and said, "Sort these. If the holes are smaller than a pea, darn them. Stains, and larger holes and rips, tear them into rags."

"Yes, ma'am," May said, reaching into the cart. A linen fingertip towel had a crimson lipstick stain. As she tore it, she imagined that a duchess might have wiped her mouth with that very towel. Who knew? Now it would polish brass doorknobs. *Snip, rip. Snip, rip.* May sighed as she clipped a damask napkin beneath the presser foot of the sewing machine. Another week of mending for eight hours a day and she might die of boredom. She wondered if it was possible, to *die of boredom*. If a person was locked into a room, say, like a room at the Roberts House, and never let out, or given anything at all interesting to do . . . And people said they *wanted to die* so cavalierly: *I'm dying for a cup of coffee*, or, *I could have died of embarrassment.* May glanced up at the big wall calendar. It was September 15th. With a sinking stomach, she realized that three months had passed, almost to the day, since she had wanted, quite literally, to die. It was hard to imagine, now, that she had felt so desperately afraid and ashamed. She had been given a second chance.

She needed to make the most of it.

Back and forth, back and forth, the fabric moved beneath the machine needle until the hole was covered by a crosshatch of stitches. A terrycloth bathrobe with a torn belt loop reminded her of the robes at the Homestead, and she thought of Byrd as she guided the thick fabric through the machine, replaying the scene in the pool. Had he *really* meant it, when he said he would marry her? And that kiss at the train station and the confusion she felt afterward . . .

What would he say if he *knew? I wanted to die.* It was too much to ask anyone to understand. Had her mother felt that blackness too? With a grinding, metallic *pop* the sewing machine stalled, and the needle snapped. Her last needle.

With an admonishment to come right back, Mrs. McPhatter gave her carfare and a list of sewing notions, with instructions to go to Lawrence & Sons in the garment district. Outside, the morning was crisp with the promise of autumn. The unanticipated freedom was a gift. May told the taxi driver the address on West 27th Street, and as he pulled away from the curb, she felt a small excitement to see a part of the city she had not been to before. Maybe she would pass some of the theaters on Broadway. Her mouth dropped open. *It's a sign! It has to be.* She dug through her handbag. *There!* She still had the newspaper advertisement.

Out on the street, May stopped at each of the shop windows. Closet-size businesses sold beads, sequins, and exotic feathers from all over the world. The Sew-Smart Shoppe at home had nothing to compare. There were bolts of handmade lace from Belgium, cones of thread in myriad shades, bins of faux pearls—some as big as an egg yolk. Crystal beads from Austria hung in sparkling strands, reminding May of her mother's costume designs. Hyman Hendler & Sons sold nothing but ribbon, with spools of plush velvet and crisp taffeta and grosgrain stacked five feet high. She found her way to the notions shop, and after she had made her purchases, she hurried down 27th Street, checking street numbers as she went.

CARLISLE THEATRICAL COSTUME MAKERS was stenciled onto a rusty metal door. May knocked, and when no one came she pushed it open and entered a narrow, tiled foyer. As she ascended the squeaky stairs, the temperature seemed to rise with each step. From the landing, she heard the sounds of machinery and someone shouting. She knocked, smoothed her hair, and waited again, then pushed the door open. Rows of tables with black sewing machines sat beneath tall, wire-mesh covered windows. Motes of lint wafted through the air as a row of women, heads bent, pushed fabric through the machines, stopping only to lift a presser foot or rotate a curve. On the opposite side of the room were taller cutting tables. Jewel-toned bolts of fabric leaned against the walls, alternating with dress forms outfitted with costumes in varying stages of completion. The sewing machines produced a steady, metallic clatter, punctuated by the occasional hiss of a steam press. A pot-bellied man in a vest undershirt operated the press, with a cigarette hanging from his mouth. He caught May's eye and winked through a curl of smoke. She looked away.

A male voice bellowed, "What?" May jumped, looking around for the speaker. Across the large room, a man in a leather apron brandished a pair of heavy-looking sewing shears. The top of his head was bald, with wavy white tufts standing out from the sides like flags. "What, miss? You here for a fitting?"

May called back, "No, sir." Her heart was racing. *This* was where it all happened. She was actually standing in a workroom. In truth, it was no more glamorous than the Biltmore laundry, and certainly not as clean.

"Then what?" He waved the shears as he spoke. "Ain't got all day."

May approached, holding her bag of sewing supplies in front of her. The seamstresses glanced up furtively, never slowing their machines. She smiled, tentatively, but none of the workers maintained eye contact. May squared her shoulders and smiled. It wasn't a spot in that line she wanted, hunched over a machine all day. She wanted to learn the business, to choose which beads went where, to work with the beautiful entertainers. "Hello, sir. I'm looking for Mr. Carlisle, or whoever might be in charge? My name is May Valentine."

When May arrived at the Roberts House that evening, she hurried to check her mail slot, and there was a letter from Byrd.

September 11

Dear May,

I sure was glad to hear from you and get your address. I've been mighty worried about you. Let me catch you up. I've told Delphina and Blue to be careful on the party line at the house. Whatever you do, <u>do not telephone us</u>.

Your Dad's trial date has been set for November 15th. The only good news there is that, if it comes to a trial, he'll probably get credit for time served. We're hoping, of course, that Beasley will take an opportunity to remove the evidence soon. Meanwhile, normal process has to continue, and the Market is still locked up.

There were some things I wanted to tell you. I wish we could talk in person, but maybe it's better to put them into writing. (That's the legal training in me, I suppose.) At least writing gives me a chance to organize my thoughts.

I find myself picking up the telephone, or else thinking of driving over to see you at the farm, then remembering you're not there. I suppose I took it as a sign when you came back from Mary Baldwin that it was a chance for the two of us. I see now that it wasn't fair for me to assume anything. Or maybe assume is the wrong word. Hope is better. I got my hopes up so high that it was hard for me to admit to myself that you weren't ready, or worse, not even interested in what I had imagined for us. That wasn't fair to you.

Now you're gone again, and I think about you more than I should. I keep wondering what might have happened in Hot Springs, thinking I missed my chance with you. But I know now, and I knew then, that it would have been for the wrong reasons. I hope you'll be able to come home soon, and that when you do, we'll be friends again. We sure do miss you here.

Love, Byrd

May blew out a long breath. Byrd's honesty was hard to see on the page. He laid himself bare. How could she possibly do the same? There was no way to write in a letter what she had done, all the mistakes and regrets. He was offering peace—friendship—and that, she needed. After some time apart, they would be natural with each other again, wouldn't they? Then there was the news of her father. If the Market stayed closed and no one tended the orchards, the farm would go under. They would lose everything.

TWENTY-TWO

For two weeks, May waited anxiously for news from home and hoped for a call from Mr. Carlisle. Except for another letter from Elsie, there was nothing. She clocked in to work on time and watched her pennies. On her days off, she went to the movie houses, but when Dora or Rocky invited her out, she demurred. She began reading novels from the Roberts House parlor library—*Jane Eyre*, and *Mary Barton*—a collection of virtuous heroines, curated by Miss Wiggins. She took up smoking. On Fridays, she stood in line at the personnel office at the Biltmore to collect her pay. On Mondays, she unlocked her suitcase and counted out ten dollars, then went down the hall to Miss Wiggins's office. When her turn came, she paid rent for the week and Miss Wiggins ticked a decisive check beside her name, then looked up from beneath her wooly eyebrows to ask, "How are you getting along, my dear?"

"Fine thank you, ma'am," May learned to say.

Despite the habit of watchfulness she had developed, May was becoming more comfortable in the city. She came to have routines and shortcuts, and a favorite spot on the Biltmore roof, where she could eat lunch with Rocky. She had learned to avoid creamed chipped beef on toast at dinner, and that waffles could remain edible for two days, when reheated with a clothes iron.

September turned to October, and before she knew it, she had been in New York for a month. The leaves were beginning to change; the nights grew cooler. May buttoned up her sweater as she left the Biltmore at six o'clock to walk home. Before she could get her key in the lock at the Roberts House, the door swung open, and a boy in a Western Union uniform pushed past her, tipping his cap, then wheeled his bicycle away, whistling.

"Miss Valentine!" The receptionist called from the desk, waving something. "Miss Valentine, you have a telegram!" Gladys held out the envelope, whispering, "I sure hope it isn't bad news." She sat forward, wide-eyed, clearly interested. "Oh, here. You've got a telephone message too."

May hurried up to her room and, with fumbling fingers, locked her door behind her. She tore the envelope and slowly pulled out the telegram. It was from Byrd.

MAY STOP ALL CHARGES DROPPED AGAINST BOTH OF YOU
FATHER RELEASED TODAY COME HOME STOP

Sagging against her door, she pressed the paper to her chest. She read the words again, tracing lines with her finger, drawing a clean breath of relief. Sparks of exhilaration ignited into giddiness. Pressing the back of her hand over her mouth, she laughed. She wanted to throw the door open and shout, *I'm safe!*

There were two quick raps on her door, and she started. A singsong voice called out, "Te-le-phone for Miss Valentine." She hurried to the hall desk and perched on the edge of the chair.

"That you, little gal?"

"Daddy! I'm so glad to hear your voice!" May sank back, cradling the telephone receiver.

"Yours too. I'm calling to tell you they let me out this afternoon."

"Byrd sent me a telegram. That's wonderful."

"Yup. They arrested Beasley this morning." Henry laughed. "Chessie Mackenzie mailed a page of that ledger to Beasley a few days ago, trying to make him sweat. Last night he took the bait. The guns he planted were in the trunk of his car. After that, things moved pretty quick. The closure order on the Market was lifted. Now things can get back to normal around here, except that I'll have to testify at Beasley's trial. Chessie says you might have to, on account of the ledger and all, but it'll be worth it, to see him locked up." Henry sighed. "Sure wish you were here. Delphina is frying a chicken right now, and Blossom is sitting here at my feet. I am glad to be home."

"I'm sure you must be." May could picture the scene. "I'm so relieved."

Her father continued, his voice bright, "Tomorrow the pickers will start in the orchard, and Blue's getting the market ready to open, first thing. Lots of rotten potatoes and moldy bread, but we'll be up and going soon enough. How soon can you get here? Should I wire you some money for a ticket?"

She didn't want to tell him that she was nearly broke. She wanted her father to proud of her, she wanted to hear him say how well she'd done, managing on her own. "I—I have enough money. I have a great job here, and I've made lots of friends. Did Byrd tell you that the place I'm living is run by an ex-nun?"

Henry chuckled. "Delphina's calling me to dinner. You let me know what train you'll be on, all right?"

There was a pause, and what May hoped to hear did not come. She said what was expected of her. "All right, Daddy. Bye."

She returned to her room and plopped onto the bed. The worry was gone—as if it had vaporized, and now they could all move forward. But to what? What was forward? Going home felt like going backward. Would she have to testify? It seemed so sordid, even if she was on the side of the prosecution. May chewed the side of her thumb and noticed the folded telephone message on the floor.

DATE: *October 2*

TO: *Miss Valentine, room 16*

FROM: *Mr. R Carlisle / Carlisle costumers*

TELEPHONE: *Herald 3880*

MESSAGE: *Position available to start October 15, call to confirm.*

May held the message slip over her mouth, hiding a silly, euphoric grin. She had tried, and they *wanted* her. Possibilities began to poke their hopeful little heads out of the ground—possibilities that did not involve working at her father's market. *This* would make him proud. She imagined sending him show programs with her name as designer, maybe newspaper photographs of famous singers and Broadway stars wearing her creations. Carlisle's might not be the top costume shop, but she could get some experience there, and move up.

There was a knock on her door, and Dora stuck her head in, looking concerned. "Gladys said you got a telegram. Everything hunky-dory?"

May sat up and hugged her knees. "Yes, but I might have to go home in a couple of days."

Dora came in, closing the door behind her. "What happened? You didn't get into secretarial school?"

"My father needs me. It's harvest time."

"Well, that sounds like tons of fun." Dora made a face and began to arrange May's belongings on her bureau, trying May's lipstick. "Harvest time. Huh. Do you have, like, a play with pilgrim costumes? Too bad, 'cause Joey just told me about an apartment that sounds perfect for us." She smacked her lips at the mirror.

May held out the message slip. "And look at this, I've been offered that job at the costumers. Rotten luck, huh?"

"Geez louise. I'll say." Dora sat on the bed and shook May's leg. "In any case, you're coming out with me tonight. We'll make it back before curfew."

At midnight, when Dora tapped another line of cocaine onto the dressing table at the Hotsy-Totsy and told May that they had missed curfew, it simply wasn't a problem. With chemically induced confidence, May believed that everything would be as peachy as Dora told her it would be. The night was theirs, and they grabbed at it.

At one, they stumbled into a cab. On the avenue, car lights streamed past like shooting stars. In front of the Biltmore, long, shiny automobiles with chauffeurs were lined up outside the main entrance. Inside, the lobby was crowded with young women in white evening gowns and long kid gloves, on the arms of self-conscious looking, slick-haired young men in white tie. Prosperous-looking fathers were paired with jewel-bedecked matrons, standing in clumps, looking pleased with themselves.

"What *is* this?" Dora asked, "What's with all the white dresses?"

May whispered, "It looks like a debutante ball. The girls are coming out into society. There's a whole season of balls and parties, and they're meant to wear a different gown every night and meet suitable young men and find a husband. Where I come from, the debs have to learn a special five-point curtsy, where their knee touches the ground. It's supposed to show how poised they are."

"Huh. Sounds like a fairy tale. Were you a debutante?"

"No." May spat the word, a bitter taste in her mouth.

As they made their way through the lobby, three debutantes approached, arm in arm. One pretty, petite redhead with a tiara and a braying laugh reminded May of Bitsy Ragsdale. The girl elbowed Dora out of the way as the trio continued past, speaking in flat, tight-jawed accents about their dance cards and escorts.

In the ladies' lounge, Florence nodded to May and Dora, saying, "Good evening, ladies, or rather, good morning."

"Florence!" May said.

Florence looked weary. She frowned slightly and said, "Hello, miss."

Like a beaming little girl showing off a new party dress, May said, "It's *me*, May. Remember? The tea sandwiches? I'm working downstairs in the laundry. This is my friend, Dora."

Florence's face lit with recognition, and she patted May's arm. "Lord, child! I wouldn't have known you. Does my heart good to see you looking so well. Only what are you doing out so late? Nice girl like you ought to be home in bed." Two of the debutantes came in and the redhead removed her long gloves, holding them out to Florence without looking at her. Her friend laid a beaded evening bag on the dressing table, then they went into stalls, still chattering. Watching them, May's mouth twisted.

"C'mon," Dora whispered, tugging at May, "Let's go."

May said goodnight to Florence, who patted her arm. "I'm going off duty in a few minutes, but you come see me again soon, hear?"

Dora strode across the lobby with May hurrying behind. As they pushed through the door to the basement, she caught a silvery glint from beneath Dora's arm. She grabbed Dora's elbow, saying, "What is that?" Dora shrugged, tucking the beaded evening bag inside her jacket. "No!" May said, "Give me that!"

"Don't be such a stick," Dora said, "That stuck-up priss won't even miss it. Bet there's some money in here." She began to open the bag, and May grabbed her arm. Dora looked up, and seeing May's murderous expression, she held out the bag and shrugged.

May turned back to the lobby, saying, "You wait here and do not move."

In the ladies' lounge, the owner of the bag was shaking her finger at Florence, who stood wide-eyed, her hands up. The redhead stood beside her friend, hands on hips. May held out the bag, saying lightly, "Does this belong to either of you? I'm awfully sorry! I have one exactly like it at home. I picked it up by mistake." She shook her head, laughing a little. *Silly, silly me!* The girl scowled and took the bag and they left, the redhead pulling on her gloves, glaring back over her shoulder. Florence slowly dropped her hands, placing one on her chest, and sat hard on her chair.

May stammered, "I'm so . . . so sorry." Florence waved her away, exhaling a deep sigh.

As May made her way back across the lobby, a deep weariness came over her. The ball was breaking up. The piano player closed the lid on the big Steinway and collected his sheet music. Dora followed her down the stairs to the laundry. The lights were low, the machines sat still and quiet. May gathered blankets and pillows, then led them to the storage room, where they unfolded roll-away cots in charged silence. Huffing, May rolled onto her side, facing the wall, then she turned over and hit Dora on the head with her pillow.

"Hey!" Dora said, covering her face with her arms. "I'm sorry, all right?"

"You could have gotten that woman fired, Dora."

They lay in the dark, and when dawn broke, May shook Dora awake. She herself had barely slept.

Dora knew how to sneak into the Roberts House through the kitchen door, if they timed it exactly, while the cook was arriving, at six. At 7 a.m., May pushed herself out of her own bed. Her mouth tasted rancid, and she just made it to the bathroom before she was sick. Changing clothes for work was an almost insurmountable task, and when she leaned over to buckle her shoes, white spots swam in her vision. Snatches of the evening came back to her—cocaine, bootleg whiskey, frenetic music, a Charleston contest? The Debutante Ball. She grimaced, and her scalp hurt.

In the dining room, Dora sat at a table alone, sipping coffee and perusing a tabloid. At the next table, four girls sat with their heads together, whispering. The newest girl, Enid, had her hand over her mouth, wide-eyed. As May sat, Dora peered over the edge of her newspaper, saying, "Well, well, if it isn't the Charleston champ herself. Jeez louise, hon, you look like something the cat dragged in. Hope you're not still sore at me. Let me get you some coffee and toast."

"Please. And see if there's any bacon or sausage." May inclined her head toward the gossiping girls and whispered, "Are they talking about me getting sick?"

Dora pushed her newspaper aside and leaned forward with her arms crossed on the table. She whispered, "Not *you*. You know Mavis, on the fourth floor?" May nodded, rubbing her temples. "Apparently, she's been getting sick too. *Every morning.* Wiggie gave her the boot. Didn't even let her say goodbye."

May blanched. "Oh. Poor thing." Her stomach roiled. "She was sweet."

"Sweet and stupid." Dora snorted. "If she'd a had any sense, she'd have gotten a Dutch cap."

"A *what?*"

Dora whispered, "A Dutch cap. Joey got me an appointment with a doctor who gets 'em from Germany. He doesn't want any, you know," She walked her fingers on the tabletop. ". . . *little Joeys* running around. It's gotta be better than a Lysol douche, right?"

She rose, patting May's shoulder. "Let me get your food."

May shuddered, silently renewing her resolve to be finished with men. She turned Dora's paper around. *The New York Evening Graphic* featured an article about a fifteen-year-old girl named Frances Heenan, called "Peaches." Peaches had recently married a 51-year-old New York millionaire, dubbed "Daddy" by the press. Altered photographs showed the plump girl smiling fatuously at her adoring husband while her overbearing mother, who lived with them, listened at the keyhole. May pushed the paper away, and Dora placed a plate of sausages and fried potatoes in front of her.

"Did you read about Peaches and Daddy?" Dora asked. "I'm prettier than she is. Why can't I meet a sugar daddy? I wouldn't care if he was fifty-one, or sixty-one." She shrugged. "Heck, he could be a hundred and one and it'd be okeydokey with me. Maybe if I got my teeth fixed . . ."

May speared potatoes onto her fork. "That girl has the right idea. He'll never break her heart."

Dora patted May's arm. "I wish you weren't going home. When are you leaving?"

"Oh. I need to call my father and get a ticket . . ." she trailed off. Thinking made her head pound. She raised her chin toward Dora's plate. "You going to eat that doughnut?"

Dora pushed it across the table. "Don't make yourself sick again."

"I need a little something sweet, to cut the grease." May put her napkin over her mouth and burped. She needed to leave for work, but what did it matter? She would be giving notice soon enough, one way or another.

TWENTY-THREE

When Mrs. McPhatter called May's name, she stopped the sewing machine. Lightheaded, she leaned against the door frame of the office, thinking longingly of a malted milkshake from the Biltmore Coffee Shop. Mrs. McPhatter rose from her desk. "Have you been to the Presidential Suite before?"

"No, ma'am, but I've heard it's grand."

"There's a private elevator, from the lobby. They wanted these by three o'clock." She held up a pair of freshly shined men's shoes and May wrapped them in brown paper and tied them with twine.

Upstairs, in the lobby, she pressed the button to summon the private elevator. Florence would come on duty at six, and she resolved to apologize again. As she waited, she was joined by two bellhops she knew, deep in excited conversation. One leaned toward her, motioning for her to listen. "May," he said, in a low voice, "You going to the Presidential Suite?"

"Only to return some shoes."

"So get this," the other bellhop said, jabbing his thumb toward his friend, "Larry took the guy's luggage up. Says he's throwing twenty-dollar bills around! A regular big cheese. Got two real dolls with him too." He dusted his knuckles across his lapel. "Hot stuff."

Larry nodded and replied, sotto voce, "Mr. Faranelli. They say he's a mobster from Chicago." Larry's eyes darted from May to his companion. "So watch your back."

The bell dinged, and the doors slid open with a heavy, muffled whoosh. Rocky stood at attention, staring stiffly forward until he saw who was waiting. May stepped into the car, giving a brief wave to the bellhops as Larry gave her the thumbs-up sign. "You don't look so hot, Kiddo," Rocky said as the doors closed.

"I went out with Dora last night." She groaned. "We missed curfew and slept on cots downstairs in the storeroom. I'm beat."

"Ah. I was going to try to get you to come to the Catagonia with me tonight."

"I couldn't possibly. And I might have to go home."

"Why? What about your new job?"

"I'll tell you about it later. I really need a milkshake. Meet me for lunch on the roof?"

"Have to be tomorrow."

"You're on. How'd you get to be in the private car today?"

"I don't know, but I'll tell you what, this guy's had people going up and down nonstop since this morning." Rocky turned and leaned against the wall, entwining his fingers, stretching his arms out in front of him. "You should *see* the food they're sending up. Smoked salmon and platters of oysters. And caviar. Ever had caviar? *Ve-ry* ritzy stuff." May groaned again, quietly. Rocky continued, "Strange thing is, these guys don't speak *at all* in the elevator. Not a word."

"Larry says they're real swells. Are they taking care of you?" May rubbed her fingers against her thumb.

"Everything's Jake. I'm not complaining," He leaned over, scrutinizing her face. "I need to trim your bangs."

She blew her hair out of her eyes. "When do you start *your* new job?"

Rocky smiled. "Next week. Official hairdresser *and* makeup artist of the Magnolia Club."

"Good for you. Is it a Black-and-Tan?"

"The help and performers are Negro; the clientele is pure white café society. So no. But you can come see the show if you're still here."

When the bell dinged again, the doors opened to reveal a formally decorated hallway. "I'd love to." She took a step out. "Gosh, this is the cat's meow. Wait for me, would you?"

The young man who opened the door was short and thick, with a shiny white scar running from his hairline to cleave his eyebrow, partially closing one eyelid. He scowled at May and called over his shoulder, "It's only the maid."

"Send her away," a voice bellowed from the salon.

"I'm returning some shoes that were shined," May said quietly, handing the parcel to the lackey. She stood stiffly; her hands clasped in front of her. *And waiting for my tip?*

"Hey, Moe," The voice bellowed once more, "Wait a sec . . . give 'er the shirts in the bedroom, tell 'er folded, with starch."

"Wait here." The lackey motioned May into the vestibule before he disappeared into the bedroom. This was one of the few rooms in the hotel that was not decorated in the modern style. The wallpaper, in muted shades, was a landscape scene that wrapped around the walls. A gilded chair held a glossy black fur coat, draped carelessly, as if it might slide off the chair and continue, catlike, to slink out the door. May wanted to touch it. Beside the chair, a table held a vase of perfect yellow roses. *Just like butter and sunshine.* The scent was overwhelmed by the blue-gray miasma of cigar smoke. She leaned closer, hesitantly. For some reason she could not name, sniffing the flowers seemed like stealing.

In the mirror in front of her, the salon was partially reflected. Off to the side, a room service trolley was stacked with dirty plates. May studied the two young women who sat on the sofa with their heads together, smoking and whispering, with martini glasses in their hands. Their makeup was heavy-handed, and the cut of their dresses—*brassy*, May concluded, as one leaned forward to grind out her cigarette in a platter of oyster shells. Three men sat at the table with tumblers and amber bottles between them. A man with black, porcine eyes and fleshy lips faced May in the mirror. When their eyes met, she had the unnerving sensation that he had been watching her. Everything about this place was unnerving. She dropped her eyes. The scarred man returned carrying an armload of shirts.

May juggled the bundle, backing toward the door. "Will that be all, sir?"

"Scram," he said, turning away as the door swung shut.

May stuck her tongue out at the closed door. *So much for the Big Cheese, throwing money around.* The elevator was not waiting, and she tapped her foot, arranging the shirts. They looked custom-made, of fine cloth, and smelled of cigars and Bay Rhum cologne. Something cold brushed her arm, and the silvery back of a cufflink gleamed, still fastened in a cuff.

The bell dinged as the elevator doors slid open. Three men charged out at once. "Watch it, sister!" one said, elbowing past.

"Sorry, miss," the second said, grabbing her upper arms briefly to steady her. They passed down the hall, then knocked on the door.

"Wait a second, Rocky." May held up her index finger, then turned to follow.

When the door opened, the men nodded at the scarred man and entered without speaking. He noticed her. "What now?"

May said, "Excuse me, you forgot . . ."

"Scram," he said. "Come back later." He shut the door.

She returned to the elevator, and as the doors closed Rocky said, "Sorry I couldn't wait for you. Those goons rang while you were in there."

"That's all right," she said, "but somebody left cufflinks in his shirt." She pulled the bundle apart. "I need to get back downstairs. We're *so* busy today. Will you drop these at the des . . ." Her voice trailed off as she hurried to disentangle the other shirt sleeve. Holding out her palm, she whispered, "Look." Each cufflink was made from a single diamond—perfectly brilliant, and as large as the iris of her eye. "Think they're real?"

"You bet," Rocky said, staring. "That guy's a real hotshot."

"What should I do? The guy at the door told me to come back later. Will you take them to the front desk for me?"

"Don't do that. Some clown from the desk will take them up there and get a big tip. Go when your shift is over. He's bound to reward you for being so honest. They're busy now. He won't miss 'em yet."

"I suppose you're right," she said. "I did hear they're big tippers."

The remainder of her shift kept May in the basement, working her way through the mending. Every few minutes she patted the pocket of her apron. At six o'clock, she pushed open the lobby door.

Flashbulbs popped like fireworks. Reporters and photographers blocked her way to the elevator bank. Her mouth went dry. Several police-men stood at the front desk, writing on pads, and police cars with rotating lights were lined up outside. She shrank back into the corridor, backing into someone. She let out a little screech. Larry, the bellboy, grasped her forearm, whispering, "Whoa, May. Calm yourself! I guess you heard."

"Heard what?" she asked, breathlessly. "What's going on?"

"That guy, Faranelli? Turns out he *was* a big gangster from Chi-cago. Came out here to meet with the local guys, only he must've done something wrong 'cause they bumped him off at a chop house over on Broadway about an hour ago."

May clutched her pocket. "Mr. Faranelli? How awful."

Larry jerked his arms, mimicking gunfire. "Yeah. They shot him *six* times, and the doll with him too. Gives me the heebie-jeebies." He af-fected a shiver. May began to walk backward, slowly, one hand on her pocket and the other over her mouth.

Hurrying back down the service stairs, she gulped air. The locker room was empty, and she sat on a bench, rocking, clutching the edge of the wooden seat. A plan would not come. Changing into her street clothes, her fingers were clumsy; her breath caught in her throat. She folded her apron with deliberate care. Still, no plan. She looked over her shoulder, then took the cufflinks from her pocket. They lay heavy in her palm. She considered leaving them in the apron, tossing it into the laundry bin. *Let someone else find them. Let someone else decide to keep them or not. And what if they go down the drain? Will anyone remember that I was the one who collected those shirts?* Two chambermaids entered, whispering about the melee upstairs, asking May if she knew any details. She shook her head. She had to decide. She had to. Dora's voice played in her head, saying, *create opportunities.* May knotted the cufflinks in her handkerchief and tucked them into the bottom of her handbag.

In the laundry room, the big, hot dryers thumped, and Mrs.

McPhatter counted off bedsheets. "Goodnight, ma'am," May said, feeling almost feverish.

"'Night." Mrs. McPhatter glanced up briefly. "Enjoy your day off tomorrow." May continued, with heavy, guilty steps to the employees' entrance. She pushed the door open, and a waft of cool air blew down the stairwell—fresh by New York standards. She closed her eyes and breathed.

"Miss?" From street level, above, two men in dark suits and hats looked down at her. One reached into his jacket. "Miss? We need to speak . . ." Their shiny shoes clattered on the stairs. May stepped back, yanking the heavy door closed with all her strength. She threw the bolt, then whipped around. *Run.* The men began to pound on the door, their calls muffled through the steel.

Mrs. McPhatter frowned. "May? What on earth?"

Stay cool and talk real slow. May shrugged. "Reporters, ma'am, from upstairs. They're everywhere. I'll go out through the lobby."

"Well!" Mrs. McPhatter said, "I never! I'm going to telephone security." The banging continued, along with the men's shouts.

Mrs. McPhatter picked up the telephone, muttering. May approached the service stairway, then turned down the basement hall. Ducking into the storage room, she closed the door and pawed frantically through her handbag, then pushed the knotted handkerchief between the ticking-striped folds of a closed roll-away cot mattress. Backing out, she shut the door behind her and hurried up the steps, trying to recall what the men looked like. One—the dark-haired one—had something wrong with his nose. It was crooked, almost smashed sideways. The other had been shorter, with red hair showing beneath his hat. She tried to remember if she had seen them in Mr. Faranelli's suite, but she could only accurately recall the man with the piercing eyes. She pushed open the lobby door. An electric tension still crackled in the air. Everyone seemed focused on the police and reporters. The piano player pounded out "Yes, We Have No Bananas", his fingers prancing over the keys. The music had the tinny urgency of a calliope. As she passed the center table, a luggage cart wheeled by and Larry waved from behind it, calling, "Have a nice night, May!"

From behind her, someone called, "Miss! Say, miss! Stop!"

She began to zigzag through the crowd and down the wide steps to street level, stopping at the revolving doors. Police cars still lined the curb. She turned back, ducking into the ladies' lounge. She would not look behind her. Florence pushed herself up from her chair, smiling, but her smile turned to a look of concern. "Lord, child, what's wrong?"

"Some men . . ." May gasped, ". . . are chasing me. I need to hide. Please, Florence. I'm—I'm so sorry about last night."

Florence frowned, peering around the doorway with her eyebrows raised. "There's some men running down the stairs now. One of 'em have red hair?" May nodded. Florence spoke out of the side of her mouth, still looking out, "Get in a stall." Two women powdered their noses at the dressing tables. May went into a stall and latched the louvered door, then crouched on the toilet lid, trying to quiet her breathing. She heard Florence wish the ladies a pleasant evening as they left.

May heard a deep, New-York-accented voice say, "Did you see a dark-haired girl? Did she come in here?"

"Gentlemen, please," Florence said, "this is the ladies'! You can't come in here. Land sakes alive! Go across the lobby."

May held her breath. Time stopped.

Florence said, "Y'all just stand aside, let this lady by. I am *sorry*, madam, please, come right on in."

Heels tapped across the floor. A pair of red women's shoes appeared below the stall door. The handle rattled, and a high, feminine voice said, "Oopsie, sorry!" The shoes tapped to the next stall. One of the men said to Florence, "How many women are in here? Answer us!"

May could hear agitation in Florence's voice. "There's so many ladies come in here every day; I can't keep track . . ."

Heavy footsteps sounded across the floor, and Florence protested. A deep voice intoned, "May Valentine? If you're in here, you had better come out right now. I am Agent Snyder, of the Bureau of Investigation."

From the next stall, there was a squeal, then, "Oh! Dear me!" A toilet flushed, and heels tapped. The woman in red shoes sounded fearful when she whispered, "There's someone in there! In that one!"

"Open the stall, or we'll kick it in." The man said. May stepped down slowly, then opened the latch. The dark-haired man stood facing her, mopping his perspiring forehead with a handkerchief. May focused on his nose. She wondered if he could breathe properly, and how his nose had come to be that way. "Miss Valentine," he said, "we need you to come with us, please."

Behind him stood the shorter man. The tips of his ears were purple, and his red eyebrows seemed ridiculous. He pulled a billfold from his jacket pocket, flashing a silver-and-blue badge. "I'm Agent Murphy. This is Agent Snyder." The redheaded man inclined his head toward his partner. Florence stood at the doorway, wringing her hands.

"Wait!" May said, "I can explain!"

Agent Murphy's voice was low and calm. "Just keep quiet for now, miss. This way," They led her outside and put her in the back of a black car.

As the agent pulled into traffic, May leaned forward. "Sir? Officer? Please, I really do need to tell you something."

"Hold your horses. When we get to the office, you can talk all you want."

Agent Snyder helped her from the car, holding her arm as they entered a granite office building. Silently, they rode the elevator to a high floor and entered a nondescript, unmarked office. They took her to a windowless room. A third man entered, also dressed in a dark suit, along with a stenographer. He nodded, then pulled out the metal chair opposite May. "Miss Valentine, I'm Agent Dickens. I work for the BOI—Bureau of Investigation. You've already met my colleagues. Can we get you something to drink? Some coffee, or a glass of water?"

Agent Murphy snickered. "Coffee's pretty bad, I'll warn you."

Wait. They're being nice to me.

"Miss Valentine," Agent Dickens said, "I apologize if we've alarmed you. We need to ask you about the events that transpired earlier today at the Biltmore. I understand that you were actually inside of Mr. Faranelli's suite?"

May nodded. *Stay cool. Talk real slow.*

Agent Dickens continued. "Now, I'd like to show you some photographs, to see if you might recognize any of the men."

"Yes," she said, nodding harder, "of course. But honestly, I don't think I'll be of much help."

"I realize this might be a little frightening for you, so please take your time. We're interviewing all of the staff who interacted with the victims. Perhaps you'd like a bite to eat? I can send my girl out to get you a sandwich."

May felt more nauseated than hungry. *Someone else can find those cufflinks. I'll just leave them where they are.* "No, thank you," she said, "I'm fine, really." *I'm fine.* Her palms were clammy, and she searched her handbag for her handkerchief, then remembered where it was. The blood left her face. She felt it drain from her forehead and cheekbones, with a dipping momentary dizziness. *Lightheaded,* she thought; *because the blood is gone from the head, it weighs less. I never understood that before.* Her handkerchief was in the cot mattress, with the cufflinks inside of it. Her handkerchief with the pink embroidery. *Oh, God. It has my name on it.*

TWENTY-FOUR

May exited the BOI office clutching her bag, fighting the urge to bolt. A Biltmore waiter and Larry the bellhop were waiting to be interviewed and she walked past them with a thumbs-up, mustering an encouraging smile. It was past nine o'clock when the agents dropped her back at the Hotel. In the lobby, the piano underscored the return to business as usual as May walked through with measured steps, determined to appear normal and calm, certain that people around her must hear the panicked banging of her heart. In the basement, the laundry room lights were dimmed. The hallway was empty and she slipped inside the storage room, her chest constricting as she saw that the dozen or more cots that had been there earlier were now only eight.

Watching the door behind her, she ran her hand between the identical folded mattresses, one by one, as desperate images flashed of her handkerchief, tumbling onto a room carpet, somewhere on the fifth, or twelfth, or fifteenth floor, begging a logical explanation. She froze, holding her breath, at the sound of a squeaking cart wheeling down the hall from the service elevator. It passed, and she continued. In the fifth cot she found it, and she closed her eyes and exhaled, weak with relief and exhaustion. Back in the hallway, a laundry cart overflowed with towels and sheets from the chute above. If she tossed the cufflinks in, no one would ever connect her to them. It could be that simple. She could walk out and buy a one-way ticket home and leave this behind. She could even write a note of resignation, right now, and slip it beneath Mrs. McPhatter's office door. May loosened the knot in her handkerchief and the diamonds tumbled into her palm, still heavy and cool, nonplussed by the drama of their recent adventure. The lobby door squealed open above, and she closed her fist.

A loud whisper; Rocky's voice. "May? Is that you?"

"Yes!"

He hurried down the steps, loosening his bowtie. "I thought I saw you. I just got back from speaking to the BOI. Larry said some men were chasing you."

She told him what had happened, then held out her hand. "I was going to toss them into the laundry cart."

"Are you *crazy*? You didn't say anything to those agents, did you?"

May shook her head. They didn't even know her real name.

"Listen, those diamonds are of no use to Mr. Faranelli anymore." May nodded. Rocky looked over his shoulder, up the stairwell. "So this is your lucky break, Kiddo!" He put his hands over May's fist and squeezed. "Hide 'em in a safe place for a couple weeks, till things die down. I'll listen out for someplace you can sell them. Now, I'm going to change, and I'll walk you home."

As May waited, exhaustion began to sink in, and her head cleared. There was logic in what Rocky had said, yet she knew she was crossing a line. She was *choosing* to cross a line. *I've been handed a golden opportunity. No, a diamond opportunity. I walked away from the Bureau of Investigation.* Fueled by exultation, little balloons of possibilities bubbled up into her throat and she laughed. *I've been looking for a sign, and this is it.*

I'm not going home.

At the Roberts House, she fidgeted at the telephone desk, waiting for her call to be connected. Nervous tension had fueled her day, but now her stomach rumbled, and it occurred to her that she had not eaten since breakfast. The operator came on the line. "Hold for your connection, please." May squeezed the handkerchief in her fist. She had made her choice; she had snatched at what was dangled in front of her. She would follow where it led and not look back.

Her father's voice sounded cautious. "Hello?"

"Daddy? I'm sorry to be calling so late."

"You all right?"

"I'm fine. I didn't mean to worry you."

"That's good. I was sitting out on the porch with Blossom, enjoying the evening. It's getting chilly already. Have you got your ticket yet?"

In the brief moments it took to form a reply, the possibilities that had entered her mind earlier turned themselves into words, and now they were making a run for it, full tilt, before she could arrange or filter them. "No. I haven't. Listen, Daddy, I wanted to tell you—I'm so glad you're home. I really am. And . . . and I'd like—I mean—I've *decided* to stay here for a while longer. Of course, I'll come home if I'm called for the trial, but I'm starting a new job in a few days, at a costumer's shop." There was silence on the line. May pushed forward, "With the Market open again, things will be all right, won't they?" Static crackled. The cufflinks had warmed in her palm, as if they were coming to life.

Her father drew in his breath, then said, "Costumer's? What kind of foolishness is that?" Instantly, she felt small and naughty. Her father's tone grew more strident. "May Marshall, you get yourself a train ticket first thing tomorrow and let me know what time to pick you up at the station."

"I know you're disappointed, but this job—it's something I really want. It doesn't mean I don't miss you all. I do." The silence on the line stretched on. May said, "This is the best thing to happen to me since I got my scholarship. I hoped you'd be happy for me."

A long sigh from Henry came over the wire. "You'll come home for the trial?"

"If they need me, of course. But I'll come for a visit, all right? For Christmas, how about that? Give my love to everyone. Tell Delphina I'll send her a letter soon." When there was no reply, she said, "Bye, Daddy."

She got into bed, ruminating over the conversation. In spite of their quarrels, she knew that her father loved her and worried about her. He would have to start thinking of her as an adult. Switching off her light, she could hear the new girl, next door in room fourteen, crying as if her heart were breaking. In the dark, May reached to her bedside and ran her fingers over the familiar curves and sharp edges of the doll's face. *Poor thing. I suppose you miss your mother. You'll get used to it, eventually.*

TWENTY-FIVE

Room sixteen of the Roberts House looked bare-boned and monotone gray. For the last time, May gazed down from her window into the garden. The chestnut tree was in its full autumn glory—an exuberant riot of yellow and orange. Bare rose canes clung to the trellises, and fallen leaves traced dry paths across the terrace. May closed her suitcase and snapped the lock. Room sixteen would soon smell of disinfectant and be purged of her presence, as if she had never been there at all. She took a pencil from her bag and wrote on the closet wall, in small letters, *M. H. M. was here, October 11, 1924.* It was her twentieth birthday.

She locked the door for the last time, and as she descended the stairs, Gladys called from the front desk, "Telephone for Miss Valentine at the first-floor desk!"

"Hello?"

"May, is that you?"

"Byrd." She set her case down, and squeezed her eyes shut. The telephone wire could not transmit her discomposure. She had meant to call him, but the days had slipped by. She made her voice light. "How are you? Tell me all the news."

"Gosh, it's good to hear your voice. I'm fine. Your dad told me you're not coming home." He sounded puzzled and disappointed.

"I've been meaning to phone you. It's true. I've decided to stay here."

"But why?"

"I told Daddy I've been offered a good job, at a costume shop. And honestly, New York suits me."

"Well, that's nice, I suppose. I mean, I'm glad that you like it there. So you've really made up your mind?"

"Yes. But I'll come for a visit for Christmas, probably."

"I was calling to wish you a happy birthday."

"Thanks." May bit her lower lip. "How is school?"

"Not bad. I was at the Fat Man's Club the other night." She wondered what he would make of the Catagonia Club and the Hotsy-Totsy. Silent seconds ticked by, then static on the line. Byrd's voice became quiet. "I wish you were here."

Was that yearning in his voice? In the space of a sentence, she wasn't sure. Was she obliged to sound the same way? She did miss him, but he needed to understand—and she needed to follow this chance and see where it led. She grasped at cheerful banter. "You're so sweet to call. I'm moving today, to an apartment with my friend Dora. It's tiny, but it's better than the rooming house—which is no fun at all—and tonight, for my birthday, we're going to a night club called the Magnolia, where my friend Rocky works."

"Oh." There was a pause. "May? Tell me something. Have you . . . met someone up there? Who's this Rocky fellow?"

"Rocky? He's just a pal. And no, I haven't met anyone. No one special, anyway. Listen, I'll write you with my new address, and really, I appreciate all that you've done for me and for Daddy." *Ugh. That sounded so . . . polite.*

Qualms, like little thorns, began to prick her skin. The things she was hiding. The cufflinks. The cocaine. He didn't even know that she was smoking. There was another pause that stretched into awkwardness. It was the space for all of the things she would not explain. When did an omission turn into an evasion? She said, "It's good to hear your voice." *Arghhh. Polite again!*

"Yours too."

May hung up, then stood staring at the telephone. She was irked with herself and annoyed with Byrd. *Why can't anyone just wish me well?* She picked up her suitcase, resolving to write him a long, newsy, polite letter. She would tell him about her new job and how excited she was to learn the costume business. At the desk, Gladys was sorting mail and handed her a letter and a parcel, wishing her luck. She turned in her keys to Miss Wiggins and said goodbye. The radio played from the visitor's parlor as she crossed the vestibule for the last time; a honeyed voice, crooning Irving Berlin:

What'll I do, when you are far away
And I am blue, what'll I do?

The elevated train jostled its way uptown. May had made this trip once already, from the Roberts House to the apartment. Her suitcase was on the floor between her knees, and she had a burning awareness of the cuff-links inside, hidden in the stuffing of one of Delphina's keep-safe sachets. Every day, she had checked the newspaper, and five days after the shooting of Alberto Luigi Faranelli an article had appeared in the *New York Post*, accompanied by a two-page spread of photographs of his funeral cortege: twenty somber, black limousines snaking through downtown Chicago, a sterling silver coffin, and ostentatious floral tributes with *R.I.P.* banners. No mention was made of anything missing. Around the train car, people read newspapers, or looked out the windows or had conversations as they rocked along. No one turned to stare at May or point at her suitcase. When a transit policeman got on at 57th Street, she busied herself pretending to look for something in her handbag.

On the sidewalk in front of 115 East 85th Street, a bare, withered tree stood forlornly in a gray square of earth. Litter and leaves blew around, settling into small, haphazard piles. A plaque for a dentist's office was mounted to the left of the doorway. Opening the front door caused little tumbleweeds of dust to wander the lobby floor and congregate against the tiles. The stairway smelled of cabbage. On the fourth floor, May put her suitcase down in front of a door with chipped green paint. With small fanfare, she inserted her key into the lock. *Ta-da! Here goes nothing!* The entire apartment was visible from the doorway: a closet, a bathroom, a tiny galley kitchen, and the main room. Two windows faced the street and two narrow beds were pushed against opposite walls. The only other furniture was a pair of spindly, mismatched chairs.

The place was smaller than she remembered, and uncomfortably hot, and she shucked off her sweater. She had not noticed the dripping sink before, nor the odor of sour rags. The radiator valve was stuck, and the soot-smeared window above it resisted opening. When the sash gave way with a bang, a startling blur of gray-and-mauve pigeons rose, then resettled themselves on the fire escape railing, preening and cooing. Small downy feathers, like snowflakes, settled after them. May leaned out. To the right, her view was impeded by the fire escape. On the left, 85th Street rolled down toward the East River.

Dora's belongings were piled on one bed; odd dishes and glassware, marked with insignias of the finest nightclubs. Her umbrella was from the Plaza, and her bathrobe bore the gold crest of the Commodore Hotel. The wrong small gold letters monogrammed her suitcase. The chintz pillows, May felt sure, had, until recently, matched the parlor sofa at the Roberts House. The ironing board was familiar too.

May made her bed with care, smoothing the chenille bedspread she had chosen for herself at Macy's, adjusting the fringed edges into a straight line. She plumped her pillow and stood with her hands on her hips, surveying her new domain with the sense of pride that comes with self-sufficiency. This place was *hers*. Well, hers and Dora's. She was humming, and realized that it was "What'll I Do?" Pushing away thoughts of her conversation with Byrd, she sat on the bed with her mail, determined to make a small ceremony of it. The letter was from her father. When she opened the flap, a five-dollar bill slid out.

October 4

My Dear May,

I can hardly believe my little gal is going to be twenty years old. I sure do wish we were together to celebrate. I've had a lot of time to

*think over the past weeks. I am sober, and glad to be. We've got the
Market up and running again, and the apple harvest looks like a good
one. So things are going well, I reckon, except that I worry about you
right much of the time.*

*Here is a little birthday money. Go buy yourself something pretty.
Please write, so that I know you are safe. We will all look forward to
seeing you at Christmastime.*

Love, Daddy

Sober. I've heard that before. But something in the tone of the letter
sounded sincere. It crossed May's mind that maybe it was easier for him
if she wasn't there. Was she a constant reminder of the child he'd lost?
Did May's resemblance to her mother cause him pain? If it did, he never
spoke of it. And he hadn't mentioned her new job at all. It was entirely
possible, May supposed, that it frightened him to think she might take
after her mother.

She untied the twine on the parcel and tore away the paper. Inside
was a pair of knitted gloves and the gray winter coat she had sewn for
herself the year before. Compared to the fashions she saw on New York
streets, her stiff wool overcoat looked frumpy and cheap. Small, wrapped
packages were tucked into the folds of the coat, along with an envelope
with Delphina's handwriting.

October 5, 1924

Chérie May,

*I was planning to bake a coconut cake for your birthday, so in-
stead, I will call it a welcome home cake for Henry. He is missing you,
and fretting, but he's awful glad to be home. I believe that Blossom is
missing you too.*

*Blue has moved back to the Market, and we are both getting along
all right. He about drove me crazy staying here while your Daddy was
gone, and I reckon we are both reminded that living separate suits us
better than marriage ever could. But he keeps asking.*

I'm proud of you, finding a job up there. Your Granddaddy Valentine used to order all his fancy fabrics and trimmings from New York City. It was a shame nobody took the business when he died. I reckon it will get cold up there soon, so here is your coat. I will send more of your winter things soon. Please write often and let me know your news.

Joyeux Anniversaire,
Delphina

May could almost hear Delphina's voice from the page. She unwrapped a small, cobalt glass bottle. The tag said: *Spirit Wash – Mix oil with soap in water, Add three broom straws. Open windows. Wash floor, starting at the door and working toward the windows. After the bad spirits get out, close windows and wash them too.*

She opened the cap, and when she closed her eyes and sniffed, the distinctive scents of lemony Van Van oil and attar of roses sparked an early memory. She was seven again.

The birds had just begun to sing. She had been waiting; checking the garden every day in the week since her mother had gone. Today was the day. She dressed herself and chose her newest hair ribbon, then crept past her father's closed door. Downstairs, Delphina was not yet in the kitchen. She slipped outside. In the laundry shed, she lined up jars, vases, and tin cans. Standing on an upturned clay pot, she was able to reach the cutting basket and clippers. Her small, bare feet left a trail through the dewy grass from the shed to the garden.

Drunk on perfume, bees droned around perfect roses. She cut dozens of them. Thorns scratched, but she continued until she had cut every rose within reach. She tied a nosegay of buds with her hair ribbon to take up the hill to baby Henry's grave. The most perfect blooms went into a crystal vase that she struggled to carry to the front hall, sloshing water in her path.

Mama would never stay away when her roses were in full bloom.

She placed roses in every room downstairs, then mopped the spilled water with a rag. When one vase remained, she returned to the garden. The only blooms left were at the top of the arbor. As she began to climb, a lattice slat gave way. She fell backward, and for a minute, she could not cry out or breathe. Her mind registered only surprise that the ground was so hard. As her breath returned, she became aware of throbbing in her shoulder; a stinging at her hip.

Delphina carried her inside, calling upstairs for her father to fetch Doctor Sawyer. Then she held May's face in her hands and spoke solemnly, "Chérie, you must listen to me. Your Mama is not coming home today." By the time the doctor arrived, Delphina had taken all of the roses away, and that afternoon she washed Ellen's bedroom, starting in the far corners and working her way toward the door, chanting incantations, or prayers. The lemon-licorice scent stayed in the house for days. Outside, the garden grew wild, abandoned.

May sniffed the bottle again. *Dear, dear Delphina, always trying to keep me safe.* A small waxed paper bag bore a tag that read: *To May, from Blue Harris, Wishing you a Happy Day.* Unwrapping it, the familiar burnt sugar and vanilla aroma of Blue's caramel candy brought a wave of homesickness. She remembered pulling taffy with Byrd when they were small; how it had stuck in their hair. They had hidden in the laundry shed with a pair of scissors to cut out the hardened taffy, and then given each other haircuts. Delphina had been very cross.

The other package was an embroidered pillowcase from Delphina. May traced the stitches. Inside, she had tucked a keep-safe that smelled of rose petals and sage and musty wool. A wave of deep emotion, like sudden grief, constricted her throat, as if she were mourning the girl who had worked so diligently on the drab overcoat and been so proud of it. She thought of her mother and wondered where she was, and if she even remembered that it was her daughter's birthday.

A key rattled in the door, and May closed the box and pushed it under her bed. The memories it held were too intimate to share. Dora came in, juggling two cups of coffee and a brown paper sack. "There's a swell coffee shop right on the corner. And they have a pay telephone." She put the bag on the ironing board and pulled out a glass sugar dispenser, a pair of metal spoons, salt and pepper shakers, and two sandwiches in waxed paper. "Just now?" she continued, "I met the little dentist, downstairs. He lives on the second floor, with his mother. He said he'll give me a special deal to fix my teeth." She affected a shiver. "I could hear somebody in his office, laughing, all *hysterical*. I bet he uses laughing gas. Or maybe he has a real funny nurse." She reached into the bag again, pulling out a pair of toothbrushes, and tossed one to May. It was imprinted: *Dr. Ronald Wracker, Painless Dentistry*. They sat on either side of the ironing board, devouring ham sandwiches and toasting themselves with coffee. Dora held out a package wrapped in tissue paper. "For your birthday, toots!" Inside was a half-empty bottle of *Amour Amour,* and a small pink cardboard box. May squeezed the atomizer. Nothing happened. "Oh," Dora said, "the sprayer is a little broken. You have to take the top off."

May dabbed her neck, saying, "You remembered how much I liked it! Thank you."

"Don't mention it. But open the small one." Dora grinned, shrugging in anticipation.

Inside the pink box was a rubber object that looked like the short half of an egg. "What on earth?" May said, turning it over in her hand. "A bottle stopper?"

Dora laughed, covering her mouth. "Geez louise! It's a *cap*."

"A cap for what?"

"A *Dutch* cap, you goose. I thought it might come in handy sometime, when you meet Mr. Prince Charming. And since we don't have a curfew anymore . . ." Flushing, May dropped it back into the box, and Dora continued, "For Pete's sake, it's brand new! I got my own. Remember when I went to that doctor? Well, the nurse left me in the room, and I had to wait a *long* time. I mean to tell you, it was like, forever and ever. So there I was, sitting in my unmentionables on this table thing, and there was this glass cabinet, with rows and rows of little pink boxes with *these* little doohickeys. So I picked up a few spares. You can thank me later." She winked. "And tonight, we are going to paint the town red! We got a lot to celebrate—your birthday, a new apartment, your new job, and best of all, no curfew!" They raised their paper cups.

Later, at the Magnolia Club, May followed a waiter to a narrow black door beside the stage. The waiter said, "He should be back there, but don't get in the way." She went through the door, and in the wings, a line of chorus girls waited to go onstage, wearing short grass skirts with sparkly seashell brassieres. The set was as a tropical island, with papier-mâché palm trees. Rocky stood with the last girl in the line, arranging flat curls across her forehead. Applause began, and May waited until the side curtain dropped back into place before she tapped his shoulder.

"This is a nice surprise!" His voice was all but drowned out by the staccato hammering of tap shoes. "Happy birthday, Kiddo! You need a haircut." He led them through a labyrinth of props, ropes, and scenery, to the stage door. "Come outside; we can hear each other out there." They sat on the steps, facing a brick wall. Rocky pulled out his cigarettes. "You alone?"

"Dora's at a table. Give me one of those, would you?" May held out her hand.

He lit her cigarette and crossed his arms over his chest. "So you're living with Dora."

"Yup. Our place is a dive, but at least there's no curfew. And she's always up for a good time." May pulled a shred of tobacco from her lip.

"You haven't told her about the cufflinks, have you?"

"God, no. I hid them in a good place. I'm dying to get rid of them, only I'm afraid a diamond dealer will take one look at me and just *know*. I mean, what if the word is out? How about if you sell them for me? I'll give you a cut. Heck, I'll split it with you."

Rocky leaned back against the steps. "Seriously?" He snorted. "Do you think that a Negro man can waltz into the Diamond Exchange with a couple of huge rocks to sell?" He laughed.

"I see your point."

"Say they belonged to your grandfather, and you inherited them—something like that. Play the belle." He pointed at her, like a teacher calling on a daydreaming student. "You could pay rent for months and months, not to mention you could take your good friend Rocky out for a steak."

"Find me a place to sell them, and that's a deal." They shook hands.

"Deal," Rocky said. "I'm glad you're sticking around. What made you change your mind? The cufflinks?"

May blew a stream of smoke. "Not really. I mean, I did think they were sort of a sign, you know? But then, sometimes, I think we *look* for things we can call signs, because it makes us believe that we've made the right choice."

"Are you having second thoughts?"

"Oh, no. No, sirree. The job at Carlisle's is a great opportunity, but I feel guilty."

"Why?"

"My father worries about me. He doesn't know that I was saving up to leave anyway. Let me ask you something—before you left home, did you feel like you were meant to be someplace else? Like you didn't fit where you were supposed to?"

"Yes."

"And there's a boy at home." May tossed her cigarette butt off the steps.

"Yeah? What's the story?"

"He's always been a friend, but then things started to get—strange between us. I feel like I've let him down too. Only I know I'm not ready to settle down. I think I'm just not cut out for marriage and a family, you know?"

"I do."

May waved toward the stage door and her sleeve slid up her arm. "This club is nice. You like it here?"

Rocky nodded. "Yep. It's definitely a step in the right direction. And who knows what's next? Some of the guys in the orchestra are talking about Paris. They're saying that's where the Jazz scene is, and colored performers are all the rage."

"Oh, I'd love to go there someday. Listen, I'd better go back inside; Dora's waiting."

Rocky put his hand on her arm. "Kiddo, can I ask you something?"

"What?"

"Have you been sniffing cocaine?"

May sat up straight, frowning. "Maybe every now and then. It isn't a problem, and it's not like I'm paying for it myself. Dora's boyfriend gives it to her. All she wants."

"May, sweetie, that stuff can ruin you. Look how skinny you've gotten." He circled her wrist with his thumb and forefinger.

She snatched her wrist away, clutching it to her chest. "It's really none of your business. You don't need to worry about me. I need to go back inside."

Rocky threw his cigarette off the stairs and gave May a small salute before he turned away.

TWENTY-SIX

The first weekend in the apartment was a blur of late-night clubs and speakeasies, where May danced to near exhaustion, fueled by Dora's cocaine. Sunday morning required aspirin and Pepto Bismol and the airing of smoke-reeking clothes and the soaking of dance-weary feet, and it was not until the third night—waking in the wee hours to the heart-stopping *whoop, whoop, whoop* of sirens and red lights flashing at the windows—that they realized that their building shared walls with the 85th Street fire station. Monday morning required strong coffee and a line of cocaine before work, with a grim accounting of what was left from Friday's pay packet. New York life, sans curfew, was intoxicating. May was unstoppable.

On October fifteenth, she stood in her bathroom, getting ready for her first day at Carlisle's. She closed the medicine cabinet and addressed her reflection aloud, shaking her finger sternly while chiding herself about responsibility and ambition, and the importance of getting started on the right foot. She told herself that she would not go out on weeknights. At least not for a while, anyway. She would set aside rent money from each week's pay and encourage Dora to do the same.

By the end of her first week, Mr. Carlisle had her taking notes at fittings and placing fabric orders. What she did not know, she figured out. He seemed to have no loyalty to long-standing employees, taking advantage of workers who did not speak English or who were illiterate. He paid low wages to pieceworkers working from home, doing beading and embroidery. He also paid someone to ignore that his employees were not members of the Garment Workers' Union.

The second week, May started arriving half an hour early and offering to stay late. Dora complained when she didn't want to go out, and they bickered over taking out the trash and cleaning the bathroom.

Each day at work was different and fascinating. May was sent to choose samples of trimmings and feathers and went from shop to shop collecting fabric swatches. Back at the workroom, she cut them into neat squares with pinking shears and pinned them to sketches. She began to offer opinions, timidly at first, and then with more conviction. Mr. Carlisle offered little praise, but when he wanted to know the progress of any particular piece, he asked her. He began to tell the seamstresses to do what May told them to do. She was pleasant and professional, but she made no effort to befriend her fellow workers. Each day brought a series of small successes and day by day and hour by hour, the conviction grew, that this was something she was meant to do, and she was going to be good at it. Now, she understood Rocky's drive. Lying awake at night, she listened to the night sounds of the city—sidewalk arguments, tires squealing, drunken laughter below her window, punctuated by the odd fire call. She slept fitfully, and her dreams often had a tactile quality. Her hands continued to stitch and pin, twitching as she slept. Some mornings she awoke having worked out a construction problem in her sleep.

When six showgirls, newly hired for *Lew Leslie's Blackbird Revue* showed up, May measured them, one by one, nervously checking and rechecking her tape measure. She consulted her clipboard, then asked, "Which one of you is Silky Velour? I need the black swan, please." The girls quieted and exchanged glances.

One of them said, "Silky's gone. They're holding auditions for a new black swan tomorrow."

Waiting idly in their underwear, the dancers encompassed a palette of tan and brown shades as varied as the velvet ribbons at Mr. Hendler's shop. Strong and beautiful and utterly unselfconscious, they stretched their long limbs and gossiped about salaries and lecherous producers and their fellow dancers. The one called Janie stood out. Tall and graceful, she moved with the blasé confidence of a cat. Her large eyes were an arresting shade of amber, and her skin had a luminous quality that seemed to cast those around her into shadow. Her wide smile transformed her features into something childlike and endearing.

It was after seven o'clock when May left the workroom. At 85th Street, she had two letters from home in her mailbox. Since the charges had been dropped and her father released, she had been consumed with moving and then her new job. Home seemed very distant.

Wearily, she dragged herself up the four flights. In the apartment, Dora was sitting on a loveseat, blowing on her freshly varnished nails. She wore a cardigan of May's. The loveseat was brown and, apparently, had no seat cushions. Dora bounced, patting the space beside her. May ran her hand over the velveteen and decided she was too tired to begin another argument about Dora taking her things. She said, "This is a definite improvement. Where did you find it?"

"Would you believe, it was out on the curb on Park Avenue? I chatted up this nice gent with a truck. He drove it up here. Doctor Wracker helped him carry it up." Dora made a face. "He might've hurt his back a little on that third-floor turn. Too bad about the cushions, huh?"

"I'm starved. Want to go to the coffee shop?" May dropped her bag on her bed, then picked up a wad of waxed paper from the floor. Holding it toward Dora, she scowled. "Dora, did you eat my birthday candy? I wasn't hiding it from *myself*, you know."

"Oopsie. Guess you'd better find a better hiding place." Dora shrugged, unapologetically. "Sorry, but it was so *good*, and there wasn't a thing here. I'm having dinner with Joey. You see my keys?" She felt around her and jumped up. "Probably, I'll stay at his place tonight. So you'll have this place *all to yourself*. Bye, doll." She winked lasciviously and waggled her fingers behind her.

After the door slammed, quiet descended, punctuated by the bubbling sound of pigeons, roosting on the fire escape. May sat, tentatively. The springs of the loveseat pinged. She put her bed pillow beneath her and settled her letters in her lap. The first was from Byrd, written the day after they had spoken on the telephone.

October 12

Dear May,

I saw your father this morning at the post office, and he looked well. I think he's been staying busy at the Market. From what I hear at the law office, preparation for this trial could take six months.

Classes are over on December 18th, and Mother and Dad are having their big Christmas party on the 20th. I hope you'll be there. Elsie has started talking about a New Year's Eve party at the River.

I understand why you want to stay up there and have your little adventure, and I'll look forward to your coming home at Christmas, if not before. Please think about what I said in my last letter. I hope you'll write back soon.

Love, Byrd

P.S. Are you going to get a telephone?

May's mouth turned down and she let her hand drop into her lap. *My "little adventure"?* Her chin jerked back. Who could think about Christmas parties? *Little adventure, indeed.* A young man going to New York to try his hand at a career would be praised for ambition, but for a woman, it became a little adventure. May was irked with Byrd, then irked with men in general. She didn't need to defend her hard work. Instead, she would show them what she could accomplish. She tossed Byrd's letter across the room, then tore open Elsie's with such force that the paper ripped.

October 11, 1924

Dear May,

Happy, happy birthday, you old hag! I'm so glad I'll always be a month younger than you. What a cosmopolitan gal you are! Your own little bachelor-girl flat. I'm absolutely consumed with jealousy.

I can't believe you're actually making costumes for chorus girls. What a lark. Of course, you always were so clever and artsy, and here I am, still in this wretched dormitory with the horrid Eunice Goode. I missed you terribly on Apple Day. Remember last year when we won the three-legged race?

Over Thanksgiving we're planning a house party at the river and oh, I wish you could be here. Mother's invited Archie's parents and his sisters! Egad, I could just die, although he's really an old dear, and Mother is awfully fond of him and she does like his people. Have you met anyone interesting?

We had the Fall Harvest Dance last night. Byrd was here with Charlotte Penrose. They won the dance contest. I suspect they got a lot of votes because Byrd is so handsome, and all the spinster teachers were judges. Must run to the gymnasium for Aesthetic Dancing. I wish you'd design some new gym suits for us!

Love, Elsie

Huh. May blinked. *Well!* Surprise pricked her, quickly replaced by a second wave of indignant irritation with Byrd. *He was at Mary Baldwin with Charlotte Penrose, the night before he called me? Funny that he didn't bother to mention it.* She told herself that he owed her nothing—not loyalty, or devotion. Still, she felt the sting of it—a feeling she absolutely refused to call *jealousy*. Was he telling other girls the very same lines? Did he have some sort of script, intended to keep them all stringing merrily along until he chose one? May paced the small apartment, inventing snide imaginary retorts that deflected humiliation. She had been a fool once. It was not going to happen again.

TWENTY-SEVEN

When the muslin toiles of the Blackbirds costumes were ready to be fitted, Mr. Carlisle sent May to the theater to obtain the approval of the costume mistress and director. When he told her to go, offhandedly, she wanted to shout and jump up and down in triumph. Instead, she nodded and asked the address.

May wheeled the garment rack from the Carlisle workshop, on 27th and Seventh Avenue, to the Liberty Theater on West 42nd Street, scurrying across the busy avenues and weaving through pedestrians. The weather had turned cooler, and a few dry leaves cartwheeled down the sidewalk. Aside from the flyers and posters promoting the upcoming presidential election: *Keep Cool and Keep Coolidge!* and, *Davis is our Man*, the view from the street was unchanged with the coming of fall. The election and other current news of the world did not concern her this week, her focus was directed solely to the successful completion of this project. Then, all going well, there would be another, and she would ask for a raise or start looking for openings at some of the larger houses. Because she wanted to appear dependable, she had not yet asked for time off for Christmas. She did not write to Byrd. She tried to put him out of her mind. *Little adventure*, indeed.

Arriving at the theater entrance at precisely two o'clock, May smoothed her hair and caught her breath, hoping to appear neat and professional.

She was right on time and had remembered to bring her pins and measuring tape and notebook . . . and the front doors of the theater were locked. She knocked politely, then banged on the glass, but no one came. A sign on the side of the building pointed to the stage door. She steered the rattling rack down the dim alley, past garbage cans and wood scraps. Two chorus girls in silky kimonos and dancing shoes sat on the steps outside, smoking and laughing. May recognized the one called Janie. "Good afternoon," she said, "Can you tell me where the costume mistress is, please?"

"Hey there. Those our costumes?" Janie asked, in a deep Southern drawl. "I remember you."

The other girl said, "She's in with Mr. Leslie. You better wait till she's through. Look around, if you want. The orchestra's rehearsing."

"Thanks. I'm May. From Carlisle's."

The girl touched her chest with long, graceful fingers. "I'm Velma, and this is Janie. We're the bookends."

"Bookends?" May asked.

"The two tallest. We're on each end of the chorus line. Bookends."

Janie's large breasts bounced, obviously untethered beneath her kimono, as she and Velma easily hoisted the heavy rack up the steps then wheeled it onto the stage. In the orchestra pit, a single trombone played scales. May left the rack and sat in the first row, wondering how her costumes would look from the audience.

Janie sat next to her, swinging her crossed leg. "Ha," she said, settling into her seat, "I never sat out here before. These chairs are itchy. Kinda hurts your neck, doesn't it, looking up at the stage?"

"It does." May said, "Where are you from?"

"Alpharetta, Georgia. How 'bout you?"

An intuition told May that she could be truthful. "Keswick, Virginia."

"Well! What do you know? We're just two little southern belles, aren't we?" Janie swished her index finger toward the rack. "Is one of those costumes mine?"

"It's only the toile. We do a fitting with muslin before we cut the actual fabric."

"Ah, 'cause I need to speak to you." Janie cut her eyes toward the stage and leaned over the armrest. "Can we talk? Regarding my particular costume? We're talking about the black swan costume, right? With the feathers? I have got to tell you that those feathers give me the big ugly creepy crawlies. I mean, I have a *real* serious problem with feathers touching my skin." She shivered—a sort of shimmy-shiver. "I can't sleep on a feather pillow, or have a pet parakeet, or even buy a hat with a feather. I didn't dare say anything to the producers, but you seem like a nice person. I feel like I can confide in you." She rested her fingers lightly on top of May's hand.

May said, "What is it, about feathers?"

Janie's gaze moved to the middle distance and her brow dropped into a glower. "I don't know you real well yet, but even if you were my very, very, very best girlfriend, well, there are some things . . . I think everybody has some things they keep hid in a dark place inside, and just can't talk about. Do you have something like that?"

May was quiet for a beat. "Yes. I do."

Janie sat forward and slapped May's leg, smiling broadly, showing her even, white teeth. "Alrighty, then. We understand each other."

"Did you audition for the black swan?"

"You bet I did! Beat out Velma and two other girls. So there is no way on this green earth that I am *not* going to be that swan. Only I need to be that swan with no feathers touching my skin, see?" She blinked slowly. "It means a whole lot to me."

"I'll see what I can do." May smiled.

"But I'll tell you something else." Janie leaned toward May and crooked her finger. "I do not have any problems at *all* with fur. I do love, love, love fur. So if you have any say-so at all? Maybe you could give them an idea, to make a mink character or a fox, instead of a swan. I'd be a pretty fox, wouldn't I?" Janie's face changed quickly to a frown. "Do you know what a mink looks like? Is it like a weasel?"

The costume mistress came out onto the stage, shading her eyes from the spotlights, and motioned for May to come backstage.

When Janie came to Carlisle's for her final fitting, she seemed delighted that May had worked the satin bodice of the swan with a feather pattern in sequins, with a tulle overskirt cut into feathery points. Janie twirled in front of the mirror. "May, you make me look so pretty! I love this."

"Don't move too much, the skirt is just basted on." May helped her out of the costume. "I'm glad you like it. You'll be a beautiful swan. What happened to the other girl?"

"Silky? Oh. She got herself into trouble. I heard she left New York. And that's a real shame, because she was good. She used to talk about this man she went with, how he was going to get her an apartment. She knew he had a wife and kids in New Jersey, but she thought she was special. She made the worst mistake."

"Getting pregnant?" May kept her face impassive as she moved away, busying herself putting the costume on a hanger.

Janie shook her head. "Uh-uh. Her mistake was depending on a man to take care of her. Those sweet-talking promises are for fools. Girls like you and me? We got to watch out for ourselves. We got to know our own worth."

"I couldn't agree with you more."

Janie pushed her breasts up. "Hey, listen, May?"

"Hmmm?"

"I sure do appreciate how you made this costume. I brought you a couple of tickets to the show. Can you come next Wednesday night? You can see me and Velma and wave to us from the balcony." Janie flapped her hands like tiny wings. "You've got to come see your own little black swan!"

TWENTY-EIGHT

On the night of Janie's show, May was finishing her makeup when Dora let herself into the apartment and immediately began to pack a bag. May leaned out of the bathroom to say, "You going somewhere?"

"Joey's taking me to Atlantic City for the night, to a prizefight. You going out? I thought you only go out on weekends now."

"One of the dancers gave me tickets to the Blackbirds Revue."

Dora came to lean against the bathroom door as May leaned toward the mirror, scrubbing a tiny brush in a cake of mascara. Dora said, "The colored show, right? You going with your colored friend?"

May caught Dora's eyes in their shared reflection and there was a momentary standoff. May said, levelly, "I'm taking Rocky."

Dora raised her chin, drawing out the phrase, "You know . . . it might've been polite for you to ask me, since I take you to the Hotsy all the time. For free."

May frowned, turning from the mirror, taking the bait. "It didn't cross my mind. You've made it pretty clear that you wouldn't enjoy that sort of show."

"Well, you could've shared with me. I share with you, don't I? You don't seem to mind helping yourself to my wacky dust." Dora raised an eyebrow.

May flushed. She had already done two lines as she dressed. *Best to turn the tables.* "I *do* share with you, whether I want to or not. You eat my food, you steal my stamps, and you wear my clothes without asking. You use all the milk and leave a quarter inch in the bottom of the bottle. For Chrissake, Dora, you wear my underwear! And look at that pile of dirty laundry! Don't you *dare* tell me that I don't share with you."

Dora narrowed her eyes then flounced to the loveseat and plopped down. She began folding clothes into her suitcase, pointedly leaving out the things of May's she had assembled with her own. "Fine, then. You go to your Blackbirds Revue. I hope you have a real swell time with your friends."

"I will. And I hope you enjoy every minute of your big fight." May collected her coat, and the door slammed behind her, echoing in the empty stairwell. She would not let Dora spoil her evening.

In the Liberty Theater, May and Rocky moved through the dense, jovial crowd. She started to take his arm, but then glanced around and dropped her hand. There were white couples and Negro couples, but no mixed couples. A gong sounded and an usher directed them to their seats. Rocky stopped on the steps and pointed, saying, "See that fellow there, going in, with the slicked-back blond hair?" May nodded and he continued, "That's Nevil Donovan. He's the manager of the Magnolia Club. He told me he was coming tonight and bringing the producer of a new revue, from Paris."

"Paris, really?" May said, "You think that's him?"

"Probably. He looks French, don't you think? They're going to the expensive seats."

From the balcony, May looked down over the assembling audience. Her heart was thumping, her eyes flitting from spot to spot. The theater seemed awash in pulsing golden light, reflecting from gilded panels and moldings. Below, orchestra seats were filling with chattering heads and top hats. Her seat was springy. She wanted to bounce on it, just a little. She flipped through the program, speaking fast. "*Lew Leslie's Blackbirds of 1924.* Look, Rocky, here's Janie. See? *Janie Mullins.* And here, *Velma Vernon*! I made both of their costumes." She tapped her feet, *rat-a-tat-tat* in a repeating tattoo. "At work," she went on, "Mr. Carlisle is horrible to everyone. He's always yelling, and most of the poor seamstresses don't even speak English. If I was in the union, I could work someplace better. Do you know about the Garment Workers' Union? That's why Carlisle's prices are lower. The Union." May nodded over and over, her feet still tapping fast. "Oh, and also, at work, the presser keeps trying to pinch my bottom. I beaned him with the tailor's ham yesterday." She giggled until she snorted.

Rocky was watching Nevil Donovan and the producer below. "Sorry to hear it."

"But I'm learning *so* much! Maybe someday I'll have my own shop. Janie tells me all the gossip in the business. There was this chorus girl called Silky . . ."

"Hey, settle down," Rocky said, frowning, "you're bouncing around like a rubber ball."

"And Janie says that her name is really Wanda . . ."

Rocky tilted his head. "Look at me."

May looked up from her program. "What?"

His mouth twitched. "You're not just excited about this show. You're high, aren't you?"

May laughed and couldn't seem to stop. It was like laughing in church. She snorted again, and her eyes watered. "What's it to you?"

"You're talking too fast and too loud. You need to sit still."

"Heck, I invite you to a show, and you're scolding me?" She sat back, crossing her arms and pouting, one leg swinging. "Maybe I should've brought someone more fun along."

"Maybe."

"Killjoy."

The music started, and the curtain began to rise. Ten chorus girls tapped across the stage. When the black swan came on, May watched Janie with a sense of maternal pride. Seeing her own design on the stage was a thrill. The embellishment, she had learned, needed to be effective from a distance—almost larger than life, and unlike a dress, a dance costume had to be highly functional. Janie's seams had to be reinforced because her breasts put so much strain on the straps and bodices. May had replaced the buttons with zippers, allowing for faster changes backstage.

Janie danced with an irreverence that played up her charm and downplayed her skill. When the number ended, the crowd applauded and whistled. Rocky still seemed irritated, and when the lights came up, the theater had ceased to glow. Without speaking, they moved with the departing crowd, slowly descending the stairs, maneuvering toward the coat check. Rocky called, "Mr. Donovan! Hello!"

May turned, and Nevil Donovan was there. He was a small, rather affected-looking man. His eyes caught hers for a second and she felt herself dismissed instantly, as uninteresting. The man with him wore a plum-colored velvet dinner jacket. He was of medium height, plump and balding, and appeared to be in his early fifties. He wasn't handsome, but he had a certain aristocratic bearing and his face had an animated, flexible quality. When he smiled toward May, his bright, yellow-green eyes disappeared into laugh lines.

"Pendergrast." Nevil Donovan spoke without enthusiasm, with a British accent that showed his bottom teeth.

Rocky stuck out his hand toward the producer. "Throckmorton Pendergrast. Good evening. How did you enjoy the show?"

In a thick accent the Frenchman said, "Philippe de Clermont. The show was *très agréable.*" He turned to May, taking both of her hands, and she noticed how soft his were. He said, warmly, "And who is this? Aren't you lovely?"

"*Merci, monsieur. Je m'appelle May. Enchantée.*"

"She speaks French! *Parfait!*" Philippe took a half step back, cocking his head toward Rocky and smiling, then he turned to Nevil. "Why did these delicious people not sit with us?"

May caught Nevil's expression of pique before he reassembled his face into a smile, saying, with a note of disdain, "Pendergrast is the hairdresser at the Magnolia."

Rocky added, "And May is a costume designer. She designed the black swan costume."

Philippe steepled his fingers and bowed slightly. "Delightful!" he said. "I am hosting a small soiree, at my hotel. You both must join us. Mademoiselle May, might you invite some of the lovely chorines, on my behalf? Such a decorative group."

"I'd be very happy to introduce you," May said.

A line of three cabs followed Philippe's car to the Ritz-Carlton Hotel. Six chorus girls poured out, along with May, Rocky, Nevil, and Philippe. They trailed up the steps, then through the lobby, chattering and laughing, the chorus girls fawning over Philippe, asking about his new revue. As they neared the elevator bank, Rocky stopped, tugging at May's arm, and whispered, "They won't let us go up in the elevator."

The elevator doors opened, and the operator began to stammer, addressing Philippe, "I'm sorry sir, but the hotel has a policy . . ."

Philippe frowned, pulling in his chin, and attempted to enter the elevator car. The operator held out his hand, then pushed a button on the control panel. Rocky leaned toward Philippe, saying, "The hotel doesn't allow Negroes to use the lobby elevators. Only the freight and service elevators."

"What?" Philippe said to the operator, "These people are my guests. I demand . . ."

A small man in a black suit with a nametag hurried up, holding his palms together, as if in prayer. "Good evening! Do we have a problem here?"

Philippe turned. "Is this true, that my guests may not use the elevator?"

"I'm afraid so, sir. It's against house rules."

"*Alors.* Then we do have a problem. Most decidedly. I shall move immediately to another hotel, tout de suite! Have my belongings sent . . ." He fluttered his hand. ". . . sent where, Nevil?"

Nevil said, "The Commodore?"

Rocky said, quietly, "They have the same policy."

People had begun to watch the exchange. Philippe sputtered, "This is ridiculous! Totally uncivilized. We shall *all* take the service elevator." He narrowed his eyes at the manager, flipping his hand dismissively. "Please, do lead on."

Silently, the group moved through the lobby to a door near the restaurant. No one spoke on the way up, and the elevator operator stared at the control knob.

Philippe's suite had three bedrooms, a kitchen, and a large living room with a grand piano. Nevil unpacked cartons of bootleg champagne and liquor. A tray was wheeled in with caviar and oysters on a bed of ice, and another followed, with deviled eggs and picnic fare, and what looked like a wedding cake. The bell rang again, and two bellmen carried in a gramophone. A third followed with a stack of records, and Velma and Janie began to sort through them. The door was propped open, and soon, exotic and beautiful people streamed in and out. Furs were tossed onto the sofa until the pile resembled a large, well-groomed bear. Jazz blared from the gramophone, and Janie had the entire party watching her dance. She was different—*freer*—May observed. Here, she danced for her own pleasure. Her hair was very short, and she wore it slicked back like a boy, showing her beautiful amber eyes to their best advantage.

As the night wore on, empty champagne bottles lined the kitchen counter, forming a squad, then a platoon. A woman curled up in the nest of furs and fell asleep. Caviar was ground into the carpet, and a pair of fox terriers wandered from room to room licking plates. Glamorous people came and went, and Philippe was gracious to them all.

The sun was up. May woke in her theater dress. Disoriented, shoeless, and dry-mouthed, she frowned up at the ceiling's elaborate moldings. It took a moment to realize that she was still in the hotel suite. *Ugh. How very awkward.* She could remember Philippe singing bawdy songs in French, while a man wearing a tuxedo with a woman's feathered headdress played piano. Tentatively, May turned her head to the twin bed next to hers, and recognized Janie's long legs. She slept with an arm thrown over her eyes.

Sitting up, May rubbed her face and tried to remember where she had left her coat and shoes and where the bathroom was. Tiptoeing across the carpet, she eased open a door that turned out to be a closet. The next was a bathroom. She splashed her face and dried it, wiping away the worst of the black rings below her eyes. She reached for a tumbler, removing a washcloth that covered the top. With a small shriek, she grabbed her throat. In the glass, a set of upper and lower pearly-white teeth looked ready to snap at her fingers. *Dear God.* She replaced the washcloth and backed away. In the room, she reached beneath the bed skirt, feeling for her shoes, praying that Janie was still sleeping.

Janie said, in a whisper, "May?"

May pulled a shoe from beneath the bed, then rested her elbows on the coverlet. Janie turned on her side and spoke with a hand over her mouth. "Don't tell anybody?"

"I won't."

"Promise?" May nodded solemnly, and Janie continued, "When I was little, my Ma would give me candy, so I would sit quiet while she entertained men in her room. I didn't have a toothbrush. When my grown-up teeth came in, they were all brown and pointy and rotten already."

"I'm sorry, Janie. That's awful."

"That's just life." Janie lay back again, covering her eyes with her arm.

"I have to go to work. See you soon?" Janie nodded.

Carrying her shoes, May crept down the hall of the suite, hesitating to switch on a light or open closed doors. On the cocktail table and living room mantel, half-full champagne glasses stood with plates of food and overflowing ashtrays. A record hiccupped on the gramophone. Low voices came from the kitchen, and May could not get to the suite door without passing. Peering around the corner she saw Rocky with Philippe at the small table, their collars unbuttoned and neckties undone, an open bottle of brandy between them. They were deep in conversation and, watching them unobserved, May perceived that she was intruding upon a burgeoning intimacy. The magnetism between them was almost palpable, and she understood something about her friend—something so complicated, and yet so simple, that it made her smile. Philippe looked up, and said, "Good morning, my dear! How do you like your eggs?"

TWENTY-NINE

In Philippe's car, on the way uptown, May closed her eyes and nearly dozed off. The driver did not speak until he cleared his throat and said, "115 East 85th Street, Miss Valentine." May was aware of the irony of being delivered home in a big, shiny Lincoln when she didn't have enough in her purse for cab fare. In fact, she was broke until payday on Friday.

It was eight o'clock, and if she hurried, she could wash her hair. It reeked of smoke, as did her clothes. She thanked the driver, and as she got out, Doctor Wracker opened the front door, apparently on his way out. He looked at the car, then he looked at May, then back at the car. "Good morning, Miss Valentine."

"Good morning."

There was no hot water for a bath. She started coffee, but the milk had soured. When she went to dress, she discovered that Dora had, indeed, borrowed her clothes for her trip. The only clean dress remaining, besides the one she had worn to the theater, was the blue summer linen she had worn on the train. As the iron heated, she wondered how to go about asking for a raise; she supposed she should come up with a list of reasons why she deserved one.

May had only a subway token to her name. Of course, there were the cufflinks, still hidden in her suitcase, and from time to time she took them out and held them to her ears as if they were earrings, or against her finger, as if one was a ring. She liked having them, knowing they were there, hidden, just in case. The idea of trying to sell them turned her hands cold.

The subway didn't arrive for ten minutes, then it stopped in a tunnel for fifteen. When she stood to get off the train, May's stocking snagged on the wicker seat, laddering a run upward from her ankle to her knee. The palms of her gloves, she noticed, were smeared with something dark and sticky. She hurried up the stairs to the street and someone touched her arm. A gaunt man, holding a dented derby hat in ungloved hands. "Spare a nickel, miss?"

May stopped, and looked into his rheumy, sad eyes. "I'm sorry, buddy. As a matter of fact, I can't today." She hurried around the corner of 27th Street.

As she came through the door, Mr. Carlisle bellowed from across the room, "Miss Valentine!" He pointed his shears at the clock. Forty-five minutes past nine. "Thank you for gracing us with your presence. We just got a commission." He scribbled on a pad and tore off a page. "The manager of the Magnolia Club called. You know where that is, the Magnolia Club? Guy sounds like an English pansy, you ask me. Name's Donovan. Wants *you* to come over there at three. Says it has to be today, on account of the producer is leaving for France in a couple days. I told him you'd be there. Take some of those sketches from Ziegfeld to show him."

At three o'clock, May entered the Magnolia Club through the stage door and told the prop manager that Mr. Donovan was expecting her. Pushing aside a heavy curtain, she found herself standing on the dance floor. With the lights turned up, the club had an aura of shabbiness, like an evening gown that had been dragged through the street. A smoky odor lingered in the air, despite the efforts of the wizened man who pushed a gray mop around the floor. May sat at a table to wait, toying distractedly with an abandoned black-satin bowtie. Exhaustion from the late night began to settle over her.

After a few minutes, Rocky stuck his head out of the curtain, grinning widely, motioning to her. "You got the message! I'm so glad you're here."

"What's going on?" May said.

"I'm not allowed to tell you. Why are you wearing that god-awful dress?"

"You don't have to make such a face. Dora borrowed the dress I was going to wear today. I can't even afford to get my clothes from the laundry. Can you lend me a few dollars until tomorrow?"

Nevil Donovan's voice called, "Pendergrast? Are the girls here?"

"Coming!" Rocky called back. He took May by the arm, saying, "*Ew.* What's that on your gloves? Never mind; come with me. And for God's sake, keep your coat on." He led her to a cramped office.

May was unsure how to address the men after the unrestrained revelry of the night before, so she opted for formality. "Hello, Mr. Donovan, Monsieur de Clermont. I appreciate your asking for me."

Philippe stood and kissed her on each cheek. "*Bonjour!* Now, where is . . ."

May perched on the edge of a chair, trying to hide her ruined stockings.

"Hi, y'all!" Janie posed the doorway, cocking one hip, bright-eyed.

"Close that door if you please, Rocky," Philippe's demeanor was now serious. "We are having a meeting." May sat forward in her chair. He pulled a gold cigarette case from his pocket, offering them around, then lit one himself. "As I was explaining last evening, all of Europe is swept up in *Le Tumult Noir*. Simply *crazed* for all things inspired by Africa— art, photography—everything." He raised his hands in emphasis. "This will be the first show of its kind—all Negro orchestra and dancers. And *bien sûr*, our *charmante* star, Mademoiselle Eugénie!" He held out his palms toward Janie. *Les Folies Noires*, he explained, was set to open in Paris, on January 9th. It would be the first big revue of the 1925 season. He continued, "I sail back to France on Monday. It is my wish that the details of this show remain a complete secret until the posters go up in Paris. This means that the acts will be planned here, and costumes made here, at Monsieur Carlisle's, *d'accord*? Auditions will be held in secrecy, this weekend."

He regarded May over the top of his pince-nez. "*Ma petite amie*, May. You are here with us because I have, at Rocky's recommendation, requested that you supervise the costumes. I was most impressed with what I saw at the Blackbirds show. I will speak to Monsieur Carlisle and tell him that it absolutely *must* be you." Rocky winked at May.

May nearly fell off of her chair. "Does that mean I get to come to Paris?" She stifled a shriek of excitement.

"*Bien sûr,*" Philippe said, "if you wish to leave your current situation. I will leave that between you and Monsieur Carlisle."

There and then, May decided she would wait until the last minute to give notice. There was just the small issue of being called to testify at home.

Philippe continued, "Nevil will take care of the details here, and since he knows Paris well, he will travel with the troupe as manager. Now, about the costumes—perhaps I should explain that the revues in Paris are more— more artistic." He steepled his fingers. "There will be some nudity."

"Oh, no," Janie said, holding up her hands. "No sirree. You didn't say anything about that last night! I've danced the hoochie-coochie and I swore I never would again. I want to be known as an artist—for my danc-ing, not for my—chest."

Nevil said, to Philippe, "We might ask Velma Vernon if she'd like the spot. She's quite good, you know."

Janie pulled back her chin, frowning. "What?" Philippe raised his eye-brows and Janie raised her chest and huffed. "My figure is much nicer than hers."

Philippe nodded slowly. "*C'est vrai.*"

Janie rolled her eyes. "All right. I'll do *one* number topless, but only if my costume has some fur on it."

May whispered to Rocky, "What about you?"

He smiled behind his hand. "I'm leaving the minute I get my passport."

Six days later, on November 11, Philippe de Clermont sailed back to Paris, with Rocky waving *adieu* from the pier. The Blackbirds show would close in early December, and the dancers and musical troupe of *Les Folies Noires* would leave New York on the *Aquitania* on December 17.

THIRTY

Following Philippe de Clermont's explicit instructions, Mr. Carlisle allowed May to work exclusively on the *Folies Noires* costumes. At the Magnolia Club, she measured and did fittings, listening to Rocky and the dancers enthuse over their plans for Paris. Nevil had been pestering her for an answer—was she going or not? He had to buy tickets. To stall him, she concocted a story about a sick grandmother back home. If she was called home to testify, Paris would be out. She consoled herself with the fallback plan that she could return to New York after the trial and look for a position at a more prestigious house.

Over the next weeks she put in long hours, and on Thanksgiving Day she took the subway to Carlisle's and worked alone. The heat was turned off, and by noon her hands were so stiff with cold she resorted to snipping the fingertips off of her gloves.

At five o'clock, shaky with hunger, she took the subway back to 86th Street. By the time she reached the coffee shop, her feet were numb. She ordered a sandwich and coffee to take out, then walked to her apartment clutching the hot paper cup, inhaling the steam. Without stopping to check her mailbox, she hurried up the stairs, not wanting to run into Dr. Wracker. He had invited her to go downtown to see the parade at Macy's and then have Thanksgiving dinner with his mother, but she had told him she was going home. Dora, thankfully, was spending more time at Joey's. May had begun to suspect that she had lost her job; she came and went at odd hours.

May ran the tub, and, shivering, debated which basic human need was the more imperative in the present moment—sustenance, or warmth? Compromising, she ate her turkey sandwich in the bath, remembering the Thanksgiving feasts Byrd's mother would supervise at Chestnut Grove, always including the Marshalls.

A hunk of bread crust dropped into the bathwater and she watched it float around. When anyone asked her about home, May described Byrd's family house, saying that her mother was disappointed she wasn't coming for Thanksgiving, then describing her pecan pies and oyster stuffing. May Valentine had a warm, loving family who wished her great success. May Valentine had no complicated, ugly secrets.

Rising from the water, she caught her naked reflection in the mirror over the sink. *How much success will it take*, she wondered, *to forgive May Marshall?* She put on socks and a sweater with her nightgown. The evening stretched before her like a blank page. She got on her knees and pulled her suitcase from under the bed and opened the lock. Sitting on her bed, she held the diamonds up to the light, twirling them, watching the reflected slivers of light refracted against the wall.

The next morning, May rose early and put coffee on to brew. She put on her overcoat and opened the door a crack. All was quiet on the landing. It was just after seven thirty, and she tiptoed down the first flight of stairs, quiet in her bedroom slippers, clutching her keys, ready to retreat. The third-floor landing smelled of roasted turkey. She scurried to the second floor. All quiet. In a burst of nerve, she continued to the lobby. As she inserted her key into her mailbox, the front door rattled and banged open, and there was Dr. Wracker, coming in from the street in his overcoat and hat, carrying an empty trash can. May backed up, embarrassed, trying to formulate an excuse for returning from the holiday early, but he was speaking to someone behind him. He called over his shoulder in a shrill voice, "The fourth floor—4B, I believe." He stopped short, his eyes widening when he saw her. He pointed at May with his trash can, blustering, "But she's right here!"

May froze. The man coming in behind Dr. Wracker had a badly healed broken nose. *Agent Snyder.* Instinct told her to run—to shove the men out of the way and fight her way through the door and down the street. But where could she go? She had bedroom slippers on.

Dr. Wracker said, "That's her! Her hair is shorter than in your photograph, but I'm certain it's her."

Agent Murphy came in last, wiping his shoes on the mat. "Miss Marshall," he said, impassively, "or should I say, Miss Valentine? We meet again."

The cufflinks were in plain sight, upstairs, on her bedside table.

Agent Snyder said, "Thank you for your help, Doctor. We can take over from here." Dr. Wracker shot May an accusing, fearful glance as he passed and hurried up the stairs.

"Miss Marshall," Agent Murphy said, taking her arm, "you'll need to come with us."

I'll give them back. I just need to think. An excuse. A plan. Something. "But I'm wearing my nightgown. Won't you let me change into my clothes first? Please? I left the stove on."

The agents exchanged glances. "We'll be right here."

Upstairs, May dressed in the same clothes she'd worn the day before. *If fine, I'm fine, I'm fine.* She wrapped the cufflinks in her handkerchief and put them in her handbag, her hands now shaking. She would just tell the truth and take the consequences. Why prolong this agony?

Back downstairs, her voice shook. "Agent Snyder, I want to explain."

His voice was calm, reasonable. "Let's not talk until we get to the office, all right? We need to get this all down officially."

In the BOI offices, May was led to the small room she had been in before. Had there been windows last time? She sat on her cold hands, frantically trying to figure out her mistake. *The Biltmore? Maybe someone had come looking for them and traced her through the laundry, or overheard her talking to Rocky? Would they go after him too? How did they learn her real name?*

Agent Dickens came in, tossed a file onto the table, then sat down without speaking. A stenographer hurried in behind him, flipping open a green pad. Dickens thumbed through pages while another agent looked over his shoulder, then he passed a file to Agent Murphy. "You've gone over this case, Murphy?"

"Yes, sir."

May sat forward, trying to grasp the agent's hands. "Agent Dickens, please, I need to tell you . . ." She took a shallow breath, telling herself that she really was not choking.

"Miss Marshall," Dickens said, "I need for you to hear me out." He sounded almost bored as he held out his hands, palms down. "Now, please, just listen. I understand you met with one of our agents, Chester Mackenzie, on . . ." He shuffled a page. ". . . September first?" May inhaled, slowly, cautiously, as if she had just been passed over by a hungry bear. The lump in her throat began to loosen. He continued, "You know that Sheriff Hiram Beasley has been accused of extortion and bribery, right?" May nodded. "We brought you in to take a statement. A trial date has yet to be set, and at present, there are—how many, Snyder?"

Agent Snyder said, "Seventy-two witnesses for the defense and eighty-four for the prosecution—that's for the whole ring. Seven arrests so far."

Agent Dickens continued, "Now, I imagine this trial is going to be a circus. They've asked us to take your statement here, and it will be entered into evidence against Beasley. You won't be called to testify. I want you to tell us everything you know, and let us decide what's important, all right? Can you do that?"

May gulped, nodding. The bear might circle back. *I don't have to testify?*

"Very well, then." He turned briefly to the stenographer. "Lily, you ready?" The woman nodded, pencil poised.

His gaze dropped and he asked, "So you outsmarted Beasley." May nodded again. Dickens tapped his chin and continued. "You have to actually answer, Miss Marshall. Lily can't record a nod."

"Yes," May gasped. *Yes. Yes! I can go to Paris!*

"There are dozens of moonshiners in your county. Why would he come after you so hard?"

May explained the chain of events. When she finished her story, she was drained.

Dickens rubbed his palm over his mouth. She could see that he was trying not to laugh. Agent Snyder looked at the floor, his shoulders shaking. "Apple butter jars. Huh," Snyder said, finally. "Best one I've heard this week."

"What happens now?" May asked.

Agent Murphy plucked at his freckled lip. "The defense has a bunch of scared, intimidated witnesses, maybe prone to lie on the stand. Our best hope at this point is that more evidence comes to light. But we're going to let you go, with your signed statement. Best if you keep all this to yourself and go about your business. We'll have one of our drivers take you where you need to go. Sorry to have inconvenienced you."

In the back of a black sedan May stared ahead, afraid the driver might be reading the skittering thoughts she could not block out: she had just been interviewed by the BOI, she was late for work, she needed to telephone home, she needed to tell Dora she was leaving, there were two big, fat diamonds in her handbag. She was going to Paris.

The driver said, "Miss, where can I take you?"

"The Magnolia Club, please."

THIRTY-ONE

An hour later, May's head was swimming with fractions. She had told Nevil Donovan to get her a ticket, now she was waiting in the dressing room with Rocky while sleepy-faced showgirls straggled in, complaining about being called before noon. As May took measurements, Rocky acted as secretary. She called out a number and heard only a deep sigh in response. When she looked up from her measuring tape, he was doodling on the page, staring into space.

Rocky was following his dream, and he was falling in love. Even though he didn't use the word, she could tell by the way he spoke about Philippe too often, and by the way his face lit up when he said his name. She had felt that way about Amory, in the beginning, after those first kisses in Gypsy Hill Park. Back then, the memory of a kiss could make her glow, and she constantly found ways to insert his name into conversations. She would replay their meetings over and over, trying each time to discern some nuance of emotion or affection that she might have neglected, savoring each one, all the while craving more. The gluttony of new love seemed insatiable. Watching Rocky, she realized how much of love was a risk. How two people offered up little bits of themselves, hoping the offerings would be accepted, praying that they might be treasured. With Byrd, she had not allowed herself that vulnerability. And now there was just so much else to think about.

With four girls still to appear, May began to thumb through a magazine. She held it up, showing an advertisement for the Cunard Steamship Line. "Rocky, aren't you excited? The boat looks huge."

"It's a *ship*." He snorted, and May threw a wad of paper at his head. He began to draw an elaborate head-dress on one of her sketches.

She held up another advertisement—a glossy double spread of well-dressed couples dancing in an opulent ballroom. "Do you think they'll have dances in third class?"

He pointed his pencil at the ad. "Nothing that swanky. But I'd sure like to have a dinner jacket and a top hat like that one. Yes, *ma'am*." He whistled.

"And look at the draping on that dress. Oh, I've just *got* to get a few things."

Rocky cut his eyes to give her a once-over. "Well, *that* has got to go. I forbid you to wear it another day."

"I made this dress myself, you know."

"I guessed that."

"Listen, I have an idea. Let's use the cufflink money. We can go to Saks Fifth Avenue and B. Altman and the swanky men's stores. I bet we'll meet some high rollers in Paris. You'll need to look the part. It's like Dora says, the right clothes create opportunities."

Rocky held up his hands. "Right. Dora the oracle. Don't spend your money on me. I'll be fine. Besides," He crossed his arms and leaned back. "I'm not sure they'd even let me try on a suit at some of those places."

May bit her lip. "But I could buy things *for* you." She snapped her fingers, the pointed at him. "What if we pretended you were my chauffeur, and . . . and we were shopping for my husband? You could borrow your old uniform, couldn't you? We could go on Saturday. It would be a lark."

"A lark for you. For me, it would be humiliating."

"Think of it as pulling the wool over everyone's eyes. You said you want a top hat."

May took the diamonds from her handbag, tossing the handkerchief to Rocky. He opened it and rolled one between his thumb and index finger, then tossed it up and caught it. "You've got a deal," he said.

On Saturday morning, Rocky was waiting for her outside the Biltmore employee's entrance, tugging at the cuffs of the familiar khaki uniform. He said, "Larry said I have to get this back by six."

May whispered, hugging her purse. "I have a *thousand* dollars in here. I put aside enough for rent and some to send home. Do you think there's a way to send money from Paris? If I send home a lot at once, they'll be suspicious."

Rocky whistled. "There must be a way. And don't forget, you owe me a steak."

"Take off that Biltmore badge." May tugged at his lapels and he swatted her hands away. "Now," she said, "where should we start?"

Rocky squared his cap. "You know how all the ritzy folks at the hotel have that luggage? With the letters on it?"

"You mean their monograms?"

"I *know* what a monogram is. Sheesh." He traced a design in the air. "It's like a pattern, with a little flower and some letters, printed on the leather. *So* swanky. I want one of those trunks."

"There's a luggage shop on Fifth. Let's go there first."

Approaching the corner of Fifth Avenue and 53rd Street, May halted suddenly, looking up at a shop sign. "Wait, Throckmorton. We have to stop here. It's Revillon Frères. The furrier. My mother had a mink muff from them." She gaped at the display window, and her voice became quiet. "It had satin lining, with a little pocket, and a mirror. She let me sleep with it sometimes, on cold nights." She looked back at Rocky. "Just a quick look?"

He shrugged and held the door. Inside, a small, birdlike woman with a tight chignon approached. She wore a severely cut black suit and white gloves. "May I 'elp you, mademoiselle?"

May stood tall in her plain coat and scuffed shoes. "*Oui, s'il vous plaît,*" she answered, then began a conversation in French. Rocky stood by the door rocking on his heels, his gloved hands clasped in front of him, as May was seated and offered tea. Within minutes, two models appeared. May and the Frenchwoman nodded, exclaimed, and pointed, then May tried on a deep-brown mink with a pegged silhouette and wide, cuffed sleeves. She stood in the three-way mirror, running her hands over the shawl collar.

Clothes were like armor, she decided, buttoning the neck. Inside of this coat, a girl could feel safe and warm, knowing that she would be perceived to be rich, and be treated accordingly. Her hands slid into the satin-lined pockets, and she imagined stepping down from the train at the Keswick depot with a fur thrown casually over her shoulders. *Just popping home for a few days, before sailing for Paris!* She wanted to see Byrd's reaction when she announced that her *little adventure* was about to get a whole lot bigger. She imagined sending him an impersonal postcard, something like—*Paris is simply divine! Spending New Year's Eve at a friend's château. Ta-ta!* But who was she kidding? She had never used the phrase *ta-ta* in her life. That was something Nevil would say.

The saleslady said, "And of course, mademoiselle, we would 'ave your name stitched inside for you, and alterations are included in the price." May tried on two more coats while the woman made notes on a pad. The models continued to show stoles, fox tippets, and wool coats trimmed with fur. When one came out in a bottle-green velvet evening coat with silver fox trim, May stopped speaking midsentence.

The effusive saleslady accompanied her to the door, clasping her hand. On the sidewalk, May held her arms up. "Woo! This is fun, isn't it? Now where?"

Rocky looked at her from beneath his eyebrows. "That money's really burning a hole in your pocket."

"I only ordered the velvet evening coat. The mink costs two thousand! Now we're going to buy *you* something. Come on." She cocked her head northward. "To the trunk store."

Inside the shop, May spoke to Rocky in an imperious tone, stifling giggles. "Throckmorton, when I'm finished here, I want you to drive me to Saks, then collect my parcels at B. Altman."

"Yes, madam, of course," Rocky said. An obsequious salesman followed May through stacks of traveling trunks in all sizes and configurations, his hands clasped, hopefully, in front of his chest. Rocky indicated what he liked with a wink or a subtle up or down of his thumb. She ordered steamer trunks for each of them, to be personalized with their monograms. She bought a matching hatbox, and for Rocky, a Gladstone bag and a black silk umbrella. In a tiny shop that sold paste jewelry, she bought mother-of-pearl cufflinks and studs for Rocky, and for Christmas, a rhinestone bracelet for Delphina. She held up a pair of dangly earrings, saying, "Do you think Janie would like these for Christmas?" Rocky nodded.

She picked up a long strand of faux pearls. Rocky said, "Don't you already have pearls?"

"They're for Dora. I haven't told her I'm going, and I feel bad about leaving her without a roommate."

"You think she'd think twice about leaving *you* with the rent if she had a chance to go to Hollywood?"

At the newly opened Saks Fifth Avenue, Rocky waited patiently while May tried on clothes, gloves, and hats for all occasions. Salespeople, she observed, were willing to overlook a homemade dress when one had cash to spend. In the shoe department, she stopped, a shoe in one hand, and gazed into the Tea Room, where well-dressed shoppers sat at small tables with pink linen cloths, sipping from gold-rimmed porcelain cups. Rocky stood, silent and attentive, behind her. She turned around and said, "I'm getting hungry. Are you . . ."

He blinked slowly and said nothing. Flushing, May looked down at the shoe she was holding, then back at the tearoom. *Everyone sitting in that tearoom is white.*

A saleswoman stood by politely. "Would you like to try those on, madam?"

"No. Thank you." May put the shoe down, conscious of a bitter taste in her mouth.

They rode down the escalator in silence. On the street, Rocky removed his cap and tucked it under his arm, then unbuttoned his uniform jacket.

"I'm heading back," he said, shaking his head and looking down. "I don't have the stomach for this."

May bit her lip. "It isn't as fun as I thought it would be. I'm sorry."

"It's fun for you—pretending to be someone you're not for a few hours." Anger flashed in his eyes. "This isn't a part for me. It's reality. No dinner jacket is worth being humiliated for a day." He plucked at the lapels of his uniform. "I swear, I can't get to Paris soon enough."

May wanted to put her hand on his arm, but she held back. "I . . . I can't tell you I know how you feel, because I don't. Honestly, I was trying to do something nice for both of us."

"I know you were. Thanks anyhow, Kiddo. Look, I've got to return the uniform. What are you going to do?"

"I'll go home. I'll come to see you off at the boat."

"Yeah." Rocky walked away, his head down.

May blew out her breath, waiting until he rounded the corner, out of sight, then, holding her handbag tightly against her body, she balanced her shopping bags and hurried toward Madison Avenue, blinking back tears. She had put her friend in an impossible position. Everything he had said was right, and it was the same for Florence, and for Delphina and Blue at home. Things needed to change—in the stores, in New York, in the South, in the whole country. She chastised herself for tolerating Dora's snide comments. *I can't change the way Rocky felt today. But I can help him get off to a good start in Paris.*

Brooks Brothers had a doorman who looked like a butler, and a hushed aura of restrained wealth. High ceilings and heavy mahogany shelves made it feel more like a library than a haberdashery. May approached a dapper, compact little clerk, explaining that her husband's luggage had been lost on a train. *I know! Can you believe it! And we're going to the Opera . . .* Armed with a list of Rocky's sizes, the efficient salesman led her through the floors, murmuring sympathetic bromides while gathering a dinner jacket and dress shirt and accessories to go with them. May fingered coarse Harris tweeds, creamy wool flannels, and seersuckers. A silky rainbow of striped ascots, paisley bowties and foulard pocket squares was arrayed on a countertop. A morning-glory blue bowtie made her think of Byrd's eyes, and she pushed it away. She chose a set of linen handkerchiefs for her father and asked to have them wrapped and sent, instructing the beaming salesman to send everything else to Mr. T. C. Pendergrast, in care of the Magnolia Club. On her way to the subway, she bought a three-pound box of Schrafft's chocolates, writing on the little card for the delivery boy: *To Florence, from a grateful admirer. Biltmore Lobby, Ladies Lounge.* On the way back to her apartment, she reflected further on the day. She hoped it was true, what Rocky had said, that Paris was more progressive.

At the door to her building she set down her bags and boxes, looking for her keys. Dora was not upstairs, and only a pile of dirty laundry on her bed indicated that she had been back earlier. May picked out her own clothes from the pile and decided to take them to the laundry up the street, and keep her new things hidden. She wanted no questions from Dora about where they came from. She shoved her boxes under her bed and locked the remaining money and gifts in her suitcase.

THIRTY-TWO

As a sort of advance penance, May took Dora's clothes to the laundry too. Continuing up the street to the coffee shop, she tried to work out exactly what she would say to Dora and to her father about Paris. She stood at the pay telephone in the back, crossing her fingers in hopes that he would pick up.

"Marshall residence." Delphina's voice came on the line. May dropped coins into the slot. "Chérie?" Delphina asked.

"Oh, Delphina." Homesick tears threatened, just hearing her voice. "Is Daddy there?"

"I'm glad to hear from you. Your Daddy's up at the cider press. Be back at suppertime."

"Oh. It's cider time, isn't it? I wanted to tell him—that I'm so glad that he's all right, and it's all over, and I wanted to tell you both—the most exciting thing—" May rose onto the balls of her feet. "I'm going to Paris, to work for a theater revue." There was silence on the line. May rocked on her feet, smiling to herself.

"Paris?"

"Yes! I talked to some agents from the Bureau, yesterday, up here. They took a statement from me and now I don't have to testify. I leave on December 17th, and, well, I'm sorry, but I don't think I can come home because the costumes have to be finished." Static crackled on the line. "Delphina, are you there?"

"I'm here." There was a long pause, followed by the sound of Delphina taking in air.

"I *really* wanted to tell Daddy my news. I'll call again tomorrow, all right? Don't tell him yet. I sent home some Christmas presents for you all."

"Oh, well, that's awfully nice . . ."

"I'll call again tomorrow afternoon."

The next morning was Sunday. May left a note on Dora's bed, saying, *Want to go out for spaghetti tonight? My treat. Big news! I've gone to work, and I'll be back around five.*

May let herself in at Carlisle's and turned on the lights and steam iron. Three dress forms stood in a row. Beadwork panels lay on the cutting table in sections. She began to pin them together. Before she knew it, it was four o'clock. She eyed the telephone on Mr. Carlisle's desk. The bill, she reasoned, would probably come at the end of the month, after she had left for Paris.

Delphina answered on the first ring. May said, "Is Daddy there?"

"I didn't tell him you called," Delphina said, her words coming in a rush. "I didn't tell him because I need to tell you something first. He won't like the idea of you going there."

May rolled her eyes and laughed. "I know! He was *so* upset when I came to New York, and I've been fine, honestly."

"Your mother is in Paris. At least, the last time I heard from her she was. But it's been years."

"What?" May's breath was shallow, her chest constricted and she leaned against the desk. She wound the telephone cord around her finger.

A sigh was audible over the line. "Your Daddy made me swear, years ago, not to tell you anything. Said he'd turn me out if I did."

"But why?" The line crackled again, and for a moment May thought the connection had been lost. She waited, wrapping the cord tighter. Her finger turned white, then purple.

Delphina's voice was resigned. "He thought it was for your own good. You know she was addicted to laudanum, and she drank. Her mother was the same."

"You mean her tonic?"

"Yes. After little Henry died, your Daddy locked her in her room—wouldn't let her have it. She ranted and raved and broke things. Then she turned quiet. Dr. Sawyer said she should have a rest cure, in a sanitarium, but she swore she would kill herself if Henry sent her away. Your Daddy struggled over it, but he believed it was for the best. Only she ran off before he could take her to Western State."

"What?" May slumped against the back of the desk, letting the cord fall from her hand. Her finger throbbed. "So that picture you have—she was in an asylum before she married Daddy?"

"Yes. That was in New Orleans. And about six months after she ran off from here, Ellen wrote to me. She was in New York then. She wrote to him too, saying she was off the laudanum and she'd come home if he would promise not to take her to Western State. He wouldn't hear of it. He couldn't forgive her—went crazy, tore up the letter and told me to close her room up and never speak her name again."

Heat began to tingle in May's fingers. It moved up through her chest. "Mama was *here,* in New York? He's lied to me. She could have come back to us."

"She was never right, after little Henry died. He'd seemed so healthy. Doctor Sawyer couldn't explain it. After Henry told her she couldn't come home she started working up there, doing what she could get. She met a Frenchman named Emile Bertillon. She lived with him. I wrote to her in secret. After about a year she wrote that they were going to Paris, and she was calling herself Ellen Valentine. I got a few letters from her there, but after the war started, my letters came back with no forwarding address. Your Daddy saw one of them in the mailbox. That's how he knew."

"How could he not tell me this?" May took small breaths through her nose. "And you?"

"I kept quiet because I felt like I needed to stay with you, to keep you safe. So much time has passed. I don't know what's become of her. That's the truth. Listen, you call back later tonight and talk to your Daddy. I'll explain to him that I told you."

"No." May wiped the back of her hand over her eyes. Her voice was stony. "I can't believe he's lied to me for so long. I have nothing to say to him."

"He's walking across the yard now. Please, talk to him."

"No. I can't. I'm going to find her."

"Forgive me, Chérie, and please, be careful. *Au revoir*." The line went dead.

May sat, clutching the earpiece of the telephone as if she could crush it, until she could hear the operator, asking if she wished to be connected. After a few minutes she replaced the receiver and gathered her things, moving stiffly, awkward with shock. She turned off the iron, and the overhead lights clicked off. The rusty door groaned as it swung shut, and she walked slowly down the stairs. On the street, she began to walk eastward. Ice gleamed on the edges of the sidewalk, and she splashed through dirty slush, clutching her arms to her chest, tucking her palms into her armpits. Snow began to fall, and icy, needle-like flakes stung her eyes. She walked on, propelled by rising anger and questions. *Why wouldn't he let her come back—baby Henry—why didn't she keep trying—or ever write again after she sent the doll?* Maybe there had been letters that her father destroyed. May's mind ran to fantasies of a joyful reunion, of an explanation of a misunderstanding that had kept them apart. The idea of finding her mother produced a sort of thrilling dread.

When she looked up, streetlights were winking on. By the time she walked the sixty blocks to her apartment, she was shivering, and her heart had hardened against her father. She crept upstairs and kicked off her sodden shoes and undressed, then crawled into bed with a hot water bottle at her feet, grateful, for once, for the tenacity of the radiator. Finally, she let herself cry, as hard as the poor, homesick girl in room fourteen had cried. She rubbed the piece of the doll's face, thinking of how some people kept stuffed bears from their childhoods, or rag dolls, but the thing she used for comfort had edges sharp enough to draw blood.

THIRTY-THREE

The next morning, May went to the Magnolia Club for fittings. Rocky was not there. His trunk and clothes would be delivered soon, and she hoped he would accept them, along with her apology. An hour later, she pushed open the door of Carlisle's. Mr. Carlisle beckoned from the cutting table, where he was cutting pattern pieces from thin cardboard. "I hope you told that French fella we charge extra for a rush job," he said. "Wait till he sees his bill. Be sure you keep track of every single sequin, hear me? And you just missed a telephone call. A *personal* telephone call."

May busied herself at the desk. If her father called and she answered, what would she say?

Mr. Carlisle scowled over the top of his spectacles. "Fella named Brad."

May looked up. "Byrd?"

"Yeah, maybe. Said it was important." He walked to the door. "But you return calls on your own time, and your own nickel." He shrugged into his coat. "I'm going to the bank."

"I'm sorry, Mr. Carlisle. Honestly, I haven't given anyone this number, except for business."

"Get to work. We got fittings at eleven thirty." He pulled his hat on, causing the flags of his hair to stick out further. The telephone rang, and May reached for it.

"Carlisle Costumes," she said, "May I help you?"

"May!"

"Byrd?" she whispered, waggling her fingers at Mr. Carlisle. *All right! Go to the bank now!* "How did you get this number? I'll have to ring you later."

"Well there's no other way to reach you! I heard you're going to Paris. Is it true?"

"Yes, it is." Mr. Carlisle watched from the door. May said, loudly, "Mr. Donovan, I'll check on that and ring you back."

Byrd said, "Why haven't you written? We all thought you were coming home for Christmas. How long have you known about this? How long will you be gone?"

"I can't talk now. I'll call you tonight."

Through the rest of the day at Carlisle's, May avoided answering the phone. She imagined Rocky, signing for a stack of boxes from Brooks Brothers, and wondered if her own steamer trunk had been delivered. It might be sitting in the lobby on 85th Street, waiting for her, along with her new evening dress and coat.

At seven, she pushed open the front door to her apartment house, dismayed to see that Dr. Wracker was in the process of locking up his office. May scanned the lobby, but there were no packages in sight. The dentist turned and smiled up at her. "Good evening, Miss Valentine. Mother and I were sorry to hear that you two lovelies will be departing the premises. Miss Dodge certainly was excited this afternoon. I do hope she has great success in Hollywood."

May's arms dropped to her sides. The floor seemed to tilt. *No. Oh, no.* Ignoring the still-chattering dentist, she hurried up the stairs. Her key fumbled in the lock and she pushed the door open. In the tiny vestibule, she grabbed for the wall with one hand, the other covered her mouth as she moaned, "No, no, *nooo.*"

Perfume hung in the air, cloyingly sweet and heavy. Her suitcase lay open on the floor between the beds, empty. Glossy boxes littered the floor, some smashed, some with explosions of tissue paper.

Dropping to her knees beside her suitcase, May tore frantically at the pinned lining, then turned it over, shaking it. With hot, sick urgency she ripped the fabric from the metal frame. The velvet pouch with her pearls was not there, nor was the Biltmore envelope with her money. The space beneath her bed was empty, her new clothes, all gone. She pushed herself up from the floor slowly, off balance, stunned by the thoroughness of Dora's betrayal—the malevolence of it.

On the loveseat, the letters May had locked away so carefully in her suitcase were spread out. The imitation pearl necklace draped across them, broken, and when May reached for Dora's note, loose pearls dropped and rolled away.

Toots,

Everybody's got secrets, right? I never would of guest that yours would be so interesting. Sorry to leave without saying goodbye. I'm off to create some new oppertunitys.

May wadded the paper and threw it as hard as she could, then kicked the suitcase across the floor, wanting to scream. The pigeons outside the window fluttered with alarm. From the bathroom, the reek of perfume was sickening. Holding her breath, she picked black glass out of the tub, then rinsed the brown residue down the drain, knowing she would forever loathe the scent of *Amour Amour*. The medicine chest stood open, and, as she expected, Dora's brown vial was gone, along with May's best lipsticks and nail varnish.

Only a day ago, the narrow closet had been so full of their combined belongings that the door would hardly close. Now, a single dress hung askew above a tangle of hangers. May's shoes were left, only through the circumstance of Dora having larger feet.

May squeezed her eyes shut. *I'm fine, I'm fine, I'm fine.* The empty closet before her was replaced in her mind's eye with the stripped armoire in her mother's bedroom. May knelt, weeping, and began to line up shoes in the bottom of the closet, desperate to bring back some sort of order she could understand—to set right this violation, all the while trying to deny the little voice in her head that told her that she *deserved* this.

A memory lit, like the flash of a firefly, and she was seven again.

Her bedroom was dim, dawn just showing around the shades. Cycling her legs, she pushed away sheets, scooting over the side of the high bed, clutching the quilt until her feet reached the security of the floor. Barefoot, she padded past the room where Daddy slept now, to Mama's room. But the bed was already made. The armoire stood open, empty, save for a single stocking, dangling from a hook. Baby Henry's empty bassinette below the window still made her feel so sad inside; she wished they would take it away. The brown bottle of Mama's tonic was gone from its place on the nightstand. Backing out into the hall, she turned and ran to her father's room. The rumpled bed was empty. In the hall she knelt on the landing, grasping the spindles, peering through to the silent hallway below. Calling for Daddy, calling for Delphie. But there was no answer.

Had everyone gone away? Had they all died in the night, like baby Henry? Descending the stairs, clutching each spindle in turn, she listened. Even the rooster was quiet. Tiptoeing down the hall, afraid of what she might find, but more afraid of being alone. Where were the breakfast smells?

The empty kitchen.

The sound of weeping.

Delphina, in her black dress, sitting on the porch steps with her apron over her face.

In a nest of dust beneath a laundry bag, the little muslin sack of Delphina's keep-safe lay on the floor. May swallowed a sob and held it to her chest, her breath heaving. When she picked up a shabby nightgown of Dora's, something clattered to the floor. It was the fragment of the doll's face.

THIRTY-FOUR

On Tuesday morning, chit in hand, May was waiting at the laundry when it opened. At the apartment, she sorted her remaining clothes with chagrin. Later that day her steamer trunk was delivered, along with the remainder of her new things. She called the luggage store and was told, with great officiousness, that since the trunk was monogrammed, it could not be returned. When she took the velvet coat to the furrier, the saleslady who had been so accommodating pointed out May's initials, embroidered in script in the lining. Saks would not take back an evening gown that had been altered.

At Carlisle's, May helped Janie into a costume, and they stood together in front of the mirror. "Turn slowly, Janie," she said, her speech garbled by the pins she held between her lips. The skirt was made from strips of gold lamé, cut to resemble long leaves, alternately covered in gold beads and large paste pearls. "Now, give it a shake," May said. "Let's see if any pearls come off. Wouldn't want to put anyone's eye out." Janie shimmied, and the pearl-encrusted flaps began to swing. "Great," May said, nodding. "Didn't lose a one."

"This one is my favorite," Janie said, looking in the mirror. "I love all of the pearls." She twirled again, exuding vitality, and May marveled that she never seemed to waver in her determination to be a star. Janie continued, "Do you really think this is going to work?"

"The costume?"

"This show. I keep worrying that I shouldn't give up what I've got. It's a big risk."

"Philippe said you can be a much bigger star in Paris than you could ever be here."

"I never even expected I could get this far." Janie laughed. "Ain't it something? If only my Mama could see me now, standing here in this beautiful costume made of pearls."

"Has your mother seen you in a show?"

Janie seemed to draw herself inward. "Not ever."

"How did you learn to dance?"

Janie flapped her hand. "That's a whole 'nother story. I'm not real proud of how I got here, but that's my own personal business, and I'm leaving it behind me when I go." She shimmied again, throwing her arms above her head and hooting, "Paris, France, here comes Janie Mullins!" She stepped out of the costume as May made notes. She didn't know whether to envy Janie's freedom or to feel sorry for her, that there was no one who would miss her when she left. Janie could go anywhere she chose, and she was only responsible for herself. And yet, May knew, that worked both ways. If the show fell flat or Janie got sick, she had no one she could count on.

"You look tired," Janie said, "You been working too much."

May smiled. "I have to get these finished."

"Hey what's in this box?" Janie lifted the heavy, chocolate-brown box top, imprinted in gold, Revillon Frères, Paris & New York. "Is this *a fur*?"

"I . . . I bought it on a whim. They wouldn't take it back, because they sewed my name into the lining."

"Ooh. Can I try it on?" Janie pulled the evening coat from the box, then stroked the fox fur and deep green velvet. "This is about the classiest thing ever." She put it on over her underwear and turned before the mirror, giving herself haughty glances over her shoulder. "I'll give you twenty-five dollars for it. Cash money. Right now. Take it or leave it."

"Oh, all right. It just kills me, but I need the money."

Janie shrugged out of the coat and folded it carefully, returning it to its nest of tissue paper. "I get the box too."

May sighed. "You get the box."

Janie put her hands on her hips. "And the muff."

After Janie left, May returned to her sewing machine. Hours later, bleary-eyed, she trimmed a thread and looked up, switching her focus to the wall calendar. It was Friday, December fifth. Her gaze moved to December seventeenth, which Mr. Carlisle had circled in red. *Twelve more days.* On either side of her, sewing machines whirred. The *Folies* costumes, nestled in their muslin covers, had begun to fill a rolling rack. Outside the windows, snow whirled, settling on the sills. She turned back to the piece she was working on and pushed the pedal, guiding the fabric beneath the needle. Her work—the creative part, at least—was her anchor. She put the finishing touches on one of Velma's costumes and pinned it into its bag.

Returning to 85th Street at six, she let herself in and wiped the gray slush from her shoes. She crept past the dentist's door, hoping that Dr. Wracker was with a patient. An envelope was sticking out of her mailbox, and she could see it was a telegram.

A familiar voice said, "That's from me." May whirled around, her hand on the envelope. "You've cut off all your hair." Byrd sat at the bottom of the stairs, holding his hat. Taken unaware, she was struck by his handsomeness. For the first time, she felt a flush of awkwardness in his presence.

"Byrd, what on earth? Why didn't you . . . ?" She hurried to where he stood and hugged him. His overcoat was damp.

"My God, May, you're thin as a rail!"

She tugged his arm. "Come upstairs. How long have you been sitting here?"

"I came up on the train and took a room at the Biltmore. I got in a couple of hours ago."

In her apartment, she glanced with dismay at the dirty dishes and pile of unwashed laundry. She fumbled to light a cigarette, saying, "Why are you here? Is everything all right?"

Byrd stood in the center of the room, still holding his hat. "You're smoking?" He looked her up and down, saying, "I can't get over how different you look. Yes, things are fine at home."

May crossed the room and pulled down the stockings that were drying over a chair back in front of the window, saying, "I was going to call you, but things have been so busy . . ." She wadded the stockings into a ball and pushed them under her pillow. "Really, you didn't have to come up here. Whew!" She backed up and began to pace. "I'm being a perfectly awful hostess, aren't I? "Let me take your coat; have a seat." The loveseat springs made pinging noises that echoed in the room as Byrd sat. May's hands were shaky. She tried to match his ebullience. "We should have a drink. I can make us orange blossoms." She moved to the kitchen and opened the closet door, shielding herself from Byrd's view as she used her foot to push dirty clothes inside. She rinsed out two tumblers and poured orange juice and gin, swigging from one of the glasses before refilling it.

She handed him a drink, then perched on the edge of the loveseat and retrieved her cigarette from the ashtray with a now-steady hand. Her new steamer trunk served as a coffee table, and she hoped he would not ask about it. She stared at the monogram above the lock with a sort of creeping dread.

His voice had an edge of hurt when he said, "I thought you'd be happier to see me. Your Dad misses you. I've missed you. It's like you've cut us out of your life."

May twirled her cigarette on the edge of the ashtray, avoiding his gaze. "Have you come all the way to New York to scold me?"

"No, but we've all been . . . concerned about you." He sat forward, arms draped over his knees in a pose May remembered.

"Why? I'm doing really well . . . I got this great job, and now Paris. I was hoping you all would be proud of me—excited for me."

"Well, I am . . . Are you even glad to see me?"

She slapped her knees. "Of course, I'm glad to see you! Let's go out on the town and I'll show you the city. It's Friday night. Did you bring a dinner jacket?"

Byrd ran his hand through his hair. "I did. I'd love to take you out, if you're free."

"I haven't been out in ages. But I do need to wash my hair. I can meet you at the Biltmore. We can go to dinner there, and then to Harlem if you like, or to a show, you name it."

At seven thirty, May stepped into her new kingfisher-blue evening dress. Why had Byrd come to New York? She didn't want to explain her rift with her father, or about the dress she was wearing, or the cufflinks, or her mother. They would have a nice evening, and she would wish him well and promise to write, then send him back home.

At the Magnolia Club, Byrd seemed to enjoy the floor show, and after the chorus girls high-kicked off the stage and the curtain fell, he said, "So that's what you've been doing up here?"

May nodded. "The costumes I've been working on are for a show that will be called *Les Folies Noires*. I helped with the design. It's opening in January. My friend Rocky has already left." The dance floor was full, and conversations buzzed around them. Byrd leaned toward her, and she swallowed the rest of the champagne in her glass. A young woman approached the table with a tray of gardenias. Byrd bought one, and when he pinned it to the shoulder of May's dress his hand lingered on her skin.

They had drunk bootleg wine with dinner, and now it was past one o'clock and they were well into a bottle of champagne. He refilled their glasses. "How on earth do they get the real stuff? It's about impossible to get wine or champagne at home."

"They bring it in on boats from Canada," she whispered, "It's all very clandestine." He held out his hand, inviting her to dance. She rose, wobbling slightly, but regained her confidence when he put his arm around her. He held her close, and she put her head on his shoulder as they swayed together. His scent was familiar, comforting. She remembered their kiss at the train station. "I see you've kept in practice," she said, "How many girls do you think you've danced with this season?"

He said into her hair, "Oh, I haven't kept count. None of them matter."

"Then why go out with so many?"

"Do you really want to know?" His hand began to trace her spine.

May murmured, into his shoulder, "Because you're looking for the prettiest, richest one with the best papers?"

He held her away, so that she had to look into his face, and his voice had the tone of a patient father explaining to a child. "No. That's not right. I go out with all these girls, hoping every day I'll find just one I can fall in love with. *One* girl who can make me forget about you. I've been trying for years now—only, so far it hasn't worked." She could not meet his eyes. He continued, "You know something, May? I've known since I was eight years old that I love you." He laughed—an unconvincing bark. "And honestly, I don't know what else to try."

The song ended. On the dance floor, they stood pressed together, unmoving. He tilted her chin up and kissed her. She put her hands on his face, returning the kiss. Without a word, they left, their half-filled glasses still bubbling on the table.

THIRTY-FIVE

On East 85th Street, gray light filtered through the shades and May squinted, trying to focus on her clock. *Half past eight?* Her mouth felt as if it were lined in bitter-tasting wool. She sniffed. *Coffee—and—something sweet. Gardenia?* She put her hands on either side of her head. Her scalp tingled painfully.

The mattress bounced as Byrd sat on the side of the bed. "Coffee?" he asked.

May opened her eyes slowly. She knew that her breath was bad, and she held her hand in front of her mouth, covering an embarrassed smile. "Please." She sat up, pinning the sheet beneath her arms, taking the cup from his hands, avoiding his eyes, wishing she could jump up and run out the door and down the stairs, but she was naked. She was sure of that one thing. "Could you get me an aspirin from the medicine cabinet?" She could hear him rooting around in the bathroom. The events of the night raced through her mind—a groping cab ride back to the apartment, smashing Byrd up against the mailboxes in the lobby, unbuttoning his shirt. It had all seemed like a good idea at the time. It certainly *felt* good.

"Here, this will help." He handed her a tablet and stroked her cheek. She sipped coffee, trying to avoid his eyes, wishing he would put his shirt on, wishing there were more space between them. She needed to use the

bathroom. *I am not about to parade across this room. I'd rather wet the bed.*
"Do you think you could get us something to eat? I'm feeling a little bit
green. All that champagne . . ."

"There's a coffee shop on the corner, isn't there? I'll be back in a jiffy."
Byrd buttoned his shirt and kissed the top of her head. He left, whistling
and jingling her keys. *So irritatingly chipper.*

As soon as the door clicked shut, May hurried to the bathroom and
stared at her disheveled reflection in the mirror, her hands flat on her
cheeks. *You are such an idiot!* She pulled her palms down, stretching her
skin. A sour pinprick of nausea threatened. Her impulse was to run, to
throw on some clothes and get away before he returned.

But he had her keys.

The kingfisher blue dress was thrown over a chair with her stockings.
She threw out the now-brown gardenia, then hung the dress in her closet.
Dressing quickly, she began to make the bed. Leaning over to tuck in the
sheets, she felt dizzy, and as the door opened, she emitted a sour belch.

"Whew!" Byrd said, "It's really coming down out there! We haven't had
any snow at home yet. I hope the doughnuts aren't ruined. May maneuvered
around the steamer trunk, away from him. She sat stiffly on the loveseat.

"Cinnamon or plain?" He held out a grease-stained bag. Gingerly, she
pulled out a doughnut and set it on her trunk. Byrd shook his head like
a wet dog and mopped his face with a dishtowel. "I got some coffee too.
That pot I made was pretty . . ." May clenched her hands together between
her knees, staring at the doughnut as if it had turned into a ring of rotting
flesh. *Must not be sick.*

"What?" Byrd asked. "Are you all right?" His face turned serious and
he sat beside her, not touching her.

She stared down, mute, knowing that the sickness that turned her
hands cold and made her breath shaky was her old, familiar companion,
Shame. It sat between them on the loveseat like a bloated beast sated from
a kill, gloating with triumph. How *dare* she think the beast would leave
her? She had slept with Byrd, knowing he loved her, and also knowing
she wasn't going home with him. In the moment she had given in to the
warmth of his love, she had let down her guard. That vulnerability had

been pure; it had been real between them. Now, in the light of morning, she did not have access to the honest words she groped for—words she desperately needed—for feelings, for regret, for confession. Inside her, the place where those words dwelt was closed over with a badly healed scar, because she had never been taught or had the chance to learn the skills of speaking one's heart. She had only learned that to be vulnerable was to be weak. When cornered, it was best to deflect, or to run.

"Last night," she said, still not looking at him, ". . . was . . . a mistake." She put her hands over her eyes.

Byrd said, "What are you saying?" Without uncovering her face, she shook her head. He pried her hands away and held them. Still, she would not meet his glance. He knelt in front of her. "Come on, don't do this." His voice dropped. "Don't keep running away."

She looked down. "You know something?" she laughed, rueful, resigned. "It works, running. It certainly worked for my mother. Run away from the mess you've made, run away when things get painful. I come by it naturally."

"My God, May, you sound so bitter. Last night was meant to happen. You wanted it to happen. Be honest with yourself." She looked at the floor. Byrd went on, "You know I love you. I came up here to take you home, where you belong."

She jerked her hands away from his. "For God's sake, Byrd, stand up, please. I gave you the wrong idea. I'm sorry. I'm not going home with you." He rose, and May spat out, "You think you know me *so* well. Guess what? You *don't*."

"May, you're . . ."

"No." She met his eyes at last. "Let me say this. I had this plan all worked out, and then you showed up. I slept with you last night because I wanted to, because it felt good. I knew that you wanted me to go back with you."

He took a step back, as if she had struck him. "I see." He looked down, shoving his hands into his pockets, shrugging into what May knew to be an affected nonchalance. His chin jerked up; his jaw was tight. "How long have you had this steamer trunk, May? It's a really nice one. Who paid for it? And who paid for that dress you wore last night?"

"I don't like what you're inferring."

"Who's paying you to go to Paris? Is it a man?"

"Yes—the man who's backing the show is tremendously wealthy . . ."

"Ah, I see." Byrd nodded slowly.

"No—he's . . . he . . . You aren't even listening to me. I'm sorry I didn't tell you last night. I couldn't face disappointing you."

"There's a name for that, you know, an ugly name for sleeping with someone because you feel sorry for them."

"No! It wasn't . . . I couldn't . . . I want you to understand, this job is something I really want to do. It's important to me." She picked imaginary lint from her skirt. "This might be the best opportunity I ever get. Can you understand that?" She raised her hands, palm up, and let them drop. "It wasn't until I had to be on my own that I realized I didn't know what I wanted for myself. I'm independent now. I'm not about to give that up."

His voice had an air of pleading. "But you don't have to take care of yourself. That's what I've been trying to tell you. I've got my practice started. I've already rented an office."

May crossed her arms. What she wanted to say was, *you can't save me. I'm damaged, I'm terrible and hopeless and empty. I will never be the person you think I am.* She said, "I'm sorry. I'm *sorry.* How many times do you want me to say it? You shouldn't have come up here. I've changed. I don't *belong* in Virginia anymore. There's nothing for me there. Don't you see?"

He turned toward the window, running his hands through his hair. His tone changed. "I understand. You've already found someone to take care of you. Say what you want—there was something between us last night. You *know* there was. Only you're afraid to admit it."

May didn't respond. *It's true. What he says is true.* She opened her mouth, but the words of explanation would not come. He didn't believe in her ambition. He didn't believe that she really could take care of herself. He believed she was involved with someone. He was upset now, but he would get over it; he would find someone else. She said, "Last night was—it was impetuous, on both our parts. And you don't need to worry, I won't get pregnant."

"What?"

"I've got a Dutch cap."

Byrd blinked. "Ah," He rubbed his palm over his mouth. "You do have it all figured out, don't you?" He stared out the window, his hands thrust deep into his pockets. His voice had a tone of wonderment. "When did you get to be so cold?"

The door clicked shut. May waited, then watched from the window as he walked through the snow, away from her. Hugging herself, she blinked back tears. She could not fall apart—not yet. She took a bath then sat by the radiator, drying her hair as the pigeons bobbed and pecked at the snow that lingered on the railing outside. Through the afternoon, she nursed her hangover, sorting through her guilt with a painful thoroughness that was like picking slivers of glass from a wound. But she did sort it, and she came to the same conclusion. She needed to take this opportunity—she *wanted* it, for herself. She deserved chances as much as anybody did. But still, the things Byrd had said played over in her mind, and she wondered, *Does that make me cold?*

THIRTY-SIX

May did not call home again. Over the next several days she checked her mail with trepidation, not wanting to find recriminations from her father or Byrd, but there were only unpaid bills of Dora's. On the fifth day, there was a small parcel from Delphina, with a letter.

December 8

Chérie,

We are all disappointed that you are not coming home. Byrd told your Daddy about your plans. I hope you will telephone him before you leave. When we talked, your news took me by surprise and I did not do a very good job of explaining how things were all those years ago. But let me try to tell you now.

When little Henry died, your father was gutted. He and Ellen did not grieve together. She only wanted her laudanum. Your poor father was left to cope, and to mourn his son. He tried hard to care for you, but he was overtaken by sadness. You would not remember. You were so small.

Ellen did not leave a note when she left. I think that was the hardest thing for him. It was hard for me too. Your mother and I had lived together since I was twelve and she was two. I loved her, and I thought I could keep her safe from herself. Then I realized I had to keep you safe.

Please, Chérie, understand that your father is a damaged man. He was always trying to protect you, and so was I.

I will miss you, but I understand what you want to do.

Love, Delphina

Delphina had enclosed a small, yellowed envelope. May's name was written on the front in ink that had turned brown long ago. On the back was an address on rue Chaptal, in Paris. Inside was an enclosure card that had been torn in two. May held the pieces together and read the still-bright blue lettering printed at the top:

Au Nain Bleu, 410 rue St. Honoré, Paris, France

Below, in gracefully flowing script, her mother had written:

2 October, 1912

Chérie May,

I was so sad to leave you behind. I miss you every day. Sometimes things happen between adults that are difficult to explain to little ones. I saw this doll in a shop window, and it reminded me of you. When you hug her, imagine that she is sending a hug from your loving,

Maman

May's hands dropped to her lap. She remembered now. In the doll's box, there had been a card. She had not been able to read the French; she only knew it was from her mother. Holding the paper to her face she tried to recall her mother's scent, but it only smelled of mildew.

The final days of preparation passed like a flash. On the night before sailing, May sat on the loveseat with no cushions, in her slip, holding two envelopes. The first letter was from her father.

December 11

My Dear Little Gal,

I hope this letter reaches you before you leave, and that you are well. I know Delphina told you some things. I suppose I knew that she would, someday. But there were things she did not tell you, which I will tell you now, so that you understand the situation with your mother.

Ellen never was a stable person. When she left, I swore her off, for your sake as well as for my own sanity. I knew I could not look at her again, because I would always wonder about little Henry. The doctor could not explain why he died. She was taking so much laudanum then, she was unpredictable. I should have tried harder to keep her from it, but it seemed to calm her.

Someday, when you have children yourself, you might understand why I did the things I did. If you decide to look for her, I don't want to know. Your mother has been dead to me for a long time.

I hope you'll let me know you are doing all right. I had hoped that we would be having Christmas together. These things weigh heavily on me, and you are always in my thoughts.

Love, Daddy

May folded the page and shoved it back into its envelope, thinking, *I want to hear her side.* The second letter was from Elsie, and when May opened it, a newspaper clipping fell out.

December 13, 1924

Dearest May,

Mother took me out of school last week to go Christmas shopping in Washington. We stayed at The Willard, and Archie came up yesterday to take me to the Ambassador's Ball. It was the first big event of the season. Byrd was there, looking impossibly handsome in his tails, and he told me you're going abroad! I so envy you!

About Byrd—he was with an English girl, called Sophie Cavendish-Boyle. Her father is some sort of diplomat in Washington and she went to the same finishing school in Switzerland that Bitsy Ragsdale went to. Anyhow, Bitsy is spreading rumors that Sophie has an absolutely scandalous past. I'll let you know what I can dig up.

This photograph was in the newspaper this morning, of all of us at the ball. But this must be dull as dirt, compared to your exciting life.

Well, au revoir and bon voyage, and all that. As soon as you get to Paris, you had better write back!

Your loving pal,
Elsie

The clipping was from the *Washington Post*, with a caption that read, *Locals mix with internationals at the Ambassador's Ball.* Elsie and Archie stood next to Byrd and a blond girl. A very pretty blond girl. May folded the clipping. Distractedly, she bit down on the side of her thumb, staring into space, then opened the clipping again. *Fun. She looks like fun. And I bet she's rich too. The perfect candidate.* May exhaled through her nose and realized she was sneering. She had not heard from Byrd at all and had not written to him. She had no idea what to say. He believed she loved someone else. She pushed her hair off her forehead. *It's simpler this way.*

On Dora's empty bed, May's clothes were piled, ready to be packed. She fingered her new evening dress—satin and chiffon, diaphanous as a whisper. Clothes were stacked on the ironing board, and the steamer trunk took up much of the space between the beds. She traced her monogram, stenciled above the lock. She had managed to get a passport for herself by going to the application office with Nevil, where he swore that he had known her for ten years and could vouch for her identity. She used her real name. In Paris, she would be May Marshall again. No one was searching for her anymore.

Her weathered canvas suitcase stood, empty, in the corner. *You served me well*, she thought, remembering when she and Byrd had run away. Next to the suitcase was a small stack of things she had brought with her. The things that Dora had not taken—darned stockings, worn-out shoes, the homemade linen dress she had worn on the train. All part of the past, all to be left behind.

PART III
BEST SOCIETY, 1925

". . . Best Society is not a fellowship of the wealthy, nor does it seek to exclude those who are not of exalted birth; but it is an association of gentle-folk, of which good form in speech, charm of manner, knowledge of the social amenities, and instinctive consideration for the feelings of others, are the credentials by which society the world over recognizes its chosen members."

Emily Post,
Etiquette In Society, In Business,
In Politics, and at Home, 1922

THIRTY-SEVEN

The travel-weary troupe of *Les Folies Noires* arrived in Paris late in the afternoon of December twenty-first. Assembling for a group photograph, each face was lit with the same hopeful anticipation. Paris was the promised land of *le jazz hot*, and they carried their portmanteaus and instrument cases proudly past the high arched windows and rows of globed gaslights of the Gare du Nord, out to the taxi stands.

Paris revealed itself to May in taxi-window-framed postcards—the Opéra, the Arc de Triomphe, the Eiffel Tower in the distance—monuments, each with a story to tell. Everything delighted her—the flower vendors with their carts of Christmas greens, the melodious taxi horns, and especially the Parisians, sipping tiny cups of coffee beneath café awnings, warmed by ugly kerosene heaters. Even the well-groomed little dogs were a delight, proudly leading chic women across the wide boulevards.

May's primary impression of the city was a soft, warm gray; the color of smooth, old stone. The river was a colder, steely gray, and the late afternoon sky a lighter shade, almost white. Yet still, the city seemed lit by a pale golden wash, unimpeded by skyscrapers. Bare trees framed the streets like skeletal sculptures, and the buildings had the serene stateliness of history, with graceful lines and tall windows. There were a depth and richness and a haughty dignity to this city, and May wanted to know it.

The Hotel Bercy was on a narrow, cobbled side street in the eighth arrondissement. The black canvas awning was torn and the neon sign only partially illuminated, flashing in spasms: *Hôt l Ber y.* The lobby was dimly lit and smelled of damp carpeting. When the music director, Cecil, rang the bell, a bead curtain behind the desk rattled. A blue cloud of smoke preceded a gray-faced woman with a saturnine expression. Her voice was a phlegmatic monotone. "Toilets at the end of the halls. Five francs for a bath." She passed a list to Cecil, then lined up keys across the counter as May translated.

"Five francs," Janie said, "to take a bath?"

The woman blinked slowly, exhaling smoke in Janie's direction. "For thirty minutes."

Janie leaned toward May and whispered, "How much is that, anyhow?"

"Twenty-five cents, I think," May said.

Cecil began to read the list. "Marshall and Mullins, room twenty-four." He dangled two keys.

"Wait a minute, Cecil," Janie said, "I'm supposed to have a room of my own."

"Sorry," he said, "Mr. Donovan's orders. We're all doubling up." Janie put her hands on her hips and Cecil shrugged. "It looked better in the brochure."

Janie poked her chest. "And are you telling me that I have got to share a bathroom in this dive, with strangers? What if I get pneumonia or some kind of skin disease? You think anybody is going to pay good money to see dancers with ringworm?" She exhaled noisily. "You tell me."

Cecil put his hands up. "We're all in the same boat. Speak to Mr. Donovan."

Janie tried to grab the list. "Damn right I will. What room is he in?"

"He isn't staying here. He's at the Ritz."

"The room is even worse than the lobby," May said, pulling off her gloves. The blotched mirror above the bureau reflected the brown shades of the walls and furniture, and a vase on the washstand held a pair of sad crepe paper poppies. Blackened channels from neglected cigarettes etched the edges of the bureau top. From the floor below came the sounds of a gramophone, the needle sticking, repeating a series of static, tinny notes. When Janie wrestled open a drawer, the knob came off in her hand. She held it up, saying, "*What* was I thinking, coming here?"

May sat on her bed, hugging a stack of clothes to her chest, grateful to be right where she was. She wanted to settle in, to make a place for herself. "It's a *start*. And they're paying you a lot to be here. Nevil says when we go on tour, you'll be world famous. You'll be able to get your own apartment."

"What about you? You took a risk coming here."

"We're all taking a risk. You want to be a star, and I want to design costumes. My mother . . . well, I haven't told anyone this, so keep it under your hat, but I found out that she's here—or at least, she *was* here. I want to find out what happened to her." Just speaking the words was a little thrill.

"She left you?"

"When I was seven."

Janie hung her kimono on a hook. Her shoulders drooped. "That's tough. But let me ask you something. What makes you think she wants to be found?" She tilted her head. "I hope you aren't setting yourself up for a broken heart, honey."

May didn't want to hear these sympathetic concerns, not from Janie, not from anyone. They sullied the pristine vision she had been forming with such care.

There was an insistent knock, and Rocky's voice. "May? Janie?"

May whispered, "Don't say anything—about what I told you?"

Janie nodded, and opened the door. "Girls!" Rocky held his arms open. "*Mes amies!* I meant to meet you at the train station, but you got in early." He kissed them on both cheeks. "The French way! First left, then right." He plopped down on Janie's bed, leaning on one elbow, and fingered the slippery fabric of the coverlet. "Sheesh. This place is a dive. The lobby smells like a subway platform, doesn't it?"

May bounced on her bed. "But we're all here now! Lucky you, you don't have to stay in this fleabag. Tell us about Philippe's house. I bet it's grand."

Janie shoved Rocky's shoulder. "Did you know that Rocky's going to Philippe's château in the country, after Christmas?"

May said, "A real château?"

"If you won't tell her, I will." Janie crossed her arms, causing her armloads of bangle bracelets to resettle with a series of clicks, like dominos. "Nevil told me that Philippe is a bona-fide *Count*. Le Compte de Clermont. Ain't that something?" Janie slapped her knee. Her bangles clacked in the opposite direction.

Rocky held up his hands. "I did *not* know that when I met him." He pointed at Janie, then rubbed his face. "Janie, you have a big mouth."

May leaned forward. "A Count? Really? Now you have to tell us *every*thing."

"You girls. I've missed you." Rocky sighed, but he was smiling. "He's lived in Paris for most of his adult life. But he comes from Burgundy— or I should say, *Bourgogne*. His family has owned a château there for a thousand years. Seriously. A *thousand* years. His parents are dead, and he inherited the estate and the house in Paris. He's the only son, but he has a sister. She's a nun."

"A *nun*." Janie whistled. "Can you feature that?"

"But we're not leaving until Christmas Day. Philippe wants to have everyone over on Christmas Eve. Y'all will come, won't you? He told me to give you these." Rocky pulled two envelopes from his pocket.

May and Janie exchanged glances, and May said, "We wouldn't miss it for anything." The envelope was heavy, the color of a robin's egg. Inside, a thick cream-colored card, bordered in the same blue, with an engraved crest. She held it with her fingertips. "I think this is the most beautiful invitation I've ever received."

Rocky said, "Nice, huh? Wait till you see the house. Listen, I heard in the lobby, a bunch of folks are going out to get something to eat and explore the neighborhood. I'm going to take them to a place I know."

"Is it really like we've heard?" Janie said, "Can colored folks get served everywhere here?"

Rocky tugged his earlobe. "I'd say . . . well, I'd say it's better than New York. The French are friendly, for the most part, but last week Philippe and I went to dinner at a nice place where there were lots of tourists. When we sat down, this tacky American woman called the maître d' over and demanded that I leave! And then the owner made *her* leave! She shouted at me, 'You should be in the kitchen!' It was pretty awful."

Janie huffed and pointed. "If anybody tries that with me, there'll be hell to pay. I want to go where folks are friendly. Just let me change my dress and powder my nose. I'll be down in two shakes. You coming, May?"

"I'm done in. I'm going to unpack. Have fun."

Janie wagged a finger at her. "Now, don't you go taking all the coat hangers and the best drawers. Share and share alike."

As soon as Janie left, May searched her change purse for francs, then hurried down to the lobby. With growing trepidation, she worked out the instructions for the pay telephone. She had already memorized the French phrases needed to ask for a listing for Ellen Valentine, then Emile Bertillon. There were none. She had arrived on French soil with possible explanations already reasoned out—her mother had moved out of Paris, she had married someone other than Bertillon, she had returned to the United States, she simply didn't have a telephone. May had a long, unwritten list. She hung up and gave the matron the requisite francs in exchange for the bathroom key. With a grim, doomsday finger, the woman pointed to a wall clock. "Thirty minutes, you send the key back down."

Back upstairs, the water ran rusty at first. May closed her eyes, shutting out the peeling wallpaper and chipped tile and the communal cube of rough brown soap. She would not entertain failure yet. Oh, no. She would simply move on in her search. She had an address, and there were official records to be explored, wherever they were kept in this big, new city.

Doors slammed, and a couple argued their way down the hall. After she drained the tub, May skulked down the hallway, clutching her bathrobe closed, then hooked the key to the cord loop that ran up the center of the stairway. The pulley squeaked as the key traveled back to the first floor, clattering on the tile below. In her room, she stretched out on her bed with her stationery box and reread Delphina's last letter, wondering where rue Chaptal was. The photograph of her mother beside the Christmas tree was in the box, and she propped it on her bedside table along with Philippe's invitation, then laid the shard of the doll's face beside the photo. She touched her mother's face in the photograph, then Byrd's little-boy face. Switching off the light, she could hear drunken singing from the floor below. It did not feel like Christmastime at all.

The following morning, May sat with Janie in the low-ceilinged breakfast room in the basement of the hotel, paddling a spoon in a bowl of gray porridge. Janie said, "You should have come out with us last night. We found this great little club in Montparnasse—that's where the really hot clubs are—and I sat right at the bar and ordered myself a glass of champagne, pretty as you please! We're going for drinks after rehearsal and try some more places. Rocky had Philippe's car, with a chauffeur. Let me tell you—you get out of *that* car in front of a club? It's tip-top treatment, all the way." She raised her hand in a tight royal wave. "He's sending the car to take us to his party too. You think it's all right if I wear the dress I'm wearing to the opening night party? I only have one evening dress."

"You look so smashing in that dress, it'll be fine. And of course, you have the *loveliest* evening coat."

Janie smiled sheepishly, then consulted her watch. "I've got to run. Nevil said you don't need to show up till noon."

May made a list of sewing supplies, then wrote identical postcards to Elsie and Delphina.

> *December 22*
>
> *I arrived last evening, and I'm excited and a little nervous about beginning my job today. Paris is beautiful, so far. I will be missing you at Christmas, but I am invited to a fabulous party at the house of a French Count, and we're going in a limousine! Please write soon, to this address. I hope your gifts from me arrived safely.*
>
> *Love, May*

Her father would almost certainly see the card in the mailbox and read it. But she would not write to him. She dropped the cards in the postbox, then

Philippe de Clermont

REQUESTS THE PLEASURE OF
YOUR COMPANY AT

A CHRISTMAS RÉVEILLON

WEDNESDAY, 24 DECEMBER 1924
AT NINE O'CLOCK IN THE EVENING
61, RUE DE MONCEAU, PARIS

— RSVP —

set out, emboldened by a map, determined to find her way to the theater. She passed a massive, classical building with stone columns on all four sides, identified on her map as the Church of the Madeleine. She continued down rue Royale to the Concorde, a sharp wind blowing off the river to whip at her coat. She continued, up the Champs-Élysées to Avenue Montaigne, stopping, now and then, to absorb the beauty of Paris. Standing across the street from the Théâtre des Champs-Élysées, May took stock. With its gray marble facade and gilded classical friezes, the theater seemed incongruously formal for something as lighthearted as *Les Folies Noires*. She wanted to capture this moment of beginning, to pause and take stock of what she had accomplished. She had been offered a chance and taken it, and now she was standing here because of her own hard work.

Inside, she was directed to the stage, where an abstract forest scene was painted on a canvas backdrop with dramatic, geometric lines and angles. It contrasted with the traditional gilt and deep-red velvet of the auditorium. Behind the backdrop, she could hear raised voices. She froze, listening.

"It will be a sensation!" a French voice said. May smiled to herself. It was all really happening, and she was here, and her designs were here, and the scenery was here.

Another voice—Nevil's, "There simply is not the time . . ."

May called out, "Bonjour? Nevil?" and ducked around the backdrop.

Unlike the gilded splendor of the entrance and auditorium, every surface backstage was painted flat black. High above, spotlights, pulleys, and ropes hung along catwalks. A rack of costumes stood on one side and several were laid out on a table. Seeing her designs in situ was the frosting on the cake. Each piece had a small bit of her heart sewn in.

Nevil was holding what May secretly considered her masterpiece—Janie's pearl costume. He addressed a sinewy, bald Frenchman with a waxed mustache, saying, "Louis, this is our wardrobe mistress. May, this *fab*ulously talented gentleman is Louis, the set designer." Nevil's voice dropped and he touched her arm. "He has an absolutely *brilliant* vision, which he will share with you. He calls it *l'Abstraction Sauvage*." Nevil's voice was falsely conciliatory. "He wants to change the costumes."

She looked from Nevil to Louis and back again, waiting, holding her breath. The black ceiling seemed to be lowering, slowly, while the walls moved in. She said, "I can get right to work, today."

Nevil dropped the costume on the table, saying, more to Louis than to her, "Salvage these, if you can." May could find no words, in French or in English. She blinked back tears.

"There, there!" Nevil said, "You know they told me not to bring someone from New York. I'll leave you two to get acquainted. Ta!" He fluttered his fingers and left. May blinked at Louis, gathering herself, pinching the soft flesh between her thumb and index finger through her gloves, pinching hard enough to stop tears.

"Mademoiselle." Louis bowed, so slightly that it was the opposite of respectful regard.

"Monsieur," May said, warily, "*enchanté*." She felt the opposite of enchantment.

He cut his eyes to the rack of costumes. "In the States, you have seamstress's guilds, yes? Do you have your papers?"

May swallowed, her palms suddenly damp, feeling like she'd been caught in a lie she didn't remember telling. "Uh, there are Garment Workers Unions, if that's what you mean, but I—I mean, Carlisle's, where I worked, wasn't really, officially . . ."

He held up a hand. "Someone should have told you, mademoiselle, that if you wish to work in this industry in France, there is a Seamstress's Guild. The regulations are very strict. An apprenticeship of three years is required." He pinched the bridge of his nose. "Now I will have to bring in a proper costume maker, and perhaps . . ." He shook his head in resignation. ". . . you can assist. Nevil tells me you are another protégée of Clermont. Hang these up, then press the shirts for the orchestra. The dressing rooms are downstairs."

"But . . . but there are twenty . . ." It was as if a trapdoor had released on the stage floor, in some sort of slapstick burlesque, and she had fallen through. This was a cruel joke, wasn't it? The French sense of humor?

"That is the work that is available to you, mademoiselle." He turned on his heel and disappeared into the blackness. The curtain settled back into place as if he had never been there, and May was alone on stage. She stood there for minutes, as numbness turned to realization. She held her arms out, silently beseeching the empty auditorium.

May waited for the grindingly slow service elevator, then found her way to the dressing rooms. The lower level of the theater was deserted, and like the flat black of backstage, it was strictly functional. Black steamer trunks were lined up, standing on end, each stenciled, *Les Folies Noires, Paris*. Each dancer and musician had one. Above the rows of mirrors mounted around the walls, some bored scenery artist had painted dream-like, watery romantic landscapes with nymph-like figures.

An ironing board was set up in a corner. She plugged in the iron, going through the motions automatically. As it heated, she stared into the middle distance, unfocused, not wanting to look past the fog. She tried very hard not to cry.

All that work. For nothing.

THIRTY-EIGHT

On Christmas Eve, May sat with Janie in the back of Philippe's long black-and-red touring car as it turned onto rue de Monceau. Despite the glass partition which separated them from the driver, May whispered, "It's *bonsoir*, at night, *bonjour*, in the day; *jour* means day."

Janie nodded. "*Oui, oui.*" She fluffed the fur of her collar. "I've never been to a party that had a fancy printed paper invitation. You sure we RSVP'd it right?"

"*Oui.* Just the way Mrs. Post says to."

"Who's Mrs. Post? Will she be here?"

"No, she's an expert on etiquette. She wrote a book about proper manners."

"I need to get that! Look, this must be the house." Janie squeezed May's knee. "We are living the high life, aren't we?"

A tall archway was flanked on either side by buildings that faced the street, creating a barrier from the rest of Paris. The car circled the gravel courtyard, stopping in front of a mansion of buff-colored stone. Lights blazed from tall windows on three stories while around the court, gaslights threw dappled shadows. The driver hurried to open their doors as May and Janie exchanged looks of subdued amazement.

As they stepped out of the car, one of the big carved wooden doors swung open. Warm light spilled from inside, casting into silhouette a tall, narrow figure stationed there. From behind the tall man, barking started from somewhere inside. What appeared to be an animated topiary bounded through the open door, with Rocky following. An elaborately clipped apricot standard poodle skidded to a stop, sniffing and wagging its sculpted tail. Janie said, "Look at his little pompoms for ears! He almost matches my dress."

Rocky called, "Well, don't you girls look pretty!"

As he neared, May was able to see what was squirming in his arms. He held out a fat black puppy. She took it, savoring its milky scent as it mouthed her fingers. "Oh," She said, "what a little darling."

Rocky said, "Philippe just gave her to me, for Christmas. Come inside."

The house was as Rocky had described—like a museum where one could sit on the furniture and touch things. The floor of the entryway was a checkerboard of black and buff stone. At one end was a stone staircase with an ornate bronze railing and at the other, a tall fir tree blazed with candles. The scent of Christmas greens blended with perfume. The houseman offered to take their coats, but Janie would not relinquish hers until they had entered a large, high-ceilinged drawing room, where guests were assembling. The walls were painted *eau-de-nil* green with gilded moldings; the curtains were of heavy red-and-gold damask. Janie strode into the middle of the room, as if it were center stage, then shrugged out of her evening coat. Her satin dress, the color of a flamingo, contrasted with the richly burnished shades of the room. Her tawny skin glowed and her amber eyes flashed. She lifted both arms and announced, "Bonsoir, people!"

From another room, the sounds of a string quartet began, discreetly playing carols. Janie looked around and said, "Hey, where's the champagne?" She kissed the puppy's head, taking her from May. "Oooh, I'm so crazy about this little dog. I might have to steal her. Her ears are like velvet, aren't they? I'd love to have a dog, and maybe some kittens too." She made a sweeping motion. "Think of all the animals you could have here. You could have your very own pony, right in the backyard! Someday, I'd like to own a place like this myself. Who knows"—she held the puppy's face close to hers, talking baby talk—"maybe I will."

When a waiter approached with a tray, May took a glass and handed one to Janie, saying, "Knowing you, you'll have something grander."

Philippe came to where they stood, kissing them both, then standing with an arm around each of their shoulders. Janie rocked the puppy, pouting at it. "This is just the darlingest puppy ever, Phil."

"She is a bulldog," he said, "I think you would call her a *French* bulldog. I have seen her every day in the window of a pet shop. The last of the litter. She seemed terribly lonely."

May asked, "What will you call her?"

"Her name is Confiture," Philippe said, "because she is so sweet."

"Fifi," Rocky added, "for short."

The sounds of convivial laughter came from the entryway. "Ah," Philippe said, "I love to hear the sounds of life in the house. When my sister and I were small, the house was always full of people—children and animals as well. We had many pets that we brought with us from the country. We kept a baby pig in the kitchen, and we used to drive a goat cart through the park. There was always much laughter, in those days."

The room filled, and at dinner, May and Janie flanked Philippe at the head of the table. May wondered if he was aware of her situation at the theater—if Louis or Nevil had mentioned it to him—but now was not the time to ask. Course after lavish course was presented on delicate china. May stopped counting after the seventh, overwhelmed at the thought of the number of dirty plates that must be piled in the kitchen. Her place setting had five forks, and she watched Philippe to discern which one to use, wishing she had consulted her Emily Post, while Janie watched and followed suit.

At midnight, they were still at table, and as the last of the chimes finished, May asked Philippe about his clocks. He answered, "There are twenty-three in all, fourteen on this floor. I have a man come once a week, to attend them. And now," he continued, "it is officially Christmas!" He dismissed the musicians and the servants, saying that their holiday was sacrosanct. "My dear ones," he announced to his guests, "I shall wait upon you myself!"

From a cabinet, he produced a small, bronze-framed mirror with a silver dish. It was passed around the table, and those who wished helped themselves to cocaine. Philippe followed, topping off champagne. Rocky looked on, with an expression of pique. When the mirror made its way back to the head of the table, he shook his head. As May inhaled a line, she overheard him whispering to Philippe, "Remember what the doctor told you."

Philippe smiled, glassy-eyed and indulgent. "But it is Christmas, and we are celebrating with our friends. *Joyeaux Noël!*" He raised his glass, and everyone cheered. Cecil played the grand piano and sang in his deep baritone, with Janie and Velma singing the chorus of "Go Tell it on the Mountain," until Velma, who had drunk too much, leaned on Philippe's shoulder and cried. Infused with goodwill and cocaine, May marveled at her surroundings. A year ago, she had been home on break from Mary Baldwin, eating Christmas turkey with her father. She wondered if he was alone at home. She looked around at the guests, at the troupe. Each of them had left something behind to come here. Or maybe they had escaped something, or someone. *Escape. Don't dwell, May. It's Christmas.* She could not stop the question that plagued her mind. Was her mother celebrating tonight too?

Against Rocky's protestations, Philippe insisted on driving them home. May and Janie helped Velma to the car. The noise of the ongoing party faded, as Velma's head bobbed against May's left shoulder and Janie leaned on her right as the car circled the courtyard. The car jostled, clipping a lamppost and Philippe exclaimed, "*Zut!*" under his breath. With one remaining headlight, he backed up, grinding the gears.

May's eyes began to close. Velma mumbled, "Mer' Chrishmuf," and they swayed along as the big Renault lurched down boulevard Malesherbes and pulled up to the stuttering lights of the Hotel Bercy.

Christmas morning looked like any other at the Hotel Bercy, with the exception of the fact that it had begun to snow during the night. May and Janie sat cross-legged on her bed, as Janie unwrapped the evening bag May had sewn for her on the voyage over, from scraps of satin and lamé. Janie gave May a compact of rouge, saying, "I am going to have a bubble bath, then spend the entire day in bed, and eat every single one of these. But you can have one." She held up a box of bonbons Rocky had given her. May told Janie nothing of her own intentions for the day. She dressed in her warmest clothes.

Outside, snow blanketed the sidewalks and muffled the chimes of church bells. A delighted toddler squealed as his parents swung him over mounds of snow. A few bars and cafés stood open, with boisterous crowds, but most were dark. May walked with purpose, glancing at—but not stopping to study—the windows of the darkened ateliers on rue St. Honoré, with their displays of furs and winter fashions. She counted down the street numbers, until there it was—number 410.

Au Nain Bleu was painted in gold on the display window. *The Blue Dwarf.* A rocking horse with a long horsehair tail and shiny brass stirrups stood in the center. Next to that was a blue doll's carriage with chrome wheels. Platoons of lead soldiers stood in lines, as stern-faced wooden nutcrackers with floss hair scowled down at them. A banner proclaiming: *Joyeaux Noël!* was strung inside the glass of the locked front door. May continued down the street, warmed by a freshly enhanced scenario in which her mother spent hours choosing the perfect doll—the one that her little girl would love best, then wrote out the card, perhaps kissing the envelope before handing it over, asking the proprietress to send it with loving care. May turned up rue de Caumartin, squinting through the snow at the street signs.

The address on rue Chaptal was a rundown building with a fruit market on the ground floor. Through a warped, unlocked door, a staircase led to apartments above. Standing outside the first door on the landing, May brushed snow from her coat. Her mother might be inside the apartment—mere yards, or even feet, from where she stood. On her walk, she had imagined her mother in an apron, flushed from cooking a Christmas goose, embracing her with grateful amazement. They would sit together, and her mother would stroke her cheek, explaining everything—how she had tried so many times to come back, and that seeing May again was the best Christmas present imaginable. She would show May a shrine she had kept, with photographs and a lock of baby hair. In May's fantasy, her mother looked exactly as she remembered her.

May squared her shoulders and raised her hand to knock. *Of course, she'll be older now.* A pinched-looking crone answered, regarding her with mistrustful cataract-glazed eyes. When she inquired, the woman shook her head and crossed herself, looking as if she might spit.

May stood blinking at the closed door; her breath steaming in the unheated passageway. *I'm fine. I'm fine.* She turned and retraced her path down the stairs, on each tread repeating to herself, *I'm fine . . . fine . . . fine.* On the sidewalk, she searched for her handkerchief, sheltering herself below the green awning that said Fruitier Chaptal.

A Closed sign hung across the door, but in the alley adjacent, a jolly-faced man with a handlebar mustache was unloading baskets and cartons from a wagon. "Do not cry, mademoiselle!" He had been watching. Walking toward her, he began to juggle oranges. When May tried to smile, he held one out, saying, "It is Christmas. Please, have one."

"*Merci,*" she mouthed, with a small sob, still rummaging for her handkerchief. The slip of paper she had carried slid from her cold glove, and he reached to pick it up.

"Bertillon?" he frowned, glancing at the paper, "You are looking for Emile Bertillon?"

"Yes. *Oui.* Well, really "—May snuffled—"I'm looking for the woman he lived with, her name was Ellen. Did you know them? I think they lived upstairs."

The man looked vaguely suspicious. "Why do you ask?"

"She is my mother."

"Your mother? Ah . . ." He rubbed his chin and his eyes flitted away. "You are shivering. Come inside." He pushed open the door. "Sit, sit," he said, "I will make coffee." He removed his gloves and rubbed his hands together. "I have just delivered the last of the Christmas boxes." Around his shop, beautiful baskets and bins of exotic fruit were placed like sculptures. May studied them, oddly fascinated by the stacks of velvety hothouse apricots and lemons from Spain, as big as a man's fist. He prepared strong, thick coffee and handed May a small cup. Placing his hand on his chest, he said, "I am Gustave."

May shook his hand. "May. My mother is Ellen Marshall, although you may have known her as Ellen Valentine? Thank you for the coffee. The woman upstairs closed the door in my face." She wrapped her hands around the hot porcelain cup.

"Ah, yes. She does not forget, that one. When they left—Bertillon and

Ellen—they owed her three month's rent. They owed all up and down the street." Gustave looked apologetic.

May sat forward. "It's been thirteen years since I've seen her. Anything you could tell me —good or bad—would help."

He nodded slowly, and there was a long pause before he spoke. "That is a long time. My memory is not so good, you know? Perhaps you do not wish to know bad news, especially at Christmas?"

"Please . . ." May reached for his arm.

"Very well. I first met your mother after the War. She was working in a *fumerie*—Drosso's, I think it was."

"An opium den?" This was not the right script. "Are you sure?"

"Yes. Many of the demobilized soldiers were smoking opium, coming off of morphine if they were wounded, or else to get through shell shock."

"I see." But it was all unclear. "What about Emile Bertillon?"

"Ah, Emile. Emile was a second-rate artist. Even I could tell that. Ellen was lovely, and he was not good for her. He left her after they had been here for six months or so, and soon after, she left Paris herself."

"Do you have any idea where she went, monsieur?" May held her breath.

"That, I do not know. It was as if Ellen Valentine disappeared." He pinched his finger together and opened them, *poof*! He looked away. "I had forgotten about her."

Disappeared. Again. May set down her cup, silently chiding herself for falling into this ridiculous holiday fantasy. She was not a character in a Charles Dickens novel, soon to discover her happy ending. Sometimes there were no endings—no resolutions. People could disappear if they wanted to. Her mother had always known where her daughter was, and she had stayed away. May rose to leave. "Thank you for your help, monsieur. Let me write down my address, in case you remember anything else."

"Gustave, please, call me Gustave. And you are as lovely as your *maman*. Here"—he flicked open a brown paper bag—"It is Christmas. Not a day for bad news; a day for nice things, no? Let me give you some of my nice grapes. Very sweet."

THIRTY-NINE

Rehearsals were running longer and tempers shorter at the theater, as the weeks flew by leading up to the opening of the show. The new costume mistress, a thin-lipped, imperious woman, assigned May the simplest sewing tasks. It was like being back in the basement of the Biltmore. May spent her time hemming yards of tulle or polishing shoes in the windowless dressing rooms. In the solitary hours, she fretted about finding another job, although she would not have the free time to look for one until after the opening. Without seamstress's papers, her career as a designer was over before it began. She fretted about writing to Byrd, and wondered about the English girl, and she fretted about how she might continue the search for her mother.

On opening night, May stood with Rocky in the wings. The stage looked like a forest. A kettle drum began to roll, and the crowd hushed. Janie's dance partner strode onto the stage wearing a rough tunic, slit low at the neck. His build was lean and muscular, his skin very dark. The new costumes, of Louis's design, were minimalistic and modern, sometimes resembling an assemblage of rags. Janie popped out from behind a papier-mâché tree, wearing only briefs of reddish-brown fur with a foxtail swinging behind. Her fingernails were varnished black. The audience roared, then quieted in anticipation. A clarinet began a solo, and with her partner in pursuit, Janie began to slink around the stage. When he caught her, he raised her onto his shoulders as if she were weightless, and the orchestra joined in, accompanying their pas de deux. Her tan skin glowed against his as their bodies moved together in a sensuous, primal rhythm, as if they were the only two humans on earth. This was not the chorus girl Janie. This Janie was a seductress, radiating sexuality and strength. She held sway over the audience. May could tell that she knew it and reveled in her power. With every leap and twirl, she manipulated the crowd a little more. May watched the faces of the men in the audience. Janie was toying with them. The women looked as aroused as the men did, and May suspected that Janie had never really minded the idea of appearing topless at all.

When the curtain finally dropped, there was thunderous applause with a standing ovation. In the crowded dressing room, hoots and elated chatter flew as bouquets arrived one after another, with invitations to dine and notes of congratulation. Velma held an armload of red roses, sent by an admirer. Chorus girls mopped sweat and wiped off stage makeup as May helped Janie into her flamingo evening dress. May observed the revelry, quietly performing her own small duties—checking over costumes and hanging them carefully, then lining up vases on the dressing tables. Rocky pinned a gardenia in Janie's hair, then she shrugged into the green velvet evening coat and was whisked away to the opening-night party.

Quiet descended after the girls left. May unbuttoned her work smock and sat in her slip and stockings at the abandoned dressing table, tracing a path through spilled face powder. She began applying makeup as Rocky had taught her to do, transforming her face from the downtrodden wardrobe assistant into what she hoped might pass for the fresh loveliness of an American socialite. Her lipstick was the color of ripe plums, and she liked to think that its intensity proved her to be a girl with nerve and style. Rocky had trimmed her hair so that it hung like black satin, framing her face in geometric planes. As she slipped her kingfisher blue dress over her head, she could not avoid thinking of Byrd. The only time she had worn it was with him, dancing in New York.

She still had not written that letter. He kept popping into her head, and she assuaged her guilt by telling herself that she *would* write, soon, and apologize. What she could not admit, in writing, was that he had been right—she had been impetuous to come here with so little experience.

As she combed her hair, she admitted to herself what she really wanted to do. She wanted to bluster past her failure, to tell everyone what a hit the show was and maybe send Byrd a card or a photograph, of herself at a party—something exotic—a sort of postal nose-thumbing. Taking one last look in the mirror before she switched off the lights, she arranged her features and pouted her plum lips. *Time to create opportunities. Tonight, something magical will happen.*

Outside of the dressing room, she found Rocky, attired in his top hat and tails. He held out his arm. "You look absolutely smashing, and so do I!"

May smoothed his lapel. "You *do* look marvelous in your tails. Where's Philippe?"

"He had to go ahead. May I escort you to the soiree, mademoiselle?"

Outside, the moon was almost full, competing with the glow of the Eiffel Tower, illuminated top to bottom with lights spelling out *Citroen*. At the Park that ran alongside the Champs-Élysées, they followed walkways il-luminated with torchieres. Above the trees, three heraldic pennants waved at the peaks of a white tent, pitched in the center of a lawn and surrounded by evergreens and classical statuary. From inside, the sounds of laughter carried over the tinkling of a piano. The cold was invigorating after the overheated theater. At the entrance of the tent, an attendant in livery checked May and Rocky's names on a list then pulled back the canvas flap.

Inside, the roof of the tent was midnight blue, painted with gold stars. Lights twinkled along the rigging and wrapped the tent poles. Gas heaters warmed the space, and silver trays of champagne and cocktails were being passed, along with exotic-looking tidbits of food.

Janie posed for a photographer while a reporter asked her questions and scribbled on a pad. "May," she called, motioning, "Help! I can't un-derstand this Frenchie." As May translated, another journalist approached, pad in hand. He nodded, apparently not wishing to interrupt, taking notes as he listened to Janie. It was the cut of his dinner jacket, May decided, or the way that his black hair fell over his forehead, that made her think he must not be French. He looked to be in his early thirties. His pale brow furrowed as he wrote, grasping his pen oddly, with the determined concentration of a schoolboy. When he squinted, May suspected that he probably had spectacles but was too vain to wear them. Observing him, she lost her train of thought and stammered. When the French reporter left, the dark-eyed man spoke. In a British accent, he introduced himself as Gerald Fournier, correspondent for the *London Times*. His photographer asked Janie to pose, then Gerald said, to May, "Mademoiselle, would you mind terribly?" The shutter snapped, and the photographer moved on.

May blinked away the white ghost of the flash. "Why do you want *my* photograph?"

He bowed and kissed her hand. "Because you're lovely. And now, I must have your name." He held up his pad. "May I ring you?"

Philippe approached, smiling benevolently. He held out his hands, palms up. "Ah, my beautiful young friends. *Bonsoir*, Gerald. Did you meet Janie and May? Have some champagne. Perhaps the three of you would care to join us afterward? There is a fete on that promises to be most amusing."

Janie nodded, and May said, "We'd love to come."

Philippe's smile dimmed. "Nevil is coming over here. Not a word to him."

"Tell me," Gerald asked Philippe, "Will the show be touring the Continent?"

"We will try Monaco, then make a decision. Rather too early to tell."

"Will you go on the tour, Philippe?" May asked.

"I think not. I usually spend the winter in the country, or skiing. Rocky and I will leave for Chamonix after the show closes."

A couple approached, asking Janie for her autograph, and she signed their program *Eugénie*, as the French reporter had addressed her. Philippe led Rocky off to meet someone, and Gerald Fournier tagged behind. May stood alone, studying the way the French women wore their evening clothes. She recognized the flutter of a clarinet, playing the opening strains of George Gershwin's "Rhapsody in Blue," and she overheard someone say that Gershwin himself was there. Nevil came to stand at May's elbow. He scanned the crowd, and May felt sure he was looking for someone more important. He spoke without facing her. "Hmm. It appears that Pendergrast has done a marvelous job of ingratiating himself with Philippe."

May continued to face forward, sipping her champagne. "Rocky's friendly to everyone."

Nevil rubbed his chin and snickered. "I've never known Philippe to go for the Americans, but one never knows. It's a different boy every year."

May lowered her glass and glared at him. "What a wicked thing to say."

"It's true." He put his hand on his chest. "*I* was one myself, years ago." He huffed a sigh. "But he tired of me. He always does. Still, he was generous enough—set me up in New York. Ah, I must speak with that man." He raised his chin and glass toward someone, smiling his tight-jawed smile. "Ta-ta, my dear."

The quai d' Orsay, at one o'clock in the morning, was harshly bright and teeming with people. Flaneurs strolled in evening clothes, drunks staggered, and the fashionable prostitutes—the cocottes—lounged against the buildings, blasé, as if they did not feel the cold, while the cheaper girls stood along the curbs, calling out to passing automobiles, laughing and opening their overcoats. Philippe's chauffeur, Bernard, stared ahead with an expression of stony determination. In the long Renault, May and Janie flanked Philippe on the back seat, with Gerald and Rocky on jump seats, facing them. When the car jostled on the cobblestones, May's knees brushed Gerald's, and she wondered if he felt the same subtle awareness of their proximity. The car stopped outside an imposing pair of carved black doors where a man in evening clothes and a tall fur hat stood sentry at the end of a velvet cordon. He opened the car door, then bowed. "Monsieur de Clermont. Please, your table is waiting."

May whispered, "What is this place? There's no sign."

Gerald leaned forward, and May felt the warmth of his breath on her shoulder. "It's called Magic City."

Inside, in the velvet dimness of the unattended vestibule, a solitary cobalt blue spotlight illuminated an arched doorway. Beyond the arch was darkness. May and Janie moved closer to the men. No one spoke. The quiet was tense and portentous, and passing through the cobalt light felt like stepping through the proverbial gates of hell, with everyone's skin glowing a momentary, silvery death-blue. They proceeded down a long passage, lit only by tiny spotlights which, at intervals, offered small puddles of cobalt light. Music and laughter became louder, and ahead, flashbulbs were going off like rapid bolts of lightning. As they entered a cavernous room, someone called, "Monsieur de Clermont! A photograph, please!" Popping flashes reflected off mirrored balls, rotating overhead, and the room appeared to spin. May was entranced, watching dots of light race around the walls, illuminating, among the people in evening dress, a shirtless matador, a Viking couple, and two *Garçonnes*—women with cropped, pomaded hair, wearing tails and top hats with matching monocles.

There were raucous cheers as, through the crowd, a pair of men in white ties processed, each with a young woman straddling his shoulders. The women wore only white briefs and turbans, with silver dancing shoes. Their torsos were painted with red bull's-eyes, centered on their navels. Simultaneously, they put their hands behind their heads, sitting up proudly as the photographer focused on them. Their bearers came to stand on either side of Philippe as more cameras flashed. Janie yelled in May's ear, over the din of the revelers, "This is really something, isn't it?" May could only nod. Someone popped a bottle of champagne and sprayed the crowd, hooting, while Philippe threw back his head and laughed. When Gerald held up his hand and tapped out a line of cocaine, May took it, relishing the familiar bitterness in the back of her throat.

Dawn was breaking when Philippe's car pulled up to the Hotel Bercy. A street sweeper pushed a wide broom, leaving striated tracks on the slush-wet sidewalk. May's head throbbed and her ears rang. She shook Janie awake. "We're home."

Janie yawned, raising her head from Philippe's shoulder. She rubbed her eyes with her knuckles. "Well, that was one hell of a night. Thanks, Phil."

FORTY

The next morning, in the breakfast room of the hotel, the bleary-eyed *Folies* troupe gathered to go through the newspapers. May translated French reviews and shouts of triumph went up. The press had christened Janie "*L'impératrice,*" after the Empress Eugénie. *Les Folies* was the talk of Paris, and it was predicted that by the end of the day, the entire run would be sold out. The musicians and chorus girls were being courted for future engagements at nightclubs and theaters. While whiskey was sloshed into cups of *café crème*, May felt removed from the celebration. In the end, only three of her costumes had been used.

Upstairs, two letters had been pushed beneath her door while she was at breakfast. She wrestled the window open, hoping fresh air might find its way down the alley and inside. She lay on her bed, flushed with fatigue, her heart fluttering as she tore open the first envelope. Her father had sent a Christmas card with a cheerful Santa Claus filling stockings at a fireplace.

Christmas, 1924

My Dear Little Gal,

My last letter to you in New York was returned with no forwarding address. I hope this reaches you and you are well.

I worry about you, and I wish that we could talk about some things. Please send me a letter. Ask me anything you want. I should have been more honest with you. I'm sorry this is not a very cheerful Christmas card.

Love, Daddy

The card dropped into her lap. Her father was at home, alone—admitting to regret, apologizing. May felt sorry for him. Then she remembered the Christmases when she had peered out of the front window, searching not for Santa Claus, but for her mother, and her heart closed to him again.

The next letter was from Delphina.

January 1

Chérie May,

 I can hardly believe it is 1925. It seems like just yesterday you were scrabbling around on the kitchen floor under my feet, banging pot lids. I hope you are safe and well. Christmas was quiet. Your father did not put up a tree. He had dinner with the Craigs, and Byrd came by to wish me Merry Christmas. He asked after you, and I was surprised that he has not had a letter from you himself. It might not be any business of mine, but I could tell that there is bad blood between the two of you. It seemed to me he made a point of letting me know that he was going to Washington for a New Year's Eve party. So I thought I'd best pass that on.

 I don't know what to say about you looking for Ellen. I don't know what kind of person she might be now.

 Thank you for my present. The bracelet is so pretty, and the package is so fancy I hate to even wear it. Please write soon.

Love, Delphina

May folded the paper and closed it into her letter box, along with her father's card. She would not write to him. The idea of putting failure into words, to anyone, was too painful. But luck could turn, couldn't it? She wrote to Elsie and Delphina, triumphantly announcing the success of the show. *All true.* She tried to describe the party at Magic City, but on paper it sounded preposterous. She put her pen down, recalling the way Gerald

Fournier's thumb had pressed against the bare skin of her back as they danced, with just enough pressure to keep her aware of its presence. She wrote on, enthusing over the charming Englishman, making a point of mentioning that she was having luncheon with him and that he had actually kissed her hand. *Also true.*

Whatever she told Elsie would get to Byrd. With her pen poised over a fresh sheet of paper, she tried to start a letter to him. How to begin? What tone to take? Maybe it was better to be light, as if nothing had occurred. They could salvage their friendship, going on as if nothing had happened. *Maybe.* She could tell him that everything was going fabulously well, that he needn't worry about her a bit. *Untrue.*

After four bad starts, May balled up the paper, squeezing it as if the right words might be wrung from the page. She found it impossible to write the truth, because if she did, she would have to admit to herself that she could not stop thinking about him. She would also have to concede, if she were being truthful, that she felt jealous of the English girl, and that her jealousy was irrational and fickle. But to admit to that would mean to admit to being irrational, and petty, and maybe in love with him, and that would mean opening a door that she had been holding closed with all her might.

When she received a letter from Elsie a few days later, with the news of her engagement and a lavish wedding planned for April, she was happy for her friend. When she read the notice from the *Richmond Times*, she felt envious of a life so neatly laid out and secure. Elsie asked her to be Maid of Honor and May tried to picture herself, holding the bouquet as Elsie recited her vows, but the vision only brought an ugly snort of self-contempt. *Maybe*, she mused, *I could be the Maid of Dishonor.*

May did not want Gerald Fournier to see the Hotel Bercy, so when she agreed to have lunch with him, she asked to meet at the south steps of the church at place de la Madeleine. From the back of a taxi, he pointed out the sights, seeming to enjoy telling her the history of every building and monument they passed. At the basilica of Sacré-Cœur, Gerald told the taxi driver not to wait. They climbed to the top of the steep steps, where all of wintry Paris fanned out below them. Gerald led her through the steeply winding streets of Montmartre, then through a narrow stone passage. Tiers of stairs unspooled below them, bordered by gas lanterns and iron railings. He said, "Two hundred ninety-four steps, last time I counted. I'll race you." They tapped down flight after flight, counting off the steps. At the bottom, breathless and laughing, he took May's hand and led her down a side street.

On the corner, a broad blue awning snapped in the wind. Beneath it, fish were displayed on a bed of seaweed. The fishmonger, in his black rubber boots and apron called, "Bonjour!" The briny sea smells were over-taken by a charcuterie next door. Further down was a *boulangerie*, where fragrant, freshly baked *bâtards* and thin *ficelles* cooled in tall baskets. At the end of the row was Patisserie Richard, with its neat rows of éclairs and tarts lined up like soldiers in the display window. M. Richard himself stood behind the window, wielding a pastry bag with scowling concentration.

At a tiny, low-ceilinged restaurant, Gerald ordered for them, then taught May how to eat an artichoke. Dried bunches of herbs hung from the rough-hewn beams and a cat sunned himself in the window. When their plates had been removed, they sat, finishing their wine. May said, "This has been such fun. Thank you for lunch, and for the tour."

He said, "I usually hate this time of year here. It can be dreadfully oppressive. I'm off to the home office in London on Monday, for a week—some work to finish up—but I'd like very much to see you again. May I take you to dinner before I leave?"

"I'd like that, but I have to be at the theater every night. I usually don't finish until after one o'clock."

"Another luncheon, then? Monday? I could take the afternoon train."

"Monday would be lovely." May felt herself flush, and she busied her-self in folding her napkin. "I wanted to ask you something. I suppose you know everyone in the newspaper offices here?"

"Not everyone. Why?"

"I need to hire a private detective, I think. Or maybe you can tell me another way to trace someone."

"Sounds terribly mysterious. Who are you looking for?"

"My mother." May explained her meeting with the fruit vendor, then said, "I've been to the embassy, and the Paris registry offices. The customs bureau has no record of her leaving France. I even checked the death records. There's nothing."

"She worked at Drosso's? Hmm. I'll get you the number of a chap who does that sort of thing—finding people."

After lunch, they stood together at the foot on the long stairs. "Now," Gerald said, "I'm afraid we have to go back up." He took May's arm and they began to climb, matching strides, falling into a rhythm. The wine and good food had inspired an ease between them. After the first two flights, they stopped trying to speak, and as they heaved themselves up the final flight, May could hear the grinding gears of a large truck laboring up the steep street ahead. With a tremendous *boom*, the truck backfired, the noise reverberating off the buildings surrounding the stairs.

May gasped, putting a hand to her chest, then laughed at herself. "That frightened me!" She squeezed Gerald's arm and felt a tremor. When he did not respond, she asked, "Are you chilled?"

He withdrew his arm from hers and hunched his shoulders, panting, shoving his shaking hands into his armpits. Sweat beaded his forehead. "Frightfully embarrassing, really," he said, not looking at her, "I must get home, right away."

May helped him into a taxi and climbed in behind him. "Are you ill? Was it something you ate?"

His lips were colorless. He held his hands between his knees, squeezing his eyes closed as he said, "Driver, cité Berryer. The Boissy d'Anglas side."

"Gerald?" May touched his sleeve.

His voice was a whisper. "I must get home. Must have quiet." He handed May his billfold and she held it until the taxi pulled over in front of a tall iron gate.

"Let me help you to your flat," she said, "You can hardly walk." She paid the taxi, then used Gerald's key to open the doorway in the gate. Upstairs, his apartment was cluttered, the shades pulled, with file cabinets and stacks of books and magazines. A typewriter sat on a desk with a view out, and a wide, leather-covered sofa faced the terrace.

"Please," Gerald said, "I'll be fine. You should go."

"You're shaking," she said, "Let me make you some tea. I'll find it."

He went into another room, closing the door quietly. She put the kettle on, foraging for tea and a pot. She wondered if there was a doctor to be called, or medicine to be administered. A marmalade cat startled her, rubbing against her legs. There was no milk, and the cabinets held only bar glasses and a few crockery cups. After a few minutes, the kettle began to boil. She carried the steaming teapot into the living room. Gerald had removed his jacket and tie and wore a heavy cardigan and needlepoint slippers. He sat on the sofa, and May heard his long, halting sigh. She sat beside him, rubbing his icy hands. He stared out vacantly toward the terrace; his pupils were pin dots. It was as if he had vacated his body. The cat settled herself in his lap and he began to stroke her back without looking at her.

"Very kind." He slurred slightly. "I've taken something, for my nerves. I'll be fine. Please, go." He continued to stare out at nothing and stroke the cat.

FORTY-ONE

A week passed, and May worked long days at the theater, listening to the chorus girls chatter about touring Europe and the job offers they were considering. On the dressing room mirrors, each of them kept a tally, marked in lipstick, of the bouquets they received. Paris was ripe, and these girls were in the right place at the right time. American Negro musicians who had stayed after the War were now buying nightclubs and opening restaurants. For anyone not in the performing arts, however, positions were scarce. Parisians resented the expatriates who sought to take jobs when the city had so many of its own unemployed. Throughout Paris, there were veterans on crutches with a rolled pants-leg or an empty sleeve, or war-torn faces, and May wondered how many cases of shell shock there were that did not even show.

She did everything the costume mistress told her to do, knowing she was only there because Philippe had told them to keep her on. No one in Paris—as May reminded herself—was looking for untrained-but-ambitious American costume designers. She read the trade papers that floated around the theater, but without documents, she had little hope.

When May rolled a rack of costumes into the dressing room, Janie looked up from a magazine, saying, "Somebody sent you flowers, honey." A small vase of white roses sat on the dressing table. May leaned to smell them, but they had no fragrance.

Velma stood in front of a mirror, shrugging into a black fur coat. She said, "You got yourself a beau, May?"

"Me? No." May reached for the card and opened it.

My dear girl,
Please forgive my wretched rudeness. Allow me a chance to redeem myself. Dinner on your next evening off?

> *Yours most contritely,*
> *Gerald Fournier*

PS The investigator chap you want to ring up is called Dickie Webber, OPERA 9 45 62

She moved the vase to a side table and tucked the card into her smock. Janie went back to her magazine while May threaded a needle and began to stitch loose sequins. The roses pleased her, but she wasn't sure how to respond. Gerald had behaved so strangely. A nice dinner would be a treat, if she could get an evening off. But she needed the wages. And how could she afford a private detective when she had started bathing every other day to save the five francs?

Velma winked, saying, "Roses are a nice start. My fella gave me this coat last week." She stroked the lapel. "Genuine sealskin. I told him I might be in trouble, then a few days later, I told him it was only a scare. He was so relieved, he bought me a Persian kitten too!"

Janie sniffed derisively, then sat up straighter. "Velma?" she said, "Did you use my cold cream? I smell my cold cream. You used my cold cream."

"Did not," Velma said, on her way out the door. "Toodles. See you gals tonight."

"I know she used my cold cream." Janie closed her magazine and looked up, frowning.

"I saw her man. He picked her up last night. Wasn't anything to write home about, I can tell you. He owns beer companies or something, and he's set her up in this swanky apartment on Avenue Haussmann. He has a wife on Avenue Foch."

May said, "Has anyone turned your head?"

"I told you before, hon, I'm not looking to have my head turned." Janie held her hands together, pointing forward as if she were about to dive. "I'm looking straight ahead, no distractions. What about you? You sweet on that fella who sent you those roses?"

May shook her head, looking down at her sewing. "He's nice, but it's nothing." She laid her work in her lap and looked up at Janie. "I've decided something. It's better to not expect anything. I thought I could be like you—work hard and get ahead without owing anything to anybody. Only I expected too much. Remember when we talked that first time at the theater, about the black swan costume? You said then that everybody has things they keep inside. Sometimes I think secrets like that can eat away at a person, like poison."

Janie nodded, and two furrows appeared between her eyebrows. She dropped her hands into her lap. Her voice went flat. "Remember, you asked me why I don't like feathers?" Her beautiful amber eyes darkened.

"Yes."

"I told you about when I was little, how my momma would entertain and give me candy? Well, there's no nice way to say it—my mother was a whore. Only I didn't understand about all that. I was about eleven when I figured it out—when I started growing into a woman.

"One night this man showed up at our house—a railroad engineer. He came to see my mother when he came through town. She told him she was indisposed, only he was mean-drunk. He pushed his way in, and slapped Momma to the floor—said he'd brought her a present and he wanted to see her wear it. It was a feather boa. He tickled her face with it, laughing all crazy, but she was out cold. I was trying to help her. He started tickling me. I was laughing, but I was crying too. Then he held me down and took what he'd come for, and I just wanted to scream." May put her hand over Janie's, and Janie looked down. "And then . . ." Janie went quiet for a moment, taking a big breath. "A few months later, Momma took me to this old lady in town. Then she sent me to live with her sister, in Alpharetta."

May whispered, "I'm so sorry, Janie. I had no idea."

"Bad things happen to everybody, right?" Janie smiled, ruefully. "I think you've got a story too."

May's first instinct was to deflect, to deny, to turn the spotlight from herself. Janie trusted her. She would listen. May started to speak, but there was a rapping on the door frame and Rocky called, "Can we come in? Everybody decent?"

"Come on in," Janie called back, gaily. She looked at May with a finger to her lips. *Shh.* In the space of seconds, Janie's face transformed from a traumatized girl back into *Mademoiselle Eugénie*.

"*Bonjour*, my dears," Philippe said. Leaning over to smell the roses, he ran a finger down the side of the vase, tracing the leaf design in the opalescent glass. "Lovely," he said, "Lalique." He turned to Janie. "Your admirer has excellent taste."

"Those aren't mine, they're hers," Janie said. "Who sent them, May?"

"Gerald Fournier," May said, absently.

"Gerald?" Philippe dropped his chin and looked over his pince-nez. "You have been seeing Gerald?"

"He took me to lunch last week."

"Ah." Philippe stood back, steepling his fingers. "I saw Velma outside. You girls! I suppose you know that there is a Madame Fournier?"

May had been studying the design of the vase. "What did you say?" *That photograph, in his wallet—three small children on a pony—needlepoint slippers with hunting dogs and tiny initials—the signature of a needlewoman. Married.* She laughed, swatting away the sting of it.

Philippe continued, "His wife has the money, and refuses to give him a divorce. I met her once—in Cannes, I believe it was. She has a face like an old horse, but her father is an Earl, and Gerald keeps her somewhere in the hinterlands of Dorset." Philippe chuckled. "I think he works as an excuse to be away. *Alors*, forgive me. Have I shocked you? You Americans can be so puritanical. In France, we look the other way." His face turned serious. "But enough gossip. I am very sorry to tell you, *mes amies*, that I will be making a rather sad announcement this afternoon. There will be no tour of *Les Folies*."

"What?" Janie sat up.

"I was speaking with Cecil, this morning. He asked, on behalf of the musicians, to meet with me. He told me that the owner of Le Grand Duc approached him and has offered to double the salaries of the entire orchestra if they will go to work there. They took a vote and decided to take the offer. I cannot see a way to pay them more than that."

Les Folies Noires closed quietly on January 30. The next day, Rocky and Philippe left for Chamonix with Rocky promising to send a photograph of himself on skis. The chorus girls were hired by the Moulin Rouge, and Janie was offered a six-week run at a casino in Monaco.

By the fifth of February, Janie and May were the last ones left at the hotel. On Janie's last morning, May lounged on her unmade bed, poking her finger through a tear in her stocking. She could think of no compelling reason to make the bed, or even to leave it. She had all the hours of the day to fill, with no job and very little money. In a matter of hours, she would be alone at the Hotel Bercy.

Janie was trying to buckle her overstuffed suitcase. "I sure won't miss this place," she said, "But who knows, Monte Carlo could be worse. Maybe I should have gone with the other girls. Dottie said she found a swell flat, all to herself, on rue Bergère, right down from Bricktop's. Maybe when I get back, we could get a little place. Unless you get yourself *arranged*, like Velma."

"I suppose she won't have to worry about getting another job," May said. The hole in her stocking began to run, and she watched, listlessly, as it laddered down her calf.

"I think that was her plan all along. And did Rocky tell you that Philippe is going to help him to open a fancy hair salon? They signed papers and everything."

"No," May said, petulantly. "Listen, at your new show, would you ask if they need any help? I'll swab the floors or darn stockings, or anything. I told the other girls to ask at the Moulin Rouge."

"Cheer up, sugar. Something will turn up. You need me to lend you some money?"

"I'll be all right, thanks."

"You know, maybe it's time to think about going back home." Janie paused, putting a hand to May's cheek. "Don't take that the wrong way . . . You're real good and all, but maybe show business isn't the best thing for you."

May blew out her breath. "Maybe you're right," she said, shrugging, trying to look as if she cared less than she did. "I thought I loved all this— the fast pace and the excitement and the glamour. But there's nothing permanent. All that work on costumes for one show, and then—poof! The skit is cut, or the show closes, and the whole thing starts again, if you're lucky. How do you do it, Janie? You never know when or where you'll find your next booking, or if the show will succeed or close."

Janie smiled and sighed. "That's easy. It's the *people*, honey. If I can make those folks love me for an hour, it's *all* worth it. I can't get enough. But you don't get that backstage. Lucky for me, I'm a hot ticket right now." She patted May's hand and glanced at her wristwatch. "Oh, I'm going to miss my train! Listen, I'll write you, soon as I know my address. Would you go down and get me a cab while I pay my bill?"

On the street, May hugged her friend for a long time. Janie waved through the back window of the taxi, smiling her bright, broad smile. May wished her friend well, but there was an edge of bitterness at being the one left behind. Her smile faded as the taxi rounded the corner, and she went slowly back up the steps, hugging herself. In the lobby, the bead curtains rattled, and the matron stuck her head out, saying, "M'amzelle? This came for you." The telegram was from Chamonix.

7 FEBRUARY

```
PHILLIPE HAD SMALL HEART ATTACK LAST NIGHT
DEPARTING WITH HIM FOR CLINIC IN SWITZERLAND
RECOVERY EXPECTED
BERNARD DRIVING BACK TO PARIS TODAY WITH DOGS
FOUR PM
SERVANTS ON HOLIDAY
STAY AT HOUSE UNTIL WE RETURN

   REPLY TO BIRCHER-BENNER CLINIC, ZURICH
```

A heart attack? May wrote out a hasty affirmative reply, then hurried upstairs. Without Janie's colorful belongings and electric presence, the room seemed abandoned, like fairgrounds after a carnival. On May's bed, Janie had left the chocolate-brown box from Revillon Frères. The velvet evening coat was still carefully folded inside and peeking from the pocket were twenty dollar's-worth of franc notes wrapped in a scrap of paper, signed with only a heart. May pressed the coat to her face, and behind the soft velvet, gratitude and anxiety and loneliness did battle with her features.

At three o'clock, she handed her key to the matron, and when she passed her the forwarding address, *61 rue de Monceau*, the matron's eyebrows shot up with a look of suspicious disapproval. She handed May a letter, and a telephone message from Gerald Fournier, saying, in French, "My towels had better be up there, or I will find you."

May glanced at the letter. It was from Elsie. She shoved it in her pocket and replied, in English, "I sincerely hope I never see you or your ratty towels again."

Outside, mist fell, and May's breath steamed. Through the window of a taxi, she had one last look at the flapping awning of the Hotel Bercy. The sky was white through the mist, all color erased. The statues along the avenues that had been so graceful before now seemed sternly disapproving. Paris—this city she thought she knew—was foreign again, and she was displaced and untethered. Paris had not welcomed her with open arms as it had Janie and Velma and Cecil and Rocky. Had she fooled herself so thoroughly, to think that she had talent and value? Close beside her on the taxi seat, Shame sat, smirking, as if to say, *Did you really think Paris was far enough?*

When the taxi pulled up to the archway in front of Philippe's house, the gates were closed. She rang the bell and waited, but no one came. The driver was beginning to make gestures, that he could not stay. He unloaded her trunk then drove off, grumbling over the modest tip. The mist had turned to freezing rain; the afternoon was waning. The lights in front of the house did not switch on, as those across the street did.

At four thirty, May left her luggage and walked up the street to the tall iron gates of parc Monceau. Following the path, she counted off the backs of the houses until she recognized Philippe's red damask curtains. Through the gate, she saw a columned terrace and a small formal garden, where snowdrops peeked hopefully from beneath the trees, but the garden gate was also locked; the wall too tall to climb. Sleet stung her face, and in an attempt to warm herself, she wandered through the park, passing frost-glazed statues and a pond, half encircled by a columned folly, its surface covered by a lacy scrim of ice. Above, the trees were bare; below, winter-brown leaves rotted in icy black puddles. She passed a man with a pair of dachshunds on leashes, all three in matching tartan coats. A uniformed nanny hurried by, holding aloft a big black umbrella while two little boys in school caps huddled close.

Circling back to the street, May passed a café on the corner. Back at Philippe's gate, she sat on her trunk and sneezed, twice. Her coat smelled like a wet cat. The sleet continued, and she decided that if someone wanted to steal her trunk, they could have it, and maybe she would end up selling matches on the street with rags wrapped around her feet. At the café, she ordered a coffee and shook out her last cigarette. She laid the damp gray envelope from Elsie on the table. The ink of the address had run. Running a knife under the flap, she guessed what problems Elsie might have to report. *Trousseau not yet delivered? Too many thank-you notes to write?*

February 1, 1925

Dearest May,

I know the overseas mail is slow, but it's been an absolute age since I've heard from you! So much has been happening! The moment I arrived home, Mother descended upon me with wedding plans.

Byrd telephoned the other day to say that Sophie was visiting him in Keswick, then he asked if he could bring her to our engagement party. He said she's invited him to Scotland. I think it sounds serious. She seems a fun sort of girl. In fact, I rather like her, and I think she might be a proper match for Byrd. I did finally unearth the gossip about her (though, really, it's common knowledge in Washington circles.) It seems that when she was a teenager, she had a torrid affair with one of her father's friends, who was married. Can you imagine? She was sixteen and he was absolutely ancient—nearly forty! When her father found out, he sent her to that school in Switzerland, Mont-Something-Something, only she ran away, so he brought her to live in Washington when he became ambassador, so he could keep an eye on her. She's got that perfect English skin and she has the most marvelous clothes from Lanvin. Byrd says she's quite the daring rider and she can shoot too.

Paris sounds too, too divine. I can't wait to hear more about your beau. Your job must be so glamorous, and you must be awfully busy, because you've been such a poor correspondent. No more news from home until you write back to your ever-loving,

Elsie

May sighed, blowing out a stream of smoke and smashing her cigarette hard into the tin ashtray. The thought of even attempting to explain her situation was utterly overwhelming. She stirred her coffee, staring into the steaming cup, as if solutions might float to the surface.

At half past five, she returned to the house. The gates were open, and Philippe's car was parked beneath the porte cochere. May recognized Bernard, the chauffeur, leaning into the trunk. "Ah, mademoiselle!" he said, looking up at the sound of her footsteps, "I was going to your hotel to look for you. But you are here." He smiled, looking tired and relieved. "I must let the dogs out. They have been in the car for some hours. Please . . ." He unlocked a tall iron gate that opened into a long alley. May followed him past what must be kitchen or scullery doors and on, into the garden. He unclipped the leashes and the dogs ran off, sniffing and joyous. The puppy had grown since Christmas. Returning to the car, Bernard said, "I am very sorry if you had to wait; I had a tire puncture."

"Tell me about Philippe. How is he?"

"When I left, they were putting him into a private room and he was giving orders to the nurses and attendants, so he must be feeling better," he said. "The Bircher-Benner is the best clinic in Switzerland. He was there last winter also. But he does not like people to know that he has a delicate heart. The doctor had told him to slow down and not to ski, but he would not listen." Bernard closed the gate. "I hope you do not mind entering through the kitchen. The dogs will be fine for a bit. I must go back for the birds; they cannot bear the cold."

The kitchen was warm from the huge gas range that stood in the center. Copper pots gleamed in the dim light, lined up like stair steps on the tiled walls. A vague odor of root vegetables and scouring powder hung in the air. Bernard returned, carrying a small cage with a muslin cover. Pulling an envelope from his pocket, he said, "Monsieur le Compte sends his gratitude and apologies to you. He asked me to deliver to you these notes on the care of the dogs and birds. The servants will return from holiday next week, but until then, the count asks you to please make yourself comfortable. The house has been unoccupied, so it will be quite cold until the furnace heats, but there is a gas fire in the blue bedroom, where he asked me to direct you. I will leave the hamper with the dog's food and coats in the kitchen, and take the birds to the bedroom, if you do not object. The heater in the conservatory is very slow. Perhaps you could move them to the large cage there, in the morning? The man who tends the clocks will be in, but otherwise, the house will be empty. I, myself, will garage the car and be on my way to the train station." He passed a ring of keys to May, along with the list, which she could see was in Rocky's handwriting.

"Tomorrow, the butcher and poulterer will deliver the dog's usual food. You may order from them anything you require." Bernard carried her bag up the stairs to the second floor, then down a long hallway, turning on lights as he went. He switched on the fire, then left to bring up her trunk in the elevator. The bedroom walls had panels of robin's-egg blue, each with a gilded crest in the center. A bucolic landscape hung over the fireplace, and the bed had a delicate lace canopy. It was like stepping into a painting. When May removed the cover from the birdcage two bright yellow canaries flitted around in distress. She placed the cage on the desk gingerly, as if it were doll's furniture. In the adjoining bathroom, she splashed water on her cold-blotched face. She sneezed. From below, she heard the front door close, and she was alone.

Later, in the strange bed with lavender-smelling sheets, she studied the lace pattern of the canopy. Her eyes began to close. Fifi nosed her way beneath the eiderdown, and Boris snuffled on the chaise lounge. May was grateful for their warmth and companionship. From the reaches of the sleeping house, an echoing of clocks rang ten, accompanied by the tinny, delicate chime of her mantel clock. Sleep came quickly.

In the morning she woke to the sounds of canary song and Fifi's crying. Scooping up the puppy, she hurried downstairs, trying to remember where the nearest door was. She let the dogs out from the conservatory and stood shivering in the doorway watching them, running one cold bare foot up her calf. The sleet had turned to icy snow overnight, and the puppy lifted her paws daintily, not wanting to venture far. May sneezed again. Her head was stuffed and achy, and she wondered if she had a fever. When the dogs came in, she went back to her room and wrapped herself in her robe and a thick pair of cashmere socks, borrowed from Philippe's dressing room. It was not yet eight o'clock, and she crawled back into bed and pulled up the covers. She opened Elsie's letter and read it again, aloud to the dogs, in her stuffy-nosed voice. In her box of stationery was Elsie's earlier letter with the newspaper clipping. May smoothed it out on top of the duvet, running her finger over Byrd's face, trying to imagine him kissing the English girl with the perfect skin.

At ten, she dressed beside the fire, in her warmest stockings and sweater. She telephoned Gerald, to tell him she had a cold and could not see him. In the kitchen, she made tea and fed the dogs. When the telephone rang, she followed the insistent trill to the houseman's office. May hesitated in answering, venturing, "Monsieur Clermont's house?" Half an hour later, a man in a clean butcher's apron arrived with a basket of raw chicken and packages of ground meat. As she was letting him out, another man arrived with a basket of fruit and a card, from Gerald. She took aspirin, and put a pot on to boil, then made chicken soup for herself and the dogs. It was only noon, and she was exhausted. When she returned the birds to the conservatory, they seemed to know they were home, flitting among the bamboo perches in their big, ornate wire cage.

Three days passed, and May nursed her cold and ate oranges and fed the birds and let the dogs out. The list Rocky had sent instructed her to walk them twice daily through the Park, but she didn't have the energy. Curled up by the gas fire in her room, she read a copy of *Great Expectations* she found in Philippe's library, taking refuge in Pip's travails.

The heating controls were so confusing as to be unworkable, and she wandered through rooms in her overcoat, touching the beautiful objects and sitting on each of the tapestry-covered settees. She counted the place settings in the china pantry (fifty-five) and read the plaques below each painting and statue. She studied portraits of generations of Clermonts and wondered if Byrd's girl had a similar background—a family castle with titled ancestors. *Byrd's girl.* She made herself say out aloud.

In the circular sitting room in the center of the first floor, large eighteenth century painted panels were set into the walls. In the six panels, the stages of love were depicted: a shepherd and milkmaid met, fell in love, were separated, then reunited. May studied the expressions of the lovers, thinking of Byrd, and of Gerald. Gerald would never look at her the way the shepherd looked at the milkmaid—with that rosy infatuation that worked so well in oil paint. She had to admit, that although he was handsome and charming, she would probably never look as bereft as the poor milkmaid did, abandoned by her shepherd. May understood how it would be between them, if she allowed it. A man like Gerald would take her to nice places, maybe buy her things. He wouldn't want to get too involved. She understood that she could be his mistress, and she began to understand how girls like herself fell into that role. It could be a victory, as it was for Velma, or it could be a capitulation. It could be the best one could do with one's assets.

May was studying the panels when Gerald telephoned, two days later, asking how she was feeling, and saying how much he wanted to see her before he left again for England. She looked at the radiant face of the milkmaid, reunited with her shepherd, and she said yes.

FORTY-TWO

In a brasserie near the Eiffel Tower, a waiter pulled out a small table so that May could slip between the tightly packed patrons to sit on the banquette. Gerald ordered a bottle of wine and their lunch, assuring May that she needed a hearty meal to get her strength back. He told the waiter not to tarry, that he had a train to catch. The man nodded and withdrew, and Gerald leaned across the table, saying, "I'm pleased to see you're fit again, and that you agreed to see me. You've been on my mind." He tapped the end of his unlit cigarette on the tablecloth. His forehead wrinkled, and he looked chagrined. "I'd like to explain, about our first outing."

May said, "You were ill. You needn't explain further."

"No, I want to. You see, in the War, I drove an ambulance at the front. One day, while my mates were loading a stretcher, I walked off to have a smoke. There was a terrific bang and a flash. When I turned round, the ambulance was gone—vaporized." He spread his fingers, making an explosion with his hands. "I went deaf, instantly. I was in a clinic for four months. And still, sudden loud noises can put me right back there." He interlaced his fingers and set his hands gently on the table, looking down at them. A strand of hair fell over his forehead, and May reached across the table and gently pushed it from his eyes.

"That must've been horrible."

He looked up with a wry smile. "We bear what we must, don't we? Or else we don't. And some chaps couldn't bear up." He rubbed his hand across his mustache. "Bloody hell, I'm being morbid. Forgive me."

The waiter came to pour wine, and May said, "There's nothing to forgive, honestly. I can't imagine." Gerald reached across the table to take her hand. She ran her thumb over his ring finger, then looked into his eyes. "I appreciate your honesty. Well, I suppose I should say, your honesty about your shell shock. You didn't mention that you're married."

He leaned back and rubbed his chin, as if they were playing chess, and May had just declared, "*Check!*"

"Does it matter?" he asked, "Oh, wait, darling, darling—don't tell me you . . ." *Checkmate!* "Oh, I do apologize." He put a hand on his chest. "I see you're upset. Let me explain my situation." He took a long sip of wine. "I was twenty-two when I went to war. Beryl and I were engaged before I left. When I returned, she nursed me through. Really, she was a brick. But the experience changed me. I realized I wasn't ready to marry, and yet I felt I owed it to her. We never did recapture that first spark, frankly. But she's a bloody good mother. She has her own interests. I pop home every couple of months to see the children. It works well enough. Forgive me, hmm? Please?" He ran his fingers over her arm. "I want to see you again, when I get back—take you to dinner, somewhere special. Don't write me off."

May wished he would stop doing that thing he was doing to her arm, but she did not pull away. She was grateful when the waiter set their plates down. Gerald said, "This is pressed duck, the specialty of the house. I hope you like it." She put her napkin in her lap and wondered if this was capitulation. Was she like Velma now? "It's good, isn't it?" Gerald asked, and May nodded. "Tell me, did you ring up that investigator?"

"I haven't had a chance yet, but this morning I went by my old hotel and there was a letter from the fruit vendor I told you about. He told me that he *had* remembered something about my mother, and I should look her up at the newspaper office. He said she had changed her name—I suppose because she was in debt when she left Paris."

"How very intriguing. What is she calling herself now?"

"Valentine. Valentine Hennessey was the name he said I should look for. Her father had a costumer's shop, on Hennessey Street in New Orleans. I suppose that's where it came from."

The waiter approached, ever solicitous, and Gerald held out his hand to halt him. He sputtered, and sat forward, wiping his mouth. "Bloody hell." He dropped his palms flat on the table, blowing out a long breath.

May said, "What is it? You have to tell me if you know something. Please."

"I haven't thought of her in years. Do you have that photograph?"

"Yes, I was hoping you might come with me to the newspaper office." She pulled the Christmas tree photo from her handbag and pushed it across the table, watching his face for a reaction.

He blanched, checking his wristwatch. "This is not the time or place." He was avoiding her eyes, seeming to puzzle something out. The waiter refilled their glasses then backed away. Gerald sighed heavily and lit a cigarette.

May whispered, "You must tell me what you know."

He reached for her hand, glancing again at the photograph. He spoke quietly. "I will tell you, if only to stop you asking around. I suppose it's better that you hear it from me. The reason you found no records was because she moved to a small village near Marseilles. She had no official identification."

"How do you know this?" May leaned forward over the table.

"The *Times* sent me to Marseilles, to cover the story."

"Go on." May was finding it difficult to breathe.

"South of here, in a village called St. Gilles, there was—there was a most unpleasant incident. Road workers found the corpse of an infant, obviously smothered, in a shoebox. It was . . . it had been left in a ditch. The gendarmerie posted notices, around the nearby villages. A woman at one of the markets saw the notice—your mother's landlady, in St. Gilles.

"The landlady came forward, claiming that your mother had become— noticeably smaller, very recently. The police searched her rooms. They found linens, very similar to those the baby had been wrapped in. They also found a pair of shoes, matching the brand of the shoebox. She was imprisoned, and tried, in Marseilles. She denied everything—said she was never pregnant. She was quite convincing, and eventually, she was acquitted. It was as if she had mentally erased whatever had happened. It was really quite shocking. The press christened her *La Valentine Noire*. The members of the jury said that they let her off because they couldn't believe anyone could commit such a crime and look at the evidence with so little emotion."

May's hands had turned cold. She pushed away her plate, sickened. *Dear God. My mother is a monster. A monster. And I . . .* She needed to retreat from this; it had to stop—to back up—five minutes, an hour, a day, to any time when she *did not know.* She looked up at Gerald and knew from his eyes that there was more.

He fumbled with his lighter, then he held her gaze with an expression of anticipatory sympathy. He snapped the lighter closed. "God, I'm sorry to be the bearer of bad news. A few years later, I heard that she had died—drowned herself in the sea. I'm awfully sorry." He squeezed May's hand. "You look unwell. I—I know this has been a dreadful shock. Most distressing. You'll need time . . . Perhaps I shouldn't have told you."

She could not take it in. The horror. *Did she kill baby Henry too? Is that what Delphina meant, about being there to protect me?* May stood up, jostling the table, sloshing wine from the glasses, and said, "I have to go."

Gerald stood. "Let me pay the check, and . . ." The waiter rushed to pull the table away.

"No. Thank you for being honest with me, but I need to be alone." She gathered her things and pushed her way blindly through the crowded tables. Outside, the sunlight was harsh. Without stopping to put her coat on, May crossed the avenue and began to walk along the Seine with no destination, hugging her coat to her chest. *My mother is dead. My mother is dead. She killed her own baby.* A cold wind blew off the river, whipping her hair into her face. Her heaving breath steamed, and the outlines of the bridges ahead blurred.

"May! Wait!" She turned. Gerald was running towards her. He dropped his valise and wrapped her in his arms. She closed her eyes, leaning into his embrace. He put his overcoat around her shoulders and rubbed her back, pressing his chin on the top of her head, and there, in the middle of the sidewalk, her heart cracked and a part of her shut down, and she fell off the edge of the world.

FORTY-THREE

Alone at Philippe's house, days passed, silent except for the chiming of twenty-three clocks. May did not answer the telephone or leave the house. She wore the same clothes every day—an old cardigan and skirt, with woolen stockings and flat shoes. After four days she tried staying in her robe all day. Her hair grew lank. Her robe needed laundering. There was no one to complain. Making each day exactly like the one before was a way to stop time, although May was unaware of having that intention.

She started letters to Delphina and her father, over and over again, and each time she did she ended up crying, using up a box of writing paper without finding a way to put her grief into words. To buy more paper would be an extravagance she could not afford. The irony of her situation was not lost on her. She could not afford letter paper, yet she could pick up the telephone and order caviar, or orchids, or expensive wine. There were numbers in the housekeeper's office for topiary trimmers, for hand-dipped Clermont blue candles, and chandelier cleaners. From the desk in her room, she picked up a heavy silver letter opener, engraved with an ornate *C* in the center. She hefted it, wondering its value, then began opening drawers, one after another, finding sealing wax in Clermont blue and a heavy bronze seal with the family crest. Another drawer had stationery—heavy, cream-colored sheets, bordered in blue.

She remembered her hesitation in taking the paper from her room at the Biltmore, and that seemed like it had happened years before, to someone else, not to this strange recluse she had become. In that dark week alone, Grief snuck up and pushed down the stairs—left her gasping, with little will to get up off the floor. She ranted, blaming her mother for her own suicide attempt and miscarriage, because maybe that same demon dwelt somewhere inside herself.

Waiting for the dogs at the conservatory door one morning, a wintry gust turned tears cold on her cheeks, and she realized she was crying again. From the Park beyond came the calls of children at play. The world was so close—just over a wall—yet she felt no desire to be in it. Over her solitary days, she absorbed the terrible truth and came to realize that she had dealt with the grief of her mother's loss years ago, as an abandoned child. What she felt most was the shock and horror of what her mother had done. The sickness that drove her to desperation.

May swiped her tears with the cuff of her robe. Behind her, the clocks began their series of chimes, echoing through the house. Time was passing, and with each hour, her heart had been healing. She had felt desperate, but she knew, beyond a shadow of a doubt that she was not like her mother.

FORTY-FOUR

The next day, Rocky telegrammed that Philippe was getting stronger, asking if she would stay on. They were leaving Switzerland for Philippe's chateâu, hoping to return to Paris mid-May. As she read his wire aloud to the dogs, they listened patiently, with Boris resting his fluffy muzzle on May's foot. His fur was becoming unkempt, and Rocky's instructions called for her to telephone the groomer to clip him every other week, but she told herself that the dog was warmer with more fur, and she did not call. In the garbage cans behind the kitchen, things began to smell. There was a telephone number she could call to have it removed, but that would require speaking to another human.

Once the servants returned, an air of mutual uneasiness pervaded Philippe's house. They each had jobs to do, whether Philippe was in residence or not. If they were disgusted by the garbage May had allowed to accumulate, they did not chastise her.

May tried her best to make no work for them and ended up wandering the rooms, feeling like an interloper. Their solicitude was unnerving, and she imagined that if she were not in residence, they might be playing cards in the salon with their feet up on the tables. She spent her days at museums and galleries and walking the dogs in the Park, trying to stay out of the way, trying to get by without money. She had a card from Janie, in Monaco, forwarded from the hotel, saying that she had been offered more money than she had ever imagined to accept a starring engagement at the Casino de Paris. She enclosed a photograph of herself, from the Monte Carlo newspaper, standing on the bow of a yacht in a swimsuit with a long mink coat, smiling and waving for the camera. She looked radiantly happy.

It was possible, May began to believe, to place the ugly secret of her mother behind her. Although *she* would always know it was there—and it would haunt her—she also possessed the power to shield others. Perhaps there could be some small redemption in that. Alone in her room, she laid out the Clermont paper and picked up her pen, and then, she began to write lies.

February 21, 1925

Dear Delphina,

I have been thinking of you often as the signs of spring start to show here. The daffodils are blooming, and at a flower shop today, I saw pansies with the prettiest little ruffled faces. They reminded me of pressing flowers with Mama. I wonder if any of them are still left in the pages of the dictionary.

I have some sad news. After all of my searching, I found someone who knew Mama. He was her neighbor. He told me that she was lovely, and she gave gifts to everyone, and everyone on the street adored her. She worked in a toy shop here, and I was able to speak to a woman who worked with her and remembered her well. She told me that they were all distraught when Mama fell ill. She died in 1918 of the Spanish Influenza. I have not found out where she is buried, but if I do, I will put some flowers on her grave. I knew you would want to know. I'm sorry to be the bearer of bad news.

May put down her pen, then picked it up again. The switch from lie to truth was a relief. She continued:

Growing up, I believed that if Mama had stayed, things would have been perfect. I didn't appreciate the care and love you gave me. I suppose little children just expect to be cared for; they don't wonder why someone stays behind.

Love, May

Dear Daddy,

I hope things are well on the farm. I often wonder what you all are doing, and I'm guessing that this week you and Otis might be pruning the Albemarle Pippins and the Winesaps. I hope business is good at the Market. Over here they have a shop for everything—one for poultry, and one for bread, and a different one for pastries.

Here, May put down her pen again. So many misunderstood years had passed between them. Now, the indirect address of paper and stamp seemed both a shield and an opportunity to express things she didn't think she could say to his face—benevolent lies and bare honesty. She continued:

Please do not worry about me. I have a wonderful job and I've been seeing a nice English fellow. I have a room in a lovely house, next to a park. There are lots of beautiful chestnut trees, and the catkins are beginning to bud.

You told me that you didn't want to know about Mama, but I think you do. She broke your heart and left you to take care of me. You couldn't help her. I was too little to understand any of that. But she broke my heart too. I understand now that it was your way of protecting—letting me hold onto the good memories.

I told you that I was going to search for her here, and I have discovered what happened to her. She died here, in 1918, of the Spanish Flu. I'm sorry to be sending sad news, but at least now we know.

Love, May

May placed the two letters side by side on the blotter. She had learned the value of truth, and yet, she also knew that she had been raised in the alley between two lies—or, perhaps, more charitably phrased, two sins of omission—that her mother had not been heard from, and that no one knew where she was. May realized now that the omissions had been protection, because the truth would have been more pain than any seven-year-old child should be asked to bear. Once the deception had begun, there was no way to go back. And now, after days of indecision, she had made the choice to shield those she loved from pain, as they had once shielded her. Delphina had been more of a mother to her than Ellen had ever been. May understood her father now, and she wondered if she could ever be a good mother herself. Elsie spoke of wanting a houseful of children, but May had never felt that pull. What if it was only a matter of finding the right person?

Maybe she already had. And she had ruined it.

She folded the letters carefully, then placed them in the cream envelopes with their blue tissue linings. Writing out the addresses, she began to feel a dissipation of the tension that arises from a decision unmade—from the hanging oppression of knowledge that demands to be released—or else locked up forever. To take no action was to continue to struggle with the beast of it. Now, the struggle was finished, and she had taken both actions—she had locked up the truth deep in her heart and she had released a white lie. There was some sort of justice in that, she thought. She took another sheet of letter paper. The thickness and heft of it seemed to lend import to her words.

She took a deep breath, and then allowed herself to write what had been hidden in the locked room of her heart. She confessed to Byrd that she loved him. She entreated him to forgive her.

The next day, May posted the letters to her father and Delphina. The letter to Byrd continued to sit on the blotter of her desk. She could not decide how to finish it. Was she going to offer to return home? Could she ask if he still loved her?

Gerald's absence had given her clarity. Now that she was out of his orbit, she could stay away. He had offered nothing, and May realized that she didn't really want anything from him. When he telephoned several days later to say he was back in Paris, she told him that she would go to dinner with him, and then rehearsed what she would say at the end of the evening—some bittersweet and wryly philosophical sendoff that might inspire him to mend his ways.

She was relieved to be able to tell the cook that she would be dining out. It was like having a house mother and Miss Wiggins and a hotel detective around. The servants looked to her for instructions. She wished she could ask *them* what she should do. She told Maurice, the houseman, with what small measure of authority she could muster, that he need not wait up for her.

After she washed her hair and put on makeup, she began to feel more like herself. She hoped Gerald would not bring up her mother. May wanted to be able to keep to her resolution to never speak of her again. No good could come of it.

At Maxim's, Gerald ordered champagne, and they danced. The singer was a beautiful Negro woman, newly arrived from Chicago. Her voice was soulful as she sang Irving Berlin, accompanied by a piano:

> *Gone is the romance that was so divine.*
> *'Tis broken and cannot be mended.*
> *You must go your way,*
> *And I must go mine.*
> *But now that our love dreams have ended ...*
> *What'll I do*
> *When you are far away . . .*

May swayed in Gerald's arms, wondering if he could sense that the song made her think of someone else. The trumpet wailed a solo, and another verse began.

> *When I'm alone*
> *With only dreams of you*
> *That won't come true*
> *What'll I do?*

She agreed to go to Gerald's apartment for a nightcap, telling herself that no matter how pleasant the evening had been, she would follow through with her intentions of breaking things off. When they walked in, the cat snaked around May's legs, mewing, and Gerald picked her up, apologizing in a baby voice for having forgotten to feed her. "Make yourself comfortable," he said, "Let me give the cat her dinner." The champagne May had hoped would give her courage had left her slightly drunk. She wandered down the hallway, and Gerald called from the kitchen, "Loo is through the bedroom. Sorry, but I'm rather a poor housekeeper." May was looking around for framed photographs. She wanted to see this Beryl, or his children, so that she might be inspired to righteousness in ending things. But there were no photographs on display.

She returned to the living room and picked up a magazine from the table. It was in English—*The Tatler*. As usual, the British society monthly featured a beautiful young film star or socialite on the cover. This one was a pretty blond on horseback, outfitted for foxhunting. She laughed at the camera, as if she had not a care in the world. *Must be nice,* May thought, idly. *Wait. That's—oh my God—that's what's-her-name!* She read the caption:

The TATLER

Tally ho! The triumphant huntress!

Miss Sophie Annabel Cavendish-Boyle, 21, daughter of Capt. Edmund Cavendish-Boyle and Georgiana Muriel Cavendish-Boyle (nee Browning, daughter of the late Earl Lyden).

London, March, 1925

May flipped the pages. From the kitchen, she could hear glass clinking, and something being poured. She read quickly.

The infamously naughty Sophie attended Heathfield, (briefly) and The Institut Villa Mont Choisi, Switzerland. She has recently been residing in Washington, DC with her father, the Ambassador. The delightfully eccentric Sophie is a terror, on both the hunting field and the dance floor. She is recently betrothed to an American, Mr. Charles Byrd Craig, of Keswick, Virginia.

Sophie's oldest sibling, the polo player and notorious rake, Angus, says that Craig is "a bloody good man. If anyone can handle my sister, this bloke can." Angus describes rumors about his sister and a certain older member of the peerage as "absolute poppycock."

The wedding will take place in Washington, and the family will host guests at the Cavendish-Boyle estate in the Highlands in July, for a later celebration. Following their sojourn in Scotland, the couple plan to reside in Virginia, where Sophie is expected to join the Keswick Hunt. Mr. Craig, 24, attends the University of Virginia School of Law and will practice in Charlottesville.

The article was accompanied by more photographs of Sophie, looking radiant in a black lace evening gown. There was also the photo that Elsie had sent her, from the Ambassador's Ball. May inhaled sharply, as if the breath were being squeezed from her chest, and her mouth twisted with a sudden, intense dislike of the English girl. She closed the magazine and turned it face down. She told herself not to think about this now, not here, not ever. But still—self-accusing thoughts, like jagged slivers of glass, began to cut her. *If I had mailed the letter . . . if I had gone back home with him . . .* A sob pushed up through her chest, as if she had been shoved. She pushed it back.

Gerald returned with two snifters and handed one to May. He swirled his, inhaling the fumes. Tears pricked her eyes; she was unprepared for the memory conjured by the scent. She said, "What is this?"

"Calvados. Apple brandy." He switched on his phonograph and a slow jazz tune began. A guitar, with a whisper of drumbeat. "Spanish. The guitarist. Do you like it?" He sat close to her on the sofa. "Did I tell you that my mother is Spanish? Castilian."

May nodded and sipped and the familiar sharp amber heat slipped across her tongue to warm her throat. It loosened the tightness in her diaphragm, and she was able to speak. "At home, we call this applejack. My father makes it. Only, this is smoother." Gerald leaned toward her and kissed her. She laid her head against the back of the sofa, wanting what he was offering. She was on her way to being very drunk, and the thought of that oblivion had a certain appeal. But if she had more brandy, she might start to cry. And if she started, she would never stop. She would cry until she turned to ash, and then she would blow away. She wanted to dissect her sorrow, but she did not want to be alone. Gerald patted her knee, then rose and went into his bedroom, returning with a blue porcelain bowl and a silver spectacle case.

"I have something special. I think you'll like it." He placed the bowl on the table and handed her the silver case. His monogram was engraved on the top, and May slowly traced the design with her finger. Inside, it was lined with purple velvet. In gold, printed on the lining was *Pravaz*. The bottom had fitted compartments. One held a glass hypodermic syringe with silver fittings. Another slot held thin needles.

"Is this for cocaine?"

"Could be, but I have something much more pleasant." He plucked a small vial from the case. "Have you ever tried heroin?" She shook her head. "It will make you feel marvelous. Like nothing else. It's best if you take it through your nose the first time, like cocaine."

May watched him tap out a line of the brownish powder, and she inhaled the promise of escape. The taste was acrid, vinegary. Her face tingled with sudden heat; she felt sick; a little panicky. She tried to stand up, but the tingle was moving from her head down her throat into her chest, fast and glowing. She sat forward, her hand over her mouth. He held up the bowl just before she vomited. "I'm sorry," she whispered. It was hard to make the words come; they echoed in her head.

"It's normal," Gerald said, "I should have told you. I was afraid you would say no. Steady on. I'll be right back." He stood, and when his hand slid down her arm it left a hot trail of stars. She let her head loll and from far away, she heard the sound of water. She closed her eyes. Was that a waterfall? Yes, it must be. So serene. So soft, and sweet, and serene.

Gerald helped her rinse her mouth. The water was thick and sweet, like warm honey. *So* warm. Everything was so very, very nice. When he stroked her neck, she arched toward him like a lazy cat. The fabric of his shirt was cool and smooth, and he smelled of limes and brandy. He led her to the bedroom and undressed her. It took hours, and she lifted her arms like a rag doll, deeply relaxed, yet aware of every nerve and muscle. Yes, she wanted this. He was speaking softly, almost cooing. His words echoed away before they reached her, yet still, she knew they were kind, and she could believe that they were loving. She wanted him to feel this too, she wanted to share, to share everything, to share the beautiful light inside her eyelids. He kissed a line down the center of her body. When he knelt over her, she held up her arms, and afterward, she knew, without opening her eyes, that her skin was luminous, like a million fireflies.

FORTY-FIVE

Two months of May's life were lost in a blur of dissipation. She spent long spring afternoons with Gerald, lolling in his bathtub, drinking gin and tonic. Their nights were spent together, connected by the rope of heroin. He sent her away when he had a deadline, and she would creep back to Philippe's house in the early hours, letting herself in through the conservatory, then padding barefoot up the servant's staircase. She slept until late afternoon, unsure, when she woke, if it was dusk or dawn. She wrote no new letters and stuffed the unfinished letter to Byrd into a drawer.

On a warm morning in the third week of May, she left Gerald sleeping and let herself out. She told the taxi driver to let her off on rue de Monceau, and not to drive through the archway into the courtyard of Philippe's house. Despite the tail end of the heroin glow, the morning sun was terrible, and she laid her head back on the seat, closing her eyes against it, longing for sunglasses. As she was getting out in front of the house, the door from the garage swung open toward the street, revealing a flash of shiny red paint. Philippe's car.

May halted. *For Chrissakes, they're back. It was supposed to be Tuesday, wasn't it? Is today Tuesday?* Bernard came out, his ears reddening at the sight of May in her evening dress at eight thirty in the morning. Tipping his hat, he hurried toward the kitchen entrance. She knew she ought to be mortified, but she wasn't. Instead, she felt irritated—intruded upon. As she let herself in the front entrance, she willed the dogs to stay quiet long enough for her to escape upstairs.

She crossed the entryway, not allowing her heels to tap on the stone, then took her shoes off and padded up the stairs. From the first turn of the stairway, she could see a curl of cigarette smoke. *Rocky.* Waiting. Even if she retreated and took the servants' stairs, she could not get to her bedroom without passing him. At the top of the landing, he was sitting on a needlepoint bench. He raised one eyebrow and did not smile.

"Well, welcome home," May said, "Were you waiting to greet me or check up on me?" She found it difficult to summon any pretense of dignity, knowing she was being judged and found lacking. And Rocky had no idea how very lacking she felt. Irritation shifted, instantly, to defensive volatility.

He shook his head and stood slowly, with an affected ease. "You know, you ought to have a good look at yourself."

The last thing May wanted was a good look at herself. She raised her chin, intending to brush past him without a response, to shut herself in her room. She couldn't think any further ahead than that. Rocky grabbed her wrist, turning her toward the long pier mirror with a jerk. She flinched at their mutual reflection. He held her there, in front of him. Her hair, reflected in the old glass, was dull, grown uneven. Days of mascara smeared her eyes. Her lips were flaking and cracked. The satin strap of her dress flopped against her bony shoulder. She reached her free hand to smooth her hair and quickly dropped it, holding it to her chest.

Rocky turned her arm over, inspecting it closely. "Stop it!" May said, "That hurts."

He sneered. "I should have known. Philippe told me Gerald's a junkie. May, this stuff will kill you!"

He dropped her arm, and she cradled it to her chest. Raising her chin, she said, "Have you got spies watching me or something? Someone skulking around with a camera?"

Rocky blinked slowly. "No. Maurice wrote to me, about the birds." May looked down, flushing. He continued, "He said you left the outside conservatory door open—all night. He came in in the morning, and the canaries were dead. He didn't want Philippe to be upset, so he told me. It's lucky the house wasn't robbed." Rocky grasped May's shoulders and shook her. "I told Philippe they died because the heater had broken. And I didn't do that for *your* sake."

When May looked back up, her friend's reflected face showed a mixture of anger and confusion and hurt. Behind Rocky, Shame stood tall, smirking, tipping a top hat.

"Leave me alone!" She shoved Rocky as a maid came from a bedroom, carrying a stack of linens. She ducked back into the room and closed the door.

Rocky lowered his voice to a hiss. "What are you doing to yourself? Answer me!"

May exhaled slowly through her nose. "Please. I don't want to quarrel. You *don't* need to worry about me. Now I'm going to have a bath and sleep."

"Philippe doesn't need anything to upset him. He's sleeping now, but he wants to have lunch with you. *I* won't be there. I don't think I could stomach it."

She went into her room and locked the door, her mood now grim. Sometimes the glow of the drug lasted all day, but it seemed that lately, it wore off faster. And each time it did, reality seemed all the more harsh. From her window, she watched the gardener working below. Spring had come without her noticing. Tulips bloomed and cherry blossoms floated down to the walkways like pink snow, while, like Sisyphus with his stone, the gardener patiently raked and raked, petals covering the path again as soon as he had finished. There was a letter on the desk, and she recognized Elsie's new stationery, with her married name. May hesitated before opening it, not wanting any news that might thaw the numbness she had cultivated with such care.

May 10, 1925

Dear May,

Well, dear one, I had really hoped to see you at Byrd's wedding. Why haven't I had a letter from you? And Byrd told me he hasn't heard from you at all! What is going on?

So I suppose it falls to me to tell you about the wedding. I had expected it to be something of a disorganized affair, coming just a week before Byrd's graduation, but it was really rather impressive. They had the reception at The Willard, and it was gorgeous. I've never seen so many roses, and even Sophie's mother, (who's a terrific snob, by the way), said it was up to snuff. And Sophie's brother Angus is too adorable. Terribly naughty. But more on that later.

Sophie wore a diamond tiara, and her dress had seed pearls. Really, much more elaborate than mine. So they're off to Scotland, and they've invited Archie and me to come for a house party in July. The men will shoot grouse and go fishing, and we'll play golf and drink Scotch, I expect. I saw a photograph of their place. I suppose you'd call it a castle—turrets and a moat, and fields of sheep and the whole nine yards.

Speaking of weddings, when will we hear something about you? What is this Gerald fellow waiting for, anyhow? You know what they say—well, actually I can't recall what they say, but you don't want to make things so easy for him, you know?

We all miss you. Now, no more letters from me until I hear from you, you naughty thing!

Love, Elsie

Naughty thing. May laughed—a short, bitter snort that was the opposite of mirth. She pulled out a sheet of paper. Tapping the pen against the desk, her mouth twisted. *Well, Elsie, I wasn't there because I wasn't invited.* She began to write.

May 20, 1925

Dear Elsie,

I loved hearing your news. I'll let you in on a little secret, and you'll be the first to know, that I'm getting married too! Gerald popped the question, and of course, I said yes. It was terribly romantic. He took me on a private cruise on the Seine and got down on one knee, then he held out the most fabulous ruby ring I've ever seen. We're going to have a quiet ceremony here, only because his schedule is so unpredictable. I'm just dying for you to meet him. It's been such ages. Love and kisses to you and Archie.

May

If only I could write it down and make it come true. I envy you, Elsie. She pushed away from the desk and went to run a bath, avoiding the mirror as she shrugged her dress from her shoulders, leaving it to form a beaded puddle on the cold tile. There was an unpleasant metallic taste in her mouth, and her body craved Gerald's silver syringe, to dull the sharp edges and float her away, if only for a few hours.

As she walked downstairs at noon, she tugged the long sleeves of her sweater. From the stairwell window, she checked the courtyard. From the bottom of the stairs, she listened, trying to discern if Rocky was still in the house. From down the hall, the telephone trilled and stopped. In the entryway, she dropped the letter to Elsie onto the mail tray then went to wait for Philippe on the terrace. As she passed the conservatory, Rocky looked up from the table and beckoned to her. Fifi jumped down from his lap, running to greet May as she sat.

"Good afternoon," May said, with sarcastic cordiality. The aroma of coffee mingled with something intensely sweet and floral, like too many gardenias, and the new canaries fussed discordantly.

Rocky blinked slowly and returned her volley. "You look like death sucking a sponge."

"How kind of you to be so concerned. I'm having my period, if you must know. I felt wretched all day yesterday. Gerald gave me some morphine for the pain, and I fell asleep." Her dishonest eyes flitted away from his. By citing female problems, she had dealt a card she knew he would not challenge. "Where's Philippe?" The telephone began to trill again, then stopped.

"He went to meet with an antiques dealer. Some Japanese lacquer cabinet has come on the market that's the mate to one he bought twenty years ago. He's mad to reunite the pair." Rocky put down his papers and glanced at his watch. "He should be back any time now. May, listen. This behavior of yours simply cannot continue. I haven't said anything to Philippe because you know he shouldn't be upset, with his heart. I'm telling you; you're going to have to straighten up or leave."

Fifi pawed at May, and she shoved her down from the settee, querulously. "No, Fifi! Not on the petit point. You know what Philippe says." The dog's ears went back, and she went to Rocky. He scooped her up. May lit a cigarette and inhaled slowly, swinging her foot, playing for time. She stared at Rocky without expression, and said, "Well, then, I'd better start packing. Only last time I checked, this wasn't *your* house."

The phone jangled again, and after six rings, Rocky put down his pen and said, "Where is Maurice?" The silent minutes dragged, thickening the air until May thought she might choke. To put distance between them, she went to the birdcage, sticking her fingers through the wires and blowing a stream of smoke through, seeking some small fragment of control over *something*, even if it was only the canaries. They looked much like the pair they had replaced, as they flitted from perch to perch, squawking in agitation.

The doors from the hall opened, and Maurice stood, holding both door handles. When he continued to stand for a few moments without speaking, Rocky said, "Was that Philippe?"

Maurice's hands dropped to his sides. He looked down at his shoes, then raised his head, looking baffled. "It was Monsieur Loo. He said—he said that the Count was at his gallery and became quite agitated . . . during their negotiations. His heart—he had a heart attack. He is—He died in the ambulance, on the way to the hospital."

"No." May and Rocky both said.

"I am so terribly . . ." Maurice choked out.

Rocky set the puppy down gently. "He was just here, two hours ago, sitting right there. He was smoking his pipe." Rocky covered his face with his hands, rocking forward. "No, no, no."

May's hand pressed against her mouth; tears welled in her eyes. She looked at Maurice, feeling lost. He said, very quietly, "What shall I do, mademoiselle?"

May went to Rocky and sat beside him, saying, "Which hospital, Maurice? Please—get them on the telephone? We should . . . we should . . .

speak to someone. There must be—oh, God—there must be arrangements to be made." Her voice rose to a nearly hysterical pitch.

Maurice said, "Monsieur Loo told me that he had taken the liberty of telephoning the Count's sister, at her convent. He has . . . he *had* been selling to the family for many years."

May nodded, over and over. "Yes. Good. That was a good thing to do."

Maurice cleared his throat. "It was she—Sister Marie Claire, who telephoned a moment ago. She is leaving the convent now, to go to the chateâu." After a long pause, Maurice said, "I was asked to relay a message ..." His voice sounded strained; he licked his lips. Rocky dropped his hands and looked up, hollowed out with shock and sorrow. Maurice continued, "Forgive me, please, if I am indelicate. You may not know that Monsieur's family has been estranged from him for many years." Rocky dropped his head, and May put her hand on his shoulder. "Sister Marie Claire instructed me to inform Monsieur Pendergrast that he is not welcome at the chateâu. The Count will be laid to rest there. I am sorry, mademoiselle, monsieur."

"I see," May said, blinking fast, "Thank you, Maurice, for letting us know."

The following afternoon, Philippe's lawyer arrived, with a clerk bearing a stack of folders. May and Rocky both wore black and stood together like a pair of Victorian orphans, waiting at the top of the first stair landing. Rocky's eyes were glassy and red-rimmed; he moved like an old man. The previous night they had sat together in Philippe's favorite room—the round sitting room with the painted wall panels. The milkmaid and the shepherd looked down, observing without comment May's sobbed apologies and the shared tears and sad laughter, until she fell asleep, curled together with Rocky on the divan, like children.

As Maurice ushered the visitors toward the sitting room, Rocky said, "I sent a cable to the château, asking Philippe's sister to call. I told Maurice that if he or the other servants wanted to go to the funeral, they could." He shrugged and it seemed to take all of his strength. "But who am I to be giving them orders? They don't work for me." He started down the steps, his head down. May stayed there, at the top of the broad stone staircase. Around her, every statue, every painting, every exquisite piece of furniture had been collected by Philippe and his family. The collection had given him such pleasure. Now he was gone, and Rocky's new life, his new love, had been snatched cruelly away.

She would hold her friend up as best she could, and he would shelter her as she returned to herself. She never wanted to see Gerald Fournier again, and she realized, with bitter clarity, that she would not miss him. She shuddered. She did not want to be in that strangling darkness ever again. Rocky had fallen to Earth from the heights of living his dream with someone he loved, and May would now begin the crawl back from the edge of a pit—the very pit that her mother had fallen into.

Maurice wore a black armband on his gray suit. He invited the men to sit on the visitor's side of Philippe's desk. May and Rocky sat facing them. The details—the business of grief—were best attended to with efficiency. Maurice poured tea and began to leave, but the lawyer addressed him. "You are Monsieur Picard, are you not? If you please, it is necessary that you remain. This business concerns you." Maurice stood at the door, his gloved hands clasped in front of him. The lawyer cleared his throat and began, "There is a provision here, benefitting Monsieur Picard." He moved the document closer, then farther away, squinting. "It reads: In recognition, for many years of faithful service, I leave to Maurice Picard, the sum of fifty thousand francs." Maurice stared at the floor as the lawyer continued, "You may leave us now, monsieur. A bank draft will be forthcoming and will be delivered to you." Maurice bowed solemnly, backing out of the room, closing the doors behind him. Beneath the desk, Rocky took May's hand. The lawyer continued, "Monsieur de Clermont's will was recently amended. Monsieur Pendergrast, and Mademoiselle Marshall, I have met with Sister Marie Claire at the Chateâu de Clermont. She had been unaware that the two of you were in residence here." He lowered his chin to peer over his spectacles at them. "She has had no contact with her brother for almost twenty years."

May looked steadily at the lawyer, reflecting on a return to the Hotel Bercy, and she supposed that Rocky had similar thoughts. The lawyer held up an index finger. "Please hear me out. I should explain first that by French law, two-thirds of any estate must be willed to any living descendants. Since Monsieur de Clermont had no children, that two-thirds portion reverts to his sister. She has signed papers bequeathing it to the Catholic Church, in accordance with her vows. The remaining third of the estate, he could leave to whomever he chose. As you have seen, he left a bequest to his manservant. When he revised his will, he left the portion that was within his control to you, Monsieur Pendergrast."

Rocky blinked and his mouth fell open for a moment. Light returned to his eyes as the lawyer continued, "It was Monsieur's wish that the estate be divided in such a way that you would retain this house. It was his intention that the two-thirds inherited by his heir include the chateâu and property. I believe that Sister Marie Claire will agree to this division. The artwork and furnishings here would have to be sold, but the house would be yours. She has agreed to allow the estate to provide severance to the servants. If you are agreeable to the arrangement, I will present it to her. A monetary settlement would, I am afraid, take many years, with the structure of the estate and the involvement of the Church. I do not foresee a problem with your remaining here in the interim."

Rocky squeezed May's hand. "He really did care for me," he said, quietly. "He did."

"Monsieur Pendergrast?" the lawyer asked.

"Yes, yes," Rocky said, looking heartbroken and incredulous, "I agree."

"I shall have the documents sent over as soon as they are prepared. Good day." His clerk shuffled papers and stuffed them into folders.

Rocky rose from his chair and shook the lawyer's hand. He seemed to May to stand taller. He leaned toward her, whispering, "Let me show them out. Take the dogs and meet me in the garden."

May remained in her seat, studying the wall panels that had become so familiar to her. The little dog, and the lovers with their expressions of longing. So many emotions had played out for her in this room. The thought of Philippe's carefully curated collection being dismantled saddened her. She was glad for Rocky that he would have the house, but mostly, she was glad that he knew that Philippe had loved him with such devotion.

She pushed herself up from the desk, then unlatched the heavy door and stepped onto the terrace as the dogs bolted out ahead. At the rear of the garden, through the gate that led into the park, she could see little boys playing tag under the watchful eye of a gray-uniformed nurse, who jiggled a sturdy blue pram. May sat on a bench, beneath a crabapple tree, pulling her sweater around her. The chilled tremor she felt was neither cold nor shock. It was the knell of a physical craving for heroin. Her crossed leg swung restlessly, uncontrollably, and she shivered.

It was time to stop. Because if she didn't, she would be just like her mother. She had shut herself off from life, and the return of emotion was like tearing off a bandage. The realization was a weight in her chest—a heaviness, as if she were aware of the weight of each of her bones. The feelings that had reawakened in her were the same she had felt after her mother left. She took no comfort in the familiarity. This was grief. It would not be ignored. It must be endured until it passed—so slowly that one could not remark that any particular day was more tolerable than the one before. After an unmeasurable time, she knew, she would feel better; but never quite the same. Those who are loved leave a space when they depart.

The afternoon was waning. Faded petals drifted down. She watched, mesmerized, choosing a single petal, then following its progress as it dipped and twisted and floated, as if suspended from a pendulum. When it landed lightly on the grass below, she started over with another, unaware of the passage of time until she heard an excited bark, and Boris was running toward Rocky as he crossed the terrace, carrying a bottle and a pair of glasses. The children and nannies had gone. He sat beside her and said, "I'd like to toast Philippe." Solemnly, they clicked glasses and drank.

May watched the bubbles rise and burst in her glass like so many little hopes and dreams. She said, "He would want you to be happy in this beautiful place."

Rocky shook his head, slowly. "Happy? I feel like I've used up all my happiness. Like I'm not allowed anymore, because I had more than my share." When he looked up, his eyes were black with sorrow. "It's easy, you know, to be greedy with happiness, when it doesn't even cross your mind that there might not be an endless supply." He laughed bitterly. "I'll have to do something to be able to keep this place up. Maybe I'll open a salon right here." He refilled their glasses, saying, "He always hated to see good champagne go to waste. He told me once that when Dom Pérignon tasted his first bottle, he shouted, 'Come quickly, I am drinking the stars!' I found out later, that was just some advertising slogan. I didn't tell Philippe that he'd got it wrong. If he were here, he would tell us that we should enjoy it before the bubbles go away."

FORTY-SIX

The library table in the Paris house was strewn with blueprints. May stood at the window, rubbing the muscles of her neck. It was late July, and the garden was badly in need of attention. She told herself that she must finish pruning the roses and trim the shrubs. But the weather had been so hot lately . . . Her heels clicked on the bare parquet floor as she moved to a makeshift desk in the center of the room, where Philippe's pipe still sat in a jade ashtray, with his letter opener and inkwell. Stacks of his papers and files still smelled of his tobacco, two months after his death. She had placed a framed photograph in the center—Philippe and Rocky at the opening of the *Folies*.

The room was far more austere than it had been when Philippe had last been there. Two days after the visit from the lawyers, a crew of six men in coveralls had arrived with an inventory from Philippe's insurance company. On the first day, May and Rocky had sat together on the stairs, watching as things disappeared, one by one. On the second day, the craving for heroin began, and Rocky held a cold compress to May's forehead as she endured bouts of chills and nausea. The vault of silver and the china pantry, which had held the Sèvres dinner service, were emptied. May ached and ranted and wept, suffering the sickness of withdrawal. A doctor came and went. The Savonnerie carpets were rolled up and carted off, the porcelains and bronzes packed into crates, all to be sold at auction, with the proceeds going to the Catholic Church. After seven skin-crawling days and nights fraught with nightmarish depression, May was spent and shaky, and she was free. The movers slammed the doors of the last van. One of them drove Philippe's car away. The grand mansion was stripped almost bare. May and Rocky slept.

For days after, the house smelled of sawdust and excelsior. Those odd pieces not included in the official inventory had been left behind, forlornly garish without the surrounding grandeur. Rocky and May closed off much of the house, combining the remaining furniture into five rooms. They ate their meals in the kitchen, on the servant's crockery plates, and moved beds and pine wardrobes from the attic quarters. On the walls, faded rectangles showed where paintings had once hung. Marble niches stood empty, as if the statues and busts that had occupied them had come to life and simply wandered away during the night. The lavish draperies and chandeliers were left, like a stage set for an as-yet-unwritten play. In the sitting room, the painted panels of the lovers remained, part of the architecture.

The door opened and Rocky stuck his head in. "I'm taking the dogs for a walk before it gets too hot. Want to come?" He looked older since Philippe's death, but it suited him somehow.

"No, thanks, but could you drop these at the bank? You need to sign, right here." She returned to the desk and indicated a blank space with her pen.

"What is this?" Rocky asked. "I feel like I've signed my life away in the past two weeks."

"You have. You're up to your neck in debt. This is to authorize payments for building materials."

"Voilà. Anything else?"

"I had a letter from Janie this morning, from Budapest. She sent another check. She's just signed a contract to advertise face cream. Have a nice walk. Don't let Fifi chase the ducks." She heard the front door close and returned to the papers before her. She and Rocky had come up with a plan, together, and May concentrated on carrying it forward, one day at a time. The salon was set to open in September. For now, she worked at Au Nain Bleu three days a week, selling toys and arranging window displays. It was a pleasant routine.

The telephone rang and May put down her pen, hoping that Maurice would pick it up. The other servants had taken their severance and gone. Maurice had brought his sister from the countryside and they lived in the servant's quarters, keeping house as best they could. The copper pots in the kitchen tarnished and the empty, closed-off rooms gathered dust.

The chiming of the remaining clocks announced the hour of three, and May realized that an hour and a half had passed since Rocky had left. Maurice knocked, and said, "Mademoiselle, you have a visitor."

"Who is it?" May rose from her desk, smoothing her hair.

"An American lady. She would not give her name. Shall I show her in?"

American? "Please. Where is Rocky?"

"He has not returned."

She steeled herself and followed Maurice back toward the door as Elsie breezed into the room, her lemon-colored linen duster flapping behind her. "May, dear God!" May was enveloped in a bear hug. "I wouldn't have known you." Holding her at arm's length, Elsie looked her up and down.

May stammered, "Elsie, what on earth . . ." Here was the reckoning she had not allowed herself to envision, personified in a yellow coat. Bluster was called for. She crowed, "I'm so glad to see you! It's been ages." Maurice waited at the door, his hands clasped. "Would you bring some tea please, Maurice? This is my very best friend from home!" He nodded and departed, and she grasped Elsie's hand. "What are you doing in Paris? Why didn't you tell me you were coming?"

Elsie pulled her cigarette holder from her bag and pointed it at May. "I decided I'd better surprise you, since you've been putting me off. Don't deny it, you naughty thing. Really, though, have you been ill?"

May smoothed the back of her hair, saying, "I have cut my hair, and I suppose I am a bit thinner."

"Well, you simply wouldn't *believe* what's happened." Elsie unfolded a piece of paper and held it out. "Here, look at this."

The TATLER

Change of course for the huntress!

London, July, 1925

The word on the street is that a certain ingénue of the smart set has thrown over her American husband of a scant ten weeks and eloped to Paris with her former lover, the recently widowed Lord B.

Shortly following the untimely demise of the Lady B. in an automobile smash, said ingénue disappeared from her own house party at the family estate in the Highlands. This young lady is no stranger to scandal, and was rumored to have been associated with the Lord some time ago, while attending a certain prestigious girl's school. Perhaps now the handsome American fox will "go to ground."

"Poor Byrd," May whispered, laying a hand on her chest. She listened to Elsie speak, and as much as she wanted to hear what her friend was saying, her mind was fixed on the news she had just read. The lovers in the wall panels seemed to be smirking at her.

"Arch and I were *there*," Elsie said, "at the house party! First, let me tell you that Scotland is dreadfully damp, and the men wore kilts and knee socks. Archie didn't, of course. I would have laughed at him. And the Cavendish-Boyle's place is really over the top.

"So Byrd had invited Arch to come fishing. Sophie's family was there, and three other couples. The men left at dawn, and when I got up there was a note under my door from Sophie, saying she had driven into town to pick up another guest at the train station. When the men came back in the late afternoon, she still hadn't returned. Then Byrd came tearing down the hall and ran out the front door and drove away. Really, it *was* awkward, because we had all been sitting in the library having tea and scones with Sophie's parents. So then Byrd telephoned, about an hour later, to tell Sophie's father that he was on his way to London. He said she had left him a letter saying she was running off with their neighbor—Lord Some-body—the old geezer she had dallied about with when she was a teenager! Byrd had gone to the fellow's place and managed to find where they were headed. He was hell-bent on going after her.

"Darling Archie was wonderfully diplomatic and suggested that all of the guests vacate, and go somewhere en masse for shooting or some other sort of *manly* excursion, but I said, 'Absolutely *not*, Archie, I am not going to be dragged around to smell sheep and damp Harris tweeds and sleep in another drafty old castle.' Although, you know, they do have some fine whiskey there. I said, 'Let's just go on to London!' So we went to the Savoy, and Byrd was there, but he left the next day, hot on the trail. Well, we couldn't get passage booked to get home for another week, so *I* said, why not hop over to Paris and visit May? So here we are!"

"Did he find her?" May felt as if the air had been sucked from the room. She waited, breathless.

"Sophie? Oh my, yes. The runaways were holed up in some little Bo-hemian love nest on the left bank. Apparently, Lord So-and-So hasn't a farthing to his name—it all belonged to Lady La-De-La, and went to the children."

Elsie took a deep breath and continued, "Anyhow, where was I? Oh. So Byrd went to the love nest and banged on the door, and when the Lord answered, Byrd broke his nose. Then he and Sophie had a long chat, and she made him a cup of tea and told him that she thought he was swell, but she really preferred the old fellow. Now I think they've gone off to Italy. Sophie and the Lord, I mean."

"How is Byrd taking it?" May held her hands out flat in front of her. She observed them as if they were someone else's.

"Well, my darling girl, ask him yourself. He's still here."

"In Paris?" May began to pace. The painted lovers in the wall panels seemed to be laughing now. The trick was up. *He's here.*

"Yes. He said this morning that he wants to go see his brother's grave. I think he just isn't ready to make explanations at home. Listen," Elsie, said, "he thought you might be . . . uncomfortable about seeing him. He wouldn't say why, but you must tell Elsie." She held May's arm, leaning in closer. "But to answer your question, he's taking it like the gentleman that he is—well, aside from the broken nose—but who could blame him? We had a long chat this morning. He thought they could be happy enough together—mutual interests, and all that."

Elsie linked her arm in May's and began to walk the perimeter of the room. "Sister," Elsie said, "this is some setup you've got here. Looks like you've fallen into a tub of butter. But are you going to get some more furniture? Forgive me, darling, but I did tell him that you're going to marry this fellow Gerald. Hope you don't mind." She emitted a low whistle, examining the painted panels. "We saw some swell pictures in London. Lots of horses and madonnas." She continued around, picking up a bronze letter opener to inspect it more closely. "This Gerald of yours must be quite the swanky gent. When do I get to meet him?" She returned the letter opener to the desk and regarded May without smiling.

"Where did you say Archie is?" May's eyes flitted to the door, desperate for some distraction, for anything that would take her out of this situation.

"I sent them to a museum," Elsie said, with a dismissive gesture. She began to loosen the fingers of her gloves and pull them off. "We're staying at the Meurice, and the Louvre is right across the street. Anyhow, Archie lets me get away with murder these days," Elsie pointed toward her abdomen.

"You aren't!" May said, standing back and holding Elsie's hands. *Happiness. Happiness is to be shown here.*

"I am. About two months along. You'll have to come home for the christening and be Godmother."

While Elsie tossed her hat and gloves onto a chair and opened her handbag, May formulated a proper response. "I'm so happy for you. You look well. How is married life?" May asked, attempting to keep the conversation away from herself.

Elsie pulled out a cigarette case. "You know, I thought it would be beastly dull. But I enjoy staying in with Arch." She fitted a cigarette into the long black holder. "He goes to work at his little insurance office every day and I do things like play bridge or go to Garden Club. Can you imagine? It's amusing to be domestic. Anyhow, life is really very civilized. When he comes home, we chat and have a cocktail, and he reads the newspaper. Believe it or not, I've actually cooked his dinner, twice, all by myself! He was really a sport, I must say. My meatloaf . . ."

Maurice entered with the tea tray. He lit Elsie's cigarette, then proffered a teacup. "Tea?" she said, slapping her leg, "Really? Come on, Elsie's here!" She winked at Maurice, saying, "I bet you've got some of that really good bubbly in the icebox. And besides, it's hot as blazes outside."

May nodded, and said, quietly, "Yes, the dog days."

Maurice bowed, and departed, closing the doors behind him. In her gravelly whisper, Elsie said, "I hope your Gerald isn't such a stiff. Can you two come to dinner with us? How about tonight? Now don't you worry, Byrd said that if you thought it would be difficult, he would bow out. To tell you the truth, he's not very good company these days. I'm sure you know the best places, so you can choose, but I really want to go to one of those clubs you told me about, with the topless showgirls? And I'm *dying* to meet your famous friend Janie. I was telling Archie, this very morning . . ."

Barking was audible from the hallway outside. The doors banged open and the dogs ran in. Fifi jumped into May's lap and Boris began to sniff Elsie thoroughly. Rocky strode in, then noticed Elsie and halted. "*Alors! Bonjour, madame,*" he said.

May rose, pushing the dog off of her lap. Her arms hung limp and her hands clutched convulsively at the fabric of her dress. "Elsie," she said, clearing her throat, "this is my friend from New York, Rocky Pendergrast. This is Elsie Nelson, from Virginia. She . . . she just dropped in! Surprised me!" Rocky seemed to pick up on the shrillness of May's tone and her desperate expression but apparently, he couldn't understand what she wanted him to do.

Elsie rose also, and cocked her head, her cigarette holder clamped in her teeth. "De-*lighted*. May's written to me about you. Sounds like you two have had some big times together."

Rocky said, "Lovely to meet you. I, uh, I'll leave you two to catch up." He backed out of the room, bobbing his head and closing the doors behind him.

"So?" Elsie said, "is there something you forgot to mention in your letters, for God's sake? Where *is* this Gerald person, May? Does he even *exist*?" Elsie held out one hand in a halting motion. "And why are you two living in an empty house?"

"It's a long story."

"Yes indeed! Spill it, sister. Gawd knows, I need a drink. I can't take much more. Where the hell is that Frenchie?"

Maurice entered with a bottle stand and glasses. He opened the champagne discreetly, with a whisper instead of a pop. "Leave it, please," May said. "That will be all, thank you." Maurice nodded and left. May smiled, ruefully. "Somehow the wine cellar was overlooked when they divided things up. Rocky's got a terrific stash of this stuff." She looked down at the bottle, then back up into her friend's eyes. There was nowhere left to run. "I'm sorry, Elsie. You always trusted me, and I lied to you. I've lied to everyone."

"So you and Gerald aren't getting married." Elsie looked pointedly at May's left hand.

"No."

"Hmm." Elsie tapped her cigarette. "This should be interesting. I thought we were chatting about meatloaf."

May crossed her arms tightly over her chest. "I made it all up. There *is* a Gerald. Only he already has a wife. I wanted Byrd to hear that I was doing fine without him. I was . . . oh, I was jealous. I tried to write to him, so many times, but I didn't know what to say." May put her hands over her face. "And then he was engaged. How could I say anything? I figured he had forgotten me." Her hands dropped into her lap in a gesture of supplication. She had no right to ask forgiveness. The truth, finally, was all she had to offer.

Elsie blew out a stream of smoke. "Hell, pour me some of that. Even if there's not much to celebrate. So . . ." Elsie struck a pose with her glass in one hand and her cigarette holder in the other. "I'm confused. What *is* going on, really?"

"Rocky inherited this house a few months ago. He lived with the man who owned it. They helped me out of . . . out of a bad time—put me up here. Now Rocky's turning the stables into a hairdressing salon, and I'll help run it. You'd be surprised how much it's like a country market, keeping the books and things. Our friend Janie is putting up some of the money. He's asked me to stay on as long as I like."

"You're going to stay here? For good? It's very nice, but it seems a bit lonely."

"I don't mind that, actually. I've been working in a little toy shop— only until the salon opens. I don't miss the fast life. One can only stay in that sort of crowd for so long without . . . without getting sucked under. And I've been working in the garden." May tried to project a dignified serenity, though she felt neither dignified nor serene.

"I see. So, since you're confessing, tell me—how do you feel about Byrd now?" Elsie refilled her glass, holding the bottle poised over May's until she was forced to meet her eyes.

May blew out a long, slow breath. The truth she had been holding tight in a clenched fist was right there, ready to fly as soon as she dared to open her hand. "Oh. He's—he's such a good man—such a gentleman. Only I didn't appreciate that, because it was always there, in front of me. When he came to New York, I treated him terribly. I was determined to come here, and I didn't think he understood. But it doesn't matter anymore, does it? Too much has happened." May returned to the settee. She stared into the bubbles in her glass. *She's right. There's nothing to celebrate.* "Oh, Elsie, I can't possibly see him. Tell them you came to surprise me, but I was out of town. Maybe you can get away and have lunch with me if you can finesse it. But don't lie to Archie if you can help it. Trust me, you don't want to go down that road."

FORTY-SEVEN

That night, May dreamed of her mother. In the dream she was a little girl, and her mother was telling her that she had to go away for a long time. *Why?* May asked, over and over, and her mother said it was because she had made too many mistakes. Her mother looked terribly sad, and May couldn't understand. She woke at dawn with a pounding heart, clenched with anxiety and dread. She rose and dressed, then went outside. In the quiet summer morning, she pulled weeds from between the cobblestones in the courtyard, then trimmed shrubs in the garden, trying to fix her concentration on the symmetry of each bush. This return to order of a circumscribed plot of earth gave her a small feeling of control. Each rasp of the shears snapping closed was like a fencer's thrust against an invisible enemy, and she took no notice of the blisters that formed on her palms. The heat increased as the sun rose in the sky, and at eleven on the dot, the dogs began to whine for their walk.

In the parc Monceau, May let them off their leashes and they gamboled ahead on the sandy path, knowing that their destination was the small stone bridge with a pond beneath it. These little rituals, she thought, were like anchors, providing stability to each day, preventing any drifting into uncharted waters. Safe. Tethered. Sheltered from storms.

Fifi stopped and picked something up in her mouth and trotted back, dropping it at May's feet, barking for her to throw it. It was a chestnut.

She picked it up, rubbing its silky surface with her thumb, remembering the trees at Keswick Farm. The dog danced around her, whining, until she said, "All right, Fifi, go get it." She lobbed the chestnut down the path and the dog raced after it.

"Hello, May."

She turned quickly, toward the familiar voice. Byrd stood on the path, ten feet away, his hands thrust into the pockets of his jacket. Fatigue and strain showed around his eyes. He did not approach her or smile.

Words would not come to her. There was no place to start. May stammered, "Elsie swore. She swore she wasn't going to tell you."

"She didn't. She told Archie."

"How did you know where I was?"

He jerked his head in the direction of the house. "Your friend told me."

"Oh."

"From what I saw at that place, you've done pretty well for yourself."

"No, it's not . . . Byrd, I—I'm so—Please, come back to the house. There's so much . . . so much I need to say to you." May started toward him but he held up both hands and stepped back. "Please," May wanted to kneel there in the sand, but she knew it wouldn't help. "I don't deserve it, I know. I wouldn't blame you if you hated me." The tight set of his mouth, the coldness in his eyes, she deserved it all.

"I don't want to hear it, May. You told me in New York that you've changed. I didn't realize how much. You've lied to everyone. I just can't understand why." He ran his hands through his hair. Watching the familiar gesture, she wanted to grab his hands—to embrace him, but he was as immobile as the statues that lined the path. Fifi began to bark, dropping the chestnut repeatedly at May's feet.

"I wrote you a letter . . ." she said, flushing with shame, knowing she sounded pathetic, "but then you got engaged. I never mailed it. Please, can we sit down? I want to tell you—I want to tell you what was in the letter." *Give me time, please, wait for me to find the right words.*

"No." He rubbed his chin, looking away, his voice resigned. "I used to think I knew you better than anyone, but I don't trust you anymore. Hell, I don't trust anybody anymore. I'm leaving Paris tomorrow. Archie said you're staying here." He backed up several steps. "I hope you find what you're looking for. I've never been able to figure out what that was."

May watched him until he disappeared through the tall iron gates. She sat heavily on a bench, staring at the gates without focusing while the dogs barked at ducks, racing back and forth to the edge of the pond. A chestnut leaf fell onto the bench beside her. *He's right. I don't deserve another chance.* She called to the dogs and walked back along the path as slowly as if she were dragging a dozen anchors behind her.

When Rocky came home that night they sat in the library, and he held May as she cried, telling him about the encounter in the park. He made her sip a glass of brandy. "You'll get through this, Kiddo. You've been through worse." He took the glass from her hand. "We've got a plan, right? You and me and Janie and the salon. You're doing fine on your own. He's got his own mess to figure out. This time tomorrow, he'll be gone."

"You didn't see his face," she said, "I think he hates me."

"If he hated you, he would have stayed away."

"What would I do without you?" May blew her nose. "Your salon is going to be the toast of Paris." She wiped her nose, smiling weakly. They walked together through the empty hallway and up the stairs.

In the desk in her bedroom, she found the letter to Byrd. She propped the unsealed envelope on the mantel beside the shard of the doll's face. The cherub clock was gone, as was the landscape that had hung above. May picked up the shard, turning it over. *This time tomorrow Byrd will be gone— and I might never see him again.* She had to tell him everything—even if he walked away again after he heard what she had to say. She pulled the letter from the envelope, and sat on the chaise lounge to read the pages:

Dear Byrd,

I have started letters to you ten times, and each time I've found it impossible to get onto paper the things I want to say. I wish that telephone wires ran over the ocean, so I could call you and hear your voice.

Before now, I wanted to write to apologize because I treated you so horribly in New York. I was determined to come here and to succeed on my own. That idea was foremost in my mind, and although things in Paris have not worked out as I hoped, I don't regret that I took this opportunity. What I do regret is that I was so selfish, and so careless with your feelings. There were things I was afraid to tell you, or anyone, because I couldn't face them myself. That's no excuse, though. There's a long, long list of apologies I need to make.

Byrd, I have missed you, and I love you. It took my sailing halfway around the world to realize it. I thought you would always be there and you were, until I pushed you away. I am full of regret and longing for you, and for the easy way we used to be together. I know I will never feel the same way about another man.

She stood and walked to the desk, then signed her name.

"Rocky?" May whispered into the dark, knocking softly on his door, "Are you still awake?"

"What is it?" He sat up in bed and switched on the light.

"I'm going to walk for a little while. I can't sleep."

He squinted at his clock. "It's almost midnight. Do you want me to come?"

"No. I want to think."

"You're going to see him, aren't you?"

From the shadow of the doorway, she said, "Yes. I love him. I have to try."

"Atta girl, Kiddo. I'll be rooting for you."

She padded down the stairs and eased open the kitchen door, then slipped out, closing it softly behind her. The evening air was balmy. In the quiet of the night, her shoes crunched in the gravel of the court-yard. She ducked beneath the scaffolding that surrounded the stables, then turned onto rue de Monceau and continued down the hill toward boulevard Malesherbes, her arms crossed over her chest, the letter in one hand, the fingers of the other worrying the edges of the doll's face. She passed through place de la Madeleine in the shadows of the great columns and continued to the river. Turning left, she followed the Seine, and at the steps of pont de la Concorde, she stopped beneath a streetlamp and threw the shard as hard as she could, into the water below. On the bridge above, Shame tipped its top hat and set off away, toward the opposite riverbank.

I'm not my mother. No more lies.

May continued down rue de Rivoli until she stood on the tile mosaic of sidewalk that spelled out *Hôtel Meurice*. Three steps up, a smiling door-man in a top hat stood at attention, holding open the door, waiting for her to enter.

Inside, she had the desk attendant call Byrd's room.

"Hello?" he said.

May clutched the telephone, turning her back to the desk clerk. Her voice was determined. "Byrd. I didn't get to tell you today, how much—how much I love you. And how stupid I've been. Please, give me a chance to explain. I'm sending up a letter. I wrote it right before I found out you were engaged."

There was a long silence on the line. Byrd said, "I'll be down."

In a quiet corner of the lobby, they sat facing each other. May sat primly, her hands clasped in her lap. He looked away from her, rubbing his palm over his mouth. She knew she needed to speak but felt unable to arrange the right sequence of words—perfect sentences—so he would understand. If she got it wrong . . . She looked up at him, but there seemed to be no clear place to start.

"Let me go first," he said, finally. "After New York, I gave up on you. I felt like the girl I had waited for was just . . . gone. I felt foolish and dis-illusioned, and hurt.

"I figured Sophie and I could make it work well enough. I was will-ing to give it a go. I think she realized from the beginning that it wasn't going to work for the two of us. We both admitted we wished we'd called it off." He laughed, "*Ha.* Neither one of us had the courage to do it. I don't like what she's done, but at least it's honest. I'm feeling pretty beaten up. I want to go home and lick my wounds."

May nodded, wishing she could assuage his pain. He said, "She gave me back the ring. That was decent of her. It was my grandmother's. It should have gone to Jimmy, by rights."

"Elsie said you're going to see his grave."

"Yes. I leave in the morning."

"I know how much that means to you." May looked down at her hands, clasped in her lap. "I'd like to go with you, if you'll let me. Let me be your friend, Byrd. I can't bear the thought of losing that."

Now it was her turn. He sat with his elbows on his knees; waiting, patient. She would match his unreserved frankness and tell him everything. There were, she realized, no magic words. What she had to say was harsh and ugly, but it was the truth. He could hate her, or not, but she had to be honest. He blanched when she explained how desperate she had been the previous June, thinking she wanted to die; and her mother's terrible story. When she told him about the heroin, he reached into the space between them and took her hand.

FORTY-EIGHT

"*Billets, s'il vous plaît, billets!*" A conductor made his way down the aisle as the train rumbled through the French countryside, stopping at small villages where washing flapped on lines and chickens pecked around doorways. Byrd sat up, frowning, uncomprehending.

"The tickets," May said to him, gently, "He needs our tickets." She asked the conductor, in French, how many more stops there were to the Château Thierry station. When he moved on, Byrd seemed to settle back into his reverie, and May did not intrude. She wanted to shield him, to create some shelter where he could experience this solemn rite in peace and begin to make sense of the reeling confluence of emotion of the recent days.

Outside, rows of bright yellow mustard blossoms flashed by in a blur, vivid against the cloudless summer morning sky. In rolling fields, white cows seemed posed in bucolic tableaux beside green ponds. Red-tiled roofs and stone churches peppered the hills. A group of women with market baskets boarded, chattering in rapid French, and May was struck by their resilience, by the fact that life—that market day—continued on, in the shadow of bombed-out shells of blackened houses and barns. May and Byrd sat facing each other, each watching the scenery, lost in thought and memory as the landscape became hillier, with patches of thick woods. She hoped that he felt easy with her, that her presence gave him peace of mind instead of further turmoil. She inhaled, wanting to absorb the vitality of the countryside. Self-forgiveness, she knew, would take time—if she ever came to it at all—but she felt grateful that she was strong enough now to help her friend. Her mistakes had shaped her, strengthened her. Rocky had cared enough to try to save her when she had nothing to offer, and now she could offer help, without expectations.

At the train station, a single taxi was parked. May explained their mission and the driver seemed appropriately solemn; no doubt he had made the same trip dozens of times. They were silent on the drive, rocking along winding roads, the breeze through the windows a relief after the hot train. Twenty minutes later they crested a hill, passing a windmill and a stone church. The driver pulled through pale stone gates, carved on each side with: Aisne-Marne American Cemetery. Beds of blooming red roses flanked the drive up to a towering chapel building of the same pale stone, set against a thickly wooded hillside. Below, acres of white marble crosses and Stars of David fanned out from the center in concentric rows. Twenty-two hundred graves.

Byrd shook the hand of the American Corporal who greeted them at the reception building, then he signed a register. May followed, clasping the bouquet she had assembled in the garden that morning, as the soldier paged through a directory. He said, quietly, "Would you like for me to lead you there?"

"No, thank you," Byrd said, "We'll find it."

As May and Byrd slowly walked the rows of graves, chimes began to peal from the bell tower, marking midday. She read the inscriptions on the immaculate stones. Some said, simply,

HERE RESTS IN HONORED GLORY
AN AMERICAN SOLDIER
KNOWN BUT TO GOD

The grass underfoot was spongy and groomed with military precision, with neither a stray leaf nor weed. There was no sign of caretakers or gardeners, nor any other visitors. When the chimes finished, echoing up into the hillside, the ensuing silence felt holy. Byrd took his pocket watch out and held it closed in his palm. Jimmy's watch.

In the fifth row, they found it:

JAMES MARTIN CRAIG
PVT. 330 INFANTRY BATT'N.
VIRGINIA AUG. 18, 1918

A young man's life, abbreviated. A crow cawed overhead, piercing the quiet. Byrd removed his hat and stood silently as May knelt to lay the flowers against the marker. She rose, her hands clasped in front of her. Tears gathered in her eyes as she remembered Jimmy. She had a crush on him, so handsome in his uniform. She and Byrd had followed the Allied campaign all that summer of 1918, moving pins across a map.

May said, "I never realized before how hard it must have been for you to be the one left when your parents lost a son." Perhaps, she thought, this shared circumstance had bound them early on, before they were old enough to understand its significance. She said, "Would you like to be alone?"

He reached for her hand. "It's the missing," he said, "and all the un-knowns, that break my heart. I feel lucky, to be able to find a headstone with Jimmy's name on it. Think of all the families who don't have that." He looked up toward the hillside. "It was in those woods up there, the battle."

"It's beautiful here," May said.

Byrd's gaze shifted out, toward the distant hills. "I'm glad he's here with his comrades. And you know, except that the trees are a little different, and they grow mustard instead of corn, it sort of looks like home, doesn't it?"

"It does." The hill at home, where her own brother was buried, flashed into her mind and a wave of homesickness took May by surprise. The sensory memories—birdsong, the warmth of a hand in hers, the scent of grass, the varied green shades of the woods—all connected back to Byrd, and to home. Being with him, honoring Jimmy, reminded her that there were good memories too, if she could sort them from the bad, instead of pushing everything away. Her vision blurred with tears.

They walked back toward the waiting taxi. Byrd said, "Do you think you'll ever go back?"

May blew out her breath. She knew it was an inquiry, not an invitation. "I don't know. I've found a life for myself here, on my own terms. I made a commitment to Rocky to help set up his salon. I want to see that through. I owe him so much. But why don't you stay a little longer?"

He smiled, wryly. "I can't. I have a trial coming up. And a divorce to see about."

"After things settle—say, in six months' time—would you write to me and let me know how you are?"

"Yes, I'll do that."

She didn't know what would happen next. But she knew that she could take care of herself. The world was a big place, full of mistakes just waiting to be made, but maybe, she thought, just maybe, there were some second chances too.

AUTHOR'S NOTE

The genesis of this story has two sources—a broken bone and a shard of porcelain. Regarding the former, don't text and walk. Just don't. In 2013, I was stuck at home for six weeks with a cast on my ankle and a course assignment to begin a novel. Regarding the latter, the farmhouse where I live was built in the 1820s and in the soil around our property I often find interesting old bottles, ironwork, and bits of pottery. While gardening around the building that is Delphina's cottage in the story, I found a broken piece of a porcelain doll's face. I wondered whose doll it had been, and what that little girl's life had been like here, a hundred or more years ago. Being the sort of person who likes to look for signs, I used that shard as a starting point, and it seemed a natural progression to begin this story here, at Keswick Farm. Another influence was a novel written in 1722. Just a few days before I walked off the asphalt I had finished reading Daniel Defoe's *Moll Flanders*. What I liked most about Moll was that she survived by her wits and she made a lot of mistakes. Defoe's Moll was an early badass, and, aside from the bit where she marries her brother, her character inspired me in imagining May Marshall.

In New York, I was able to place May at the boarding house where I lived as a graduate student. The Roberts House rules were about the same in the early 1980s as they were in 1924, minus the hats and gloves. Now, the building is a dormitory for Yeshiva University. May's apartment on 85th Street is also taken from personal experience, complete with pigeons, creepy lobby dentist, and neighboring fire station.

I knew I wanted a grand New York hotel as a setting in this novel and I settled on the New York Biltmore. The Biltmore opened in 1913 and stood where the MetLife building is now, adjacent Grand Central Terminal. In 1981 it was demolished and unfortunately, despite the last-minute efforts of conservation groups, none of the interiors were saved. F. Scott Fitzgerald's story, *Bernice Bobs Her Hair* is set at the Biltmore, and the area below the ornate gilded clock in the lobby was a popular meeting spot. The clock now stands in the lobby of the building that replaced the hotel.

Originally, my character Janie was going to be Josephine Baker. I was advised, wisely, to change that. Initially, I was crushed because I had done so much research on Miss Baker, but in the end, it was the right choice. I did, however, have the good fortune to be granted a private tour of the Théâtre des Champs-Élysées in Paris and see the backstage, dressing rooms, and theater almost as it was in 1925, when Miss Baker premiered there in *La Revue Nègre*. Also, in Paris, I used my favorite museum as the setting for Philippe's house. The Musée Nissim de Camondo is a mansion, left to the city of Paris with the proviso that it be left in situ, and it still looks as if the de Camondo family will come back at any moment and sit down to lunch in the dining room. Tragically, however, Moise Camondo's beloved son and heir, Nissim, died in World War I, and later his daughter and her family died in concentration camps in World War II.

I took a few small liberties with time. The tabloid headliners Peaches and Daddy did not get up to their hijinks until 1926. The Sheriff Beasley storyline is based on an actual trial known as "The Great Moonshine Conspiracy of 1935," which happened in Virginia, only it was ten years later than my story. And finally, the stone gates and chapel of the Aisne-Marne American Cemetery in France were not constructed until 1929.

ACKNOWLEDGMENTS

I bear debts of gratitude to the following people and institutions:

My writing teachers and mentors: Sarah Kennedy, Mary Kay Zuravleff, Connie May Fowler, Clint McCown, Jacqueline Mitchard, and especially Barbara Jones, who threw me to the ground early on and stomped on me, then patiently taught me how to get up again.

My stellar agent and agency, Mark Gottlieb and Trident Media Group; and Rick Bleiweiss and the amazing crew at Blackstone Publishing for bringing this manuscript out into the world.

Jennifer Pooley and Ciera Cox, editors whose keen eyes made these pages better in important ways.

Clara Coscia, who corrected my terrible French.

Early readers: Mary Catherine Amos, Linda Hewitt, Ray Nedzel, Ron Harris, Charles Heiner, Robin Traywick Williams, and the late Catherine Coiner.

My grandmother, the first, inimitable Elsie.

Stefanie Lieberman, who helped this story along its way.

The late Mrs. Drue Heinz and the Hawthornden Fellowship Committee and Hamish Robinson, administrator at Hawthornden Castle in Lasswade, Scotland, where I read these pages to my fellows on cold spring nights in 2018. Also, my Hawthornden Fellows: Selina Fillinger, Sheena M. J. Cooke, H. S. Cross, and T. Sean Steele.

Erowid Center Experience Vaults, (with permission) for research on cocaine and heroin.

Dr. Eric Foner, DeWitt Clinton Professor Emeritus of History at Columbia University.

Dr. Jennifer Fronc, University of Massachusetts, Amherst, Dept. of History.

Dr. Karen E. Huber, Wesleyan College, Macon, GA, for her dissertation on infanticide in France.

Dr. Chin Jou, Senior Lecturer in American History at The University of Sidney.

Musée Nissim de Camondo, Paris.

The New York Historical Society Library, for period photographs and research.

Dr. Marcy Sacks, Professor African American History, Albion College, Albion Michigan.

The Schomberg Library, especially librarian A. J. Muhammad.

Théâtre des Champs-Élysées, Paris, and Tony Rouleau and Ophélie Lachaux, Public Relations.